THE
WIZARD
OF RONDO

THE WIZARD OF RONDO

EMILY RODDA

SCHOLASTIC PRESS   NEW YORK

Library of Congress Cataloging-in-Publication Data

Rodda, Emily.
The Wizard of Rondo / Emily Rodda. — 1st ed.
p. cm.
Summary: Cousins Leo and Mimi return to the world of Rondo through their family's
enchanted music box to rescue a missing wizard and foil the plans of the evil Blue Queen.
ISBN-13: 978-0-545-11516-2
ISBN-10: 0-545-11516-7
[1. Space and time — Fiction. 2. Adventure and adventurers — Fiction. 3. Magic — Fiction.
4. Kings, queens, rulers, etc. — Fiction. 5. Wizards — Fiction. 6. Music box — Fiction.
7. Cousins — Fiction.] I. Title.
PZ7.R5996Wiz 2009
[Fic]—dc22
2009004375

10 9 8 7 6 5 4 3 2 1   09 10 11 12 13

Printed in the U.S.A.   23
First edition, October 2009

FOR KATE, HAL, ALEX, CLEM, AND BOB

CONTENTS

THE
WIZARD
OF RONDO

CHAPTER 1

THE MUSIC BOX

Leo Zifkak stood at his desk, staring down at the painted box that had changed his life. A shadowy face stared back at him from the shining black surface of the box's lid. It was Leo's reflection, but it seemed to float in darkness far below the mirror-smooth lacquer. It was as if it wasn't a reflection at all, but the face of a darker and more mysterious Leo enclosed within the box.

Thoughts like this made Leo extremely uncomfortable. Eager to break the illusion he grabbed the box and lifted it up. The oval silver ring set into the center of the lid flashed dazzlingly.

Leo jerked back, nearly dropping the box, and instantly felt ashamed. *Idiot*, he told himself, as his thudding heart slowed. It was just the sun shining through the window above the desk, hitting the silver ring. *What's the matter with you?*

But he knew what the matter was. Just over a week ago, his pleasant, ordered, *ordinary* life had changed. Just over a week ago, the music box that had been a family treasure for hundreds of years had arrived in this house, and taken its place in Leo's room. Great-Aunt Bethany Langlander had left it to Leo in her will, because she thought that he was the most sensible, the most responsible, of all her great-nephews and great-nieces. She was sure that Leo would look after the music box, and that he would be as careful as she had been to keep the rules laid down by her own uncle Henry when he had left the box to her.

This time ignoring the flash of the silver ring, Leo lifted the box again and squinted at the yellowed strip of paper stuck to the bottom, just above the key you turned to make the music play. For about the hundredth time he read the faded words Henry Langlander had written so long ago.

Turn the key three times only.
Never turn the key while the music is playing.
Never pick up the box while the music is playing.
Never close the lid until the music has stopped.

If the rules had been kept, the first rule especially, Leo would never have learned the secret of the music box.

And left to myself, he thought, *I'd probably have kept the rules till the day I died, and left the music box to whoever in the family I thought would keep them, too. If it hadn't been for Mimi . . .*

If it hadn't been for his cousin Mimi — prickly, interesting, infuriating Mimi Langlander . . .

The sound of voices drifted through his open window. Down below, in the back garden, his parents and four of their oldest friends were sitting around the long table relaxing after their leisurely Sunday lunch. They were waiting for Leo — waiting for him to bring down the music box. And by this time they must have been wondering why he was taking so long.

Just get it over with, Leo told himself. *It mightn't be as bad as you think. They might just look at it quickly. They mightn't ask you to make it play.*

Oh, sure. Holding the box gingerly, he left his room, plodded down the short hallway that led past Mimi's room and the bathroom, and went down the stairs.

His father's distinctive bark of laughter floated in from the garden, and despite the churning in his stomach Leo had to smile. Tony Zifkak always grumbled about having to entertain, but as soon as the first people arrived he started enjoying himself, and by the end he was the life of the party.

Tony was the one who had heard Leo come into the kitchen after arriving home from his friend Nathan's house. He was the one who had jovially shouted to Leo to go get the music box to show to Ana, Peter, Horst, and Will.

Leo's heart had given a peculiar little jump. Excuses had skittered through his mind, every one of them feeble. "Okay," he'd called back. What else could he do?

"Suzanne's old aunt left it to him," he'd heard his father say as he left the kitchen. "Antique . . . should be in a museum . . . extraordinary piece of work . . ."

Extraordinary isn't the word for it, Dad, Leo thought now, moving slowly to the back door and feeling as sick as if he were going to his own execution. He looked down at the box clutched in his hands. His dim reflection stared back at him, floating in darkness.

Ana, Peter, Horst, and Will called cheery greetings to him as he walked out into the garden and put the music box down on the table. His mother beamed at him as they oohed and aahed, admiring the incredibly detailed paintings that decorated the front, back, and sides of the box. Naturally she thought Leo would be as pleased as she was to have the family treasure admired.

She turned the box on its short rounded legs, so that everyone could see the busy town scene at the front, the forest and farms on one side, the rolling green grass and fairy-tale castle on the back, and the sea and golden sand on the other side.

Leo watched her, his heart in his mouth. But Suzanne didn't seem to see the hundreds of changes that to him were so very obvious. She didn't notice that the tall policeman had disappeared from the steps of his police station, for example. Or that a large pink pig wearing a flower-laden hat had moved from the field beside the biggest of the farmhouses on the side of the box to the door of the tavern in the street scene on the front. She didn't even notice that the proud, blue-gowned queen no longer stood on the drawbridge of her castle.

Maybe Mom's not expecting changes, so just doesn't see them, Leo thought. *Or maybe she sees them, but just assumes she's remembering wrongly about the way things were before.*

He knew that he would have done the same thing until a week ago. He would have told himself anything rather than believe the evidence of his own eyes, because it was evidence of something that was simply . . . impossible.

"Does the music still play?" asked Horst, and Leo's heart sank.

"Oh, yes!" said Suzanne. "Leo?"

Trying to appear unconcerned, Leo lifted the box and turned the key on its base three times.

"You can only turn the key three times," he heard his mother explain. "The box is so old and delicate, you see."

That's not the reason, Mom, Leo told her silently. He put the box down and opened the lid. The strange, chiming music began. The guests murmured with pleasure. Leo felt his smile grow fixed.

"It's beautiful," breathed Ana, peering in fascination at the forest scene facing her. "I've never seen anything like it. The painting is exquisite! So detailed. You can almost see the trees moving in time to the music, can't you?"

"When I was little I used to think they did," said Suzanne. "And I used to think I saw tigers in the shadows — bears as well."

Tony and Peter laughed indulgently.

Standing there, his stomach in a knot, Leo suddenly wondered what would happen if he said, quite casually, "There *are* tigers and bears in the forest, actually, Mom. And the trees *do* move. They're alive. There's another world inside the music box. It's called Rondo. Aunt Bethany didn't know about it, but the Langlanders who owned the box before her used to visit Rondo all the time. Two of them even ended up staying there for good! I know because a week ago Mimi and I went to Rondo, too."

Would the laughter die straightaway? Or would it just trail off, before being replaced by strained smiles, because intelligent, sensible, mature Leo had suddenly stepped out of character to make a rather weak joke?

The music was running down. The adults smiled, pointed, discussed the value of antiques. Leo waited, stiffly smiling.

"You get in and out of Rondo by using a magic thing called the Key," he imagined himself saying conversationally to his father, the scientist. "It looks like an ugly old pendant. Aunt Bethany left it to Mimi without knowing what it was. The Key can create things in Rondo — change them and destroy them, too. The Blue Queen — the evil queen who lives in the castle on the back of the box — got hold of it once and caused what Rondo people call the Dark Time. So we have to make sure she never gets it again."

That would go down well with Dad, Leo thought. *Next thing, I'd be in the hospital having blood tests.*

The last chime struck. The music box was silent. Trying not to seem too eager, Leo shut the lid, picked up the box, and backed away from the table, mumbling about homework.

"Thanks for showing it to us, Leo," said Will. "It's a treasure."

Ana, Horst, and Peter chorused agreement. Grinning and nodding madly, Leo reached the back door and escaped into the house. The moment he was out of sight he stopped and scanned the box, looking frantically for changes and hoping he wouldn't find too many.

"Leo looks more like a Langlander every day, Suzanne," he heard Ana murmur.

"Don't let him hear you say that," his mother said, laughing.

"Aunt Bethany used to insist he looked exactly like her boring old uncle Henry. 'It's the eyes,' she used to say. 'The steady, responsible eyes.' Poor Leo *hated* it."

Yes, I did, Leo thought, feeling his face grow hot. *I used to wish I looked like wicked Uncle George, instead.* And he thought ruefully of George Langlander, whose name in Rondo was Spoiler, who was a thief and a cheat.

Now I'd hate to look like him, Leo thought. *And I'm* glad *I look like Uncle Henry — Hal. Hal's not boring at all. He's the opposite of boring.*

"Which reminds me — where's your little houseguest?" he heard Will ask. "I thought you had her for a month."

"No sooner did Mimi get here than she had to rush off to some weeklong music thing," Suzanne said. "It's a series of workshops for promising young violinists. That famous violinist — Takeshi Sato — is running it."

"Sato!" Horst exclaimed, obviously impressed.

"Yes, it's all quite high-powered," Suzanne said. "Sato's keen on encouraging young talent, apparently. The workshop idea was a last-minute thing, tacked on to the end of his tour, and it wasn't certain Mimi could go. It all depended on whether the organizers could find a host family who'd agree to her having Mutt — that's her little dog — with her. She wouldn't go without him."

"Ludicrous!" Leo's father snorted.

"She's a bit insecure, that's all," Suzanne said peaceably. "Anyway, someone rang last Sunday night and said it was all fixed, so off she went. Sato had heard a recording of her playing and wanted her in the group, so the organizers moved mountains to make it happen. She'll be back tonight."

And about time, Leo thought, slipping out of the kitchen and hurrying to the stairs. The week had seemed like a year to him, though as Mimi's return drew closer, he was becoming more and more nervous about the confession he was going to have to make to her.

Regaining the safety of his room at last, Leo put the music box on his desk and snatched up the magnifying glass that for the last week had lain on his desktop instead of inside a drawer. His heart beating fast, he peered at the box through the glass.

The town scene on the front looked almost exactly the same as it had before. There was the police station, the art gallery, the bank, the flower stall, the toy factory, the tavern with its sign reading THE BLACK SHEEP.

But it wasn't the same. People had moved or disappeared from sight altogether. Posy the flower seller was rearranging the flowers in the buckets on her stall, instead of passing a posy of violets to an elderly gentleman in knee britches. And the pig in the flower-laden hat was no longer at the tavern door, but was standing on the balcony of one of the upstairs rooms.

Why are you in the tavern, Bertha? Leo thought uneasily. *Why did you leave the farm? Are you looking for us? I know we promised to come back to Rondo as soon as we could, but Mimi had to go away, and without her . . .*

He heard the doorbell ring at the front of the house. He knew his parents wouldn't hear it from the garden. He sighed, got up, and ran downstairs. He opened the door cautiously, expecting to see the bright smile of someone selling something or wanting to talk to him about religion.

But there on the doorstep, clutching her violin case and her little mustard-colored dog, and weighed down by a bulky backpack that made her look like a small, skinny tortoise in baggy jeans and sneakers, was Mimi Langlander.

CHAPTER 2

CHANGES

"Mimi!" Leo exclaimed, pulling the door wide. "What are you doing here? We weren't expecting you till tonight. Hi, Mutt!" He put out his hand to the little dog, then snatched it back as Mutt gave one of his miniature gargling snarls.

Mimi turned and waved vaguely at the dark blue car idling by the curb outside the house. The car gave a little toot of acknowledgment and drove away.

"There was only some stupid farewell party this afternoon," Mimi said, staggering into the house and making for the stairs. "Sato-san wasn't staying for it, and there were going to be *games*. So I told them I wanted to go home, and they got someone to drive me."

"Right," Leo said, thinking disloyally that the organizers had probably been quite glad to be rid of Mimi, who would have made it very clear that she was not going to be an asset to the jolly event they had planned.

"A couple of the others left, too," Mimi snapped, peering up at him from beneath her long bangs as if she'd read his mind. "I wasn't the only one."

"Give me your pack," said Leo, closing the door behind her. "I'll take it up while you go tell Mom and Dad you're home. They're outside. They've got some friends here."

Mimi wrinkled her nose. "I'll see them later," she mumbled. "When everyone's gone." Without even pausing to give Leo something to carry, she started toiling up the stairs, bent nearly double.

Leo followed her, determined not to fuss. *If she wants to stagger upstairs carrying everything, then let her*, he thought, knowing full well that half his irritation sprang from the fact that Mimi had come home early, and he would have to admit a few things sooner than he'd thought.

Mimi swung into the spare bedroom that was hers while her parents were away in Greece. Leo stood at the door and watched silently as she put the violin case down on the desk, dumped the backpack in the middle of the floor, and picked up the white china bowl that Suzanne had provided for Mutt's water.

"I'll do that," Leo said. He took the bowl and went to the bathroom to fill it, mentally rehearsing what he would say to Mimi when he got back. *Mimi, I wound the music box a few times while you were away, and then just now Mom made me wind it again, so . . . Hey, Mimi, you'll notice that there've been a few changes in Rondo since you left, because . . .*

He still hadn't quite worked out how best to break the news when he returned with the filled water bowl, but as it happened there was no need to say a thing. Mimi was no longer in her room. Uninvited, she had gone into his. Sighing, Leo put the bowl down and went to his door. Still clutching Mutt, Mimi was sitting at his desk, examining the box. She swung around to face him, her eyes accusing.

"When I left, Bertha was at Macdonald's farm," she snapped. "Now she's in the tavern. And there's smoke coming out of the Blue Queen's tower. You've been winding the box!"

"So?" Leo snapped back, furious at being spoken to like a naughty child however much he might have been expecting it.

She stared at him, her sharp little face tight with anger. "When you wind the box, life in Rondo goes on, Leo!" she hissed.

"I know that," he said coldly. Of course he knew it. In fact, at first that had been the whole point. It had been horrible to think of everyone in Rondo being frozen, of time in Rondo stopping, when the music box ran down. Hal had said that for people in Rondo the pauses were unnoticeable — just the space between one blink and another — but Leo still couldn't cope with the idea. Thinking about it had made him feel queasy, and so guilty that he'd been compelled to wind the box the day after Mimi left. In fact, it had been all he could do to stop himself from closing the lid while the music was still playing, so that life in Rondo could go on and on.

He hadn't done it. He'd let the music run down. Then it had occurred to him that by examining the changes in the pictures that only seemed noticeable after the music had stopped, he might be able to find out where Spoiler was hiding. Spoiler had broken his agreement with the Blue Queen — tried to get the Key to Rondo for himself. He'd run from the castle afterward, and disappeared.

But he can't stay hidden forever, Leo had thought, peering through his magnifying glass at the smooth green grass and the willow trees on the back of the box. *He'll have to move. He'll need food, and shelter, and money, and for sure he'll cause trouble trying to get them. I've got a bird's-eye view of the whole of Rondo. I should be able to find him. Then I can tell Hal where he is.*

But though he wound the box every day after that, and examined the pictures with the glass till his eyes watered, he didn't get what he regarded as a confirmed sighting of George Langlander.

On the second day he did see a tiny figure in a checked jacket and what looked like pale pink trousers right at the top of the front of the box — just outside a village nestled in a cleft between two low hills. Spoiler had a checked jacket, and he had been wearing pajamas covered in faded red crowns when Leo had last seen him. But the figure was too small to be recognizable, and anyway was half hidden by a horse pulling a large cart loaded with furniture and trunks.

So Leo went on winding and searching, winding and searching as the days passed. The man in the checked jacket disappeared from view. The horse and cart turned and began a slow journey back down toward the town at the bottom of the box. A sea serpent rose to the surface of the water on the coast side of the box and menaced a small fishing boat. Dragons flew across the sky and perched on distant mountaintops. Preparations for a large party began in and around the glass-towered palace high on the front of the box. Life went on in the town.

It was only toward the end of the week, when Leo noticed faint blue-gray smoke drifting from the Blue Queen's tower room, that he began to wonder if he was doing the right thing. Everything was changing so fast — much faster than he'd thought it would. And when Bertha disappeared from the farm and became visible in the center of a crowd outside the tavern, he felt a twinge of real panic.

It had just occurred to him that if life went on in Rondo for too long without him and Mimi being present, the Blue Queen might start wondering why her butterfly spies were failing to find any sign of them. The queen thought Mimi and Leo were stranded in Rondo because the Key had been destroyed. If she couldn't find them, she might begin to suspect she'd been tricked.

And that would be a disaster. If the queen realized that the Key still existed she'd never stop trying to get it. Never, ever . . .

Leo hadn't wound the box again — until this afternoon, when he'd been forced to do it. He fervently hoped that it wasn't too late to repair any damage he might have unwittingly done. What did the blue smoke mean? Why had Bertha left the farm?

Mimi caught sight of the magnifying glass on his desk. "You couldn't help yourself, could you?" she said bitterly. "You had to experiment . . . wind up the box, then watch to see how long things took to happen, whether you could actually see people moving, and all that. They aren't lab rats, Leo! They're living, breathing people! And some of them are supposed to be our friends!"

The unfairness of this took Leo's breath away. If Mimi Langlander wanted to put the worst possible interpretation on what he'd done, then let her. And to think he'd actually been looking forward to having her home!

14

Angrily he watched Mimi turn the box so that she could look at the back. She was acting as if the box were hers, instead of his.

"The Blue Queen's up to something," she said, pointing to the trail of smoke drifting from the tower of the castle on the hill.

Leo wouldn't give her the satisfaction of saying "I know." He wouldn't tell her he'd been worrying helplessly about the smoke ever since he'd first noticed it. He wouldn't admit that he'd been longing for her to return so that they could use the Key to take them into Rondo and warn Hal, Bertha, and their other friends.

Mimi spun around to face him, her eyes dark with fury. "Don't you even *care*?" she demanded.

Something inside Leo seemed to snap. "Shut up, Mimi," he said, in a low, dangerous voice he hardly recognized as his own. "You don't know what you're talking about. You've got no idea what it felt like, being here alone with this for a week. You've been somewhere else, doing whatever 'promising young violinists' do."

He put as much venom into the last few words as he possibly could, and with satisfaction saw Mimi's face close up as it always did when she felt threatened or insulted. It crossed his mind that the best thing he could do now was turn around and stalk back downstairs, but he quickly dismissed the idea. Mimi would be quite capable of winding up the music box and taking herself into Rondo without him, and he wasn't going to risk that. So he stuck his hands into his pockets and stayed where he was, glaring at her.

"We'd better get changed and go straightaway," she muttered, getting up and moving away from the desk. "We have to let the

Blue Queen's spies see us, and anyway I want to find out what's been going on. We'll go see Bertha at the tavern — send a message to Hal from there."

Leo felt a tingle of excitement, but it wasn't enough to quench his anger, or to override his natural caution. "I agree we have to go," he said in a formal voice. "And I know we'll have to stay two or three days to convince the Blue Queen we're still stranded. But this time we're not going to get into any trouble or take any risks. We're going to stay safely in town with Conker, Freda, and Bertha. We'll get beds at the tavern, and wander around the streets during the day. That way we'll be quite safe. Right?"

Mimi shrugged and looked bored. "Don't worry, Leo," she said. "Whatever happens, we'll be quite safe."

The tone in which she said this was immensely irritating. "And Mutt isn't coming with us," Leo snapped, more out of a desire to provoke her than anything else.

To his surprise, Mimi shrugged again. "As if I'd take Mutt," she said scornfully. "The Blue Queen stole him once, and she'd do it again if she got the chance. Anyway, he's really tired. He didn't sleep much while we were away. Neither of us did."

She pushed past Leo and disappeared into her own room, shutting the door behind her.

She's impossible, Leo told himself. He strode to his wardrobe and pulled it open. The clothes he'd brought back from Rondo were rolled up at the back of the very bottom shelf, behind his winter pajamas. He pulled the bundle out and put the things on his bed.

The soft white shirt was creased, but not too badly. The dull green trousers were fine. The boots, belt, and brown leather jacket were just as they had been when he put them away last Sunday night. He pulled everything on and instantly felt different — stronger and more alive, as if he'd just had a megadose of vitamins.

He looked in the long mirror on the inside of the wardrobe door and saw that he even looked different. He looked taller, older, and just more . . . interesting.

Another reflection appeared in the mirror behind him — the reflection of a poised, elegant young woman wearing slim black trousers, soft black shoes, and a long green and gold Chinese-style jacket fastened with tiny covered buttons. The Rondo clothes had worked their magic on Mimi, too.

She was still small and thin and pale. Her fine mouse-brown hair was still cut very short at the back and above the ears, and her bangs still reached all the way down to her eyebrows. But somehow the clothes that had chosen her in Rondo made all these things look attractive and unusual, whereas the baggy jeans, the battered sneakers, and the hand-me-down pink blouse with puffed sleeves had just made her look like a gawky child.

"That's *so* much better," Leo blurted out, then could have bitten his tongue.

But Mimi didn't seem to feel insulted. She looked at herself in the mirror and nodded soberly. "I wish I could wear these things all the time," she said.

A gale of laughter floated up from the back garden. Mimi

looked at the window impassively. "We'd better go, while they're still having a good time down there," she said, and walked to the desk.

Leo closed his wardrobe doors and went to join her. She watched as he took a small notebook and a pen from the desk and shoved them into his pocket.

"Good idea," she said. "We really needed a pen and paper last time."

"I'm sorry I wound the box," Leo said impulsively. "I was looking for Spoiler. I didn't think of —"

"It's happened," Mimi interrupted. "Don't worry about it. We can make it right once we're there."

Leo picked up the music box and wound it. One, two, three, four, five, six times. Even now, even knowing the real reasons for the music box rules, it wasn't easy. He had to force himself to make those last three turns.

Turn the key three times only . . .

(Because even one more turn opens the way into Rondo.)

He opened the lid just to check the music was playing, just long enough for a couple of chimes to sound, and shut it again.

Never close the lid until the music has stopped . . .

(Because then the music never runs down, and life in Rondo goes on.)

Mimi took his hand, and with her free hand grasped the pendant hidden beneath her jacket. "Think of the tavern," she murmured. "Focus on it."

"Where? Where in the tavern?" Leo gabbled. "It has to be somewhere the blue butterflies won't see us arrive."

Mimi hesitated, but only for an instant. "Inside," she said rapidly. "Beside the storeroom, at the bottom of the stairs that lead up to the bedrooms — near the hooks where we got our Rondo clothes. Have you got it?"

"Yes," Leo muttered. He fixed the image in his mind. The dark little hallway. The rows of red hooks on the wall. The storeroom door. The stairs curving up into darkness. The smell of stale cider, old clothes . . .

"Let us in!" he heard Mimi say. And he felt his hand torn away from hers as they plunged into a tunnel of chiming rainbows.

CHAPTER
3

TROUBLE AT THE BLACK SHEEP

"Gotcha!" a triumphant voice bellowed in Leo's ear. He had barely registered that he was on his hands and knees on a wooden floor when someone seized his arm and hauled him to his feet.

Leo forced his eyes open. Dim, hazy shapes swam around him. For a split second he didn't know where he was. Then he remembered.

He was in Rondo. He was — or he was supposed to be — inside The Black Sheep, where he'd be safe. But someone was shaking him, shouting at him.

Spoiler, Leo thought. Desperately he tried to free himself.

"Oh, no you don't!" the voice yelled. "You're not getting away. You're going straight to Officer Begood, you are!"

It took a moment for the words to penetrate Leo's panicking mind. When they did, he realized that his attacker couldn't be Spoiler. Spoiler wouldn't go near Officer Begood, the Rondo policeman.

Leo stopped struggling and blinked in the dimness, trying to get his bearings. He could hear the dull roar of voices and the clinking of glasses from somewhere not too far away. He could smell spices, apple cider, and the faint, lingering odor of cooked cabbage. As his eyes slowly came back into focus, he saw that he was standing beside a door marked STOREROOM. Pinned to the door was a large notice reading: NO ADMITTANCE EXCEPT ON TAVERN BUSINESS. TRESPASSERS WILL WISH THEY HAD NEVER BEEN BORN. THIS MEANS YOU!

Dismayed understanding flowed through Leo. Groaning softly, he twisted his neck to see who had grabbed him.

His captor was a lanky young man with popping pale green eyes, straw-colored hair that stuck out at odd angles all over his head, and very large ears that had turned bright red with excitement.

"Yoo-hoo, Master Jolly!" bawled the young man. "Master Jolly, come quick! I got one!"

"Wait! I'm not —" Leo gasped, but it was too late. A gray glass door at the other end of the corridor burst open, releasing a blast of light and sound from the room beyond. A very stout, balding, red-faced man came hurtling through the doorway. He had reached Leo and his captor before the door had swung shut again.

The man's shirtsleeves were rolled up to his elbows. A purple scarf was knotted jauntily beneath his second chin. His trousers were held up over his round belly by wide green suspenders.

It was Jolly, the landlord of The Black Sheep, blue eyes snapping, chest heaving, his usually happy face distorted into a ferocious snarl.

"I caught him red-handed, Master Jolly!" yelled Leo's captor, jiggling up and down and grinning so broadly that it looked as if his thin face had split in half. "Crawling around in the shadows, he was, like the sneaking thief he is! But I spied him, I did, with my little eye. And I grabbed him!"

"Good work, young fellow-me-lad!" shouted Jolly, slapping him on the back. "I had my doubts about hiring you, I'll admit, but you've earned your pay today, dallybuttons you have!" He lunged forward and took charge of Leo with gleeful efficiency.

"Shall I run and get Officer Begood?" the young man asked eagerly.

"Begood's still out of town," Jolly said. "He went straight up north from the Crystal Palace ball last night to fetch a prisoner, they tell me. There's been some kerfuffle in Hobnob."

"Kerfuffle?" gasped the young man. "What kerfuffle, Master Jolly?"

The door at the end of the corridor swung open. "Jolly!" a female voice shrieked over the din. "I need *help* in here!"

"I hear you, Merry!" Jolly bawled. As the door swung shut again, he jerked his head at his assistant. "Get back to the bar and give Merry a hand," he ordered. "What were you doing out here, anyway?"

The young man's ears went so much redder that they looked as if they were about to burst into flames. "I — I just came to see how the g-glowworms were feeling, Master Jolly," he stammered. "I was that worried about —"

"You're here to *work*, not fiddle around with the light fittings, you silly young parrot!" roared Jolly. "You get back where

22

you belong and leave those glowworms alone! They only got sick after you came — it's probably you that's upset them. Go to Merry! Go!"

The young man wheeled around, loped rapidly along the corridor, and shot through the glass door, falling over his own feet as he did so and landing on the other side with a thump.

"Right, you young villain!" Jolly growled to Leo. "You can go into the cupboard under the stairs till Begood gets back. We'll see how you like it alone in the dark with the big black spiders. Ha!"

"We weren't trying to burgle your storeroom, Master Jolly," Leo managed to gasp. "We were just —"

Jolly's eyes bulged. "*We?*" he roared, looking wildly around. "You mean there are *more* of you? Where are they?"

Dragging Leo with him, he strode to the storeroom and threw open the door. Dozens of small, golden-brown creatures that looked exactly like gingerbread men, right down to their black currant eyes and the three currant buttons dotting their chests, scattered, squeaking and giggling. "Pesky dots!" Jolly growled, slamming the door again. "So, your gang isn't in there, you villain. Where is it?"

"Here," said a voice coolly. And Mimi moved out of the shadows at the bottom of the stairs, looking very elegant and composed.

Jolly goggled at her. Mimi obviously didn't look like his idea of a burglar. *I suppose that means I do*, Leo thought gloomily. *It must be the leather jacket.*

Mimi lifted her chin. "We came to see Bertha, your model,

Master Jolly," she said in a severe tone. "We're *very* good friends of hers. But this corridor is so dangerously dark that my cousin tripped and fell. He could have hurt himself *very* badly."

Jolly glanced uneasily at Leo, who tried to look like an innocent victim.

"And then," Mimi went on, "before he could even get up, your assistant *attacked* him!"

Jolly dropped Leo's arm as if it were scalding him. He pulled a large white handkerchief from his pocket and hastily began to scrub at the greasy finger marks clearly visible on Leo's jacket sleeve.

"Many apologies . . . unfortunate misunderstanding," he mumbled. "The boy . . . all his fault . . . only started yesterday . . . can't get good help these days. And the lights . . . all the glowworms back here have gone off sick. Tummy trouble — and that's a powerful bad business inside a light fitting, let me tell you. I've been meaning to get some substitutes, but I've been rushed off my feet since —"

"Can you show us to Bertha's room, please?" Mimi broke in crisply.

Jolly, however, wasn't a man to be pushed too far. He made an obvious effort to pull himself together. "Bertha's not seeing anyone just at present, lass," he said stiffly. "She's fair tired out, she says. All the interviews, and so on."

"Interviews?" Leo exclaimed, temporarily forgetting his "innocent victim" role.

"One after the other!" said Jolly, unbending a little. "This place has been crawling with reporters ever since Bertha got here."

"*Reporters?*" Leo wished he could stop repeating everything Jolly said, but he couldn't help it. He felt very confused.

"Reporters from everywhere," said Jolly. "*The Rondo Rambler, The Herald, Palace and Bower, Coast Watch, The Vampire* . . . There's even a mouse from *The Squeaker* here — this business has kept the messenger mice hopping, as you can imagine."

"Oh — yes," Leo said weakly. "So — the tavern's full of —"

"Full as a goog!" said Jolly with great satisfaction. "I couldn't give you a room if you offered me a bag of gold and three wishes on the side."

Leo glanced at Mimi. He wasn't surprised to see her glaring at him. Life in Rondo had gone on without them all right — and gone quite a long way, by the sound of it.

"Why are the papers so interested in Bertha all of a sudden?" Mimi asked bluntly.

"Don't you *know*?" Jolly demanded, with a slight return of his former suspicion. "I thought you were friends of hers."

"We've been out of town," Leo said lamely.

"For much too long," Mimi snapped, frowning at him.

Jolly reached behind him and pulled a folded newspaper from the back pocket of his trousers. He shook out the folds and thrust the battered paper at Leo. "There," he said. "This was the first report. There have been loads of others since then, of course."

The page, boldly headed *The Rondo Rambler*, featured a large and very badly painted picture of Bertha smiling coyly beneath her flower-laden hat. The headline above the picture read: HERO PIG FOILS BLUE QUEEN'S KIDNAP PLOT.

"Oh!" Mimi squeaked, and clapped her hand over her mouth.

"That gave you a shock, didn't it?" Jolly chortled. "Yes, the Blue Queen's been made a fool of properly — and that rotten apple Spoiler with her, by all accounts."

Feeling dazed all over again, Leo began to read the story below the picture.

A hostage was rescued and seven enchanted swans were changed back into people last night when the Blue Queen's castle was stormed in a midnight raid. The raiding party, comprising seven heroes and a hidey-hole, was led by Bertha, popular artist's model, fearless wolf and troll fighter, and, in her spare moments, highly valued watch-pig at Jack Macdonald's farm.

"This was my very first quest, and I'm thrilled it turned out so well," the multitalented pig confessed, when The Rambler *tracked her down at the thriving Macdonald property.*

Bertha insists she doesn't deserve all the credit for the heroic rescue. "I couldn't have done it alone," she said with a smile. "I was just one small part of a wonderful team of heroes like myself. But I must admit that it was my appearance on the scene that caused the Blue Queen to faint with fright, thus freeing the swans she had bewitched in the Dark Time."
(Continued on p. 3)

Leo went cold at the thought of the Blue Queen's rage as she read those words. Her image rose before him — a terrifying figure in a rich blue gown, her jeweled crown glittering among the coils of her white-gold hair and her pale eyes burning with spite.

He forced the picture out of his mind and glanced at Mimi. Her mouth was set in a straight, hard line.

Leo didn't think he could bear to read whatever was on page 3. With a murmur of thanks, he gave the paper back to Jolly.

"What do you think of the picture?" Jolly asked, carefully casual.

"Oh, it's *very* good," said Leo untruthfully. "It's one of yours, isn't it?"

"It is, as a matter of fact." Jolly beamed. "The paper bought the right to copy it. Of course, the black and white doesn't do it justice. But on the whole . . ."

The door at the other end of the corridor swung open a little. "Jolly," bawled the same female voice as before, "if you don't get back in here soon, there'll be a riot!"

Jolly jumped guiltily. "Coming, dear!" he yelled. He turned to Leo and Mimi. "Look, I'm sure Bertha will want to see you, if you've been away," he said rapidly. "She's in Room Nine. Turn left at the top of the stairs. It's dark, so mind how you go. I'd never have put glowworms in if I'd known they were so sickly. They're cheap enough to run, but the inconvenience isn't worth it. Well, cheery-bye."

He trotted away. As he pushed through the glass door into the noisy room beyond, there was a loud chorus of cheers.

In grim silence, Leo and Mimi made for the stairs. In

silence they climbed through the dimness, reached the top, and turned left.

Sunlight streaming through the window at the end of the corridor helped them find their way to Room 9. A sign reading DO NOT DISTURB hung from the doorknob. Leo knocked loudly.

"I'm resting," trilled Bertha's voice from inside the room.

"Bertha! It's Leo and Mimi!" Leo called.

There was a squeal, and the next moment, the door had been flung open, and Bertha, wearing a large pair of sunglasses, was welcoming them joyfully and ushering them inside.

CHAPTER 4

A VERY STRANGE MESSAGE

The room had been painted a rather bright pink. White lace curtains hung at the glass doors that led out to the balcony, and a rose-patterned rug covered the floor. There was a bed with a frilled pink satin coverlet, a white chest of drawers with a heart-shaped mirror hanging over it, two plump armchairs, and a low table heaped with newspapers and magazines. The cover of the magazine on the top of the pile featured another of Jolly's paintings of Bertha and the bright yellow headline: MY QUEST AGONY: BERTHA TELLS. Bertha's favorite hat lay on the chest of drawers, wreathed in flowers and trailing long pink ribbons.

"Oh, Mimi, Leo, it's so good to see you!" Bertha babbled, pushing out the chairs for Leo and Mimi to sit on. "Conker and Freda will be *so* pleased. They're out on a dot-catching job at the bank, but they'll be back soon. Now, what do you think of my room? Isn't it *gorgeous*? Jolly had it redecorated just for me."

"Very nice," said Leo politely. "But Bertha —"

"A bit different from the farm, isn't it?" Bertha said, throwing herself down on the bed and stretching out luxuriously. "Oh, moving to town was the best thing I ever did! No more rooster waking me up at the crack of dawn. No more gossiping hens wasting my time. No more grumpy old Macdonald ordering me around . . ."

She broke off, gave a shrill laugh, and adjusted her sunglasses. "But that's enough about me. Tell me about you. Why haven't you come back to Rondo before this? We were all getting quite anxious. I mean, by now the Blue Queen must be starting to wonder why her spies haven't been able to find you anywhere."

"We couldn't come before. Mimi had to go away," Leo said, ignoring Mimi's thunderous expression. "Bertha, is everyone all right? Hal and Tye? Jim and Polly —?"

"No problems at all, Leo," Bertha assured him. "We're all on constant alert, of course, but the queen hasn't made a move against anyone so far. Everyone's fine. Except me, of course. I'm *absolutely* —"

"Bertha, you've been talking to the newspapers about what happened at the castle," Mimi broke in abruptly. "The tavern's full of reporters —"

"Oh, I *know*," groaned Bertha, flinging off her sunglasses. "Isn't it *awful*? I'm absolutely *drained*. I had no idea that being a celebrity could be so exhausting."

It was true that she didn't seem her usual bright self, Leo thought. Though she was obviously pleased to see them, her chatter sounded strained. And now that she'd taken off her sunglasses, he could see that she had bags under her eyes and that the eyes themselves were more red than blue.

"But now the queen must be even angrier than she was before!" Mimi said furiously. "And she knows the swans are free, too. Bertha, how could you *do* it?"

Bertha stiffened. "I didn't!" she snapped. "For your information, by the time *The Rondo Rambler* reporter came to the farm to see me, he already knew the whole story."

Mimi blinked in surprise, but it didn't seem to occur to her to apologize.

"That vulgar hidey-hole we took with us boasted about the quest to all its forest friends," Bertha told her haughtily. "The story spread like wildfire — you know what forests are like for gossip. It's just very lucky that this *particular* hidey-hole *is* vulgar. It was so interested in the fighting and things getting smashed and so on that it didn't even notice all the talk about the Key to Rondo, and said nothing about it. So *that* secret is still safe, at least."

Leo sighed with relief.

"Still, you shouldn't have given an interview, Bertha," Mimi said stubbornly. "You should have told Scribble 'no comment' or something."

Bertha tossed her head. "I *did*," she said. "I may be new to questing, but I *am*, after all, a famous model. I know how to deal with the press. But Scribble said that it would be a *very* bad idea not to speak to him."

"Oh, yes?" Mimi muttered.

"Yes," said Bertha with dignity. "Scribble said that he'd have to write the story whether I spoke to him or not — it was his duty to the public. He said that if I didn't talk to him — if the story was just based on forest gossip — it might be full of all sorts of embarrassing errors that could *ruin* my reputation."

"He *blackmailed* you?" exclaimed Leo.

"Of course not!" cried Bertha, very ruffled. "He just wanted to *help* me. He's been a fan of mine for ages, apparently."

"Oh, Bertha!" sighed Leo, torn between irritation, sympathy, and a strong desire to laugh. Mimi snorted.

"Hal *quite* understood my position," Bertha said. "In fact, after he got over the shock of the first headline, he decided that more interviews would be a good idea. He said the publicity would divert the queen's attention from Suki and the other ex-swans, and focus it on us."

"Oh, right," Leo said weakly. Then he remembered something and sat up straight in his chair. "I have to get a message to Hal, Bertha," he said. "I've seen smoke coming out of the Blue Queen's tower."

"Oh, Hal is well aware of the smoke, Leo," Bertha said, with the rather irritating air of one who is in the know. "He says there have been traces of it around the tower before — before you and Mimi came the first time, I mean. He was sure the queen was working on a new spell then, and she's obviously gone back to working on it now."

"Working on it harder than ever, I should think," Mimi muttered, glancing meaningfully at the heap of newspapers and magazines.

"Oh, I'd say so," Bertha agreed blithely. "It's probably some-thing really nasty, too. Anyway, Hal and Tye are staying on at the house at Troll's Bridge so they can keep a close eye on the castle. They'll let us know if anything strange happens. We send mice to one another every day — sometimes twice."

"What about Spoiler?" Leo asked. "I thought I —"

"Who cares about Spoiler?" Mimi interrupted irritably. "I can't understand why you're so obsessed with him, Leo!"

"Hal's obsessed as well," Bertha told her. "He's asked Conker and Freda and me to keep our ears open for any gossip about odd happenings, or money being stolen — anything sneaky that might be Spoiler's doing and give us a clue about where he is. But we haven't heard a thing."

"Hal should stop feeling responsible for what Spoiler does," Mimi said, shaking her head. "And so should Leo. It's stupid. Just because Spoiler's a Langlander —"

"It's not just that, Mimi," Bertha said earnestly. "Spoiler's been out of sight so long that we've decided he must be in disguise. And Hal thinks it's quite possible that he's planning to stalk you and Leo and try to capture you. I mean, what better way to get back in the Blue Queen's good books than to make her a gift of her two deadliest enemies?"

Mimi became very still. An unpleasant fluttering began in Leo's stomach.

"There was a ball at the Crystal Palace last night, to welcome Princess Pretty and her new husband home from their honeymoon," Bertha went on. "I was invited, but I was just too *exhausted* to go. The princess was sure Spoiler would turn up and steal the wedding presents, so Officer Begood went to guard them. But nothing happened, apparently."

"Spoiler probably stayed away because he heard Officer Begood would be there," Leo suggested.

"Possibly." Bertha sighed. "Or maybe he just had something better to do — something worse, I suppose I should say. Anyway, Hal says you mustn't go anywhere on your own while you're here. There are a lot of strangers in town, because of the school holidays. And Spoiler might be *anywhere*. He could be *anyone*!"

"I'd recognize him whatever he was wearing," Mimi said. "He attacked me twice. I saw him really close-up." She wrinkled her nose in distaste.

They all jumped as there was a sharp knock at the door.

"I'm resting!" called Bertha. "Can't you read the sign?"

"Dots to the sign!" roared a familiar voice. "Bertha, open up! Urgent quest business!"

Leo threw open the door. The stocky, wild-haired figure of Conker strode in, closely followed by Freda the brown duck, who was looking even more disgruntled than usual. Two weapons that looked like large flyswatters swung from Conker's belt. Leo noticed with a shudder that they were still clogged with currants and dot crumbs.

"Leo!" bellowed Conker. "Mimi!" He shook their hands warmly. "Oh, this is perfect! Isn't it perfect, Freda?"

"Perfect," the duck drawled. "Now all five of us can make geese of ourselves together."

"What is it?" Bertha demanded.

"A job," whispered Conker, his little black eyes glittering with excitement. "Freda and I were just leaving the bank when a mouse came with *this*!" With the air of a magician producing a bunch of flowers from a hat, he held out a very small, crumpled piece of mauve paper.

Leo took the paper. It was covered on both sides with large, round, purple writing. Slowly he read the words aloud.

Dear Master Conker,

I saw in the paper that you do quests and I hope you can help us whatever Clogg says about papers telling lies. My poor young nephew is in terrible trouble with the law but he didn't do it. It's not Simon's fault that the wizard disappeared.

That was the end of the first page. Leo turned the paper over and read on.

He was sometimes very irritable Simon says but Simon would not have hurt him let alone drowned him in the pond and as for vanishing him well Simon couldn't have done that if he tried. All this worry is very bad for my health so please come

And that was it. There was nothing else on the paper at all.

"Well?" cried Conker. "What do you think?"

"It doesn't give much information," Leo said doubtfully. "It doesn't say where you have to go. It isn't even signed."

"Well, that's the cleverness of it!" said Conker, rubbing his hands. "If it had fallen into the wrong hands, the enemy wouldn't have been able to tell what it meant."

"But . . . do *you* know what it means, Conker?" asked Mimi.

"No idea," Conker said happily. "But it's obviously urgent, and that means there's no time to waste. We'll just have to set off and work out where we're going on the way."

"How's that for a plan?" Freda asked the others sourly.

"Conker, I don't see how you can set off if you don't know which direction to set off in," Leo said as gently as he could.

"Oh, my heart, liver, and lungs!" Conker puffed out his cheeks irritably. "You aren't thinking, Leo! All we have to do is work it out from the clues!"

"What clues?" Mimi asked.

With a snort of annoyance, Conker snatched the message from Leo and scanned it. "There!" he said. "'Clogg says' — that's the first clue. Wherever this place is, a person called Clogg lives in it."

"You can't assume that," Bertha pointed out — very reasonably, Leo thought. "Clogg might have written that silly opinion about the newspapers in a letter."

Conker ground his teeth. "Forget about Clogg then," he snapped. "There are lots of other clues. Wherever this place is, for example, there's a wizard —"

"Not anymore, apparently," said the duck.

"There *was* a wizard," Conker plowed on with a scowl. "A crabby wizard, who's disappeared. And this crabby wizard has — had — a friend, or an assistant, maybe, called Simon, who's being blamed for doing away with the wizard, and who is the nephew of the person who wrote this note."

"That's right," Mimi agreed, clearly becoming interested in Conker's clue hunt. "And wherever the wizard and Simon are — were — there's a pond!"

"Oh, that's *very* helpful," snapped Freda. "There couldn't be more than a few thousand ponds in Rondo."

"And a few thousand Simons, probably," said Bertha.

"I met a frog once who called himself Prince Simon," Conker said thoughtfully. "Later on I heard that his real name was Plop, and he just pretended to be an enchanted frog to make himself look important. Still . . ."

Leo felt desperate. "Listen," he said, leaning forward. "We're wasting time thinking about Simons, and ponds, and so on. We should be thinking about *wizards*. There can't be so many of those."

"Brilliant!" Conker thumped his fist on the low table, making several newspapers slide flapping to the floor. "Right! Let's think of all the wizards we know." He knitted his brow in furious thought. "Well, there's Wizard Zargo on the coast . . ."

"Dead," Freda snapped.

"Oh, that's right." Conker nodded. "One of the Blue Queen's monsters ate him in the Dark Time. Right . . . well, what about Wizard Nerklan? No, he's dead, too — drowned trying to invent a bottomless teacup, they say. All right . . . ah . . ." His face brightened. "Wizard Wurzle, in Flitter Wood. Now, *he's* a possibility!"

"No he's not," Bertha objected. "I know Wizard Wurzle. He goes to Macdonald's farm to get eggs. He's *very* shy and timid. He bites his nails and jumps sky-high when anyone speaks to him. I can't imagine him *ever* being irritable."

"Right," said Conker. "So. Zargo's out, Nerklan's out, Wurzle's out. Wizard Plum's out, too, by the way — I ran into him at the bank."

"Head-butted him in the belly, as a matter of fact," Freda told the others, smirking. "Plum went down like a big fat bowling pin."

"He should have known better than to get in the way of a dot-catcher in the lawful pursuit of his duties," Conker said loftily. "Who else is there?"

There was a tense silence.

"Oh, I can't *think*!" complained Bertha, fanning herself. "This detecting business is *exhausting*!"

"What about Wizard Bing?" Leo asked suddenly. "You know — that wizard who once tried to train lizards to carry messages, so that the messenger mice could be replaced? You told us about him, Conker, when we were here last time."

"Oh, yes!" exclaimed Conker, his enthusiasm returning instantly. "Bing! I'd forgotten about him. Well, most people have, since the lizard disaster. But it *could* be him. He's *very* irritable — or so I've heard. They say he's fallen out with everyone in Hobnob at one time or another."

"Hobnob!" Leo and Mimi gasped.

The others turned to look at them.

"What?" demanded Bertha.

Leo swallowed. "Jolly said that there'd been some sort of trouble at Hobnob. He said that Officer Begood had gone there . . . to bring back a prisoner!"

"Aha!" Conker said, his beard and eyebrows bristling with excitement. "A prisoner called Simon, I'll bet my boots! Charged with murdering Wizard Bing! Oh, my heart, liver, and lungs, this is it! We've got it!"

CHAPTER
5

CONKER LOSES HIS TEMPER

Conker threw the note down on the bed, stuck his thumbs under his belt, and puffed out his chest. "So there you are!" he declared. "We've broken the code. Perseverance, brainpower, and teamwork! That's all it took."

At that moment, a skinny brown mouse slid from beneath the mirror that hung over the chest of drawers. A small mauve square dangled from a gold chain around the mouse's neck.

"Message for Conker," the mouse drawled. "Immediate reply requested." Skirting Bertha's hat, it slouched to the edge of the chest of drawers, unclipped the mauve square from the chain, and gave it to Conker.

"What's this?" Conker hissed. "It looks like . . ."

As he unfolded the mauve paper, everyone could see that it was covered on both sides by the same purple, rounded writing as the first note had been.

Conker frowned at the paper for a long moment. Then he turned it over and read the other side. He began to breathe heavily through his nose.

"What is it?" exclaimed Leo, unable to bear the suspense.

Conker looked up, his face a picture of baffled fury. He glared at the messenger mouse, which had sat down, crossed its legs, and begun to whistle tunelessly through its teeth.

"Why didn't I get this before?" Conker demanded, shaking the paper in the mouse's face. "Why wasn't it delivered with the other one?"

"One page only, of the officially approved size, to be carried by any one messenger," the mouse droned. "Should a message require more than one page, of the officially approved size, separate messengers, if and when available, are to be used for each and every extra page, such extra pages also to be of the officially approved size."

"What!" Conker bellowed. "Since when?"

"Since the stop-work meeting this morning," the mouse replied, yawning. "The vote was unanimouse."

Mimi gave a shout of laughter. The mouse uncrossed its legs and looked at her severely.

"It's no laughing matter," it said. "It's all a matter of weight. Certain persons, namely newspaper reporters, have been abusing the service. We've got eleven members off with neck strain, fourteen with severe claw fatigue, and fifty-two on stress leave. You can read all about it in *The Squeaker.*"

"The day I use *The Squeaker* for anything but wrapping the garbage is the day I'll give the game away!" roared Conker, beside himself with rage.

"Conker, just read us the note," Mimi urged.

Conker squinted at the mauve paper in disgust. "'To Hobnob at once and find Wizard Bing,'" he read in a flat voice.

"What?" exclaimed Bertha.

"Oh, my heart, liver, lungs, and *gizzards!*" Conker exploded. "Don't you understand? This is the second page of the message we've just spent endless time trying to decode!"

"I understand *perfectly*," Bertha said huffily. "And I'll thank you to leave your internal organs out of this. I have simply temporarily forgotten how the first page ended."

Leo snatched up the first note from the end of the bed and read out the last line. "'All this worry is very bad for my health, so please come . . .'"

He nodded to Conker, who glared ferociously at his own paper and went on:

. . . to Hobnob at once and find Wizard Bing. Officer Begood has arrested Simon, and I don't know what the neighbors will say. Clogg says it was to be expected because Simon is a hopeless case but what I say is poor Simon has tried very hard

Conker cleared his throat irritably and turned the note over.

to be a good apprentice and stayed longer than any of the others, which I admit isn't saying much, but still. Don't worry about the money, I will pay your fees whatever Clogg says as we are very rich if I do say so myself and my nephew can't do

anything not being quite himself at the moment not to men-
tion in jail as well by now I expect.

    Yours very faithfully,

    Muffy Clogg (Mrs.)

    Upstairs, Clogg's Shoe Emporium, Hobnob

"Well!" Bertha exclaimed. "So all that exhausting detecting and remembering and so on was a complete waste of time! All we had to do was wait for the second page of the message."

Freda gave a harsh quack of laughter. Conker glowered at her.

The mouse yawned. "Is there going to be a reply or not?" it drawled. "I can't wait around all day. We're *very* short-staffed and I'm due for my cheese break."

Conker gritted his teeth, felt in his pockets, and at last pulled out a tiny notebook and the stub of a pencil.

The mouse closed its eyes and began its tuneless whistling again. Making an obvious effort to ignore it, Conker wrote laboriously, then tore the page out of his notebook and held the ragged paper up for everyone to see.

Quest team will be with you as soon as possible, if not before.

"Brief and to the point," said Freda with approval.

Conker handed the folded note to the mouse. Sighing, it clipped the note to its neck chain, then sauntered back to the mirror and disappeared behind it.

Conker rubbed his hands. "So!" he said. "We leave for Hobnob at dawn."

"I don't see why you're so obsessed with dawn, Conker," Bertha complained. "You might as well be a rooster."

"If you want to be a true quest hero you've got to respect the questing traditions," Conker declared. "Dawn it is. But we've got a lot to do before then. We've got to buy supplies, for one thing — not to mention interviewing the prisoner when he arrives. Come on!"

He strode to the door and wrenched it open.

"What about the thing?" Freda inquired loudly. "The thing Mimi has to put in a Safe Place before she goes anywhere?"

Bertha bounced on the bed and gave a startled squeak.

Conker froze, slammed the door again, and spun around. "I didn't forget," he snapped, looking very flustered. "I was just testing you."

"So was I," gabbled Bertha, whose ears had gone very red.

Leo saw that Mimi's hand had crept up to cover the pendant hidden beneath her jacket. Her lips were pressed into a straight, stubborn line.

"Mimi, Hal doesn't want you carrying the Key while you're here," Bertha said, scrambling off the bed. "He wants you to put it in a Safe Place, and collect it again just before you go home."

"The Key is perfectly safe with me," Mimi snapped.

"It's — ah — not so much a matter of its *safety*, Mimi," Conker said with a feeble smile. "It's more a matter of . . . ah . . ."

"Of the damage you might do with it," Freda said flatly. "You don't realize how dangerous the Key is, Mimi. There's *nothing* the Key can't do."

Patches of bright color appeared on Mimi's cheekbones. "I won't do any damage," she said, barely opening her lips. "I promised Hal I wouldn't use the Key to change things or create things, and I won't."

"You mightn't be able to help it, Mimi," Bertha said earnestly. "You're like me — very sensitive and creative, and all that sort of —"

"I can control my imagination if I want to," Mimi interrupted, the scarlet spots on her cheeks glowing even more brightly. "I'm not a baby!"

Leo bit his lip. He thought that Hal was perfectly right to worry about Mimi being on the loose with the Key to Rondo. Anything could happen if Mimi became frightened or angry or lost concentration for even a minute. And yet . . .

"I don't like the idea of hiding the Key, either," he said. "Someone might find it and steal it. And it's our only way home."

Mimi looked at him coldly. "I see," she said. "Getting home is all you care about, Leo. It doesn't matter to you if I'm accused of being an idiot who can't control the Key."

Leo felt a wave of fury. "Can't you think of anything but your precious feelings?" he shouted. "You're prickly as a — a pineapple! You should be glad I'm on your side, whatever the reason is, you —"

"Stop it!" squealed Bertha.

As Leo gaped at her, she shook back her ears, breathing hard. "We'll have no more shouting, if you please," she announced in a trembling voice. "My nerves are shattered as it is. Conker, it's perfectly obvious that Mimi and Leo have no idea what a Safe Place *is*."

Conker stared. "Oh," he mumbled. "Right."

Bertha turned to Leo and Mimi. "I will now demonstrate, if I can," she said. She cleared her throat and spoke respectfully to the room in general. "If any Members of the Ancient Order of Safe Places are present and available for guard duty, could they please reveal themselves?"

For a moment, nothing happened. Then, over by the window, there was a soft creaking sound and a small square of the rose-spattered carpet lifted like a trapdoor, revealing what looked like a red velvet cushion.

"At your service," said a dry, cracked voice from the depths of the cushion.

Mimi gave a little shriek. Leo jumped violently.

"There, you see?" Bertha said. "*That* is a Safe Place."

"At your service," repeated the dry voice, and the little square of carpet dipped in a slight bow.

"It's just a different sort of hidey-hole," Mimi muttered, recovering a little from her shock. "I'm not going to leave the Key in a —"

"Sshh!" Bertha hissed, aghast. "Lawks-a-daisy, Mimi, don't say things like that! Have the proper respect!"

She glanced nervously at the red cushion, which was rippling gently and making a slight humming sound. "Thank goodness! It doesn't seem to have heard you," she whispered. "Mimi, Members of the Ancient Order of Safe Places must *never* be confused with common hidey-holes. They are *very* distant relations. In fact, Safe Places prefer to pretend they are no relation at all."

"Snobs!" jeered Freda, though Leo noticed she kept her voice down.

"They *are* a bit snooty," Bertha agreed. "They don't think hidey-holes are respectable, because they move around and tend to be — well, flighty. Safe Places stay in one spot, and their Order is governed by very strict rules. They only guard valuables — they wouldn't dream of hiding anything alive. And, unlike some hidey-holes I could name, they're *utterly* trustworthy."

She turned to Leo. "So you needn't worry about thieves, Leo," she added. "Once a Safe Place is filled, it won't open again till someone stands right over it and whispers the password. Safe Places are also impervious to dots, mice, spells, quakes —"

"Then why didn't Hal use one to hide the Key in the first place?" Mimi interrupted. "Why did he bother taking it back to our world? If Safe Places are as safe as you claim —"

"I knew she'd say that!" Freda remarked.

Conker sighed. "In those days Hal didn't trust Safe Places any more than you do, Mimi," he said. "He knows better now."

"Odd there's only one Safe Place in here," Freda commented, considering the rippling red cushion with interest. "Tavern bedrooms usually have at least three."

"The others are probably already occupied," Bertha said. "Jolly was complaining about it just the other day. He says this tavern has only a fraction of the Safe Places it used to have. It comes of folk forgetting their password, or even forgetting where their Safe Place is. That happens a lot, apparently."

Leo looked quickly at the red cushion, memorizing its distance from the window and the pattern of the carpet around it. He noticed that the cushion had stopped patiently rippling and was now pulsating in a slightly irritable way instead. The raised square of carpet had begun to sag a little.

"Please present the item to be guarded," said the dry, cracked voice. "Please have your password ready."

"They don't like to be kept waiting," whispered Bertha to Mimi. "Oh, Mimi, *please!*"

Mimi frowned for a moment, then suddenly gave in. "Oh, all right," she said ungraciously. She tugged at the chain around her neck and drew out the ugly old pendant that contained hairs from the brush that long ago had created Rondo. Conker, Freda, and Bertha stared at it in awe.

"Choose a password you'll both remember," Bertha urged, suddenly anxious.

"But nothing too obvious!" warned Conker from the door.

Leo and Mimi walked over to the red cushion and knelt down in front of it.

"Password, please," said the dry voice. "Speak distinctly to avoid disappointment."

"Marion," said Mimi in a low voice. She glanced quickly at Leo with her eyebrows raised, and Leo nodded. Only he and Mimi knew that Marion was her real name. As a password, it was perfect.

"Marion," the Safe Place repeated softly. "Very good. Please place the object . . . now."

Mimi put the pendant and its chain on the red cushion. Instantly the cushion shot downward into the gloom, leaving a hollow darkness in its place.

"Thank you for your custom," the dry voice whispered from the depths. "Please stand back."

The trapdoor thudded shut, the line around it sealed, and in moments there was no sign at all that the carpet had ever been disturbed. The Key was gone.

"So — that's that," Leo said. He was determined to sound cheerful, but he felt rather empty inside. It had been unsettling to see the Key disappear.

"That's that," Mimi repeated. Her face was unreadable.

"Excellent!" exclaimed Conker. "Now, let's go shopping!"

CHAPTER 6

SPLITTING UP

"Wait!" Bertha cried, as Conker threw open the door. "I've just thought! It's broad daylight outside. If any of those reporters see me in the street I'll be mobbed."

"Disguise yourself, then," Conker said impatiently. "Put on your sunglasses. And don't wear your hat."

"I can't go out without my hat!" Bertha cried. "My complexion —"

"Dots to your complexion!" roared Conker. "It's only skin, isn't it?"

Bertha drew herself up. "It may be only skin to you," she said in a high voice. "But modeling is my livelihood. My *only* secure livelihood now, I'd like to remind you!" Her lips quivered.

Conker looked helplessly around the room. His gaze fell on the rumpled bed and his eyes brightened. "I've got it!" he exclaimed. He rushed to the bed, snatched up a pillow, and pulled off the frilled satin pillowcase. He wrapped the pillowcase around Bertha's head like a scarf and knotted it firmly under her chin.

"There!" he said. "Perfect!"

Bertha trailed to the chest of drawers and looked in the mirror doubtfully. Pink satin ruffles framed her face and flapped limply over her eyes. "I suppose it might do," she said.

"Of course it'll do!" cried Conker. "You look —"

"Like a pig in a pillowcase," Leo heard Freda mutter under her breath.

"— marvelous!" Conker finished loudly, glaring at the duck.

"Actually, it *does* rather suit me, doesn't it?" said Bertha, tilting her head this way and that so she could see herself in the mirror from every angle. "Could someone get my sunglasses?"

Full of misgivings, Leo fetched the sunglasses and fitted them over her nose.

"Wonderful!" said Conker. "Your own mother wouldn't know you. Right, let's go! There's no time to lose!"

They crowded out into the corridor and Conker led the way toward the stairs.

"Conker, Hobnob's in the north, isn't it?" Leo asked suddenly.

"Keep your voice down!" hissed Conker. "We don't want pesky reporters catching on to where we're going, do we? Yes, Hobnob's in the north. It's an out-of-the-way little place — nice scenery and all that. People go there for holidays."

"I think I might have seen Spoiler in the north," Leo said, determinedly not looking at Mimi. "He was just outside a village that's between two hills. Is that — ?"

Conker shook his head. "That's not Hobnob. It sounds like Innes-Trule, farther east. Spoiler might well have been there. A Gap — you know, a Rondo shortcut — runs from Troll's Bridge to Innes-Trule. Spoiler might have used it to get away from the castle as fast as possible. But he's not in Innes-Trule now. Tye went there and couldn't find a trace of him."

"What if he went on to Hobnob?" Leo persisted eagerly as they reached the stairs. "It sounds like a good place to hide, if it's so out-of-the-way. And now this wizard has disappeared from there . . ."

Mimi sighed and rolled her eyes.

Conker tugged at his beard. "That's a very good thought, Leo," he said kindly. "But it's unlikely that Spoiler would bother to abduct Wizard Bing. Bing's not exactly a huge professional success, and he's as poor as a squirrel."

They went downstairs and left the tavern by a back door that led into a lane lined with the shabby backs of buildings. The lane was deserted except for a few dots, rather crumbly around the edges, poking listlessly in garbage cans and scuffling through the dead leaves in the gutters.

They hurried along the lane till they reached the mouth of an alley that ran between buildings. At the other end of the alley was the bustling main street, and the flower stall, with its red-and-white striped awning and its buckets of bright blooms. Leo felt a tingle of excitement.

"We'll split up to save time," said Conker. "Bertha and Mimi can buy the food, and the rest of us will go to the camping shop. We need some new equipment. My old cooking pot's insisted on retiring."

"About time, too," said Freda sourly. "It leaked whenever it coughed."

"True," Conker agreed. "Anyway, it's gone, and it's taken the spoon with it — they were always very close — so we need replacements." He heaved a very false-sounding sigh.

"Any excuse," Freda muttered to Leo out of the side of her beak. "He's wild about the camping shop."

"Turn right at Main Street, and go along to Dinah's Dotless Delicacies, just past the wing repair place," Conker instructed Bertha and Mimi. "We'll meet back in your room."

Bertha looked uncomfortable. "Ah — I'm afraid I don't have any money just now," she said in a small voice.

"No problem," Conker told her. "Everything can go on my account."

"An *account*!" squealed Bertha, brightening up at once.

Conker eyed her warily. "You just leave everything to Dinah," he ordered. "She knows what we need. Just tell her there are five of us this time, for a three-day quest."

Five of us?

"No, Conker," Leo said quickly. "Not five. Three. Sorry — I thought you realized. Mimi and I can't go to Hobnob."

Conker's mouth fell open in dismay. Bertha gave a wail of disappointment.

"What are you *talking* about, Leo?" Mimi demanded.

"We agreed not to go anywhere," Leo said doggedly. "The plan was to see Conker, Freda, and Bertha, and keep safe in town . . ."

"But that's all changed now, hasn't it?" Mimi retorted. "Conker, Freda, and Bertha are going away."

"Mimi, we *decided* —" Leo began furiously.

"*I* didn't decide!" Mimi snapped. "*You* did. You stay here if you want to. I'm going with the others."

"Leo, you have to come with us!" Conker groaned. "The team's missing Tye and Hal as it is! I was depending on you!"

"If Leo won't come, the quest is off," Freda said flatly. "We can't leave him alone here. Hal's orders."

Conker made a strangled sound.

Bertha's lips trembled. "It seems very unfair," she said in a high voice, "that after all I've been through, my new career should be blighted before it even begins! But if Leo insists on staying, I'll stay with him. The rest of you can go find the missing wizard and be hailed as heroes and earn lots of money and so on. I don't mind."

Leo felt dreadful. "I'm really sorry," he said miserably. "It's just . . . we decided not to do anything dangerous this time."

"But this isn't dangerous, Leo!" Conker exclaimed. "Not *dangerous* dangerous. The Blue Queen isn't involved in this. And even if she was, what could she do to us in Hobnob? Ever since she lost the Key and the Dark Time ended, she's only been able to change people into things and enslave them, and create monsters to tear them apart, and so on inside her castle!"

"Are you sure?" Leo asked doubtfully.

"Oh, my lungs and kidneys, of course I'm sure!" roared Conker. "Do you think I'd be standing here talking to you now if the queen could do anything about it? Oh, she can still disguise herself and go around poisoning folk or sending them to sleep for a hundred years — little things like that — by using some potion or other. But that's all."

Freda nodded. "You have to be inside her castle, right in the center of her power, before she can do anything *really* bad to you," she agreed. "And she can't *make* people go into her castle, even if she knows their names. They have to go there willingly or be brought there by someone else."

"The queen can't use Leo's or Bertha's or my name to bewitch us anymore anyway," Mimi said unexpectedly. "I fixed that with the Key before we left Rondo last time."

Leo stared at her. So this is what she had meant when she'd said there was nothing for him to worry about! He told himself that he should be grateful . . . relieved . . . and he was, in a way. But it gave him a weird, uncomfortable feeling to think that Mimi had put a sort of spell on him — even a good spell — without saying a word to him about it.

"Mimi, you promised Hal you wouldn't use the Key for *any-thing*!" scolded Bertha.

Mimi tossed her head. "When Hal had it he used it to protect Tye and Conker and Freda and himself," she said. "I didn't see why I couldn't do the same thing for *my* friends."

Leo felt a rush of warmth. It didn't quite extinguish his sense of having been somehow invaded, or his fury with Mimi for refusing to support him about staying in town, but it helped.

"There, you see, Leo?" Conker wheedled. "All we have to do is take the usual precautions, and none of us has anything to fear."

"Oh, leave him alone, Conker," Freda said carelessly. "Let him stay here with Bertha. You, Mimi, and I will manage all right on our own. Of course, it might get tricky if Spoiler *is* behind the Bing business, as Leo suspects, but that's how it goes."

She looked meaningfully at Conker, whose eyes suddenly widened with understanding. "Of course," Conker said with very false heartiness. "If we have to deal with Spoiler, we'll do it." He heaved an exaggerated sigh. "Mind you, it won't be easy — with just the three of us."

Leo knew perfectly well what Freda and Conker were up to. They were just trying to lure him into joining the quest. Neither of them thought for a minute that the mysterious disappearance of Wizard Bing had anything to do with Spoiler.

The trouble, nagging at the back of Leo's mind, was the suspicion that they were wrong.

Hadn't Hal said to be on the watch for any odd happenings? Having lost the favor of the Blue Queen, wouldn't Spoiler be attracted to the idea of a wizard whose magic might provide him with protection and an easy life? And wouldn't it be just like Spoiler to do something wicked, then sit back and let someone else take the blame?

None of that is proof, Leo told himself. *Rondo's affecting you, like it did last time. You've just got a hunch, and you despise hunches! You don't believe in them!*

But what if Spoiler *were* in Hobnob? What if he *had* done something to Wizard Bing and the quest team could prove it? Then they'd be able to hand him over to Officer Begood. The people of Rondo would be safe from him for a while, at least.

And so would we, Leo thought. *We'd be able to enjoy Rondo without looking over our shoulders all the time. We'd be safe.*

It was a very tempting prospect. It made going to Hobnob seem almost like a duty. And *that* gave Leo the perfect excuse to do what he had really longed to do all along. He glanced at Mimi, who raised her eyebrows and grinned wickedly.

55

"All right," he said. "You win. I'll come."

Bertha squealed with joy. Freda smirked.

"Excellent!" Conker said, rubbing his hands with great satisfaction. "And bear in mind that we're not expecting you and Mimi to come for nothing, Leo. We'll split the fee five ways."

"After deducting expenses," Freda put in.

"Now, let's get moving," Conker went on. "You and Mimi go first, Bertha. We'll attract less attention if we don't move in a bunch. Stay together now. And watch out for Spoiler!"

Leo watched uneasily as Bertha and Mimi set off toward the crowded main road. He didn't like the idea of splitting up. It was bad enough that the Key was no longer under his eye, without Mimi disappearing as well.

"I think I'll go with them," he said suddenly. He started forward, but Conker grabbed his arm and held him back.

"No, Leo," Conker said. "I want Bertha and Mimi to have some time alone. A bit of girl talk might help, and Mimi's a girl."

"What am I then?" snapped Freda. "A bunch of waterweed?"

"You might be female, Freda, but, let's face it, you couldn't do proper girl talk if you were paid for it," said Conker, refusing to be bullied. "If Bertha told you her troubles you wouldn't say 'I know, I know' and 'how awful, you poor thing,' and stuff like that. You'd just tell her to stop whining."

Leo thought uneasily that Mimi might easily say exactly the same thing. In his opinion, Mimi Langlander and Freda the duck had a lot in common.

Mimi and Bertha reached the main road, turned right, and disappeared from view.

"Our turn," Conker said briefly, and set off along the alley with Freda at his heels. Leo hurried to keep up.

"Why does Bertha need to talk?" he demanded. "What's wrong with her?"

Conker sighed gustily. "I suppose she told you she came to town of her own accord," he said. "That's what she told us. But it's not true. Freda heard all about it, from this crow she knows who saw the whole thing."

"Marjorie," said Freda.

"Marjorie," Conker agreed. "Well, it turns out that Macdonald got sick of all the reporters trampling over his fields night and day. He said Bertha was more trouble than she was worth, and gave her the sack."

"That's terrible!" Leo exclaimed, very shocked. He would have said more, but they had almost reached the main street, and at that moment Posy the flower seller saw them and waved a brawny arm in greeting. Four of the blue butterflies dancing around Posy's buckets of flowers rose into the air and fluttered purposefully away.

"Gone to report," muttered Freda.

"Well, it's what we want, isn't it?" Leo said, trying to ignore the little chills running up and down his spine. He looked quickly to the right, but Bertha and Mimi had already vanished into the crowd.

CHAPTER 7

THE PRISONER

Conker led the way out to the street, turned left, and clicked his tongue in annoyance. A huge dappled gray horse was clip-clopping very slowly toward them, pulling a cart. With a start, Leo recognized the horse and cart he'd first seen at Innes-Trule, then watched slowly making its way south. It had finally reached the town.

The cart was piled high with old furniture, overflowing trunks of clothes, and boxes of dusty household goods. It was so wide that it blocked the road almost completely. People in its way were jumping aside, flattening themselves against walls and stalls.

"We'll have to wait till it goes by," said Conker, ushering Leo back into the mouth of the alley. "Botheration!"

As the cart drew level with the alley, Leo saw that the words WINKLE & CO. — OLD GOODS BOUGHT & SOLD were painted on its side. The cart's driver was a tiny, bent man with a long white beard and very large ears. He was hunched over the reins and swaying slightly. His eyes were closed, his mouth was open, and he was snoring gently.

"That Winkle fellow's a menace," Conker fumed. "He shouldn't be allowed on the road. Can't stay awake for five minutes at a time. Where's Begood when you need him? Off arresting perfectly innocent people, the big lummox!"

The cart trundled by with agonizing slowness. The sleeping driver had developed a slight tilt to the left.

"He'll fall off in a minute," Freda said gleefully.

"Wake up, Winkle, you dunderhead!" Conker shouted, shaking his fist. The horse turned to look at him and snickered offensively, but the tiny driver snored on, his drooping mustache fluttering with every puff of breath.

"We should talk to Winkle before we leave," said Leo urgently. "Spoiler was standing right behind that cart when I saw him in Innes-Trule. Maybe he was stealing a disguise from one of those trunks of clothes."

"Maybe," growled Conker. "But Winkle wouldn't have a clue what was missing. He's dead to the world most of the time. It's a miracle he gets back to town with any goods at all. Right! He's clear! Come on!"

He plunged into the crowd of people milling about in the wake of the cart. As Leo and Freda hurried to catch up with him, Leo looked around nervously. He couldn't see anyone who looked like Spoiler, but that didn't mean anything if Spoiler was in disguise. He worried briefly about Mimi, then told himself it was unnecessary. Spoiler wouldn't risk attacking Mimi while she had Bertha for a bodyguard. Bertha in fighting mode would terrify anyone.

"How *could* Macdonald sack Bertha?" he wondered aloud. "She's so good at her job."

"She's only got herself to blame," Freda muttered.

"That's not fair!" Leo said hotly. "It wasn't Bertha's fault that the reporters —"

"Freda's not talking about the reporters," Conker interrupted. "What she means is that, according to the crow —"

"Marjorie," said Freda.

"According to Marjorie," Conker continued, "Bertha made it easy for Macdonald to let her go. She told him to get a fox to control his dots, see, and he did. Well, you know what foxes are."

"Sly," said Freda darkly.

Conker nodded. "This one's even *called* Sly, by all accounts," he said. "That should have put Bertha on her guard, but she didn't suspect a thing. She showed him all around, told him everything he wanted to know, and soon he started moving in on her job, sucking up to Macdonald, suggesting he could guard the farm just as well as Bertha could, acting all smarmy and polite . . ."

Freda made a vomiting noise. A beautiful, fragile-looking young woman who was drifting by glanced at her in horrified disgust and twitched her frothy, pale pink skirts aside.

"Oh, go sit on a pea and bruise yourself, why don't you?" Freda said rudely.

The woman gasped, tossed her golden ringlets, steadied her tiara, and hurried on.

"I wish you wouldn't insult princesses, Freda," Conker complained. "They're all potential quest clients, you know."

They passed Crumble the pie seller, who was dealing with a long queue of people eager to buy his tasty-looking pies while dots skittered around his feet snatching up flakes of golden pastry.

"Getting plenty of holiday business, I see, Crumble," Conker called. "Managing to palm off those old turnip and chili mash pies on the tourists, are you?"

A few of Crumble's customers looked quickly at the pies they'd just bought.

"Nothing wrong with those pies," Crumble retorted. "The chili preserves them, doesn't it? And as for tourists, at least tourists can pay, which is more than I can say for *some* people. You wouldn't believe what I've been through the last couple of days. Pestered for free samples at every turn."

"Yah! You've never given a pie away in your life!" jeered Freda.

"And never will," said Crumble, slapping a scorched apple pie into a bag and pushing it toward the mild-looking woman at the head of the queue. "I'm not a public convenience. But some people won't be told. Hanging about, all sad and big-eyed and dribbling — it's a disgrace! You'd think Begood would do something about it — but oh, no. Begood's too busy at the jail with big-time criminals, isn't he? He's got no time to do the really important —"

Conker stiffened like a dog that had just caught the scent of a passing rabbit. "Are you saying that Begood's back in town already?" he demanded.

"Oh, he's back all right," Crumble said sourly. "But he's too high and mighty for dribble control these days! From what I've heard, he's questioning a prisoner he's just brought in for murder of a wizard and resisting arrest and general rudeness and I don't know what else!"

"Tallyho!" Conker yelled. He seized Leo's arm and took off down the street, weaving recklessly through the crowd with Freda half-running, half-flying at his heels.

Familiar sights flashed past Leo's eyes. Pop the balloon seller. Spoony's Coffee Shop. Brown's Chocolates. The little shop without a name, its window covered by a thick gray curtain. Ahead there was adventure and a mystery to be solved. Panting, hot, and jostled, Leo found himself grinning broadly. Suddenly he felt supremely happy.

The police station came into view. A lot of people had gathered outside it and were trying to peer through the windows.

"Make way, if you please!" ordered Conker, barging through the crowd with Leo in tow and Freda complaining bitterly behind him. "Official quest team! Make way!"

He reached the police station door, threw it open, and strode inside.

The police station office was very cozy. A fire crackled merrily. A teapot swaddled in a knitted cover was keeping warm on the hearth. A vase of flowers stood on Officer Begood's battered desk. The only things that made the place look like a police station were the official-looking posters stuck to the back wall, where there was also a door that bore a sign reading: JAIL. AUTHORIZED VISITORS ONLY. PLEASE WATCH YOUR STEP.

Officer Begood was sitting by the fire in a comfortable armchair, drinking tea. His feet were snugly encased in tartan slippers.

He hastily tucked them under the chair and raised his eyebrows at the newcomers.

"Greetings, Begood," Conker said importantly. "We are here to inform you that our quest team has been appointed by Mistress Clogg to investigate the disappearance of Wizard Bing and the wrongful arrest of her nephew."

"Master Tact," Freda muttered.

Officer Begood's cup clattered onto its saucer. His eyebrows shot up.

"Before leaving for Hobnob, we naturally have to interview the prisoner," Conker went on. "When would be a convenient time for us to see him?"

"Can't be done, I'm afraid," Begood said, pursing his lips. "Simon Augustus Humble is not allowed visitors. He *is* a violent murderer, after all, and he's having a real temper tantrum at the moment as well."

Conker seemed to swell. "I insist on seeing my client!" he roared. "I'm a registered quest hero and I've got my rights. The law's the law!"

"Don't you talk to me about the law, Conker!" Officer Begood said severely. "I know all about the law, and what I know is I've got a prisoner in here who's guilty as sin and no slippery quester in the pay of the prisoner's auntie is going to prove otherwise!"

Conker stepped forward menacingly, his hands on the handles of his dot-swatters. Officer Begood put down his cup and saucer, stood up, lifted his chin heroically, and put up his fists like an old-time boxer. Freda gave a resigned quack, and took aim at Begood's ankle.

Leo knew he had to do something. Quickly he moved in front of Conker and faced Begood himself.

"Sorry, Officer Begood," he said in the reasonable voice he'd usually found successful when dealing with furious teachers and his father in a bad mood. "We're just trying to do our job. Simon's aunt is sure that he's innocent, you see."

Begood smiled in an infuriatingly smug way and shook his head again. "Of *course* he's not innocent," he said. "He won't talk. He hasn't answered a single one of my questions. If that doesn't prove he's guilty, what does?"

"He might be in shock," Leo suggested. "His aunt says he's not himself."

Begood gave a short, pitying laugh. He frowned at the windows that were now completely blocked by dozens of curious faces pressed against the glass. He moved smartly across the room and plunged it into gloom by closing the curtains, ignoring the howls and boos of the frustrated onlookers.

Conker was making a sound like a simmering kettle. You could almost see steam coming from his ears. He kept glancing at the jail door.

"Forget it," muttered Freda. "It'll be locked for sure."

Officer Begood began lighting the candles that stood in jars and on odd saucers all around the room.

"People say I should install that modern glowworm lighting," he said to Leo. "But what I say is, you know where you are with a good old-fashioned candle. The glowworms at the tavern have all gone down with some plague or other, they say. But you never hear of candles going on sick leave, do you?"

"No," said Leo politely. Out of the corner of his eye, he noticed that Conker had put his hands behind his back ,and, pretending to study the posters on the back wall, was moving casually toward the jail door. Freda, muttering under her breath, was following him.

Officer Begood paid no attention to them. He was still lighting the candles, making sure each one was perfectly straight before moving on to the next. He had begun humming gently to himself.

Conker sidled on. Leo hurried to join him, hoping to stop him from doing anything rash.

By the time Leo reached him, Conker was staring at the last poster, which displayed the face of a villainous-looking gnome. THIS GNOME IS DANGEROUS! the words beneath the picture warned. IF YOU SEE HIM, CONTACT OFFICER BEGOOD OR YOUR LOCAL REGISTERED HERO IMMEDIATELY. DO NOT APPROACH HIM YOURSELF. DO NOT TRY TO GUESS HIS NAME. DO NOT OFFER HIM YOUR FIRSTBORN CHILD.

"Good advice," Leo murmured. He heard a tiny sound and looked around quickly to see Conker furtively trying the knob of the jail door.

As Freda had predicted, the door was locked. Conker cursed under his breath and put his eye to the keyhole.

Leo glanced nervously over his shoulder at Officer Begood, but the policeman was standing at the mantelpiece, carefully straightening the last of the candles and still seemed quite oblivious to what was happening behind his back.

Conker remained motionless at the keyhole for a long moment, then stepped back, looking stunned. He turned to Leo and Freda. His mouth opened and closed but no words came out.

"What's the matter?" Freda hissed impatiently. "Is he dead?"

Conker shook his head. Again he tried to speak, and failed. He gestured helplessly at the keyhole.

Leo bent and looked through it. He found himself staring into a cell that was directly opposite the door. He could see a section of barred gate fastened by a huge padlock. Something red was bobbing behind the bars.

Leo closed one eye and pressed the other more firmly to the keyhole. His jaw dropped.

Jumping up and down furiously in the middle of the cell was a giant mushroom in a red-and-white striped beanie.

CHAPTER 8

A CHANGE OF PLAN

Leo gave a shout of shock. He jerked up from the keyhole just in time to see Officer Begood swing around, his eyebrows raised.

"You peeked!" Begood accused. "After all I said, too! That was very, very —"

"You've jailed a mushroom, Begood!" roared Conker. "A *mushroom!*"

Officer Begood raised his chin. "I have it on excellent authority that the prisoner is not *usually* a mushroom," he said coldly. "His aunt made a sworn statement to that effect, and so did various other Hobnob shopkeepers."

"Well, of *course* he's not usually a mushroom!" Conker stormed. "How could a mushroom be a wizard's apprentice?"

"I wouldn't know anything about that," said Officer Begood, folding his arms. "The work practices of wizards are not relevant to this case. All I know is that Wizard Bing has disappeared and Simon Humble, in his present mushroomial form, was found behaving in a highly suspicious manner at the scene of the crime. It's all in my notes."

Before anyone could say anything he pulled his notebook from his pocket, flipped it open at a page covered in tiny writing, and began to read in a slow, flat voice:

"'On my arrival at the scene of the crime, that is, the home of Wizard Balthazar Bing, also known as "Bats" Bing, I discovered Simon Augustus Humble, hereafter known as "the accused," attempting to push himself through an open window in an attempt to escape the house. I deduced that as in his present mushroomial form the accused has no hands, he had been forced to use the window because he had been unable to turn the knob of the door.'"

At this point, Officer Begood gave a little nod of satisfaction and glanced up at Conker, Leo, and Freda to see if they were suitably impressed by his detective skills. Receiving nothing but stony looks from Conker and Freda and a fascinated stare from Leo, he cleared his throat, referred to the notebook again, and read on even more slowly and deliberately than before.

"'When challenged, the accused refused to give any explanation for his actions, or to say where his employer was,'" he droned. "'I formed the opinion that he was the obvious suspect, and accordingly attempted to take him into custody. The accused violently resisted arrest and had to be restrained. As handcuffs were not effective, because of the accused's lack of wrists in his present mushroomial form, a chain was fastened around his waist — or, more accurately, his stem — to keep him from hopping away. Since his arrest the accused has failed to cooperate with police in any way, has stamped on the official cookies and milk offered to him on arrival at the jail, and has refused to respond to questioning.'"

Begood raised his head and, with the air of having proved his case once and for all, snapped the notebook shut.

"But how can Simon answer any questions?" Leo asked blankly. "He's got no mouth. He can't talk! He's a mushroom!"

"Is that my fault?" demanded Officer Begood, growing pink in the face. "Goodness gracious, you people are never satisfied!"

He strode to the front door and held it open. "Out!" he ordered.

He stood silent and ramrod straight as they trooped past him out into the open air, then slammed the door hard behind them and turned the key in the lock.

The crowd outside had thinned considerably. Presumably most people had gotten bored staring at a closed door and four tightly curtained windows. When the few who remained saw that Conker, Leo, and Freda were free of chains and had no apparent injuries, they looked disappointed and began to drift away.

"Right," said Conker. "This turn of events calls for a revised plan."

"Why?" Freda asked. "The old plan was all right. Leave at dawn, go to Hobnob, find the wizard, get paid, come home. It still sounds good to me."

"What's wrong is the timing," Conker explained earnestly. "Now that we know Simon's a mushroom and can't tell us anything, it's vital for us to get to the scene of the crime as quickly as possible. We have to investigate while the trail is still hot. That means we have to leave now."

"Now?" Leo exclaimed. "But what about Mimi and Bertha?"

"*Now?*" exploded Freda at the same moment. "What happened to the tradition of leaving at dawn and all that?"

"Tradition has to bow to necessity in perilous times," Conker said firmly. "Don't worry. I'll arrange everything."

He pulled out his notebook, stuck out his tongue, and began to write, frowning in concentration. At last he tore the page out, folded it small, then bent and rapped sharply on the road three times.

After a moment a mouse appeared from beneath a nearby cobblestone. It was limping and heavy-eyed.

"Yes?" it said in an exhausted voice.

"To Bertha the pig at Dinah's Dotless Delicacies, please," said Conker.

"Oh, all right," said the mouse hopelessly. It clipped the note to the chain around its neck, limped back to the cobblestone from which it had come, and disappeared.

"What was in the message?" Leo asked, feeling that everything was going too fast for him.

"It just told Bertha and Mimi to meet us on Woffles Way, at the turnoff to The Tavern of No Return," Conker said.

"The Tavern of No Return?" Leo repeated, hoping he'd misheard the name.

"Why go that way?" Freda demanded. "There's a Gap from Flitter Wood to Hobnob, and we can get to Flitter Wood through the Gap in The Black Sheep. It'd be much quicker to —"

"We can't go to Flitter Wood, Freda," Conker said seriously. "It's much too close to Macdonald's farm. It would upset Bertha."

Freda made a disgusted sound. Conker began scribbling another note. When he had finished it, he rapped on the cobblestone again.

It took quite a while for this second summons to be answered. Conker was stamping with impatience by the time a fat mouse with a sagging belly crawled out from beneath the cobblestone and ambled toward them, picking its teeth with a very large toothpick.

"To Polly and Jim at Grandma's cottage off Troll's Bridge Road, thanks," said Conker.

The mouse sighed, put the toothpick behind its ear, fastened the message to its chain, and slouched away.

"Really," muttered Conker. "The standard of messengers these days . . ."

"Conker, what was in *that* note?" Leo demanded, before Conker could get going on one of his familiar rants about the faults of the Rondo mail service. "Why did you write to Polly and Jim?"

"You'll see," said Conker infuriatingly. "Now, we've got to hurry to the camping shop. The Tavern of No Return's not too far from there, but we don't want to keep Bertha and Mimi waiting too long, do we?"

The camping shop was a large square building on the corner of a dusty road called Woffles Way that stretched off through thick trees into the distance.

The shop's enormous, shambling owner, who wore a vast sheepskin jerkin and who had a narrow face, a very long nose, small dark eyes set rather close together, and a mane of coarse brown hair, greeted Conker like a long-lost brother.

"Leo, meet Peg," Conker said, emerging, breathless, from his huge friend's welcoming hug, which had lifted him high off the ground.

"Peg!" agreed the camping shop owner, punching her chest with enormous force and laughing as if she'd made a great joke.

Leo smiled uneasily. Peg looked friendly enough, and she was obviously very fond of Conker, but her tremendous size was unnerving, her voice was very deep, and there was something about her eyes . . .

"Any news for us, Peg?" Conker asked.

Peg shook her head. "I been checking the Merks' place every night, but no sign of Spoiler there so far," she rumbled. "You sure he's a friend of theirs?"

"He used to be," Conker said. "Before he took up with the Blue Queen and got too grand. Have you heard any whispers from anywhere else?"

"Not about Spoiler," growled Peg. "Other things, but. Be some funny rumors coming back from the north."

"About Wizard Bing?" Conker asked eagerly.

"Him?" Peg shrugged her massive shoulders. "Heard he been murdered by a mushroom. That nothing. Other rumors more interesting." She bent toward Conker and lowered her voice.

". . . is on the move," Leo thought he heard her say. "Young ones seen it . . . two, three times . . . at night . . . different places . . ."

Conker shook his head. "Imagination!" he declared firmly. "Children with too much time on their hands trying to scare one another. It's always the same in the school holidays."

"Maybe," rumbled Peg, sounding unconvinced.

"Is Peg a giant?" Leo whispered to Freda.

"Shh! Of course not!" muttered Freda. "She's a bear."

"What?" Leo squeaked, far more loudly than he'd meant.

Peg looked over her shoulder inquiringly.

"Leo stubbed his toe," called Freda.

Peg nodded and turned back to Conker.

"Freda, what do you *mean*?" Leo gasped, feeling sweat break out on his forehead. "Peg's not a bear. She's got no fur."

"She's only a proper bear at night," Freda said impatiently. "She changes at sunset. But don't mention it. She gets embarrassed. And we don't want to upset her. Peg's one of the best sources of gossip we have."

She moved to join Conker and Peg, but Leo hesitated, staring nervously at Peg's broad back, her slightly bowed shoulders, her gleaming dark brown hair.

"Come on!" Freda ordered, looking back at him. "She's harmless at present. And she's very responsible — always closes the shop before sunset. Just in case she gets carried away and eats a customer — you know."

Leo nodded feebly.

When Peg heard that Conker wanted a new cooking pot, she

frowned. "Not many left," she growled. "Waiting for a new delivery. Better you come back tomorrow."

"Can't do that, Peg," Conker said briskly. "We're leaving for Hobnob tonight."

Peg sighed and led the way to a large cage. Inside the cage sat three round, black pots. One was small, one was large, and the third was medium-sized. As Conker moved closer, all three pots stood up on wiry bowed legs and began whimpering and jumping up and down.

"These all half-price special," said Peg, the corners of her mouth turning down.

"Good," said Conker. "I'll have that one." He pointed at the medium-sized pot, which jumped up and down even harder.

"You don't want that one," Peg said flatly. "That one no good for my friend. It good for tourists only."

The medium-sized pot raised its handle indignantly and redoubled its leaping and whimpering.

"It looks all right to me," said Conker, smiling at it encouragingly. "Plenty of energy and just the right size. I'll take it."

Peg sighed and flipped open the cage lid. Using a pole with a hook at one end, she caught the medium-sized pot by its handle and lifted it out. The two rejected pots looked depressed. Leo felt sorry for them, especially the little one.

"Not to worry," Peg said, noticing his expression. "Is school holidays. Tourists will buy, no problem."

She clipped a long chain to the cooking pot's handle and gave the free end to Conker. Then she helped Conker select a large cooking spoon, a coil of superstrong yellow cord, two backpacks with lots of special pockets, money pouches for Mimi and Leo, and many other things, including a natty device that combined compass, tape measure, nail clipper, and poison-testing kit.

"We've got most of this stuff back at the tavern," Freda grumbled as Conker divided his purchases between the two packs. "What's the point of spending our hard-earned money on —"

"Time is money," Conker said grandly, passing a large number of coins to Peg. He shouldered the heavier of the two packs and pushed the other toward Leo.

"See you, then," said Peg amiably, shambling with them to the door and opening it for them. "You take care in Hobnob. Like I said — funny things happening up north."

She swatted at a couple of blue butterflies that had incautiously flown too close to her head, and glanced at the sky. "Sunset very soon," she added casually.

"Oh, right!" Conker exclaimed. "Well, see you later, Peg!"

He bolted through the door with the cooking pot. Leo and Freda hurried after him.

CHAPTER 9

WOFFLES WAY

Conker, Freda, and Leo set off along Woffles Way at a brisk jog. Nothing was said, but they were all keen to put plenty of distance between themselves and Peg before the sun went down. After only a few minutes, however, the new cooking pot began whimpering and dragging its feet. "Legs sore, Conkie," it wailed in a tinny voice. "Carry me?"

"Don't be silly!" scolded Conker, glancing at Freda, who was rolling her eyes. "You're a big grown-up cooking pot and you can walk. Now hurry up. Do you want the bear to eat you?"

"Won't eat me," said the cooking pot. "I not made of meat. Only eat you. Carry me?"

"No!" Conker roared. He jerked the chain and jogged on, dragging the pot behind him. The cooking pot stubbornly drew up its legs and bumped along on its base in the dust.

"It'll dent itself at this rate," Freda remarked to no one in particular.

Conker looked up at the slowly dimming sky. "Oh, my liver, lungs, and *gizzards*!" he exploded. He snatched up the cooking pot and set off again.

"Conker, what was Peg telling you back there?" Leo asked. "Something about some rumors? I couldn't hear properly."

"Oh!" Conker glanced nervously over his shoulder at the mention of Peg. "Nothing important. She's heard some travelers' tales about folk in the north claiming that the — ah . . . the S-T-R-I-X had woken, and was on the move."

"The what?" Leo demanded. "S, T, R . . . What's the Stri —"

"Don't mention it!" Freda quacked.

Leo glanced at her. She was cruising along in her usual half-running, half-flying style, but her head was up and her eyes were alert as she scanned the mounds of red-rimmed clouds gathering on the horizon.

"It's . . . a monster, sort of —" puffed Conker. "Supposed to drift around in the sky — in a cloud palace — high up — out of sight. Supposed to come down and — carry off children and so on. Bad luck to speak its name — in case you summon it. Nothing to worry about. Probably just a myth, anyway."

"I wouldn't be too sure of that," Freda said darkly.

"Are we there yet?" whined the cooking pot.

"One — more — word out of you and I'll drop you and leave you here to rust!" wheezed Conker. "Freda, anything behind us?"

"Not so far," Freda said.

Conker slowed to a walk. "There's probably — no real danger," he said as he caught his breath. "We've known Peg for years. She'd probably recognize us, even when she's a bear."

"I wouldn't be too sure of that, either," Freda said.

"Conker, let me carry that for a while," Leo offered, holding out his arms for the cooking pot.

Conker passed the pot over to him, but no sooner had Leo taken it than it began to whimper and struggle. "Conkie, carry me!" it wailed.

"Be a good pot now," Leo said, feeling ridiculous. "Conker's tired." He walked on, but with every step the pot's struggles grew more violent and its cries grew louder, rising at last to a crescendo of earsplitting metallic shrieks.

"That's it!" bellowed Conker, stopping short. "That's enough! I'd rather starve than put up with this."

He grabbed the screaming pot from Leo. Holding it at arm's length, he stalked to the roadside and dumped it under a tree. Then he strode back to Leo and Freda, brushing his hands together.

"That's that," he said. "Come on. Not far to go now."

He began walking again, very rapidly. Leo and Freda hurried after him. The cooking pot's shrieks filled the air. Leo looked back. The pot was having a full-blown tantrum, rolling around on the ground under the tree and flapping its handle hysterically.

"How much did that thing cost, again?" murmured Freda.

Conker stuck his clenched fists into his pockets and, chewing his mustache furiously, strode on.

The screams of the pot grew fainter, and at last Leo couldn't hear them anymore. Either he, Conker, and Freda had moved out of earshot or the pot had finally exhausted itself.

The road stretched ahead of them, straight as a ruler. The birds had stopped singing and the sun was sinking rapidly. Leo saw that Freda was still glancing frequently at the sky, and remembered the conversation about the Strix.

A monster who lived in a castle in the clouds — it did sound like a fairy tale, of course. But then there were lots of things in Rondo that sounded like fairy tales and were true. And though Conker seemed determined to dismiss Peg's warning, Freda was obviously taking it very seriously.

Leo looked at the heavy clouds building on the horizon. For an instant he thought he saw the shapes of walls and towers, and his stomach fluttered.

They're just clouds, he told himself firmly. *Cumulus clouds. Nothing else.*

His father had told him all about clouds. Clouds were just collections of water vapor, and the different shapes had different names. The rounded fluffy clouds that looked as if they were made of cotton wool were cumulus clouds. The long straight ones were stratus clouds. The feathery ones were cirrus clouds. Then there were stratocumulus clouds, altocumulus clouds . . .

Repeating the names in his mind, Leo looked down at his feet. Gradually his stomach settled, but he still felt uneasy. He kept thinking he could hear the faint sounds of twigs snapping and leaves rustling. He thought of Peg and looked over his shoulder, but the road was deserted and he could see no movement among the trees.

Then, with shocking abruptness, the silence was shattered by a tremendous crash and the sound of splintering wood. As Leo spun around, his heart in his mouth, there was a bloodcurdling shriek.

"Stop!" a shrill voice screamed. "Thieves! Cheats! Stop!"

The voice was floating from the mouth of a path that yawned beside a signpost on the right-hand side of the road not far ahead.

"Oh, my liver and lungs!" roared Conker, lunging forward. "They *didn't*! Oh, *tell* me they didn't . . ."

There was the sound of thudding feet, and the next moment two familiar figures hurtled out onto the road. A third figure, very large, was hot on their heels, screeching and swearing.

"Mimi!" Conker bellowed. "Bertha!"

Mimi and Bertha pelted toward him. Bertha's eyes were wild. The frills of her pillowcase scarf whipped around her head, and she was carrying a large pink bag in her teeth. Mimi was staggering under the weight of several bulging carrier bags marked DINAH'S.

Their pursuer, an immensely fat woman in a stained red velvet dressing gown and a red turban, caught sight of Conker and Freda and skidded to a halt, glaring malevolently. Leo thought he'd never seen such an unpleasant-looking person. Her dressing gown was stiff with dirt and crumbs, and the edge of her turban was black with grease. What made her particularly repellent, however, were her tiny, malicious eyes and her thin gray lips, which reminded Leo irresistibly of a metal trap.

"You again!" she snarled at Conker, as Mimi and Bertha dropped their burdens with relief and collapsed on the ground.

"I tell you we haven't *seen* Spoiler! Why don't you leave us alone?"

"And a very good evening to you, too, Misery," Conker replied coldly.

"It's Mistress Merk to you, Master Impertinence," the woman snapped. "And these thieving friends of yours owe Grim and me for two drinks plus a broken door, so pay up!"

"You're not getting a dib out of me," said Conker. "Take yourself off."

"That criminal pig broke down the door of the ladies' lounge!" shouted Misery. "And she knocked Grim flat!"

"I had no choice," Bertha cried. "They were keeping us prisoner!"

"They said we couldn't leave till we gave them all the bags of food, because we didn't have any money," Mimi gasped. "And we hadn't even *asked* for a drink! We just went in to sit down."

"We run a tavern, missy, not a waiting room!" spat Misery Merk. "You come in, you're expected to have a drink. That's how it is."

"There were dot crumbs in mine," Bertha said. "Also a hair. I'm not accustomed to drinks of that sort."

"Well, I'm not accustomed to having dirty great pigs sprawling all over my good lounge!" shrieked Misery Merk. "So there! Ha!"

"You're a really, *really* horrible person, you know," panted Mimi. Her eyes were narrow. Her fists were tightly clenched.

Misery Merk smiled smugly. Instantly a very large, very

angry-looking pimple appeared on the end of her nose. Leo clapped his hand over his mouth to stifle a yell of shock.

"What are you staring at, goggle-eyes?" jeered Misery, apparently unaware of any change in her appearance. She turned away and began stomping back toward the path.

Leo looked at Mimi. She met his eyes defiantly.

She *did it*, he thought in shock. Mimi *made that pimple appear. And that means . . . she's got the Key! Somehow she gave Bertha the slip and went back for it. And I'll bet that's what she meant to do all along!*

Anger swept through him. He told himself that he should have known. Never had he met anyone as stubborn and irresponsible as Mimi Langlander. She'd do anything, anything at all, to get her own way.

He looked quickly around. To his relief, none of the others had noticed what had happened.

"You'd better watch it, you lot!" Misery shouted over her shoulder as she reached the signpost. "There's a big brown bear prowls these parts at night, you know. Not to mention the S-word."

"What?" squeaked Bertha.

"Oho!" Misery hooted. "Not so snooty now, are you? Oh, yes, the S-word's on the prowl, they say, looking for new exhibits for its Collection. It wouldn't surprise me a bit if it came down for the likes of you, either. It likes weirdos." She spat contemptuously and lumbered off into the shadows.

"Lawks-a-daisy!" quavered Bertha, as Conker began stuffing the food bags into Leo's pack. "I've never been so glad to get out of anywhere in my life — and that includes the Blue Queen's castle. Why in Rondo was the meeting place changed? You've had bad ideas before, Conker, but if this one wasn't the worst *ever*, I'm a mushroom."

"Don't *say* that!" Leo, Freda, and Conker shouted together.

Bertha gaped at them.

Conker cleared his throat. "We've got a lot to tell you," he mumbled. "And we *will* tell you — when we're on our way."

"You'll tell us right now!" Bertha snapped. "After all we've been through —"

"You were supposed to meet us at the signpost!" Conker broke in crossly. "Blood and bones, *everyone* knows not to go into The Tavern of No Return!"

"Well, we didn't," Bertha retorted. "Oh, that place was filthy! It must be *crawling* with germs. And I've got a nasty feeling the sofa had fleas." She scratched her side thoughtfully.

"Why do you think it's called The Tavern of No Return?" said Conker, pushing the filled pack over to Leo. "One visit's enough for anyone."

"Except Spoiler," said Freda. "He used to —" She broke off, cocked her head as if listening, then swung around to stare at the bushes on the other side of the road, opposite the signpost. "Something's moving in there," she warned.

"Aha!" Conker exclaimed. He shouldered his pack, darted across the road, and, beckoning excitedly, vanished into the bushes. The others cautiously followed.

"Misery Merk said a bear lived around here," Mimi whispered.

"I'd put bears right out of my mind if I were you," Leo muttered savagely, and she shot him a look that was a strange mixture of guilt, fear, and resentment.

They emerged from the bushes to find themselves in what seemed to be a small field. It was very dim now, but Leo could see an uneven whitish gleam on the ground not far away. A darker shadow moved beside the gleam. It was Conker, beckoning furiously.

"What's he up to now?" Freda complained. "Oh, I'm getting too old for this!" She darted forward.

As Leo, Mimi, and Bertha crept after her, they distinctly heard leaves rustling somewhere ahead. Mimi drew a quick breath and stopped short.

"It's not a bear!" Leo snapped, sincerely hoping it wasn't.

"And it can't be the — the thing Misery mentioned," Bertha whispered. "The S-T-R-I-X doesn't hide in bushes." But Leo noticed that she glanced nervously at the sky all the same.

"Come on!" Conker called impatiently.

"Conker, watch out!" Leo called back. "There's something . . ."

His voice trailed off. Mimi and Bertha squeaked in surprise. They'd all finally seen what the whitish gleam on the ground beside Conker was.

It was a black-and-white patterned rug, exactly like the rug in Leo's room at home. It was hovering fastidiously just above the lank grass, its fringe fluttering slightly. Freda was already sitting on it, rocking gently, her wings peacefully folded.

"The flying rug!" Bertha squealed in delight.

Conker was grinning broadly. "What do you think of my surprise?" he crowed, patting the rug. "I got Polly and Jim to send it to meet us here. It's been with them since it took the ex-swans home from the Blue Queen's castle, you know."

Leo hadn't known. He hadn't even thought about what had happened to the flying rug that had saved his life during his first visit to Rondo.

Mimi ran to the rug and climbed on with Bertha's pink bag. Leo loaded his pack and then got on himself. As he felt the familiar, rippling sensation beneath him, visions of the Blue Queen's cruel smile flooded his mind. He pushed them away.

"What a brilliant idea, Conker! I hope Polly and Jim don't mind lending it to us," said Bertha, climbing onto the rug in her turn. The rug dipped under her weight, then straightened again.

"Oh, no," said Conker. "Hal says it's been giving them a bit of trouble lately, as a matter of fact. Restless, you know. Curling up so furniture falls over, thrashing around at night and keeping the family awake, and so on."

He clambered onto the rug and settled himself next to Freda. "Polly and Jim haven't got time to exercise it properly, that's the trouble," he went on. "And of course they can't let it outside by itself in case it goes wild in the forest. Feral rugs can do a lot of damage. Still, this trip should tire it out and settle it down for a while."

He looked around happily. "Everyone sitting comfortably? Right, then. Rug — to Hobnob, if you please!"

As the words left his lips, and the rug slowly began to rise, there was a shriek from the bushes. Something round and black shot from the shadows, hitting Conker squarely in the chest. He fell back, gasping. The rug rocked violently.

"Conkie!" shrieked the cooking pot, wrapping its legs tightly around Conker's waist and bouncing up and down. "Don't leave me, Conkie! Take me with you!"

CHAPTER 10

NIGHT RIDERS

Dipping and flapping wildly, but intent on following its orders, the rug rose into the night sky. Conker bellowed, his roars punctuated by oomphing sounds as the cooking pot bounced on his stomach. Freda, her wings spread wide as she struggled for balance, snapped at the pot's legs, trying to make it loosen its grip. Clinging helplessly to the bucking rug, Mimi, Bertha, and Leo could do nothing but watch as the wind whistled around them, tearing at their clothes and hair.

Leo knew that their situation was perilous. He knew that any minute he might lose his grip, slide off the rug, and plummet to the ground that was now so terrifyingly far away. He knew that Mimi, Bertha, and Conker were in exactly the same danger. And yet instead of yelling in fear, he was laughing. He couldn't help it — it was all so absurd.

"Stop laughing!" Mimi shrieked. "Leo, are you mad?"

"Leo, what's that thing on top of Conker?" Bertha squealed.

"It's a — cooking pot!" Leo gasped, then drew up his knees as another gale of laughter overwhelmed him. He clung to the fringe of the rug, his stomach aching, tears streaming down his face.

"Well, *really*!" Bertha snapped. "Rug! Stop climbing! Go down!"

The rug didn't respond. Either it couldn't hear Bertha's voice over the sound of Conker's roars or it was too flurried by the struggle in its center to pay attention.

"Get — oomph — off me!" shouted Conker. With a tremendous effort he rolled over, pinning the cooking pot beneath him and nearly crushing Freda, who flew out of the way just in time. The rug tipped dangerously.

"Eeek!" Bertha shrieked as she began to slide down the steep slope, her front trotters scrabbling uselessly, her sunglasses falling from her nose. In an instant, her back legs were kicking in the air beyond the rug's fluttering fringe.

The laughter died in Leo's throat. He flung himself toward Bertha, clinging to the rug with one hand and reaching out with the other. Mimi moved at the same moment. They both managed to catch hold of a ruffle of Bertha's scarf. The terrible downward slide stopped, but Bertha's back legs still hung perilously over the edge of the rug. "Pull me back!" she squealed.

But Leo and Mimi couldn't. She was far too heavy. All they could do was hang on.

"Oh, lawks!" Bertha wailed. "Oh, *do* something, quickly! The ruffles won't hold! The stitches will break. You won't —"

Mimi screamed. In horror Leo saw that the ruffle she was gripping had begun to tear away from the main part of the pillowcase in a long, frilly strip. At the same moment, he distinctly felt threads breaking beneath his hands, and his own part of the ruffle began to pull away. Bertha slid farther over the edge.

"Conker!" Leo yelled, looking over his shoulder.

Conker was beyond hearing anything. He was facedown on the rug, punching the sides of the cooking pot beneath him, trying to make it loosen its grip. But Freda, fluttering over Conker's head, heard Leo's cry. She looked around and took in the situation instantly. Without hesitation she flattened her wings and dived at Conker's back, straight as a spear.

Her beak stabbed the sole of the cooking pot's right foot. The cooking pot howled and let go. Conker bellowed in triumph and sat up.

"Conker!" Bertha, Leo, and Mimi shouted together. "Help!"

Conker turned to face them. His eyes bulged in horror. He lunged across the rug and took hold of Bertha's front trotters. "Heave!" he yelled.

His strength made all the difference. In moments, Bertha was lying fully on the rug again, gasping and shaking but safe, with the ruffles of her pillowcase scarf tangled around her head like frilly pink streamers.

Leo sat up, weak with relief. Conker was flat on his back, panting hard. On Bertha's other side, Mimi had collapsed into a trembling heap.

And only then did Leo remember the Key. Why hadn't Mimi used the Key to save Bertha? Even Hal wouldn't have objected to her using it for something so important.

Mimi's hands were pressed to her eyes. A ragged strip of pink ruffle was still caught between her fingers. Leo remembered her terror as they struggled to hold Bertha, remembered her agonized scream as the ruffles started to tear away . . .

And in an instant of clarity he suddenly knew exactly what had happened, and understood why Mimi was still curled up with her hands over her eyes.

Conker groaned, sat up, and glowered at the cooking pot. It was whimpering in the center of the rug with Freda, looking very severe, on guard beside it.

"Right!" Conker growled. He began crawling toward the pot with a murderous look in his eye.

"Sore, Conkie!" the pot wailed, holding up its bruised foot. "Kiss better?"

Conker bared his teeth. "The only kissing to be done around here is when you kiss the ground, cooking pot," he snarled. "You've made my life a misery for the last time." He grabbed the pot's handle and swung his arm back. The pot shrieked piteously.

"No, Conker!" Leo begged. Abandoning the cooking pot by the side of the road was one thing. Throwing it screaming from a great height was another. It seemed like murder.

Conker scowled. "It's just a cooking pot, Leo!" he snapped. "A *cooking pot* — and a faulty one at that!"

"It — it might hit someone," Leo stammered, seizing on the only argument that he thought Conker might accept. "If it fell on someone's head, it could kill them!"

"He's right, you know," Freda said regretfully.

Conker sighed and lowered his arm. He set the cooking pot on the rug again. The cooking pot gave a squeak and rolled over with its legs in the air. Conker nudged it with his foot but it didn't move.

"Fainted," said Freda with contempt.

"Well, that'll keep it quiet for the moment, anyway," said Conker. "We'll get rid of it in Hobnob."

"Will someone *please* tell me what's been going on?" Bertha interrupted. She had managed to sit up and was blinking dazedly in the wind. Mimi had moved a little away from her and was sitting with her knees drawn up to her chin, her shoulders hunched defensively.

"In my opinion," Bertha said, her voice trembling with indignation, "this quest has got off to a *very* bad start. Mimi and I have been forced to walk a long way, carrying a lot of heavy bags. We've been insulted and exposed to gruesome diseases — and fleas. And *I* have narrowly escaped death. Plus my disguise is *ruined*." She tossed a strip of ruffle out of her eyes.

"Yes, well, sorry about that," Conker mumbled. "But every quest has its ups and downs, you know. There have certainly been a few unfortunate events —"

"*Unfortunate!*" squealed Bertha.

"Conker, just tell her," Leo said quickly.

"You tell her," grunted Conker, who seemed to have decided to sulk.

So while the rug flew steadily on through the cool, starry night, Leo told the story. Conker preserved an insulted silence for a while, but Bertha's exclamations and questions soon drew him out of his bad mood. In no time he was chiming in, adding details and explanations to everything Leo said.

"So," he said rather pompously, when Leo had finished. "Now, I hope, you see why we had to get to Hobnob without delay."

"Certainly," Bertha said, in a crisp voice that showed she hadn't yet quite forgiven him. "Imagine Simon being a mushroom! No wonder his auntie said he wasn't himself. The question is, how did he get to *be* a mushroom? Who changed him?"

"It's a mystery," Conker said, shaking his head. "I've racked my brains but I can't think of anyone who's got that sort of transforming power these days."

"Spoiler certainly doesn't," Leo said ruefully.

"I never heard that Bing had it, either," Freda put in.

"Well, no one who had the power would advertise it, would they?" Bertha retorted, still sounding rather distant. "Transforming spells *are* illegal."

Conker shrugged. "That was always a pointless law," he said. "Who's going to arrest someone who can turn you into a toad at fifty paces? A few of the registered heroes tried, and where did they end up? Croaking and catching flies for a living, that's where."

"Yes." Bertha sighed. "Isn't it *tragic*? Though Scribble — my special reporter, you know — says they seem to quite enjoy it. The healthy outdoor life, freedom from stress, and so on. Scribble once did a series of interviews . . ."

Leo caught a slight movement out of the corner of his eye. He looked around and saw that Mimi's hand had crept up to cover the pendant hidden beneath her jacket. Leo's skin prickled.

"Mimi," he whispered sharply. "Don't —"

Mimi's head jerked up and with a quick, guilty movement she snatched her hand away from the pendant. "Shut up, Leo!"

she hissed, glancing furtively at their companions, who were still talking about toads. "If the others guess I've got it they'll just start fussing."

Leo stared at her, seething. He didn't trust himself to speak.

"Stop looking at me as if I'm some loony with a loaded gun," Mimi muttered. "I wasn't going to *do* anything just now. I was just thinking that if only I'd been with you at the jail I could have turned Simon back into himself. Then he'd have been able to tell us who —"

"Mimi, you're incredible, do you know that?" Leo's voice was shaking with anger. "How many times do you have to be told? The Key is dangerous! Using it is dangerous! Even *thinking* about using it is dangerous! But you know better, don't you? No one's going to tell *you* what to do, are they? So you sneak, and lie —"

"I didn't lie," Mimi snapped back. "I agreed to put the Key in the Safe Place, but I didn't promise to leave it there. Hiding the Key was a stupid idea. Who knows when we might need it?"

"We needed it just now!" Leo hissed. "And you couldn't use it, could you? Not to help, anyway."

Mimi's face froze into a stiff, expressionless mask. Leo knew by now that this meant she was very upset, but he was far too angry to care.

"You were in such a panic, you couldn't think!" he went on remorselessly. "Then Bertha said she was afraid the ruffles would tear, and lo and behold, they did! Because the moment she said it, *you* couldn't stop yourself from imagining it! You nearly made

Bertha fall! And what about Misery Merk's nose? That's exactly the sort of thing Hal's afraid of. If the Blue Queen hears rumors —"

"She won't," said Mimi, her lips barely moving. "Misery Merk won't think anything of that pimple. She probably gets them all the time. Anyway, it was an accident and I won't make the same mistake again. Just leave me alone."

She turned away from him and stared out into the night. Her hair flew wildly in the wind. *She could do anything,* Leo thought suddenly. *She could turn this rug into a dragon. She could change us all into messenger mice.*

You realize how dangerous the Key is . . .

Only now did Leo fully understand how true those words of Freda's were. So much depended on Mimi's being calm and sensible. And Mimi Langlander just wasn't a sensible sort of person.

Not like me, Leo thought, and for some reason felt angrier than ever.

At that moment, the rug passed over a mass of twinkling lights so bright that it lit up the sky. Everyone looked over the side at a fairy-tale vision of gleaming glass spires.

"The Crystal Palace," Conker said, straightening up and smoothing his ruffled beard. "Hobnob's not far now."

I'll have to tell them about the Key, Leo thought. *If I don't I'll be as responsible as Mimi if anything bad happens.* He winced at the thought of the scene that would follow his announcement. What was more, he couldn't shake the feeling that he would be betraying Mimi, telling tales on her. Mimi would certainly see it that way.

Oh, if only I'd never seen that pimple pop out on Misery Merk's nose, he thought dismally. *If only I'd been looking the other way like everyone else! Then I wouldn't have this problem.*

He looked out at the sky, struggling with his conscience. *I'll have to tell,* he thought, *but I'll wait till after we've landed. It would be safer.*

Immediately, everything looked brighter. The problem still had to be faced, but at least it didn't have to be faced right at this moment. He pushed it out of his mind and tuned into the conversation going on around him.

"Still, law or no law, transforming spells have gone out of fashion since the Dark Time, haven't they?" Conker was saying. "I think the old Wicked Witch of the West was the last real expert, and she exploded ages ago."

"Wanda specialized in frogs, anyway," said Freda. "She did the occasional newt, toward the end, but I never heard of her going in for vegetables."

"Mushrooms aren't vegetables," Leo put in automatically. "They're a kind of fungus."

"Really?" exclaimed Bertha. "Oh, I can't wait to tell my know-all brother! He always puts mushrooms in that vegetable soup he's so proud of. Just wait till I tell him he's been wrong all along."

"He hasn't been wrong!" Mimi snapped. "You *use* mushrooms like vegetables, and they're *sold* with vegetables, so you might as well *call* them vegetables. It's just boring to go on about them being *fungus.*"

I'd rather be Mister Boring than Little Miss Weird, Leo thought savagely. He turned away from Mimi, looked ahead, and jumped in shock. "What's that?" he yelled.

A strange cloud formation had suddenly become visible as the rug lost height. Spearing up through the inky blackness of the sky was a cluster of tall, weirdly luminous gray-green shapes, narrow and pointed like towers. As the rug dipped again, everyone could see that the towers rose from a bulky, billowing mass that reared up from the ground like castle walls.

"The Strix's castle!" Bertha quavered. "It's here! Misery was telling the truth! And we're heading straight for it! Oh, lawks! Oh, help!"

"Oh, my blood and bones!" muttered Conker, his eyes bulging.

"No worries," drawled Freda, whose feathers were standing up like spines. "It's just a myth, remember?"

"I don't believe it," moaned Conker. "I just — don't — *believe* it!"

"Conker, turn the rug around!" Leo shouted.

But before Conker could say a word, the rug stopped dead in the air, then dropped straight down with stomach-churning speed.

Bertha, Conker, Freda, Leo, and Mimi screwed up their eyes as the wind roared past their ears, smothering all other sound. They gasped for breath, flattening themselves against the rug, clinging to it for dear life, bracing themselves for the crash they knew must come . . .

Then there was an abrupt jolt, and silence.

CHAPTER 11

HOBNOB

Cautiously Leo opened his eyes. He found himself staring up at a string of lights that spelled out the words OGG'S HOE EMPORIUM. It took him a moment to see that the lights were fixed to the front of a large shop that seemed to be made up of several smaller shops joined together. Shortly after that, he realized that the rug was hovering a hairsbreadth above the cobblestones of the Hobnob village square.

Slowly he sat up. Around him, Conker, Freda, Mimi, and Bertha were doing the same. They all looked very shaken and windblown.

"I think my stomach got left behind up there," groaned Bertha.

"If I'd known this thing was so skittish I'd have thought twice about borrowing it," grumbled Conker. He clambered off the rug, and the others gingerly followed.

A muffled rattling sound, like the pattering of rain on a metal roof, was coming from behind the closely shuttered windows of the hoe emporium.

"Ogg has obviously got a big dot problem," said Conker, fingering the handles of his dot-swatters. "My blood and bones, listen to those pests — there must be hundreds of them!"

They looked around the deserted square. A spindly little tree bearing a few limp white flowers drooped in a pot in the center, and lamps, only one of which was alight, hung from poles at each corner. All the quaint two-storied buildings were as tightly shuttered as the hoe emporium. Leo noticed an antiques shop, a sweet shop, a bakery, and a small shop called Stitch the Tailor. On every door there was a notice reading CLOSED, and the windows above the shops were dark.

"Lawks-a-daisy," Bertha whispered nervously. "Folk go to bed very early in Hobnob."

"I'd say they're just being cautious," Freda said. "Who wouldn't be, under the circumstances?" She jerked her head at the cloud mass that brooded over the outskirts of the village.

Leo stared, and his stomach turned over. From the air, the cloud had looked very like a palace. On the ground, it looked exactly like one. Menacing and faintly luminous, it rose high behind the rooftops, its turrets and towers glimmering palely green against the blackness of the sky.

"It's so strange," Mimi breathed. "I wonder what it's like inside?"

"Don't, Mimi!" squealed Bertha. "That's how it catches you!"

"Stop it, all of you!" Conker snapped. "Whatever that — that *thing* is, it's not going to distract us from our mission. We're safe as long as we don't go near it, and there's no reason why we *should* go near it. It's got nothing to do with us."

"But, Conker, it might have *everything* to do with us," Leo said reluctantly. "Maybe it's — the answer."

Conker's jaw dropped. "Of *course!*" he gasped. "Oh, my blood and bones, no *wonder* Begood arrested the mushroom and rushed home saying the case was closed. He didn't want to face the thing in that cloud!"

"Ooh!" Bertha squeaked. "You mean — Wizard Bing might have been . . ." She swallowed.

"Collected," Freda said flatly. "Well, if he has, no one will ever see him again. We might as well say good-bye to our fee and go straight home."

"How can you say that, Freda?" Leo exclaimed impulsively. "If Wizard Bing's been taken prisoner, we can't just let him rot! We've got to try to save him!"

The moment the words left his lips, he longed to snatch them back. But it was too late. Freda was frowning in disgust, but Mimi was nodding vigorously, Bertha's eyes were shining, and Conker was looking deeply moved.

"You're right, Leo," Conker said in a choked voice. "What better way to die than to lay down our lives in such a noble cause? What hero could ask for anything more?"

"This hero could," Freda said tartly. "This hero would prefer not to die at all, for example."

"Oh, we'd all prefer *that*, I daresay," cried Conker, flapping his hands. "Still, you can't have everything. All right! We storm the palace at dawn."

"There you go with that dawn business again!" Bertha complained. "After breakfast is surely quite early enough to —"

99

"We shouldn't wait till the morning," interrupted Mimi, gazing at the palace in fascination. "The cloud might drift away in the night."

"Taking Bing with it!" Conker shouted, electrified. "Oh, my lungs and liver! Right! We storm the palace at once."

"We haven't even had dinner yet," Freda grumbled.

"It's a wicked waste of good food to eat it just before you're going to die," Conker said sternly. "I'm surprised at you, Freda!"

"Wait!" Leo said desperately. "We mustn't — we *can't* attack the cloud palace!" He felt his face grow hot as everyone turned to look at him in surprise. *Just say you didn't mean what you said*, he told himself. *Just say you've changed your mind.*

But he couldn't bring himself to do it. *It's the Rondo effect*, the rational part of his brain told him. *It's what made you suggest a rescue mission in the first place. Ignore it! Say what you have to say. You're the only responsible one here. It's up to you to save them all.*

They were all staring at him, waiting. He had to say something. He *had* to!

Delay. The little word floated into his mind, as welcome as a life preserver in a stormy sea. "I mean — we can't attack the palace just yet," he said in a rush.

"Why in Rondo not?" Conker demanded.

Leo thought furiously and was suddenly inspired. "We have to report to Muffy Clogg first," he said. "She's expecting us. If we go off to the cloud palace without telling her and then disappear, she'll never know we were here at all. She'll think we let her down."

Conker deflated a little. "That's true," he muttered. "It would be very bad for our reputation."

"It would be dreadful!" Bertha cried. "I mean, it will be bad enough to die on only my second quest, without dying a heroine and no one even *knowing* about it!"

"True quest heroes aren't in it for the glory, Bertha," Conker said loftily. "Still . . . it does seem a pity."

"I wonder where Clogg's shoe shop is?" murmured Leo, fervently hoping it would be so hard to find that the Strix's palace would drift away while they were still looking.

"Fan out!" Conker ordered. "We'll find the woman before midnight if we have to knock on every door in Hobnob to do it!"

As if to set an example he pounded on the main door of the hoe emporium. The pattering noise behind the shop windows stopped abruptly and an instant later a pair of shutters flew open above the friends' heads.

A round-faced woman with a frilly lace cap perched on her very curly, very golden hair leaned through the window, one plump hand pressed to her heart. "Mercy, what is it?" she gasped. "Oh, you gave me such a fright!"

"My apologies, madam," Conker said, baring his teeth in what he no doubt thought was a winning smile.

The woman gave a little scream and shrank back. Conker frowned. "This is urgent quest business, madam," he said. "Please pay attention. We need to see Mistress Muffy Clogg. Do you know where she lives, by any chance?"

"Oh!" said the woman, her china-blue eyes widening. "Why, yes! She lives *here*. I mean, I am her . . . she is me . . . I mean — *I* am Muffy Clogg!"

Bertha exclaimed in amazement. Leo glanced up at the lighted sign and shook his head, unable to believe his bad luck.

Conker narrowed his eyes suspiciously. "If you are who you claim, madam," he said coldly, "why are you living *here*?"

The woman looked at him blankly. "We've always lived here," she said. "Of course, the shop was much smaller before . . . before our fortunes changed for the better."

"They must have the glowworm plague here, too, Conker," Leo whispered. "See? There are letters missing from the sign."

Conker blinked up at the glowing letters spelling out OGG'S HOE EMPORIUM. His lips moved silently for a moment. Then he cleared his throat and looked back at the woman at the window.

"So!" he said heartily. "*You* are Mistress Clogg of Clogg's Shoe Emporium?"

"Indeed I am!" the woman said breathlessly. "And would I be right in thinking that you are the quest team, come to save my poor young nephew from wrongful arrest?"

"Indeed we are!" Conker said, gesturing grandly behind him at Freda, Leo, Mimi, and Bertha.

Muffy Clogg blinked into the shadows, clearly unable to see anyone but Conker himself. "How do you do?" she said faintly. "So good of you to come. I must say, I didn't expect you so soon."

"Let it never be said that our team drags its feet when duty calls," said Conker. "Now — may we come in?"

Muffy Clogg glanced nervously behind her and lowered her voice. "Actually, it's not *quite* convenient just now," she whispered. "Could you come back tomorrow? After breakfast? When my husband has gone down to the shop?"

"After *breakfast*?" Conker bawled, swelling with indignation. "Madam, this is a matter of life and death!"

Muffy Clogg's hands flew to her cheeks. "Mercy!" she squealed. "Don't tell me that poor Simon is going to be — *executed*?"

"No, no, Mistress Clogg!" Bertha cried as Conker scowled ferociously. "Simon's fine — other than being a mushroom, of course. What Conker means is that we have to invade the — um — the thingy's cloud palace before it leaves. Otherwise we'll have no chance of saving Wizard Bing, will we?"

"We've got no chance anyway," Freda muttered to Conker. "Listen, if the Clogg woman won't let us in, get her to throw down a bread roll or something, will you? I'm starving."

Muffy Clogg blinked shortsightedly in Bertha's direction, her rosebud mouth hanging slightly open. Clearly she was utterly bewildered.

"Don't you see?" Conker bellowed. "Bing's been collected!"

"*No!*" gasped Muffy Clogg. "You mean Wizard Bing came *back*?"

"The woman's feebleminded," Conker said under his breath.

But Leo had just been struck by an idea so wonderful that it almost took his breath away. "Mistress Clogg!" he called urgently. "When did the cloud palace arrive in Hobnob?"

Muffy Clogg's cheeks were now bright pink with indignation. "Early this evening, it was," she said breathlessly. "Around sunset.

It came down right over Tiger's Glen. It wasn't at *all* a nice thing to happen — very bad for business, and *very* bad for my nerves, which —"

"What?" exploded Conker. "The palace only arrived a few hours ago? But . . . . Bing disappeared last night! Oh, my heart, liver, lungs, and *gizzards* — if Bing wasn't even *here* when the palace came down, how could he have been *collected*?"

Muffy Clogg had clasped both hands over her heart. "Well, I'm sure there's no need for you to shout at *me*, Master Conker," she said in a high, trembling voice. "*You* were the one who said Wizard Bing had been collected."

"She's right, you know," muttered Freda.

Conker's eyes bulged. "I apologize, madam," he mumbled to the pink-faced woman. "It seems our deductions were, for once, incorrect. Wizard Bing is *not* in the cloud palace after all."

"Then where is he?" wailed Muffy Clogg, wringing her plump little hands. "Oh, mercy, my nerves can't take much more of this!"

"Muffy, my love, what's keeping you?" a male voice called plaintively from somewhere behind her. "Who is it?"

Muffy Clogg gave a little start of alarm. "No one, dearest," she trilled over her shoulder.

She leaned a little farther out of the window. "You can stay at the Snug tonight," she whispered. "It's right beside Tiger's Glen, but I'm sure you're so brave you won't mind that." She pointed vaguely over their heads, in the direction of the looming cloud towers.

"But — but —" Conker spluttered.

"Come back tomorrow," the woman said. "Not too early, mind. And don't come through the shop. Use our private door — the green one with the brass knocker. Good evening to you."

She jerked her head back, pulling the shutters closed behind her with a click. It was exactly like seeing a cuckoo pop back into a cuckoo clock.

"Well, I like that!" growled Conker.

"How rude!" exclaimed Bertha. "Imagine her treating us like that! When we were just about to risk our lives, too!"

Freda gave a quack of laughter. "She just doesn't want her husband to find out she's hired us. Clogg thinks her nephew's a hopeless case, so she knows he won't want to spend money on trying to prove he's innocent."

"That's all very well," Conker began crossly. "But —"

"There's no big rush now, remember," Leo broke in, trying not to sound too happy about it. "Bing can't be in the cloud palace. We don't have to go save him anymore."

"Oh, yes!" exclaimed Bertha, cheering up a little. "So we don't have to face certain death after all. Well, that's something to be grateful for, isn't it?"

"I'll be grateful when we can have a bite to eat," muttered Freda. "And I wouldn't say no to a roof over my head and a locked door, either. That cloud gives me the spooks. Let's find the Snug quick smart."

"We'll have to take the rug," Conker said gloomily. "We can't leave it parked in the square all night."

They trooped wearily back to the flying rug. When they reached it they found that the cooking pot had recovered from its faint and was sitting up, leaning weakly against Conker's pack.

"Foot *very* sore, Conkie," the pot whined, lifting one of its legs pitifully. Freda snapped her beak and it shrank away from her.

"Poor thing," said Bertha, as she, Mimi, and Leo took their places among the luggage. "Don't be too hard on it."

Conker snorted. He climbed onto the rug himself and sat down as far away from the cooking pot as he could. The rug's fringe quivered and it bulged slightly in the middle as if readying itself for a quick takeoff.

"Listen to me, rug!" Conker said sternly. "We're going to the Hobnob Snug. You're to rise gently, fly smoothly, and when we get there, you're to land *slowly*. No nonsense, or it will be the worse for you. Dot-swatters make good carpet beaters, you know, and I've got two of them!"

The rug stiffened sulkily, but it rose quite sedately into the air, sailed over the square, and began to glide silently over the rooftops toward the edge of the village. The glimmering towers of the cloud palace loomed closer and closer. Leo saw that Mimi was staring at them, transfixed, and wished very much that the Snug had been in the opposite direction.

"Is that it?" Bertha shrilled, looking over the side of the rug.

Clusters of lights twinkled below, and a faintly illuminated sign read: OB OB NUG — VA A CY.

"Hobnob Snug — Vacancy," Leo interpreted, filling in the letters that were missing because of glowworms on sick leave.

Mimi stirred. "Now that we've come this far, why don't we take a closer look at the cloud palace before we settle down for the night?" she suggested lightly. "Just in case —"

"No!" Conker, Bertha, Freda, and Leo shouted. Mimi's casual tone hadn't deceived anyone. Everyone could see that her fascination with the cloud palace hadn't grown any less. If anything, it had strengthened.

"Put it out of your mind, Mimi!" Conker ordered, as she pressed her lips together in annoyance. "I was right all along. The cloud palace has nothing to do with us, so none of us is going anywhere near it, and that's final."

He raised his voice. "Rug! Snug below! Commence your landing."

CHAPTER 12

THE SNUG

The rug had obviously taken Conker's dot-swatter threat to heart. Its smooth descent toward the round field of worn grass at the center of the Hobnob Snug was as different as possible from its stomach-churning drop into the town square.

"Well, this *is* nice!" Conker said with satisfaction, as the rug sank decorously between the whispering tips of the giant trees that ringed the grass. "And a fine piece of luck, too. I hadn't expected to be able to stay here. I thought we'd have to make do with a bed in the tavern. Ah, there's nothing I like better than a Snug."

"I've never been so keen on them, personally," said Bertha, wrinkling her nose. "A bed in a tavern would have suited me."

Leo, who had decided by this time that "Snug" was just a Rondo name for a camping area, silently agreed with her.

We don't even have a tent, he thought glumly, as the smoky scents of campfire cooking drifted to his nose and he began to hear the muffled sounds of music and the faint, high-pitched squeals of children far below. Like Bertha and Freda, he had been looking forward to sleeping between four sturdy walls and behind a locked door. The night wasn't cold, but the idea of spending it in the open air while the Strix's palace loomed so near was nerve-racking, especially with Mimi acting so strangely.

He stole a glance at Mimi, wondering if she were still angry, and saw that clearly she was. She was staring into space, her mouth set into that straight, stubborn line that was only too familiar.

She's so annoying! Leo thought in irritation. *She's always complaining about being treated like a baby, so why is she acting like one? She's curious about the cloud castle. Well, so am I. But I've got more sense than to want to go near it.*

He was just about to look away when he saw Mimi's eyes widen, and her tight mouth fall open in surprise. Quickly he turned his head to see what had startled her, and his mouth dropped open in turn.

The trees of the Hobnob Snug might have looked like any other trees from above, but now Leo could see that they were far from ordinary. Sprouting from the thickest of their gnarled, spreading branches — actually *growing* out of the living wood like weird, upright fruit — were small, perfect, nut-brown cabins, each with a rounded roof and walls, two round windows like knotholes, and a round front door. Light shone from some of the windows, and Leo could see the shadows of people moving about.

He was still staring up in astonishment when the rug

completed its landing, settling to rest beside an old stone well with a wooden bucket and a canopy that looked like the cap of a red-and-white spotted toadstool.

"Very good," Conker told the rug. The rug's fringe fluttered modestly.

The field seemed deserted. Small fireplaces made of stones were spaced evenly around it, but only one fire was still glowing. The smell of fried onions and slightly singed sausages drifted in the air.

A plump little man carrying a large clipboard emerged from the shadows behind the fire and trotted toward them, hastily pushing the end of a sausage into his mouth. He was wearing a woolly green dressing gown and a close-fitting green cap with earflaps that hung below his chin.

"That'll be the caretaker," Conker muttered. "Now, whatever you do, be polite. Snug caretakers can be very picky. We don't want him to take against us."

Everyone clambered from the rug. The cooking pot jumped up eagerly and began to follow, apparently forgetting all about its sore foot.

"Stay!" Conker ordered, pointing at the pot and scowling. The cooking pot seemed about to argue, then obviously thought better of it and sank back down against the pack, muttering to itself.

As the little man reached the rug, fussily dabbing at his lips with a green-spotted table napkin, Leo saw that the "clipboard" was actually a piece of bark covered in fuzzy black writing. The writing seemed to be some sort of list. Many of the entries were smudged, and there were many crossings-out.

"Welcome to the Hobnob Snug, ladies and gentlemen," the little man squeaked, in a perfect gale of sausage and onions. Everyone took a quick step back, but fortunately he didn't notice. He was looking with interest at the hovering rug.

"That is a most *interesting* conveyance, if I may say so," he said. "As I watched you land I said to myself, I have never seen a flying carpet with a pattern quite like that before, I said. And I never have, you know. Most unusual."

"We'd like to stay here tonight, if you please," Conker said, carefully keeping his distance as the little man turned toward him again. "Possibly tomorrow night as well."

"Certainly, certainly," said the little man. "That can be arranged. I am Woodley, the Snug caretaker — caretaker, you know." He suddenly became aware that he was still holding the table napkin, and tucked it quickly into his dressing gown pocket.

"I was just having a tiny bite of supper — supper, you know," he said self-consciously. "And thinking of my bed, to tell you the truth. I said to myself, it is far too late for any more visitors to arrive tonight, I said. But here you are, here you are. And most welcome — most welcome, you know."

Bertha's stomach rumbled loudly. Everyone pretended not to notice except Freda who laughed coarsely, earning a warning scowl from Conker and a haughty stare from Woodley.

"Pardon," Bertha murmured.

"It's lucky for us that you have some vacancies," Conker said hurriedly. He looked around at the trees, many of which were dark and silent in contrast to the lighted trees from which faint squeals and chatter could still be heard.

"It is most unusual at this time of year," Woodley responded, looking very put out. "*Most* unusual, you know. But as perhaps you may have noticed a — ahem — a small unpleasantness has occurred in Tiger's Glen."

He pursed his lips and jerked his head slightly toward the place where the sinister towers of the cloud castle spiked into the darkness of the sky above the treetops.

"It'd be hard to miss it," Freda said dryly.

"Yes." Woodley sighed. "Imagine the Snug having such a neighbor! In school holiday time, too — holiday time, you know! And Tiger's Glen is a most *beautiful* little woodlet, filled with the most *unusual* wildflowers and birdlife, and it's one of our most *famous* tourist attractions. A large group of children on a nature tour spent the day there only today. Tourists may stay as long as they like in the Glen, provided they do not stray off the marked paths — the paths, you know. Fortunately the children and their leaders had returned to the Snug before the — ahem — unpleasantness occurred, or the results could have been . . . yes, well . . ."

He cleared his throat. "I did explain to our visitors that there was no danger here in the Snug — no danger at all," he went on. "The public picnic area lies between the Snug and Tiger's Glen, after all. All you have to do is keep away from the Glen, I said, and you will be perfectly safe. But . . ."

He shrugged hopelessly and tapped his list with its many crossings-out.

"The vacant trees are very upset," he added, lowering his voice. "Snug trees take things very personally. They can't cope with rejection — with rejection, you know. Well, most of us are just the same way, aren't we?"

"I'm not," said Freda. "Listen, can we just get on with this? We need to get a fire going and rustle up some grub."

Bertha's stomach growled in ferocious agreement.

Woodley looked down his nose. "Well, *really* —" he began.

"At least *some* families decided to stay, Master Woodley," Leo said quickly.

"What? Oh, yes," said Woodley, turning to him with exaggerated courtesy after giving Freda and Bertha a last, hard stare. "About half of them stayed, determined not to spoil their holiday, and to ignore the — ahem — unpleasantness as far as possible — as far as possible, you know. Very sensible, as I told them. But I fear the children are all *extremely* overexcited. I hope they don't wake you too early. I will put you as far away from them as I can — as far away as I can, you know. Now, shall we get on? I can see that *some* members of your party are becoming impatient."

He consulted his list, running his finger down the entries and smudging them even further. "Mirth is the most isolated," he murmured, "but unfortunately Mirth only has the one cabin — one cabin, you know — and I gave that to another unexpected visitor who arrived not long ago. A single gentleman — a very charming fellow — very charming."

Leo's heart skipped a beat.

"*He* was *most* interested in hearing about the problems we're having here," Woodley continued, shooting a reproachful look at Freda, who yawned and closed her eyes.

"This gentleman," Leo asked, as casually as he could. "Is he — quite tall, with dark, wavy hair?"

"Oh, no indeed," said Woodley, studying his list. "The gentleman in Mirth is of ordinary height — of about my height, you know. Quite ordinary. Perfect for Mirth, whose cabin is not as large as some."

His eyes brightened and he looked up. "Are you perhaps expecting another friend to join you?" he asked hopefully. "Should I wait up a little longer?"

"No, no," Conker said firmly, shooting Leo a reproving look. "We're not expecting anyone else."

"Ah." Woodley looked disappointed, then gave a little sigh and returned to his list. "All Glee's cabins are vacant," he murmured. "All her cabins, you know. But sadly the folk who were staying in the largest of them left in such a hurry that they forgot to pack their snake."

"Snake!" Bertha squeaked.

"It's in there somewhere," Woodley said, shaking his head in annoyance. "It was asleep when I popped in to tidy the place up — asleep, you know, coiled around the lamp stand — Glee does not have central lighting, unfortunately — but I'm afraid I startled it when I opened the door. It hissed at me *very* rudely, then slid away and hid, quick as a flash — quick as a flash, you know. I wasn't able to find it, though I wasted a lot of time searching. It has probably gone back to sleep by now, but it was rather bad-tempered, and *very* large for a six-fanged rock serpent — very large indeed — so perhaps we had better leave Glee unoccupied for the moment."

"Perhaps we'd better," Leo agreed fervently. He glanced at Mimi, hoping she wasn't imagining large snakes with six fangs, and was relieved to see that she appeared not to have heard what Woodley had said. She had wandered over to the well and was peering curiously over the side.

"Yes," Woodley murmured, running his finger down the list again. "Poor dear Glee. I really wish people would be more careful — more careful, you know. It's so *awkward* when they leave their belongings behind. Do you know, there is not a single vacant Safe Place left in the whole of the Snug? Generations of forgetful guests have filled them all. *Most* inconvenient! Ah, here we are. Bliss!"

He turned and pointed to a huge tree standing a little back from the clearing. As he did so, Leo saw with a shock that two stubby wings protruded from neatly bound openings in the back of his green dressing gown.

"Bliss would be ideal for you — ideal, you know," Woodley chattered on, turning back to blast his guests with his sausage and onion breath once more. "She is one of our older Snug members, and has two cabins quite close together on the one branch — on the one branch, you know. You will need to take two, won't you? Some of you are rather *large*."

He eyed Bertha. She returned his stare indignantly, but couldn't speak because she was holding her breath.

"Rather large, you know," Woodley repeated, absentmindedly patting his own round belly.

Bertha tossed her head, turned, and stalked away to join Mimi at the well.

"The Bliss cabins are our deluxe accommodation," Woodley ran on, apparently oblivious to the fact that he'd insulted one of his guests. "Their features include central lighting, a double fireplace, dot-proof curtains, and goose-feather quilts."

"*Goose* feathers?" muttered Freda. "What's so deluxe about them?"

"Leo," Conker said in a strained voice, "why don't you, Mimi, and Bertha get some water from the well, then take the rug over to Bliss and start cooking dinner? I'll fix things up here. We shouldn't be much longer."

"I wouldn't count on it," Freda muttered.

"Just one thing!" called Woodley, as Leo gratefully began to turn away. "Ahem — about the well . . ."

"What about it?" snapped Conker. "Not poisoned, is it?"

"Oh, no, no, no!" gabbled Woodley, his hands fluttering nervously. "It is perfectly safe — the water is perfectly safe to drink, I mean, but —"

"Spit it out, man!" bellowed Conker, finally losing patience. "Oh, my suffering nostrils, what's *wrong* with the fool well?"

"It's — cursed!" Woodley squeaked, jumping back in fright.

"*Cursed?*" gasped Leo.

"CURSED?" roared Conker. "Oh, my heart, liver, and lungs, why didn't you say so before, instead of blithering on about —"

"Wak!" Freda exploded, flapping her wings in shock. She was gaping at the well.

"Oh, dearie, dearie me," sighed Woodley, who was facing the same way.

Then Mimi screamed, there was a mighty thump, and an eerie, high-pitched squeal split the air.

CHAPTER 13

BIG MISTAKE

Leo and Conker spun around. Mimi was squeezed against the well, her hands pressed to her mouth. In front of her, almost hiding her from view, lay what looked like a monstrous, oval pink balloon with four tiny kicking legs.

The thing was so grotesque that for an instant Leo couldn't take in what his brain was telling him. He could see a head, wrapped in pink satin and looking absurdly small, sticking out of the huge balloon at one end, and a curly tail twitching at the other, but he had to force himself to believe that what lay on the ground, crushing Mimi against the side of the well, was Bertha.

"Help me!" Bertha squealed in that strange, high-pitched voice. "Oh, help! Oh, what's wrong with me? I fell over, and now I can't get up!"

"Oh, my heart, liver, and lungs!" Conker muttered, goggling at her and tearing at his beard as if he were trying to pull it out by the roots.

Leo tore his horrified gaze from Bertha and met Mimi's eyes. They were huge and dark with shock. Her hands still pressed against her mouth, she shook her head slightly. She was telling

118

Leo that she had nothing to do with what had happened to Bertha — that the Key had nothing to do with it.

"Did I faint from hunger?" moaned Bertha. "Oh, I feel *very* strange."

"You *look* very strange," said Freda, recovering from her shock and waddling over to stare at Bertha with interest.

"What do you *mean*?" screamed Bertha in fright. Her trotters paddled the air as she desperately tried to roll herself over and stand up, but her huge, swollen body was far too heavy for her to move. She waggled her head violently and the last rags of the pink satin pillowcase flew off and fell to the ground in a crumpled heap.

"Stay still, Bertha!" Conker roared at her. "You might make it worse!"

"I don't see how it could be worse," said the duck.

"Dearie, dearie me," a voice behind them mumbled. "Most unfortunate."

Leo, Conker, and Freda jumped and looked around. For a moment they had forgotten all about Woodley.

Woodley had pulled the table napkin from his pocket and was mopping his forehead with it. "It's the well," he said faintly. "As I was telling you — ahem — just now. Or as I was about to tell you when —"

With a ferocious growl, Conker sprang forward, seized Woodley by the shoulders, and began shaking him violently. "What *about* the well?" he roared. "What's it done to her?"

Woodley's teeth chattered. His plump cheeks wobbled. His mouth opened and closed but no words came out.

"Let him go, Conker!" Leo shouted, grabbing Conker and trying to pull him away from the little caretaker. "He can't talk while you're shaking him. Let him go!"

"Someone help me up!" wailed Bertha from the ground. "What's wrong with you all?"

"Stop it, Bertha!" Leo heard Mimi call out, her voice sharp with panic. "Stop struggling! You're crushing me against the well."

Don't use the Key, Mimi, Leo begged silently. *Don't try to shrink Bertha with the Key. We don't know what's caused this. You might hurt her if you try to . . .*

He made a huge effort and finally managed to pull Conker away from Woodley. Panting, Woodley straightened his dressing gown and tightened its cord with trembling hands. "Naturally you are upset," he said breathlessly. "*I* am upset. Very upset. We are *all* upset. But there is no need for violence. Only yesterday I was saying to myself —"

"Master Woodley," Leo broke in, holding Conker back with difficulty, "please tell us right now what's happened to Bertha. Tell us what we can do to help her!"

"Oh," Woodley said blankly. "Well, she will have to reverse her wish, won't she?"

Everyone stared at him. He blinked at them and absent-mindedly mopped his brow with the table napkin again.

"Are you saying that this well is a *wishing well*?" Leo asked at last.

Woodley frowned. "Well, it never used to be," he said crossly. "Guests often *thought* it was, because of course it's a very old well — ancient, really — ancient, you know — and its appearance is — well, 'quaint' is the word our guests often use. But it was always just an ordinary well — a well for water, you know — until just before the last school holidays, when that interfering Wizard Bing —"

"*Bing?*" shouted Conker.

Woodley jumped back in fright.

"It's all right," Leo told him, keeping a firm grip on Conker's jacket. "Go on, Master Woodley."

Woodley wet his lips and cleared his throat nervously. "Wizard Bing came here to the Snug saying that he had just perfected a new spell — a new spell, you know — that could change our well into a wishing well. And I said to myself — well, folk are always making wishes at our well anyway, I said, and it might be an added attraction if the wishes came true. And the trees were very keen — *very* keen, you know. So I paid Wizard Bing what he asked, and he cast the spell. He only told me afterward that it was irreversible."

He shook his head mournfully. "I should have known. After the sandwich tree fiasco, and that lizard business, I should have *known* something would go wrong. Bing wouldn't refund our money or even apologize! He said I should just put a sign on the well to warn people to wish carefully. A vulgar sign! On an antique Snug well! Oh, the villain!"

He clenched his plump little fists. His stubby wings whirred in agitation, lifting him a short way from the ground, and for a moment his pleasant face looked quite ferocious.

"So Bing did the spell, and something went wrong . . ." Leo

prompted. He was seething with impatience, but he knew that he had to let Woodley tell the story in his own way if they were ever going to get any useful information out of him.

"*Everything* went wrong," said Woodley, twisting the table napkin into a corkscrew. "It is hard to imagine how the whole dreadful business could have turned out *worse*. Either he put the spell in *backward*, or it was backward to start with — I don't know. But the fact is, if anyone makes a wish at our well now, the *reverse* of what he or she wishes for comes true!"

Freda gave a harsh quack of laughter. Conker swore under his breath.

"The — the reverse," Leo murmured, thinking it through. "You mean . . . that if I wished to be, say, taller, the well would make me shorter?"

"Quite." Woodley sighed. "Or if you wished to be the most handsome man in the world, you'd become so terribly ugly that folk would scream at the sight of you. If you wished to be rich, you'd lose every penny you had in the world. It's quite frightful. Why, I myself —"

But Leo had already turned away and hurried to Bertha's monstrous side, beckoning for Conker and Freda to follow him.

"Well, at last!" Bertha cried indignantly as she caught sight of them. "What have you been doing, wasting time arguing and fighting while I lie here so frail and weak with hunger that I can't get up —"

"That's not it, Bertha," Leo said, kneeling down beside her

head. "Bertha, when you were looking into the wishing well, did you wish to be slimmer?"

"What?" Bertha gasped, instantly going crimson in the face. "How did you — ? I mean, how *dare* you, Leo! Why would I wish a thing like that? Are you saying I'm *fat*?"

"Wak! Wak! Wak!" Freda laughed.

"No, no!" said Leo urgently. "I mean, yes. I mean . . . listen, Bertha, this wishing well doesn't work properly. You can't get up because it's made you *gain* weight, instead of losing it. You're enormous!"

Bertha screamed in horror and burst into tears.

"Oh, Leo!" Mimi groaned in exasperation.

"You could have told her more tactfully, Leo," Conker said uncomfortably.

"Bertha, please listen," Leo pleaded. "It'll be all right. We can fix it. *You* can fix it. All you have to do is wish again. But this time you have to wish for the *opposite* of what you really want. Do you see? You just have to look into the well and think, 'I wish I were fat' and —"

"No-o-o!" Bertha wept, beside herself with misery. "Never! I could *never* wish such a thing! I'd rather die!"

"Bertha, you aren't listening," Leo said desperately. "Calm down and listen! You wouldn't *really* be wishing you were fat. You'd really be wishing you *weren't* fat — or at least, that you were only as fat as you were before."

"So!" shrieked Bertha. "I was fat before, was I?"

"Well, you *are* a pig, Bertha," Conker put in helpfully.

Bertha howled and burst into fresh floods of tears.

"Dearie, dearie me," murmured Woodley, glancing worriedly up at the trees, which had begun rustling and creaking. "This is *most* disruptive — most disruptive, you know."

Leo looked up, too. The doors of all the occupied cabins had been flung open and light was streaming out onto the tree branches, where groups of chattering people stood staring down at the scene at the well as if it were an entertainment put on especially for their benefit. Small children in pajamas were squealing and jumping up and down recklessly. Older children were being stopped with difficulty from sliding down to the ground to get a closer look.

"Bertha!" Mimi said sharply, digging her elbow into Bertha's side. "Take no notice of the others — they're just being idiots. You've got to pull yourself together. You're causing a scene. It's embarrassing!"

Bertha's wails abruptly stopped. Leo shook his head in annoyance. He knew he should be glad that Mimi's harsh tactics had succeeded in calming Bertha, but it seemed very unfair that they had when his kindness had failed. And what did Mimi mean by calling him an idiot, when his advice to Bertha had been perfectly sensible?

"Right," Mimi said. "Now, Bertha, we're going to get you up so that you can look into the well again. Then you're going to make another wish. The wish has to be the opposite of what you really want, because the well works backward. Have you got that?"

"Ye-es," snuffled Bertha. "But I can't *bring* myself to —"

"You don't have to wish to be fat," Mimi said crisply. "That would probably be dangerous, anyway. You might end up so skinny that you *still* couldn't get up. What you have to do is think: *I wish* not *to look the way I did before.*"

Bertha drew a shuddering breath. "Well, I suppose I could do that," she said in a quavering voice.

After that, the crisis ended quite quickly. While Freda and Mimi supervised and the crowd in the trees called out advice and encouragement, Leo, Conker, and Woodley removed the luggage from the flying rug, urged the rug close to Bertha, and managed to roll her onto it with so little effort that Leo suspected Mimi was using the Key to help.

For once, he approved of her breaking Hal's rule. Mimi hadn't tried to use the Key's magic to reduce Bertha's size. She'd shown great self-control about that, considering how uncomfortable she must have been, squeezed between Bertha's huge body and the wall of the well. But making Bertha roll easily onto the rug was something she felt she *could* do with safety, and she'd done it. *Very sensible*, Leo thought with some surprise.

Free to move at last, Mimi edged out of the narrow space between Bertha and the well. Then, sagging deeply under its huge burden, its fringe quivering with effort, the rug struggled gamely upward till it reached the well's rim.

Bertha twisted her neck until she could look down into the water. As everyone watched, frozen with tension, her lips moved silently. The next moment, her enormous body had shrunk like a deflating balloon and she was herself once more.

As the rug sank to the ground with obvious relief, the crowd in the trees whistled, cheered, and stamped. The trees rustled their leaves disapprovingly.

"All right, ladies and gentlemen," cried Woodley. "The excitement is over now. Quiet in the Snug — quiet in the Snug, you know!"

The people in the trees shouted even more loudly, waving, whistling, and clapping. Bertha looked up in dazed surprise. She shook back her ears and bowed graciously.

"I think we should retire to our tree at once," she said to Leo, Conker, Freda, and Mimi in a low voice. "People have obviously recognized me from the newspapers. They'll be coming down wanting autographs next, and I'm really just too, *too* exhausted to meet my fans tonight. Oh, if only I hadn't lost my sunglasses!"

CHAPTER 14

FREEDOM OF THE PRESS

Woodley escorted them to the tree called Bliss, introduced them courteously, and left them to return to his dinner. By this time everyone was very hungry, but Conker refused to consider a simple meal of bread and cheese. He was determined to get some use out of the cooking pot before abandoning it for good. He started a fire in one of the twin fireplaces that sat side by side beneath Bliss's spreading boughs. Then, grimly ignoring Freda's muttering and Bertha's loud complaints about being famished after her ordeal, he filled the pot with dried meat, chopped onions, herbs, and water from the well, and set it on the fire.

The pot wriggled in the flames, giggling and flapping its handle up and down. "Tickles, Conkie!" it shrieked. Water and shreds of dried meat and onion slopped onto the fire. Most of the flames went out, and smoke billowed from the charred, wet wood, making everyone cough.

"Now look what you've done!" Conker roared at the pot. He kicked at it furiously. It screamed and dodged, spilling most of its remaining contents over the last struggling flames, which died at once.

"Fire all gone," the pot said in surprise, shifting uncomfortably in the black, watery mess of dead coals, meat, and chopped onions that now filled the neat little fireplace.

Wreathed in smoke, speechless with rage, Conker bared his teeth.

"Never mind," Bertha said brightly. "Bread and cheese is fine with me."

Without a word, Conker turned to the second fireplace. He lit the fire and dumped the cooking pot on top of it. The pot jiggled and tittered in the flames just as it had done before, but by now so little stew remained that none splashed out.

Doggedly Conker filled the kettle and put it beside the fire to warm. Then he plopped himself onto the ground, folded his arms, and sat glaring at the flames in stubborn silence.

Freda sighed and wandered off into the shadows. Leo had the distinct impression that she was heading for the glow of Woodley's fire, from which the smell of sausages was still faintly drifting.

After a while, the cooking pot stopped giggling and started fidgeting in a bored sort of way instead. The stew inside it had begun to bubble, and soon the delicious scent of cooking meat, herbs, and onions filled the air. Bertha's stomach growled.

"All done, Conkie," the cooking pot said hopefully. It bounced on the coals, and sparks sprayed from the fire, showering the kettle and Conker's boots.

Conker jumped up with a curse, shaking off the sparks and stamping them out on the ground. He pointed a quivering finger at the cooking pot. *"I'll* say when it's done," he snarled. "And if you move again, pot, it will be the last thing you ever do."

He turned his back on it and glowered at Mimi, Bertha, and Leo as if daring them to say anything about being hungry.

Bertha's stomach rumbled again.

"Well," Leo said, desperate to break the tense silence that followed. "This is great, isn't it? We're in Hobnob, we've got a safe place to sleep, and tomorrow we can start investigating!"

Mimi gave a snort of amusement. Conker sniffed. But Bertha nodded approvingly.

"You're quite right, Leo," she said. "As my dear mother always told my brothers and me, whatever happens you should always count your blessings. I must say, after that wolf blew my house down and then started chasing me and trying to eat me, it was quite difficult to think of any blessings to count. Still, I thought of some eventually."

"What were they?" Mimi asked curiously.

"Well, one was that my house had been made of straw, so it hadn't crushed me to death when it fell down," Bertha told her. "And another one was that the wolf hadn't bitten off any of my legs yet, so I could still run."

"Some blessings," Conker grunted.

"Well, they were better than nothing," Bertha said defensively. "I think a positive attitude is very important — especially when a wolf is chasing you."

"That's true enough," Conker agreed, and Leo was relieved to see that he had begun to look a little more relaxed. It was also a relief that Mimi was acting normally again. The drama at the well, and Conker's struggles with the cooking pot, seemed to have driven thoughts of the Strix's castle from her mind.

Leo was just about to say something about Wizard Bing, hoping that a discussion of the quest would cheer Conker even further, when he saw a light bobbing toward them through the trees. Someone was approaching, carrying a lantern.

"Evening, all!" called a harsh, scratchy voice.

A scrawny gnome with a long nose and shiny, slicked-back hair stepped into the firelight and put down the lantern. He was wearing a purple shirt and tight black trousers, both of which looked very new, a black belt with a large gold buckle in the shape of a snake biting its own tail, and patent-leather shoes with pointed toes. A flashy gold chain hung around his neck and a huge gold ring with a purple stone winked on his finger.

"Oh, my heart and heaving stomach!" growled Conker in disgust.

"Scribble!" Bertha cried. "What are *you* doing here?"

"Wherever you go, I go, dear lady," said Scribble, bowing with difficulty in his tight trousers. "I just can't keep away."

Bertha giggled and blushed. "But how did you know where I *was*?" she asked breathlessly. "We didn't tell a *soul* where we were going!"

"Ah, there's no stopping an ace reporter on the trail of a story," said Scribble, tapping his nose with a bony finger. "As a matter of fact, that straw-haired, rather dim-witted new assistant at the tavern was cleaning your room when I popped in to see you this afternoon, and he let me in to wait for you."

"Oh, *did* he just?" snarled Conker.

"I happened to see some messages lying on the bed and had a tiny peep at them," Scribble told Bertha with a repulsive wink. "I saw your team had been asked to Hobnob to investigate the disappearance of Wizard Bing — *very* exciting! *Then* I saw your hat was missing, and realized you must have dropped everything and set out at once."

Bertha sighed with admiration. Conker cursed under his breath.

Bertha's hat! Leo thought. *That's what's in the pink bag. I'll bet Mimi sweetly offered to run up to Bertha's room for it — so she could pick up the Key at the same time.* He winced at the thought of how Bertha would feel when she realized how she'd been tricked.

"I left for Hobnob at once," Scribble was telling Bertha. "And it was lucky I did. If I'd delayed I'd be a prisoner in the cloud palace right now."

"What a load of old dot mush!" Conker sneered.

"A lot you know!" Scribble retorted. "I'd only just left Tiger's Glen when the palace landed. You'll read all about it in *The Rambler* tomorrow morning. What an escape! What a story!" He blew out his cheeks and fanned his face with his hand in exaggerated relief.

"But what were you doing in Tiger's Glen, Scribble?" asked Bertha in bewilderment.

"Why, that's where I arrived," Scribble told her. "That's where the Gap ends."

"A Gap?" Bertha gasped. "You mean — there's a shortcut from

town to Hobnob? You mean we had that long journey and got exhausted and half-killed for *nothing*?"

"You came the long way, did you?" Scribble smiled at her pityingly. "What a shame you didn't take me into your confidence, Bertha, instead of trusting the dot-catcher to guide you! I took two Gaps, to be precise — one from the tavern to Flitter Wood, and the other from Flitter Wood to Tiger's Glen."

"Oh," Bertha said in a small voice. "Flitter Wood."

Scribble nodded brightly. "Oh, yes! Very near your old farm, Bertha. I was in too much of a hurry to stop long in the wood, of course, but I did get a few words with a couple of squirrels, and I know you'll be happy to hear that Sly the fox is proving to be an excellent replacement for you. In fact, he's making a *huge* success of the job. There's not a dot left in the place."

"How nice," said Bertha miserably.

Scribble's long nose twitched. Leo was sure that he knew the whole story of Bertha's sacking, but was saying nothing for the moment so she would go on giving him interviews.

"What's the matter with Bertha?" Mimi whispered in Leo's ear, as naturally as if their bitter argument on the flying rug had never happened.

"Didn't she tell you?" Leo whispered back, a little startled by how good it felt to be on friendly terms again. He briefly repeated what Conker and Freda had told him about Sly stealing Bertha's job. Mimi listened impassively, her eyes hardening as she gazed at Scribble.

"Both of the Gaps I used are quite secret, but ace reporters have their ways of finding out these things," Scribble boasted, with a malicious glance at Conker. "It was a *very* fast trip."

"Only authorized persons are allowed to use The Black Sheep Gap, Scribble," Conker snapped.

"Oh, I'm sure you'll go running to Jolly telling tales on me when you get back," Scribble said nastily. "But I think you'll find that he's quite happy for me to use *all* the tavern facilities, as long as I keep buying his portraits of Bertha."

He beamed at Bertha, Leo, and Mimi, showing a mouthful of brown, crooked teeth that didn't match his fine new clothes at all. "I hope you don't mind my dropping in," he said. "I just *couldn't* wait till the morning to find out if Bertha had recovered from her terrible ordeal at the well."

"Oh," Bertha murmured, looking disconcerted. "You know about that, do you?"

"Of course!" said Scribble. "Mirth, my modest little abode for the night, has an *excellent* view of the clearing. I'd love to have your comments to go with the story. If we're quick, I can send it to *The Rambler* in time for tomorrow's edition."

Ignoring Conker's growl of protest, he whipped a notebook from his pocket. "I'm sure you must hold the Snug caretaker, Master Woodley, personally responsible for your stressful experience, Bertha?" he prompted smoothly. "No doubt you feel that he should be sacked, and the Snug should be closed down until the matter of the cursed well can be dealt with by the proper authorities."

"Oh!" mumbled Bertha, very flustered. "Well, I —"

"I thought so," said Scribble, writing busily. "But knowing you as I do, Bertha, I'm sure that despite this frightful episode, not to mention the terrifying presence of the cloud palace in Hobnob, you are still determined to lead the quest to locate Wizard Bing and prove the innocence of Simon Humble, helpless victim of police incompetence and brutality?"

"Oh!" Bertha gulped, glancing nervously at Conker. "Well —"

"Say no more, dear lady," crooned Scribble, making another note. "Don't distress yourself any further. I have it all down here, and as usual I'll report your statements with perfect accuracy. Trust me."

His tiny eyes sparkling, he flipped over another page of his notebook and turned to Mimi. "And you are Bertha's little friend Mamie, I presume," he said, lowering his voice to a husky croon as if he were speaking to a pet or a small child. "Where have you been hiding yourself for all this time, Mamie?"

Mimi glowered at him.

"It's Mimi, not Mamie, Scribble," Bertha put in anxiously.

"Of course," Scribble said, making a note. "Well, Mimi, I can see that you're not very happy with the state of affairs here. What a pity to see divisions in the team so early in the quest."

"I'm not —" Mimi began angrily. But Scribble had already turned to Leo.

"And you must be Leo," he said. "Or Leo the Lionheart, as you prefer to be called, I understand. How do *you* feel about Bertha as a quest leader? Do you share Mimi's doubts?"

"W-what?" stuttered Leo in great embarrassment and confusion.

Scribble's eyes brightened again. "Ah!" he said, making another note. "I understand completely. It's only natural that a fine young man like you might have ambitions to be the leader yourself — very natural!"

"Scribble, I don't think Leo meant —" Bertha began.

"Of course you're distressed about Mamie's and Leo's comments, Bertha," said Scribble, writing busily. "You feel betrayed, after all you've done for them. But it's best to get these things out in the open. And of course the public has a right to know."

He looked around. "I see the fighting duck has abandoned the team already," he said. "Or was she expelled for laughing during the embarrassing incident at the well?"

"Freda was *laughing*?" exclaimed Bertha, outraged.

"Naturally you couldn't put up with disloyalty like that," said Scribble, nodding as he wrote. "I presume the duck will try to join a rival team. How would you feel about that? Would you approve?"

"Well, no, of course not!" Bertha spluttered. "I mean —"

"You'd warn any rival team not to even consider employing her," said Scribble, flipping over yet another page of his notebook. "You want her banned —"

"Scribble," said Conker in a low, dangerous voice. "If your rag of a newspaper prints one word of this rubbish, I'll have your guts for garters." He lunged forward, drawing his dot-swatters.

"Conker!" Bertha cried in fright. "Don't —"

Scrawling a last, rapid note, Scribble skipped backward, out of swatter range. He squeezed his notebook back into his trouser pocket and picked up the lantern. "It's dangerous to attack the freedom of the press, Conker," he said defiantly. "You're seen as a hero now, thanks to me, but public opinion can change very quickly, you know."

"Don't you threaten me, you worm!" Conker spat. "Who do you think you are? Until you made a fortune out of Bertha you were sneaking around the forest with your trousers tied up with string, scratching out a living by picking up gossip from squirrels!"

Scribble smirked at him and flicked a speck of ash from his purple shirtsleeve. "All that's in the past," he said. "The public loves me, so my boss does, too. These days I can name my price for a juicy story. And just wait till my readers hear what's going on at Hobnob! It will curl their hair! It will line my pockets with —"

He broke off with a start as Freda walked out of the shadows, her wings half-raised, her eyes gleaming coldly behind their black mask.

"Everything all right here?" Freda asked mildly, and snapped her beak.

Scribble turned and ran.

CHAPTER 15

BLISS

Dinner that night was not a great success. After Scribble's abrupt departure it was discovered that during his visit all the liquid in Conker's stew had boiled away, leaving only a scorched brown sludge at the bottom of the cooking pot.

"I *told* you it was done, Conkie," the pot whined as Conker lifted it from the fire and began scraping out the sludge in silent rage. "I *told* you! Ow! Ow! It hurts!"

"Good!" snarled Conker. He divided the frizzled mess between the five tin dishes he'd laid out in readiness for the feast. The servings were very small, and looked more like little heaps of crushed beetles than helpings of beef and onion stew.

"We'll fill up on bread and cheese," Conker muttered, looking at no one. He crammed a spoonful of sludge into his mouth, grimaced, and chewed determinedly.

"Oh, I'm fine with this," said Freda, pecking at the scraps on her plate without much interest. Conker looked at her resentfully. Freda's beak shone with grease, and a spicy odor hung about her. Leo wondered how many of Woodley's sausages she had stolen. She wore the satisfied expression of a very well-fed duck.

For Conker's sake Leo ate what was on his plate, except some really blackened bits that he managed to tip onto the ground while Conker was looking the other way. He had hoped that some of the dots scuttling around Bliss's roots would dart in and carry the fragments away, but none of them seemed interested. Mimi didn't even pretend to eat. She passed her dish straight over to Bertha, who had finished her share in one gulp and was only too glad to have more.

"I itchy, Conkie," complained the cooking pot. It began scratching uselessly at its sides with its toes, making a horrible rasping sound that set everyone's teeth on edge.

"Its insides are covered in burned stew," Freda told Conker. "You'd better soak it. You'll never get it clean otherwise."

"I'll soak it, all right," growled Conker, throwing his dish aside and grabbing the pot's handle. "I'll throw it in the well, that's what I'll do!"

The cooking pot screeched, shattering the silence of the night. All around the clearing, branches creaked and leaves rustled in indignation.

"Quiet in the Snug, if you *please!*" called Woodley's disapproving voice from the distant shadows.

"Oh, shut up," Conker muttered. But he stomped away from the fire and began rummaging in Leo's pack, pulling out bread and cheese, and pretending not to notice as Leo half-filled the cooking pot with warm water from the kettle.

"All better." The pot sighed gratefully as the blackened stew scraps began to loosen and float to the surface of the water. It snuggled more deeply into the dust, gently lowered its handle, and appeared to go to sleep.

"It's rather sweet, really," said Bertha gazing at it sentimentally as Conker, looking thunderous, doled out chunks of bread and cheese. "You shouldn't be cross with it, Conker. After all, it's very young, and this *is* its first job."

"You wouldn't be making excuses if it had ruined all the food we had!" snapped Conker.

"Possibly," Bertha agreed with her mouth full. "But fortunately it didn't. Could I trouble you for the pickles?"

After the bread and cheese had been eaten, Leo washed the dishes while Conker scribbled a note telling Hal where they were. The note was collected by a mouse so old and shaky, and so gray about the nose, that it had obviously been brought out of retirement to help during the staff shortage.

After that, there seemed little to do but to put out the campfire and go to bed. Mimi and Leo were yawning. Bertha was very obviously ignoring Freda. Conker was too dispirited by the night's events to talk about plans for the morning.

"Time enough for that tomorrow, when things will look brighter," he said. Leo nodded, gloomily thinking that the quest so far had been nothing but a series of disasters, and a good night's sleep couldn't change that.

The flying rug, very tired after its heroic effort at the well, managed to rouse itself enough to carry everyone up to the huge branch on which Bliss's cabins grew side by side. They took all their belongings with them except for the cooking pot. It was sound asleep, making tiny, tinny snores, and Conker refused to wake it.

"Someone might steal it in the night," Bertha fretted, looking down at the pot sleeping all alone beside the twin fireplaces.

"We can only hope," snarled Conker.

It was agreed that Bertha would sleep in the smaller of the two cabins with the luggage, while the rest of the team shared the larger cabin.

"I just know I won't sleep a wink!" Bertha said. "I never do in a Snug, whatever my brother says — and this time I have that awful cloud castle practically on my doorstep as well. I'll toss and turn all night long, and I don't want to keep anyone else awake. Just be sure and call me if there's a fire, in case I happen to drop off toward dawn."

Bliss's leaves rustled in agitation.

"Don't worry, there won't be any fire," Mimi said reassuringly. Leo thought she was comforting Bertha and was surprised and touched by the gentleness in her voice. Then he saw that Mimi was looking up at the trembling leaves above her head and realized that she was talking to Bliss.

Typical, he thought, shaking his head. *Mimi wouldn't dream of comforting Bertha, who's her friend, but she's happy to comfort a tree she hardly knows!* Then, as Bertha began loudly worrying that the snake hiding in Glee's cabin would somehow find its way to *her* cabin and bite her during the night, he sighed and made himself admit that, after all, Mimi was right. Bertha's babblings about fire were just Bertha's usual fussiness, whereas to Bliss, who had probably seen the horror of forest fires firsthand in her long life, the fear of fire was very real.

It annoyed him that he hadn't realized this at first. It annoyed him that *he* hadn't thought of reassuring Bliss. It was just so hard to think of trees as beings you could talk to, but he should have remembered that everything was different in this world. It still embarrassed him to think of that time in Flitter Wood, during his and Mimi's first visit to Rondo, when he had thought the flying fairy creatures called Flitters were green moths. If it hadn't been for Mimi he might never have seen what they really were.

Mimi only recognized them because she was carrying the Key, he told himself grouchily. *That's how she knew to talk to Bliss, too. The Key makes her more sensitive to magic.*

But as he watched Mimi murmuring to Bliss, lightly stroking a small branch in a perfectly natural way, he wondered if the Key was the only explanation. It was quite possible that Mimi had *always* talked to trees — and maybe watched for fairies, too, while he, of course, would never have dreamed of doing either of those things. In that sense, he thought rather bitterly, Mimi was more fitted for Rondo than he was. She understood it in a way he didn't, and maybe never could.

He found this idea very irritating. It seemed very unfair that he wasn't as competent in this world as he was in his own, just because he was sensible and normal instead of being a dreamy loner like Mimi. After all, *he* was the owner of the music box, not her.

She's got the Key though, he thought resentfully. *And it definitely does make her more sensitive to magic. For sure it's because of the*

Key, for instance, that she's so fascinated by the Strix's palace, and that's dangerous for all of us. I'll have to tell the others about the Key first thing tomorrow. I've got no choice.

As Mimi went on murmuring to Bliss, and Conker and Freda saw Bertha safely into her cabin, Leo moved to the cabin he was to share. He felt jittery and overtired, and the knowledge of the troublesome secret he had to tell in the morning was like a large cold stone in his stomach.

He wished he didn't have to share a room with Conker, Freda, and Mimi. Conker would snore. Mimi would complain about Conker's snoring. Freda, her stomach full of Woodley's sausages, would probably wake up with indigestion. And Leo would be expected to keep the peace.

But I'm sick of keeping the peace and making everyone else feel better, Leo thought. *I'm sick of disasters and fights. All I want is to be alone! If only we'd gone to a tavern instead of this place! If only I was home in my own room, my own bed!*

"Take off your boots, Leo," Conker called over his shoulder. "Leave them outside the door. Snug rules."

Wearily Leo did as he was told. Then he opened the cabin door.

Soft light flooded the round room beyond. It illuminated curved pale brown walls as smooth as the inside of a china bowl, a rounded gold-brown ceiling, windows shrouded in thick green curtains, a pile of white quilts, and a floor covered with a thick, pale, spongy substance that looked as soft as thistledown.

And that was all. There were no beds. There was no furniture of any kind. It was just a plain, bare space.

And yet . . . Leo had never seen a place that looked more inviting.

Welcome, Leo, a hushed voice breathed in his mind. *Enter, and leave your cares behind.* .

Leo knew that it was Bliss. The ancient tree was speaking to him — he felt it without a moment's doubt or even wonder — and her invitation was irresistible.

He stepped across the threshold. His feet sank deeply into the soft, spongy floor. The air was fresh and faintly scented, something like the inside of the carved wooden chest in which his mother kept the spare blankets at home.

Home . . .

The light seemed to dim a little.

You are home with me, the soft voice whispered. *And it is late, very late. Time to sleep now. To sleep . . .*

And before he knew it, Leo was curling up on the feather-soft floor and snuggling into a white quilt as his eyelids fluttered closed. The light was still on. He hadn't washed his face. He hadn't cleaned his teeth. He was still wearing his jacket, his belt, his . . .

Sleep well, Leo, the voice whispered. *Sweet dreams.*

Soft darkness flooded Leo's senses. And the next thing he knew, it was morning.

He opened his eyes and blinked in golden sunshine. Conker and Freda were sitting up, stretching, and yawning. Mimi was standing at one of the cabin windows. She had opened the green curtains, and dappled light was streaming in. As Leo sat up, she turned around, her face glowing.

"Have you *ever* had a sleep like that?" she cried. "Ever in your whole life?"

Leo thought he had. Not for a long time, though. Not since he was very young, and life was very simple.

"I always say there's nothing like a Snug to set you up for the day." Conker grinned, jumping to his feet and running his fingers through his tangled hair.

Leo couldn't understand what had happened. He felt twice as alive as before he went to sleep. He could feel energy running through his veins like bubbling water. He was filled with a feeling of boundless goodwill that made him want to hug everyone in the room.

"Is it — magic?" he asked stupidly.

"Just trees," Conker said. "Snug trees, anyway. They love having guests, and they've got a real talent for it."

"No doubt about that," Freda agreed, energetically preening her right wing.

It took quite a time to wake Bertha, who finally staggered to the door of her cabin smiling and blinking and exclaiming at how quickly the night had passed. No one could convince her that she'd been asleep. She said she couldn't possibly have been, because she never *could* sleep in a Snug.

When finally they'd coaxed her outside and gathered their belongings together, they whistled to the flying rug. It sailed up to fetch them, then sank to the ground again without a single bump or tremor. The night beneath the Snug tree seemed to have done it good.

The cooking pot was still asleep when they landed, and they didn't disturb it. They lit the fire again, made tea, and toasted the last of the bread, spreading the toast with honey that Dinah had added to their supplies.

"Excellent!" said Conker, lying back on the rug and wiping crumbs from his beard with the back of his hand. "Bless my bones, that was the best breakfast I've ever had!"

"Me, too!" Bertha, Mimi, and Leo agreed. And Leo knew it was true.

Just after breakfast, however, while he was packing the honey jar away, Leo saw some blue butterflies hovering watchfully just outside the shade of Bliss's spreading boughs. He wondered nervously how long they'd been there. He wondered if he should mention them to the others. Then he suddenly remembered that he'd planned to break the news about the Key to Conker, Freda, and Bertha this morning. He'd been feeling so happy and content since waking up that he'd forgotten all about it.

He glanced at his friends. They were sprawled on the rug, chatting amiably and not even bothering to brush away the dots that had begun scurrying around, attracted by the toast crumbs. Conker had just presented Mimi with her money pouch, and she was very pleased with it. It seemed too cruel to spoil the cheerful, peaceful atmosphere by upsetting them just now.

I'll tell them later, he thought. *There's no rush.* And with a sense of relief he again put the Key to Rondo out of his mind.

CHAPTER 16

THE BATHING PARTY

"Well," said Conker, scratching his beard luxuriously, "it's still too early to visit Mistress Clogg, so I'm for the bathhouse. Anyone want to come with me?"

Leo had expected just to wash his face and hands in water heated on the campfire, but he wasn't going to miss the chance of seeing the Snug bathhouse. Mimi obviously felt the same, and Bertha was also keen to join the bathing party, though she was careful to point out that she had had a bubble bath at the tavern only the day before.

Freda shook her head. She said that baths were a waste of time when all you had to do to keep your feathers free of dust was to preen after every meal. "Someone should stay and guard the packs, anyway," she added. "That Scribble fellow might come calling again, and I wouldn't put it past him to go through our stuff."

"Oh, I'm sure he wouldn't do that!" Bertha exclaimed. But she didn't protest too loudly when Freda, Conker, and Mimi laughed derisively. The events of the previous evening seemed to have shaken her faith in Scribble.

"If he does come, Freda, you won't do anything . . . *rash*, will you?" she asked nervously.

"I won't kill him, if that's what you mean," yawned the duck. "That would cause too much trouble. I'll just damage him a bit."

"Good thinking," said Conker, and ignoring Bertha's cries of distress, he led the way out into the sunshine.

As they emerged from the shade of Bliss's broad canopy and moved into the clearing, they saw that people had begun to stir in most of the other cabins. Round front doors were flying open, curtains were being pushed aside, and cheery good-mornings were being shouted from tree to tree. A few people were cooking breakfast, and three very slim, pale green creatures in gauzy clothes were working together to draw a bucket of water from the well. A small, red-haired girl was dragging a long skipping rope across the grass, calling up to friends who were still in their cabins to come down and play.

And behind the treetops on the Snug's western side, looking much too close for comfort, the towers of the Strix rose jaggedly into the light blue sky.

"It's still there," Leo said uneasily.

"Yes," Conker muttered. "Don't look at it. Especially you, Mimi!"

"Why especially me?" snapped Mimi, as if she hadn't been transfixed by the cloud castle the evening before.

"Oh, look at that!" Bertha whispered in scandalized tones. "Lawks-a-daisy, what are they *thinking* of?"

Twin girls in identical blue overalls had joined the girl with the skipping rope. All three girls were pointing up at the cloud towers and jumping up and down together, chanting some sort of rhyme. Leo felt a little shock run through him as he made out the words.

"Dare to call the Strix," the girls were chanting. "Show the Strix your tricks!"

The green creatures at the well looked horrified. Quickly they dipped jugs into the bucket of water they pulled out of the well and flitted out of the clearing, disappearing into the trees with a flash of gossamer wings.

"Those sprites have got the right idea," Conker growled. "All this open space would make anyone nervous, with those silly children carrying on like that. I'm going to report this." He stomped away, heading for Woodley's fireplace. Bertha, Mimi, and Leo hurried after him.

Woodley, still cozily encased in his dressing gown, his cap pulled firmly over his ears, was sitting by the fire on a canvas stool, frying half a dozen eggs in an old black pan that still smelled strongly of sausage and onion. A pile of toast was keeping warm at the edge of the fireplace. A round table covered in a green-and-white spotted cloth and neatly set for breakfast stood nearby.

Woodley greeted his visitors warmly, asked if they had slept well, and beamed proudly when they said they had. When Conker told him about the girls' chanting, however, his brow puckered and his wings whirred, lifting him off his seat.

"Oh, dearie, dearie me!" he squeaked, kicking his short legs and waving the dripping spatula with which he'd been tending his eggs. "Oh, I was afraid something like this would happen! I will deal with it immediately after breakfast."

"In my opinion, you should deal with it right now!" Bertha exclaimed.

Woodley blinked at her. "I cannot possibly do it now," he said gently, sinking back to his stool. "My eggs are nearly ready."

"*Eggs?*" Bertha squealed. "Master Woodley —"

"The children are overexcited, that's the trouble," Woodley said fretfully. "And they have no fear. The Ancient One is just a story to them — just a story, you know."

The Ancient One, Leo thought, and shivered. Somehow he found that name far more frightening than Strix.

"You'd think their parents would warn them," Bertha said indignantly. "My mother told my brothers and me, over and over again, that the S — I mean, the keeper of the cloud palace — would come and carry us away if we were naughty."

"Well, that sort of thing is just the problem, in my opinion," Woodley said in a lecturing tone. "That is *exactly* what has made today's children treat the Ancient One as some sort of joke, like a Langlander tale told around the fire at night. It is quite ridiculous — ridiculous, you know — to claim that the Ancient One cares if children go to bed on time, or eat their vegetables!"

"Oh, quite," Conker said, clearly sick of the whole discussion. "Well, we've told you what's happening. What you do about it is up to you. Would you be so kind as to direct us to the bathhouse?"

"Oh!" cried the little caretaker. "Did I not show it to you on your arrival? That was *very* remiss of me — very remiss, you know. The bathhouse is directly behind my dining room here — directly behind it, you know — just a few steps away." He pointed with his spatula to a narrow path that wound into the trees beyond his picnic table.

"Thank you," Conker said curtly. "We'll leave you to your breakfast, then."

Woodley gave a little jump, as if the mention of breakfast had reminded him of something. He looked around in rather a furtive manner. "Take care not to leave your possessions unattended," he said, lowering his voice. "I hate to say it, I really do, but it seems we have a sneak thief in the Snug."

"A thief!" Leo exclaimed, his thoughts flying immediately to Spoiler.

"I fear so," Woodley said, looking very embarrassed. "It cannot be one of our *guests*, of course — oh, dearie me, no. But there has been quite a little crime wave in town just lately, they tell me — and now it seems that the wrongdoer has taken to creeping into the Snug."

"What's been taken from here?" Leo asked eagerly.

Woodley lowered his voice even further. "Well," he said, "last night, while I was fetching water from the well — for tea, you know — three of the seven sausages I had been keeping for breakfast were taken from my pan. *Three* perfectly cooked sausages! Can you believe it?"

"Lawks-a-daisy!" cried Bertha, very shocked. "That's *awful!*"

"Dreadful," Conker said solemnly.

"Terrible," Mimi murmured, without a tremor.

Leo muttered awkward agreement and looked down at his boots, not daring to let the little caretaker see his face in case his expression gave him away.

"As only four miserable sausages remained, I was forced to eat them there and then," Woodley confided. "I decided that there was no point in keeping so few. What sort of breakfast would four sausages make?"

He glanced at the frying pan again, saw that his eggs were done to his liking, and began lifting them onto a plate. "It is just fortunate that I had an egg or two put by," he added. "Otherwise I might have starved this morning — *starved*, you know. Oh, by the way, will you be wanting the Bliss cabins again tonight?"

Conker nibbled at his mustache. He was obviously very tempted, despite what they'd seen in the clearing. "Ah — do you have regular newspaper deliveries here at the Snug?" he asked, darting a meaningful look at Bertha, Mimi, and Leo.

"Why, of course!" Woodley exclaimed, carrying his loaded plate to the table and sitting down. "Several copies of *The Herald* arrive around lunchtime for the use of guests, and lately we have been taking *The Rondo Rambler* as well. It is rather a *sensational* paper, I know, but it has become very popular. "

"Oh, really?" Bertha said faintly.

"We probably *won't* be back, now I come to think about it," Conker said, beginning to edge away. "Our business will be taking us elsewhere."

"Far elsewhere," Bertha put in hurriedly.

"What a pity," sighed Woodley, picking up his knife and fork. "Bliss will be very sorry to lose you. Still, I hope we will see you here at the Snug again very soon."

He began eating his eggs and toast with gusto, merely nodding and waving his fork as the four friends gabbled farewells and moved quickly past him onto the path that led to the bathhouse.

"He didn't recognize me without my hat," Bertha whispered as soon as Woodley's table was safely behind them. "And he doesn't seem to know that Scribble is a reporter, either."

"He'll know it soon enough when he reads Scribble's story about your trouble with the wishing well in *The Rondo Rambler* today," Mimi said grimly.

"That's right." Conker groaned. "Oh, my heart, liver, and lungs, it's lucky I didn't pay for two nights in advance. Wait till Woodley reads what Bertha said about how he should be sacked, and the Snug closed down and all that."

"I didn't say that!" Bertha squeaked indignantly. "*Scribble* said it."

"Well, no one who reads *The Rondo Rambler* will think that," Mimi told her. "Scribble will make it sound as if it was you."

"Lawks-a-daisy," sighed Bertha. "Being a media megastar is far more difficult than I'd thought it would be. Life was so much simpler on . . . on the farm."

Her voice quavered a little as she said the last word. Leo glanced at her sympathetically. He wanted to comfort her, but how could he, when he wasn't supposed to know about her trouble?

"Ah!" Conker exclaimed loudly. "Here we are!"

They had rounded a bend, and there before them, in the middle of a shady clearing, was the Snug bathhouse.

It was nothing like Leo had imagined. For one thing, it wasn't a house at all. It was a clear pool wreathed in mist, surrounded by a narrow border of thick green moss and ringed by trees whose topmost branches met over it, making a leafy roof.

It was dim beneath the trees, but as Leo moved into the clearing, the air felt warm. It took him a moment to realize that the heat came from the pool itself. The mist that hung over it wasn't mist at all, but steam rising from the water.

Conker plopped himself down on the ground. He pulled off his boots and began unbuckling his belt.

Are we all supposed to have a bath together? Leo thought nervously. He saw that Mimi was turning away, rather pink in the face.

"Take off your jacket and belt as well as your boots, Leo!" Conker called, throwing his belt aside and stripping off his leather jerkin. "Leather and Snug water don't mix. I ruined a belt and two perfectly good swatter holsters before I worked that out."

Leaving his belt, jerkin, and boots on the moss, Conker waded into the pool. Bertha followed and was soon wallowing in the steamy water with little cries of appreciation.

"We have a bath in our *clothes*?" Mimi burst out.

"Of course!" Conker said in surprise. "How are you going to get them clean otherwise?" He lay back in the water and floated, his hair and beard drifting around his face like brown seaweed.

Mimi laughed. Without a moment's hesitation, she kicked off her shoes and plunged into the pool. "Oh, lovely!" She sighed. "Come in, Leo! It's so *warm!*"

Leo hesitated. The pool looked inviting, but it would be very uncomfortable to spend the next few hours in wet clothes. At the same time, he'd feel very odd stripping down to his underwear while everyone else was dressed.

"Hurry up, Leo," shouted Conker. "We can't stay here all day, you know!"

Reluctantly Leo took off his jacket, belt, boots, and socks and stepped gingerly into the pool. He felt smooth pebbles beneath his feet. Steam swirled around him. The water, deliciously warm and somehow smoother than ordinary water, rose to his knees, to his thighs, to his waist, till finally he was chest deep. His trousers and shirt flapped softly against his skin like the fins of fish. It was a strange feeling, but not unpleasant at all. In fact, the more he relaxed into the water, the better he felt. His worries about the chanting girls, about the Key to Rondo, about Scribble, about Bertha's troubles, drifted away.

"Ah," sighed Conker, closing his eyes. "This is the life! I feel as if I haven't a care in the world!"

"I am surprised to hear it," a cold voice said from the trees.

Conker jumped, sank, and came up spluttering. Battling the waves he was creating, half-blinded by steam, Leo, Mimi, and Bertha blinked up in astonishment at the tall, slender figure, the tiger-striped face, the angry golden eyes of Tye the Terlamaine.

CHAPTER 17

THE ANCIENT ONE

"Tye! What are you doing here?" Bertha squealed.

"I might ask you the same question," Tye said, unsmiling. "When Freda told me you were lolling around in the bathhouse, I could not believe my ears!"

"Oh, well," mumbled Conker, climbing hastily from the pool. "A Snug bath, you know, Tye. A rare treat — and included in the cabin price." Water poured from his clothes, hair, and beard and sank into the moss.

Tye regarded him in silence.

Bertha tossed her head. "There is no need for you to apologize, Conker," she said loftily. "There's no law against having a bath, I hope! We had a *very* tiring day yesterday, and our first interview regarding the disappearance of Wizard Bing is not until later in the morning."

Tye prowled forward. In the dim green light her black leather garments and her spiky black hair were almost invisible, but the jeweled hilt of the dagger on her hip gleamed, the golden markings on the smooth fur that covered her face seemed to glow, and her eyes were burning. She looked even more dangerous and startling than Leo remembered.

"I care nothing for the wizard, or your quest to find him, Conker," she hissed, ignoring Bertha completely. "I came here only because Hal asked me to. We have still had no news of Spoiler. Hal finds this ominous. He wishes me to keep watch over the Langlanders and see they do not come to harm. The Blue Queen would give much to have them in her power, and here in the north you are closer to her domain than Hal thinks wise."

Leo's stomach turned over. He caught sight of three blue butterflies flitting in the shadows at the edges of the clearing, and wondered uneasily if they were the same ones he'd noticed near Bliss.

It doesn't matter, he told himself. *They can watch us all they like. We might be closer to the queen's castle here than we were in town, but there's no way we're going to let ourselves be kidnapped and taken to her — by Spoiler or anyone else.*

"Leo and I don't need looking after, Tye!" Mimi snapped, climbing out of the pool and shaking her wet hair from her eyes. "We're perfectly all right with Conker, Freda, and Bertha."

"Oh, I see you are," Tye said in a silky, sarcastic voice. "That is why you play in the bath while in the field the young ones summon the Ancient One."

Despite the warmth of the water, a chill ran down Leo's spine. He tore his eyes away from Tye, glanced at Conker, and stared, dumbfounded.

Conker was looking crestfallen, but this wasn't what made Leo gape at him in amazement. Water was still running in sheets from Conker's trousers into the moss, but the upper half of his body was already completely dry. His hair and beard were crisp masses of gleaming curls. His red shirt was several shades lighter than it had been before, and looked as if it had just been freshly ironed.

Astounded, Leo waded to the pond's edge. By the time he reached it, Conker's trousers were dry down to the knees. By the time Leo climbed out, the last of the water was draining from Conker's heavy socks — which had turned out to be brown instead of black — and the moss around Conker's feet was covered in a thick layer of sooty flecks, brown dust, hairs, carpet fluff, burrs, one of Freda's feathers, some bits of dry grass, a few tiny twigs, and quite a lot of toast crumbs.

Conker looked down, grunted, and stepped off the moss, leaving behind him a black circle with two gray footprints in the middle.

Tye curled her lip fastidiously.

"I wasn't *that* dirty," Conker said defensively. "We had a bit of trouble with the fire last night, that's all."

"This is great!" exclaimed Mimi, looking down at herself with pleasure. She stepped off the moss in her turn, her short hair shining like a brown satin cap, her green and gold jacket and straight black pants looking fresh and new. The damp, dusty circle she left behind her was smaller and fainter than Conker's, but it still showed clearly on the bright green of the moss.

Water was pouring from Leo's hair and clothes, streaming down his arms and legs. It was a weird feeling — like standing in a shower, in a way, except that there was no new water beating down on his head. *No wonder the pond stays so crystal clear,* he thought. *We carry our dirt out with us!*

He found himself trying to work out the scientific principle that would make this possible. Was the Snug bathwater heavier than normal water? Did it contain some substance that had made the dirt and dust cling to his hair and clothes while he was in the pond, but released it as soon as he was standing in the air? Was the moss important in the process?

He wished he could take a sample of the water home — maybe give it to his father to analyze. Then he looked up. He saw Conker tugging at his freshly washed beard, Tye standing very upright and scornful, and Bertha clambering from the pond, a haughty expression on her face.

Forget it, Leo, he told himself. *This is Rondo. There are lots of things here that just can't be explained. You just have to accept that they* are. Almost guiltily, he felt a little thrill of excitement run through him. It made him feel strangely free not to know, or even be able to predict, what was going to happen next.

He looked down at himself again and realized that he was quite dry. He stepped off the moss and turned to look at the dark circle he had left behind him, the lighter marks of his bare feet clearly visible in the center. He found this evidence of how dirty he had been a bit embarrassing. It also seemed a shame that the moss had to be marked and spoiled.

Then a thought struck him. Why wasn't the moss completely covered in grubby circles? There were dozens of guests in the Snug, and all of them probably used the bathhouse.

He was just about to ask Conker about this when he realized that the dark circle was fading rapidly. The flecks of dirt were sinking into the moss. In seconds all that remained of the circle was a spotty patch of scattered grass seeds, some large fragments of ash, a burr or two, and some threads of carpet fringe. Then these, too, sank below the moss's surface, leaving no trace behind.

"Conker," Tye said in a soft, dangerous voice. "Why did you not mention in your note to Hal that the palace of the Ancient One had appeared in Hobnob, covering Tiger's Glen?"

"Well, I don't know! I didn't think of it. Why should I have?" Conker blustered, turning away from her and beginning to pull on his boots. "It's got nothing to do with us, has it?"

"It very nearly had a great deal to do with me," Tye snapped. "As it happens, I chose to come here by taking the Gap that leads from Troll's Bridge to Innes-Trule, and walking the rest of the way. I did not care to visit Tiger's Glen, where the quicker way — the Flitter Wood Gap — comes to an end. But if I *had* taken the Flitter Wood Gap, Conker, I would have stepped straight into the cloud castle and been lost in the dreams of the Ancient One, as others of my tribe have been lost in their time."

Her expression didn't change, but Leo saw the muscles tensing beneath her skintight leather tunic. *She's had a bad shock*, he thought suddenly. *That's why she's so angry. She's afraid. Tye's afraid.*

Yet even in the Blue Queen's castle, when she believed that her world was being undone, Tye had not been afraid. Why was she fearful now?

The Ancient One . . .

"Oh, my liver and lungs, you can't blame *me* for not warning you, Tye!" roared Conker. "I didn't know you were coming, did I?"

"Part of your duty is to tell Hal what is happening in Rondo," spat Tye. "You are supposed to tell him of anything unusual that has occurred, tell him if there is any sign of Spoiler —"

"There *hasn't* been any sign of Spoiler!" Conker bellowed, slapping his belt on the ground in rage. "We haven't seen hide nor hair of him! No one has, as far as I know, though Leo is as jumpy as a dot, seeing him under every rock and —"

"Then Leo is wiser than you," snapped Tye. "Spoiler could be anywhere. For all you know he is watching us at this very moment, waiting his chance to strike. But leaving Spoiler aside, your bringing the Langlanders to a place that has been invaded by the Ancient One is inexcusable, Conker! Hal trusted you, Freda, and Bertha to guard them, and yet —"

"Stop it, Tye," Leo cut in, as Conker spluttered and Bertha bridled. "It isn't fair. None of us had any idea the cloud palace was in Hobnob. It arrived just before we did."

"That's right," Mimi said, moving to stand shoulder to shoulder with him. "And anyway, we came here to do a job, and I don't see why the cloud palace should scare us off."

"I agree," Leo said rashly.

"Here, here!" boomed Conker, recovering. "After all, the palace of the Ancient One is only dangerous if you go inside it."

Mimi narrowed her eyes. "And just because *you're* tempted to do that, Tye," she said shrewdly, "that doesn't mean *we* are."

To Leo's astonishment Tye froze. There was a long, uncomfortable silence. Then, at last, Tye bowed her head and all her tension seemed suddenly to drain away.

"It is true that Terlamaines have always been drawn to the idea of the Ancient One," she said quietly. "The Ancient One is as old as Rondo. It existed before the Terlamaines existed. It remembers the time when only the Artist walked in Old Forest, listening to the silence."

She scanned their serious faces. "For some reason I do not feel its lure at this moment," she said. "But I must still beware. And you must not forget that the palace of the Ancient One can move where it wills, in the blink of an eye, and enclose the ones who have summoned it whether they feel its lure or not."

"But who is it? *What* is it — the Ancient One?" Leo burst out.

Tye half smiled. "I only know what I was told, long ago. It was said among the Terlamaines that the Ancient One was the first creation of the Artist's brush. One version of the story claimed that it was an error — a smudge or blot. Another version held that it was a test. Whichever it was, it was not — or perhaps it could not be — erased. The Ancient One was covered and hidden as our world grew beneath the Artist's hand, but still it had life — of a kind."

The familiar chill was running down Leo's spine. He felt cold inside. He pulled on his jacket and huddled into it, but it didn't help.

"The Ancient One bides in the deepest layers of the sky, where the clouds are thickest, and there are birds who never touch land,"

Tye said. "It dreams there, lulled by the music of the clouds, and time passes. Sometimes it wakes and comes closer to us. It becomes curious if it feels strong magic or if someone calls its name, and its curiosity draws it to land. This happens rarely, and according to the legends, that is just as well, for if the Ancient One takes you back above the clouds you can never return to the life you knew."

She looked directly at Mimi. "And you would be wise not to deny its fascination, Mimi Langlander. If I am in danger from the Ancient One, then so are you. More so, it seems, because while I do not yet feel its spell, you do. I see it in your eyes, however you try to hide it."

Mimi didn't answer. Her face remained stubbornly expressionless.

Tye's eyes flashed. She swung around to Conker. "Did you follow the orders about the Key?" she snapped.

"Of course we did," Conker grunted. "What do you think I am? It's in a Safe Place in the tavern."

"Well, that is something, at least," Tye muttered grudgingly.

Mimi's expression didn't change. Not by a single flicker did she betray herself.

She's not going to tell, Leo thought, his heart thudding. *I'll have to do it. I can't wait any longer. If I don't speak now, I'll never be able to do it. It'll be too late.*

But even as the thought crossed his mind he knew it was already too late. He had waited too long. To announce now that Mimi had the Key to Rondo would be to betray Conker, Bertha, and Freda as well as Mimi. It would be to expose them to Tye's anger and withering scorn. And Tye would of course inform Hal at once. Cónker, Freda, and Bertha would have to face Hal's fury, too. They'd be devastated to think they'd failed him — this man they all loved and admired so much. And they had done nothing, nothing at all to deserve it.

Except to trust us, Leo thought miserably. Resentment surged through him, heavy and sour. How could Mimi have put him in this position? He couldn't look at her.

"We must leave the Snug at once," Tye said crisply. "It is not safe. As you will learn, if you come with me now."

She turned on her heel and led the way back into the trees.

CHAPTER 18

DANGEROUS GAME

Now that the friends were away from the still, steamy air of the bathhouse, they could again hear sounds from the clearing — a rhythmic, thudding noise and children's voices chanting.

Conker gave a muffled exclamation. Bertha squeaked nervously.

"There!" snapped Tye. "Do you see?"

She had paused at a gap in the trees, and was frowning out at the field in the center. Conker, Bertha, Leo, and Mimi crowded around her to look.

Several other girls had joined the three with the skipping rope, and a game was in progress at the far end of the field. A girl with a long braid hanging down her back was jumping the rope while two other girls turned it. As the rope turned, rhythmically thudding the ground, all the girls chanted in time. There were so many voices that the companions could hear the words quite plainly.

Dare to call the Strix!
Show the Strix your tricks!

One, two, buckle your shoe,
Who will meet the Strix?

At the third line, the girl with the braid deftly bent and touched her shoe, just straightening in time for the next turn of the rope. The chanting went on, a little more loudly.

Dare to call the Strix!
Show the Strix your tricks!
Three, four, knock on the floor,
Who will meet the Strix?

At the third line, the girl with the braid crouched and knocked on the ground. This time, however, she didn't manage to get up and regain her balance before the rope came around again. She missed her jump and was out. Laughing in an embarrassed sort of way, she ran to take the place of one of the girls who had been turning the rope, and the game began again with another jumper — one of the twins this time.

Dare to call the Strix!
Show the Strix your tricks!
One, two, buckle your shoe . . .

"This is bad," said Conker uneasily.

"This is *very* bad," Bertha mumbled.

"It is worse than bad," Tye hissed. "Those young ones will call the Ancient One to them if they do not stop."

"No," said Mimi, staring at the twin jumping the rope. "None of them will be able to stay in till the end of the rhyme. They're too young. It's too hard."

Leo glanced at her nervously. He saw that Tye was looking at her, too.

"What does it matter if no one gets to the end?" Bertha asked in a high voice. "They're saying the name over and over. Isn't that enough?"

Mimi shrugged. "In a story it wouldn't be," she said. "In a story, they'd have to get to the end."

"This is not a story!" Tye hissed.

Mimi shrugged again.

The twin had managed to touch her shoe and knock on the ground without tripping over the rope. As she continued to jump, flushed with triumph, her friends chanted on:

> *Dare to call the Strix!*
> *Show the Strix your tricks!*
> *Five, six, pick up sticks,*
> *Who will meet the Strix?*

At the third line, the jumping twin bent and pretended to pick up objects to the right and then to the left of her feet. She was fast, but not fast enough. The rope thudded into her legs, and she was out. Pouting in annoyance, she stood back as her sister took her place.

"I told you," said Mimi. "It's too hard. They'll never get to ten."

Tye glanced at her sharply. "Let us move on," she said. "Freda is waiting."

When they reached their campsite they found Freda pacing around the flying rug, which was rippling perkily and turning up slightly at the corners. The cooking pot was huddled against one of Bliss's roots looking very sulky.

"At last!" Freda snapped at Conker. "Do you *hear* those children?"

"Freda was mean to me, Conkie," whined the cooking pot.

"I just made it wash itself," said Freda dismissively. "I only had to peck it twice."

"There was no point in getting it clean," growled Conker, shouldering his pack. "It's not coming with us. We're tying it up and leaving it here."

The cooking pot began to wail and drum its heels on the ground. Bliss's leaves rustled anxiously.

"Make it stop!" Tye hissed at Conker. "We cannot afford to attract unwelcome attention."

Scowling, Conker strode to the pot and picked it up. The pot stopped wailing and snuggled into his chest, making metallic purring sounds.

Freda snapped her beak at it. "No sign of Scribble," she told Conker. "He must be sleeping in."

"He was probably up all night writing his lying story and sending it to *The Rambler* page by page," Conker said sourly. "Still, we'd better sneak out of the Snug through the trees instead of taking off in the field. It will take longer, but if Scribble wakes up and sees us leaving he'll try to follow. How can we make discreet inquiries with a slimy reporter tagging along wherever we go?"

Tye nodded agreement. "I would also prefer not to be seen," she said. "There are too many children here."

"Why — ?" The question died on Leo's lips and his face grew hot as Tye looked at him impassively. Of *course* Tye didn't want to attract attention in the Snug. Many people in Rondo feared and distrusted Terlamaines, and parents might react violently if they saw Tye near their children.

"Right," said Conker. "Rug, roll yourself tidily and —"

"Wait a minute!" cried Bertha. "I'm not dressed. Mimi, can you get my hat?"

Conker stamped impatiently, Freda muttered something rude under her breath, and Tye stood frozen-faced as Mimi took the flowery hat from the pink bag and helped Bertha put it on.

"I thought you were worried about being recognized," Conker growled.

"Lawks-a-daisy, it's too late to worry about that now!" Bertha exclaimed, suddenly more confident now that her hat was securely in place. "Once folk read today's *Rambler* they'll know there's a celebrity in town. Anyway, I was obviously recognized last night — you heard all that cheering. Ah, well. That's the price of fame, I suppose."

With the neatly rolled rug floating behind them, they began threading their way through the trees. They kept as far away from the field as they could, but it wasn't always possible to avoid it completely. The sounds of the skipping game grew louder by the minute, and every now and then they would catch a glimpse of the turning rope between the trees.

They were almost opposite the game when the chanting grew suddenly louder and more high-pitched. All of them stopped and turned to look.

The small girl with fiery red hair was jumping the rope. She jumped with a fierce, determined air, her eyes fixed straight ahead, her mouth set in concentration. Her friends chanted excitedly.

> *Dare to call the Strix!*
> *Show the Strix your tricks!*
> *Seven, eight, lock the gate . . .*

As the third line began, the red-haired girl spun around in a circle. She almost made it, but not quite. The rope thudded down just before she'd completed her turn and she tripped, falling to the ground with a squeal. The chant broke off in a chorus of groans.

"Out," Mimi murmured with relief.

"Still," said Bertha, looking worried, "that girl got further than anyone else. Next time she tries, she might —"

"What's 'lock the gate' got to do with turning around?" Leo asked, frowning.

"The spin mimics the turning of a key," said Tye unexpectedly. "It is an old skipping trick and not too difficult, with experience."

She had spoken without thinking. When she became aware

that everyone was looking at her in surprise, her face became expressionless. "Even *I* had a childhood, strange as that may seem to you," she said coldly. "In Old Forest, when I was young, my friends and I played similar rope-jumping games."

Friends who are all dead, Leo thought, swallowing the lump that had suddenly risen in his throat. An ancient forest destroyed. A whole tribe — a whole way of life — obliterated by the Blue Queen.

How would it feel to be the last of your kind?

Lonely — so lonely . . .

Tye's not alone, though, Leo told himself. *She's got Conker and Freda and Bertha. And Hal — especially Hal. Last time we were here Tye said that* he *was her tribe now.*

But Tye's past had vanished. Her people were gone forever. When Tye herself died at last, there would be no one to remember what it was to be a Terlamaine.

Leo looked down at his boots. He didn't want to meet Tye's cold, golden gaze. He knew she didn't want his pity. She'd probably be insulted by it.

"Did you ever play *that* game, Tye?" Mimi asked, nodding toward the clearing, where the chant had started again from the beginning.

"We were not so foolish," Tye said harshly. "We had more sense, and more respect, than to chant the name of the Ancient One in mindless play. These children are soft and protected. They treat danger as a game because they have never known real danger and think they will always be safe. We in Old Forest knew better."

Dare to call the Strix!
Show the Strix your tricks . . .

The rolled rug nudged the backs of Leo's knees impatiently. He was just about to suggest they move on when Woodley came into view, whirring sedately across the clearing. He called out in his squeaky voice, but the girls, intent on their game, didn't hear him.

Obviously outraged at being ignored, Woodley picked up speed. "Stop it at once — at *once*, I say!" he squeaked, buzzing in circles over the heads of the skipping girls like an angry beetle.

The girls squealed and scattered. Three of them, the twins and the small red-haired girl who had snatched up the abandoned skipping rope, headed straight for the place where the companions were standing.

"Move on!" Freda said urgently.

But it was already too late. The girls saw them, skidded to a stop, and stood staring, transfixed, at Tye.

"What are you?" the red-haired girl asked Tye curiously.

"I am a Terlamaine," Tye said, unsmiling. "What are you? Other than extremely impolite."

The twins each took a step back, but the red-haired girl stood her ground.

"I'm a girl," she said. "I'm called Skip."

"You should *never* tell strangers your name, little girl," Conker growled.

Skip sighed in an exaggerated fashion and rolled her eyes. "Skip isn't my *true* name," she said. "It's only what I'm *called*."

"Skip," one of the twins whispered, tugging at her arm. "Let's go!"

"Yes," Tye said coldly. "Go, before your parents come looking for you. And do not use that jumping rhyme again. It is dangerous."

The twins giggled behind their hands, but Skip regarded Tye solemnly. "I got right up to 'Seven, eight, lock the gate,'" she said.

"I saw you," said Tye. "You did well. But save your efforts for another game. If you play that one again it may be the last time you ever jump the rope. Tell your friends the same."

The twins stopped giggling. Skip bit her lip. All of them looked scared, though Leo suspected that it was not the Strix but Tye herself who frightened them.

"You're teasing," Skip said, rallying a little.

Tye shook her head. "I am not," she answered softly. "Now, be off with you!" She hissed and made a sudden shooing movement with the black-gloved hands.

The three girls turned on their heels and ran, the twins screaming shrilly. Instantly Tye moved on, walking fast.

"They'll go straight to their parents and tell," Mimi warned.

"Of course," Tye said. "And their parents, who care not at all that they risk summoning the Ancient One, will panic at the thought that they spoke to a Terlamaine."

"Triple-dyed fools!" muttered Conker.

Tye gave a short, bitter laugh and glided on, a shadow slipping through the green shade of the trees.

By the time they found a clearing large enough for the rug to unroll itself and take off, there was an uproar in the Snug. As they sailed over the treetops, the sounds of angry adult voices, excited children's chatter, and the anxious squeaks of Woodley drifted up to them from below.

"Down, if you please," Tye said to the rug after only a few moments. The rug hesitated and then, with a petulant tweak of its fringe, began settling to land.

"But we haven't gone nearly far enough yet," Bertha protested, looking over the side. "We're only just out of the Snug, and the Shoe Emporium is right in the middle of town!"

"I do not propose to walk through the streets of Hobnob with you," Tye said calmly. "Tongues will soon be wagging about my presence at the Snug, and the sight of me will cause aggravation. You will be safer without me, as long as you remain together."

"Oh!" mumbled Conker, shifting uneasily as shame and relief warred on his face. "Well, as you like, Tye."

Tye smiled wryly.

The rug landed on a narrow road that ran beside the Snug. Trees grew thickly on the other side of the road, but they were very different from the Snug giants. They were slender, with pale trunks and whispering light green leaves. The moss and ferns that covered the ground were puddled with sunlight and striped with flickering shadows. Somewhere not far away there was the glint of water.

Tye slid lithely from the rug and stepped into the trees. "Come to me at sunset, or earlier if you need me," she said, and melted away into the shadows.

CHAPTER 19

GOSSIP IN THE SQUARE

Conker glanced up at the sun and gasped. "We're late!" he shouted, batting away the cooking pot, which was trying to climb on to his knee. "Rug! To the village square! On the double!"

He regretted his order to speed as soon as it was given, but he had no time to take it back. Thrilled, the rug shot up into the air, leaving everyone gasping for breath, and hurtled toward the village center, its fringe flattened to its sides. The cooking pot rolled and shrieked. No one else could utter a word.

In what seemed only a few seconds, the rug halted in midair and dropped like a stone. Even through the roaring of the wind in his ears, Leo could hear people shrieking below.

The rug jerked to a stop just as the tips of its dangling fringe touched the cobblestones. Its center bulged violently. Freda flew upward with a squawk, and Conker, Bertha, Leo, Mimi, the packs, and the cooking pot rolled off onto the ground.

"Well, have you ever seen the like?" a woman's scandalized

voice shrieked. "If that's not dangerous driving, I don't know what is!"

"Out of the sky like a thunderbolt!" cried another voice. "If we'd been standing underneath it we'd have been squashed flat, Bodelia!"

Dazed, bruised, and blinking, the friends crawled to their feet. Bertha's hat was hanging below her chin, Conker's newly washed hair was standing on end, the cooking pot had a small dent in its side, Leo and Mimi were windblown, and everyone was smeared with dust. Even Freda, fluttering to land beside them in a small shower of loose feathers, was in disarray.

They were right in the center of the square, beside the sick-looking tree that Leo had noticed the night before. Several blue butterflies were dancing around the limp white flowers. On seeing the quest team, two flew quickly away.

It doesn't matter, Leo told himself, trying to ignore the sick feeling in his stomach. *It doesn't matter.*

Still, he looked closely at the four chattering people in front of him, and was relieved to see that none of them looked remotely like Spoiler. From their conversation they all seemed to be shopkeepers who had run out to see what the commotion was all about.

A large, gimlet-eyed woman encased in a beaded purple dress, her steel-gray hair so stiffly arranged that it looked as if she were wearing a helmet, was talking to a meek, wispy little woman in a pink-striped apron.

"Scruffy-looking lot, aren't they, Candy?" the large woman said, glaring at Conker as he snatched up the cooking pot to stop its wailing. "What are they doing with a rug like that? You can see it's valuable — look at the pattern on it! In my opinion, they've stolen it."

"Ooh! You're probably right, Bodelia," her friend breathed. "We should send for Officer Begood." Her faded eyes grew a little misty as she said the policeman's name. She obviously had a soft spot for him.

Leo brushed his clothes hastily. As he did so, his elbow bumped one of the branches of the little tree and one of the drooping white flowers fell limply onto his boot. He looked down and was startled to see that it wasn't a flower at all, but a sandwich, soggy with tomato and slightly curled at the edges. He shook it off furtively.

"We are *not* rug thieves!" Bertha announced in a high voice. "I'll have you know we are *very* famous heroes, on a quest to —" She broke off with a gasp as Conker dug her in the ribs.

The woman called Bodelia gave a humorless snort of laughter. "Heroes!" she said with the contempt Conker reserved for dots. "I might have known! As soon as that cloud palace appeared it was dabs to dibs there'd be heroes here next, trying to get rid of it and make a name for themselves."

"Madam, we are *not* —" Conker began indignantly.

"Barging around the place full of their own importance, expecting three free meals a day and all the ale they can drink," Bodelia went on loudly. "Keeping us up all night singing songs about how brave they are, then half the time getting mortally wounded and expecting us to clean up the blood."

"Hmm," said a gloomy man in black, looking at Conker, Freda,

Bertha, Mimi, and Leo in a calculating way, as if he were measuring them up for something.

"*Heroes!*" sneered Bodelia. "Do you remember that time we had a dragon, Candy? And that hero came to kill it? That knight, or whatever he called himself?"

"Ooh, yes," breathed Candy, her eyes becoming misty again. "Sir Clankalot. He was so *gallant!*"

"Gallant my big toe!" Bodelia said rudely. "He ate us out of house and home, used up every tin of metal polish in the town, and in the end he never killed the dragon at all. It just flew away by itself. The cloud castle will do the same, you mark my words. All we have to do is ignore it."

"Not *all* heroes are useless, Bodelia," said a thin little man with a voice almost as squeaky as Woodley's. "What about those heroes in the paper who defeated the Blue Queen the other night? The ones led by that glamorous wolf-fighting pig in the hat?"

"As if first-rate heroes like that would ever come to Hobnob!" Bodelia said resentfully. "We get the dregs, that's what we get."

Mimi snorted with laughter.

Bodelia's nostrils tightened as if she smelled something bad. "The dregs," she repeated, glaring at Mimi. "The scum of Rondo!"

"Steady," muttered Freda, as Conker made a strangled sound and the tips of Bertha's ears went bright pink.

"Larrikins on flying rugs, claiming to be heroes!" Bodelia grumbled, turning her back on them. "Why we should put up with it, I really don't know."

"We *could* send for Officer Begood," Candy put in hopefully.

"Begood wouldn't come back so soon," said the man in black. "He only left yesterday."

"With poor Simon Humble," added the thin little man.

Bodelia pursed her lips. "I always said that boy would come to no good," she announced balefully. "I told Mayor Clogg so, to his face. 'Your wife's nephew,' I said, 'will come to no good.' And now look at him! A mushroom, and under arrest for murder!"

"Did you see how he jumped on Begood's foot?" the man in black said. "And I always thought Simon Humble wouldn't say boo to a goose. It just goes to show, you never know about people."

"Let's run for it," Freda muttered out of the side of her beak.

But Conker shook his head. "We could learn something useful here," he whispered. "They'll talk more freely among themselves."

"Well, I must say I'd never have thought that Simon was the murdering sort," Candy was saying breathlessly. "He never showed *me* his violent side anyway, though I must say he drove me wild begging for free lollipops whenever he came to town. He never seemed to have any money, poor chap. I told him he should ask Wizard Bing for more pay, but he said he'd be too scared to do that."

"Every worm can turn," Bodelia said darkly.

"If you ask me, Humble did us all a favor," the man in black declared, picking a sandwich from the tree and munching it gloomily. "Bats Bing was nothing but trouble. Hobnob is well rid of him."

"Oh, Master Sadd, that's a terrible thing to say!" Candy gasped, her eyes sparkling with pleasurable horror.

"It's true, though," the man retorted. "And well you know it, Mistress Sweet, after what Bats did to you with that superchewy toffee he invented. How long were your jaws stuck together when you tried it?"

"Three days," said Candy Sweet ruefully. "I had to eat and drink through a straw. He wouldn't give back the chocolate I'd traded him for that toffee, either."

"He'd probably already eaten it," said Bodelia. "He was a chocolate addict, in my opinion. You should have sued him for everything he had."

"He didn't have much," Candy murmured. "He was very slow in paying his bills."

Everyone groaned and nodded.

"You should never have let him have an account, Candy," Bodelia said. "I've told you time and again you should never give credit."

"But you let Count Éclair take that silver trinket box without paying for it, Bodelia," Candy protested feebly.

"Expensive antiques are *rather* a different matter from bars of chocolate, my dear," Bodelia said with a patronizing smile. "And customers of noble birth are *very* different from broken-down wizards. Count Éclair's bill will be settled by messenger in due course — that's the way the gentry manage such things."

"Bing owed you money, too, didn't he, Stitch?" said Master

Sadd, turning to the thin little man. "He never did pay for that new cloak you made him?"

"No, he did not!" squeaked Stitch. "He'd insisted on best-quality double-sided velvet, too. I had to order it in specially."

"Bing said that cloak fell to pieces the first time he wore it," Bodelia told Candy in a loud whisper. "He had to go back to wearing his old cloak — you know how he never went *anywhere* without his cloak and hat — and he said he had no intention of paying for shoddy workmanship."

Stitch glowered at her. "There was nothing wrong with that cloak when I delivered it," he said. "Simon told me that Bing dipped it in a dirt-repellent rinse he'd invented and all the thread dissolved."

"Well, you won't get your money now," said Master Sadd with a mournful sigh. "And neither will Mistress Sweet. Bing's gone for good. I only wish Humble hadn't hidden the body so well. I've got my living to make, and what's the use of digging a grave if there's no one to put in it?"

"I don't think Bing is dead at all," Stitch said stoutly. "He was working on some mysterious new invention, you know, just before he disappeared. Simon told me so, the last time I saw him, though he wouldn't say what the invention was, or what it was supposed to do."

"Aha!" hissed Conker, digging Leo painfully in the ribs. "An invention! A *transforming* invention, or I'm a mushroom!"

"Don't *say* that!" snapped Freda.

"Simon wouldn't tell me what the invention was, either," said Candy with a sigh. "He just kept dropping hints. He was so excited to have a big secret, poor boy. It made him feel important."

"Well," said the little tailor, "we all know how Bing's inventions always turn out. My theory is that he transformed poor Simon with this new one — by accident, probably — and just panicked and took to his heels."

"Nonsense!" Bodelia said scornfully. "Bing wouldn't have run away. He's always thought he had the right to do anything he liked."

"He might have thought he'd gone too far this time," said Master Sadd. "We've put up with a lot from him, but he must have known that turning the mayor's nephew into a mushroom would be the last straw."

He looked dismally at the half-eaten sandwich in his hand. "This is stale," he commented. "And I'm so sick of tomato I could scream. How long has it been since we had anything else?"

"I got an egg and lettuce one just before the last school holidays," said Stitch. "At least, I *think* it was egg and lettuce."

"You shouldn't eat those sandwiches, Master Sadd," Bodelia snapped. "They're unwholesome. The tree's diseased — anyone can see that. We should never have allowed Bing to put it in the square, let alone paid him good money for it. I said that from the first. But no one listened to me, oh, no!"

"Free sandwiches *sounded* like a good idea," Sadd said gloomily.

"Bun didn't think so," said Stitch. "If the sandwich tree had been a success it would have put Bun's bakery out of business. But poor old Bing couldn't invent anything that worked if he tried.

Look at that wishing well in the Snug. What a disaster *that* turned out to be!"

Candy Sweet gave a little start. "Oh!" she cried. "Oh, speaking of the Snug, you'll never guess what I heard just before I came over here! Some girls were attacked by a *Terlamaine* that was lurking among the trees."

"*No!*" everyone gasped.

"Time to go," muttered Conker, edging away as the shopkeepers began chattering excitedly. "But I told you it was worth staying. We found out more from eavesdropping than we'd ever have learned by doing interviews, and now we've got a handful of suspects."

"Lawks-a-daisy, yes!" Bertha whispered. "Candy Sweet. Master Sadd. The little tailor fellow, Stitch. Bun the baker. Even that woman Bodelia. Every one of them had a grudge against Wizard Bing, and they all knew about his new invention. One of them could easily have disposed of him and stolen it."

Conker tucked the whining cooking pot under one arm and rubbed his hands gleefully. "Plenty of suspects plus a good, solid theory already," he said. "Excellent! We'll have this mystery solved in no time. On to the Shoe Emporium!"

CHAPTER 20

STRAWBERRIES AND CREAM

The shopkeepers were too busy giving their opinions on Terlamaines to notice the friends backing away toward the Shoe Emporium, pulling the rug along with them by its fringe.

"Of all the suspects, I think Bodelia is the most likely," Bertha said.

"Bodelia's certainly the meanest," Conker agreed. "But Sadd has a nasty, creeping look. And that tailor . . . he's skinny, but he's got hidden depths. I'd say he could lash out quite violently, if he was angry enough."

"He doesn't look as if he'd hurt a fly to me," Bertha objected. "Whereas Bodelia —"

"Candy Sweet *acts* timid," Mimi broke in. "But in a book she'd be the one, because she's the least likely. And we shouldn't forget Woodley. He's obsessed with his Snug, and Bing messed up its well."

"My money's on this Bun character," said Freda.

"You're all forgetting what Stitch said about Bing transforming Simon by mistake and then running away," Leo put in. "That made sense to me."

"Bing wouldn't have run," Freda said, shaking her head decisively. "The Bodelia woman was right about that. Bing's a lunatic."

"What if someone found out about Simon being a mushroom and took advantage of the situation?" Mimi said thoughtfully. "It would have been hard for anyone to get to Wizard Bing and his invention normally, because Simon lived in the house and would be a witness to anything that happened. But once Simon was a mushroom and couldn't talk . . ."

"Brilliant, Mimi!" Bertha exclaimed, looking very impressed.

Leo was quite impressed, too, though he wasn't going to admit it.

The Shoe Emporium's CLOSED sign had been turned around to read OPEN. The shutters had been pushed back, and now they could see the huge range of shoes that filled the large windows and lined the many shelves inside the shop.

"Mayor Clogg must be a *very* hard worker," said Bertha, gazing through the windows. "Lawks-a-daisy, he must stay up all night every night to make so many shoes!"

Leo stared. He had never seen so many shoes in one place — even in a large department store. There were thousands of them, in every imaginable size, color, and shape. Several eager young men and women wearing red blazers with C.S.E. embroidered in gold on the breast pockets were dealing with the few customers, who were sitting on red velvet chairs arranged in rows in the middle of the shop, or paying for their purchases at an elegant desk.

At the back of the shop, right in the center, a man with a bristling white mustache sat with his chin on his hand. He wore a dark pin-striped suit, a crisp white shirt, and a striped tie that looked as if it were strangling him. He had a red rose in his buttonhole, and a gold mayoral chain hung around his neck. To his left was a pedestal on which stood a very handsome and expensive-looking pair of tall yellow boots and a sign reading 7-LEAGUE BOOTS! EXCLUSIVE TO CLOGG'S EMPORIUM! To his right was a glass case marked FOR DISPLAY PURPOSES ONLY — NOT FOR SALE in which two glittering red shoes were dancing all by themselves.

The man's eyes were blank with boredom, and didn't even flicker as the cash register rang out, signaling a sale.

"That must be Mayor Clogg," said Bertha with interest. "He doesn't look very happy, for a man whose business is doing so well."

"Who cares?" snapped Freda. "Let's get out of sight before those loonies in the square turn around." She started for the shop door with Conker, who was looking appreciatively at the yellow boots, and Mimi, who couldn't take her eyes off the dancing red shoes.

"Not in there," Leo whispered. "Clogg's not supposed to know about us. Muffy Clogg told us to knock at the green door — the one at the end."

With a snort of annoyance, Conker wheeled around and strode to the door at the far end of the Shoe Emporium. Bertha, Mimi, Leo, and Freda hurried after him, the rug flapping limply at their heels.

Glancing over his shoulder at the crowd in the square, Conker lifted the brass knocker and rapped sharply three times.

"Don't want to go into nasty house," whined the cooking pot.

"Too bad," Conker muttered, tightening his grip on it as it struggled to get down. "Rug, roll yourself up, and make it snappy."

The rug, clearly aware that it was in disgrace, wasted no time in doing what it was told. It had just finished, and Leo had just managed to put Bertha's hat back on her head, when the door was opened by a pretty but rather sad-eyed maid wearing a pink gingham dress and a white cap and an apron edged with lace. She drew a quick breath when she saw the visitors, and her eyes brightened.

"Quest team to see Mistress Clogg," Conker said importantly.

The maid pulled the door wide, revealing a grand flight of stairs. "You're expected," she said, sounding quite excited. "Please follow me."

Quickly she led the way up the stairs and through a spacious, light-filled room decorated in pink and white and filled with squashy chairs and sofas, plump cushions, and spindly tables covered with boxes of chocolates, magazines, balls of wool, and half-finished pieces of knitting. French doors opened onto a large balcony, where Muffy Clogg sat at a white wrought-iron table eating strawberries and cream with a silver spoon.

This morning she was wearing a mauve-flowered dress with puffed sleeves, and mauve lace mittens. Matching bows were tied in her curly golden hair. She raised her head as the maid ushered the visitors through the doors and gave a little start as she saw how disheveled Conker, Leo, and Mimi looked. Then her eyes fell on Bertha and her face broke into a delighted smile.

"The quest team, ma'am," said the maid, bobbing a curtsy.

"Oh, yes. Thank you, Tilly," Muffy said breathlessly. "Bring tea, if you please, and perhaps some more strawberries. I'm sure Mistress Bertha would like to try some of our strawberries. Tell Cook to add a little more sugar, this time. These are not as sweet as they could be."

"Yes, ma'am," said the maid. She bobbed again and left the balcony with a swish of pink gingham skirts.

"You have a beautiful home, Mistress Clogg," Bertha said politely, staring after the maid with a slightly puzzled expression on her face. "I *love* your color scheme."

"Why, thank you," Muffy gushed. "*We* like it. And may I say what an *honor* it is to be able to welcome you here, Mistress Bertha. When I wrote asking for help, I naturally addressed my note to your assistant. I hardly dared *hope* you would come to Hobnob yourself! You must be so very busy dealing with the press."

Bertha fluttered her eyelashes modestly. Conker scowled and muttered under his breath. Muffy Clogg eyed his wild hair, touched her own perfectly arranged curls, gave a nervous little cough, and turned back to Bertha with obvious relief.

"I've seen your picture in so many magazines, Mistress Bertha," she confided. "It's such a *thrill* to meet you face-to-face. Won't you please sit down?"

Everyone crowded around the table. The flying rug meekly wedged itself against the balcony rail. Mimi, Leo, Conker, and Freda sat down. Bertha said she'd prefer to stand.

"Good choice," Mimi muttered to her, wriggling, because though the wrought-iron chairs looked like white lace, they were extremely hard and uncomfortable. Leo noticed that Muffy Clogg's chair was well padded with a large silk cushion.

"It is most kind of you to come see me so early," Muffy said, delicately spooning a particularly plump strawberry into her mouth. "Though I must admit I'm surprised. I thought you'd visit the scene of the crime first, since you were so close."

"Were we?" Bertha asked blankly.

"Why, yes!" Muffy said, opening her blue eyes wide. "Wizard Bing's house is in the center of a little wood that lies just across the road from the Snug. Didn't I tell you?"

"No," Freda said sourly, and snapped her beak.

Muffy looked frightened and unconsciously ate another strawberry.

"It doesn't matter," Leo said quickly. "We saw that wood on our way here. We can go back to it easily enough."

"Of course you can," Muffy agreed, recovering. "Take very good care, though, at Wizard Bing's house. They tell me it's full of old spells and poisons and . . . spiders!" She shuddered.

Conker cleared his throat, leaned forward, and put his elbows on the table with the air of getting down to business. "Now, madam," he said. "Please tell us, in your own words, all you know about the disappearance of Wizard Bing."

Muffy looked at him blankly. "Mercy, I don't know anything about it at all," she cried. "All I know is, my poor innocent young nephew has been dragged off to jail *most* cruelly and with no respect at *all* for my nerves!"

She put down her silver spoon, pulled a lacy handkerchief from her sleeve, and dabbed at her eyes, which had suddenly filled with tears. "Oh." She sniffed. "Just *thinking* about it makes me *so* upset."

"Your nephew is quite upset as well," Freda remarked. "Plus, he's a mushroom."

Muffy Clogg began to sob in earnest.

"Fat lady's face leaking, Conkie," said the cooking pot conversationally.

Conker crushed it to his chest in an attempt to smother it. It wriggled, but at least it fell silent.

"Could you tell us how Wizard Bing's disappearance was discovered, Mistress Clogg?" Leo asked, thinking that this at least was a straight question to which he might get a straight answer. "I mean, how did you find out about it? Who gave the alarm?"

"Oh," Muffy quavered, dabbing her eyes. "Well, that was the chicken."

"Chicken?" Bertha repeated with interest.

Muffy nodded tearfully. "I'd gone to bed early that night," she said. "My knitting was making my head ache *frightfully*, and Clogg had suggested that an early night might do me good. Well, I'd just managed to fall into a fitful doze when I was woken by the most terrible explosion! And while I was lying there, calling out to Clogg and Tilly and wondering what in Rondo had happened, one of Wizard Bing's chickens came running into the square calling out and carrying on *dreadfully*. It's done that sort of thing before — it's always been high-strung — but this time it was quite *hysterical*! It kept running around in circles, flapping its wings, and screaming that the world was coming to an end and the sky was falling and Wizard Bing had been murdered and Rondo knows what else. Feathers were flying everywhere — oh!"

She pressed her hand to her heart. "It just wouldn't stop. In the end Clogg had to throw a bucket of water over it."

"I bet that calmed it down." Freda smirked as Leo and Mimi exchanged horrified looks.

"Well, it did stop screaming," Muffy agreed. "It fell over and just lay there with its beak open."

"In shock," said Bertha, nodding sagely.

"I suppose so, the poor thing." Muffy sighed. "I had a lot of sympathy for it, I must say. I'm a martyr to my nerves as well. But I couldn't do anything for it, could I? I was in a terrible state myself. I'd been dreading something awful happening ever since poor Simon started working for that frightful, bad-tempered wizard. I begged him not to take the job, but he was wild to be a wizard's apprentice, poor fellow."

She looked down at her strawberries. "These really do need more sugar," she said fretfully.

"What happened then, Mistress Clogg?" Leo prompted gently.

"Well, the chicken was too stiff to talk, so everyone except me went to Bing's Wood to see what had happened," Muffy said resentfully.

" 'Everyone'? " Conker said sharply. "Who's 'everyone'?"

Muffy jumped as if she'd been stung. "Well, *everyone*," she babbled in confusion. "Everyone who lives in the square. Clogg, Candy Sweet, Stitch the tailor, Bodelia Parker from the antiques

shop, Bun and Patty from the bakery, Master Sadd the gravedig-
ger — he lives in Bodelia's cellar — as well as a lot of other folk
from the streets around. No one could possibly have slept through
all that noise."

"And were these folk all at home in bed when the chicken first
arrived?" Conker demanded, his eyes narrowing.

"Well, of course they were!" Muffy exclaimed, opening her
blue eyes very wide. "Where else would they be? It was the middle
of the night!"

"But did you see them?" Conker persisted. "In their nightclothes, I mean?"

"Certainly not!" squeaked Muffy, turning pink. "Naturally
everyone got dressed before they came out. People don't go pranc-
ing about in the streets in their nightclothes in Hobnob, whatever
they might do where *you* come from, Master Conker!"

Feverishly she applied herself to her bowl of strawberries
and cream, scooping up massive spoonfuls and swallowing
heedlessly.

"So any one of our suspects could be the guilty one," Conker
muttered to his friends under his breath. "Any one of them could
have killed Bing, hidden his body, then joined the crowd milling
around in the square. Who would ever know?"

"No one!" gasped Bertha, wide-eyed.

"Unless the guilty one left evidence behind him — or her!"
Mimi pointed out with relish.

"Exactly," murmured Conker. "And that's our next job. To
examine the scene of the crime."

CHAPTER 21

TOO MANY SUSPECTS

"What are you all whispering about?" Muffy Clogg demanded, throwing down her spoon hysterically. "Are you talking about me? Don't I have a perfect right to finish my breakfast? I have to keep up my strength."

"Lawks-a-daisy, of course you do, Mistress Clogg," Bertha said quickly. "We weren't talking about you. We were —"

"We were wondering who sent the message to Officer Begood," Leo broke in, sure that Muffy's state of mind wouldn't be improved by finding out that the team suspected one of her neighbors of murder.

"Oh," Muffy said, calming down a little and smoothing her curls with a trembling hand. "Well, you only had to ask me! It was Tilly, my maid, who sent the mouse. And when Officer Begood arrived, Tilly *insisted* on going out to Wizard Bing's house with him, though I'm sure he could have found his way on his own. He *is* a policeman, after all. How Tilly could have left me in the state I was in, I do not know! I was all alone for ages, with only Cook to look after me."

"Oh, dear," Conker said, with unconvincing sympathy.

"It was a frightful ordeal," Muffy said, blinking at him pathetically. "And then, when at last Tilly and Clogg came back, they broke the news to me that Wizard Bing was gone and that Simon — wasn't himself, and had been arrested. I don't know what happened after that, because naturally I fainted."

"Naturally," said Freda.

The pretty maid arrived with a tray covered in a white lace cloth and crowded with cups, milk, sugar, a very elegant silver teapot, and another bowl of strawberries.

"The master is coming up the stairs, ma'am," she murmured discreetly as she set down the tray.

"Mercy!" Muffy dropped her spoon with a clatter and jumped up so fast that her silk cushion fell on the floor.

She goggled at the quest team. "Stay here!" she hissed. And with amazing speed for such a well-padded woman, she darted into the sitting room, closed the doors, and pulled the curtains shut, leaving the friends alone on the balcony with Tilly.

"Oh, my blood and bones!" growled Conker. "This is no way to conduct an investigation!"

Tilly gave what might have been a sigh and began pouring tea. "Milk, ma'am?" she asked Bertha. "Sugar?"

"Both, thank you," said Bertha graciously. "Do you know, Tilly, it's very strange, but I keep thinking I've seen you somewhere before."

"I think you may know my sisters Gilly, Lily, and Milly, ma'am," said Tilly, without looking up. "Folk say we look very alike."

"Oh!" breathed Bertha, her face suddenly alive with a mixture of powerful emotions. "Oh, of course! Your sisters are maids at Macdonald's farm where I"— she swallowed —"where I used to work myself before — before I gave it up to become a quest heroine. Have you heard from your sisters lately? Is all well at the farm?"

"Quite well, ma'am, I think," said Tilly, placing a cup of tea in front of her. "Mistress Mary is a little quiet, the girls say, and the chickens seem depressed and aren't laying so well. But the mistress's garden is flourishing because the new watch-fox — your replacement, you know — has got rid of all the dots. The girls say he's very efficient."

"Oh, yes," Bertha replied, her voice hardening a little. "He's very efficient. If you like that sort of thing."

She looked down at her tea and began blowing on it miserably. Conker, Freda, Leo, and Mimi exchanged uncomfortable glances.

"I thought I'd find you having breakfast on the balcony, my love, on a fine day like this," a man boomed in the sitting room. Everyone jumped and looked at the curtained doors in alarm.

It's not our fault we're here, Leo thought, crossly fighting down the urge to hide. *Muffy Clogg invited us!* But still he dreaded the thought that Clogg might come out onto the balcony and discover them, and by the tense looks on his companions' faces he could tell that they felt the same.

"Why in Rondo are you lying there in the dark, Muffy?" the man went on, his voice suddenly even louder as he moved closer to the balcony doors. "Here, I'll open the curtains for you."

"No, no! Please leave them, Clogg!" Muffy's voice cried plaintively. "I can't bear the glare. I have *such* a headache!"

"Oh, dear," said Clogg, his voice suddenly full of concern, and fainter as he turned away from the curtains. "You've been fretting about that nephew of yours, I suppose, but you really mustn't trouble yourself, my love. Are you comfortable on that sofa? Do you need another cushion?"

Her face a well-trained blank, Tilly passed a cup of tea to Leo. He murmured his thanks and she nodded and forced a tiny smile.

"I'm as comfortable as can be expected, thank you, dearest," sighed Muffy. "But why have you come upstairs at this time of day? Are you tired? I hope you haven't been overdoing it down in the shop."

There was a heavy sigh and a soft thump, as if the man had thrown himself into one of the armchairs. "There's not much chance of overdoing it," he said dully, "sitting there like a dummy without a thing to do. I came up to tell you it might be as well for you to stay indoors today, my love. Now, don't be frightened, but apparently a Terlamaine's been causing trouble in the Snug."

"*No!*" Muffy exclaimed, as the quest team exchanged rueful glances.

"So Stitch says," Clogg said. "He was in the shop just now. He says there's nothing to worry about, but I thought it was best for you to know."

"Thank you, dearest," Muffy said warmly. "You're so thoughtful. Now, you run back downstairs. I don't want to keep you from your work."

"*Work?*" Clogg scoffed dismally. "What work? There are hardly any customers, and even if there were, the shop could run perfectly well without me. Ah, Muffy, I can't help remembering the old days when —"

"When we were poor and hungry!" Muffy said, a sharp note entering her languid voice. "When we had a tiny little shop and one room above, and you made all the shoes, and sold them, too, and I had to do all the washing and cooking and cleaning myself *and* ruin my eyes embroidering handkerchiefs for tourists *despite* what you promised me when we were married! Surely you can't really wish those days back again, Clogg? I certainly don't!"

The man sighed again. "No, I don't wish them back, not really," he said in a defeated voice. "But I'm a shoemaker, Muffy, like my father before me. I *enjoyed* making shoes. And ever since those dratted elves took over my shop —"

"Shh!" hissed Muffy, and Leo could almost see her glancing at the balcony doors in alarm. "Clogg, what are you thinking of? What if someone is listening?"

"Who could hear us up here?" Clogg said drearily. "And who cares, anyway? Folk must know there's something funny about this place. They must hear the work going on behind the shutters every night."

Leo remembered the tapping sounds he'd heard behind the shuttered windows of the Shoe Emporium the night before. It hadn't been dots. It had been elves! Elves busily making shoes!

He glanced at Mimi. She was smiling with fascinated delight. She met his eyes and put her finger to her lips.

"Everyone thinks you have special, secret machines that help you make shoes faster," Muffy said from the sitting room. "I told Bodelia Parker that ages ago — in strictest confidence, so naturally she spread the word."

"Naturally," Clogg said miserably. "But, Muffy, I don't know how much longer I can take this. I promised you a soft life if you married me, and I meant what I said. But I never thought I'd have to sit back and watch while a bunch of elves took over my workshop and made all my shoes a lot better than I could — not to mention leaving me a rich man with nothing in Rondo to do!"

"Well, the elves weren't *my* fault, dearest!" Muffy exclaimed. "I didn't ask them to come help us, did I? They came of their own accord."

"Maybe," Clogg muttered. "But you know what I think, Muffy — I've told you often enough. It was that wizard who brought this plague down on us. It was Bing!"

His voice was venomous. Leo, Conker, Freda, Mimi, and Bertha exchanged startled looks. Even Tilly paused in the act of pouring tea and put her head to one side, listening.

"Now, now, Clogg!" Muffy cried in alarm. "You mustn't —"

"Didn't Bing come to our little shop wanting a pair of tall boots?" Clogg fumed. "Didn't I have to tell him I only had one piece of leather left, and it wasn't enough for boots, only for shoes? Didn't Bing go off muttering I wasn't a shoemaker's bootlace, and Hobnob deserved better? And didn't those pests turn up that very night?"

"Yes," quavered Muffy. "But —"

"How you could have let your nephew go to work for the man who ruined me, I do not know!" Clogg shouted. "It drove me wild, Muffy, to hear you talking about it. 'Simon says this about Wizard Bing. Simon says that about Wizard Bing. Simon says Wizard Bing is working on a wonderful new invention.' A new invention to blight the life of some other poor soul, I suppose! It drove me wild, I tell you!"

"Oh, mercy," Muffy cried tearfully. "How can you say such things, Clogg, when Wizard Bing is in a hidden grave, and Simon is in a dungeon?"

"Best place for both of them, as far as I'm concerned," roared Clogg. "You'd have thought with Bing gone those dratted elves would have disappeared as well. But oh, no! Last night they were hard at it just the same. Snip, snip, snip, tap, tap, tap! When will it all end? Hundreds of shoes. Thousands of shoes! More than we could ever sell in a lifetime, half of them magic and every one perfect! It makes me sick!"

At that, his wife burst into a storm of sobs so violent that he was forced to pay attention to her distress.

"Oh, Muffy, my love," he said hastily, in quite a different voice. "Forgive me. I didn't mean to upset you. Sometimes my feelings just get the better of me and I can't help . . . Muffy, please stop! You'll make yourself ill."

Muffy's sobs rose to a crescendo of choking wails.

"Tilly!" shouted Clogg in panic. "Tilly, come quickly!"

Tilly put down the teapot. This time she didn't even try to suppress her sigh. "Please excuse me," she said politely. "Madam is having hysterics again. I must take charge of her before the master panics and throws a bucket of water over her. It's all he can think to do, but it ruins the carpet." She hesitated, then went on in a rush. "I think you should forget about madam for the moment. She really can't tell you anything and will just delay you."

She moved swiftly to the French doors and slid through the curtains into the room beyond. In moments her cool, soothing voice was mingling with Muffy's wails and Clogg's desperate shouts.

"Lawks-a-daisy!" exclaimed Bertha. "We've got another suspect!"

"A good one, too!" Conker said, his eyes glittering with excitement. "If anyone had a better motive to dispose of Wizard Bing and frame his nephew than Clogg, I don't know who it is! Tilly realizes it, too. She was very anxious to get rid of us."

"We still haven't seen this Bun character," Freda reminded him. "Let's drop in on the bakery on our way to Bing's."

"Good idea," Bertha agreed. "I could do with a snack. These strawberries *are* a little sour."

"Right," said Conker. "Rug, unroll yourself! We're leaving!"

The rug struggled to do as it was told, but failed because it was still wedged against the balcony rail. Finally Leo and Mimi managed to pull it free, and it flattened itself eagerly, its fringe quivering with excitement as everyone climbed on.

"To the bakery on the other side of the square," Conker instructed, gingerly putting aside the cooking pot, which had fallen asleep under his jacket. "And this time, rug, go quietly, or it will be the worse for you!"

The rug rose meekly into the air, cleared the roof of the Shoe Emporium, and sailed over the square, self-consciously rigid and level as a tabletop.

Leo looked down at the people standing on the cobblestones below. He couldn't see Stitch the tailor or Candy Sweet, who had presumably returned to their shops, but Bodelia and Master Sadd were still deep in conversation beside the sandwich tree. Occasionally Bodelia looked sharply around, as if wondering where the ruffians with the flying rug had gone, but luckily she didn't think of looking up.

"We'd better land at the back and walk around," Leo said quietly.

Conker nodded and gave the order. The rug flew carefully over the bakery and settled into the narrow street that ran behind it. The street was deserted except for hundreds of dots, most of which were vainly attempting to burrow their way through the bakery's tightly sealed back door. The dots scattered as the rug landed.

"Very good," Conker told the rug, stepping off. "Now . . ." He glanced at the sleeping cooking pot and then at the bakery door. His eyes glittered.

Very gently he lifted the pot and slipped its handle over the bakery doorknob. The pot didn't stir. Hanging peacefully from the doorknob, it slept on, its skinny legs dangling.

"There," Conker whispered with satisfaction. "Problem solved. Now all we have to do is get out of sight before it wakes up."

"Conker!" Bertha said reproachfully, but Conker frowned ferociously, put his finger to his lips, and tiptoed with exaggerated care to the corner, dragging the rug behind him.

"Wait for us here," he told the rug when everyone was safely around the corner. "We won't be long." And closing his ears to Bertha's accusations of cruelty to cooking pots, he led the way up to the square.

Chapter 22

Bun the Baker

As the friends turned the corner and approached the bakery door, appreciatively sniffing the delicious aroma of baking bread, they saw that an elegant red fox was sitting beside the doorstep, keeping a watchful eye on the dots scurrying about on the cobblestones.

Bertha made a small, choked sound that she tried to turn into a cough as everyone looked at her anxiously. "It's all right," she said. "I got a little shock, that's all. That fox reminds me of — of another fox I know."

"All foxes look alike to me," Freda muttered.

"Good morning," Conker said to the fox with forced heartiness as they reached the doorstep. The fox nodded graciously without taking her eyes off the dots.

A bell on the door tinkled as Conker hurriedly ushered Bertha into the shop. Mimi followed, then Freda, slapping her feet loudly on the step and giving the fox a challenging look as she passed. As Leo hesitated, glancing over his shoulder to make sure that Bodelia and Sadd weren't looking in the bakery's direction, a dot made a break for the open door.

The fox moved so fast that she was a red blur. The dot didn't even reach the doorstep. Snip, snap, swallow, and it was gone. The fox licked her lips with a long pink tongue and went back to her post.

"She's fast, I'll give her that," Freda said grudgingly, as Leo quickly stepped into the shop and closed the door behind him.

"Fastest fox in the north," said a cheerful voice. "A treasure! I'd be lost without Renée."

A chubby bald man wrapped in a spotless white apron was beaming at them from behind the counter. Wire racks behind him were loaded with loaves, rolls, pies, and cakes. There couldn't be any doubt that this was Bun the baker.

"We're wasting our time here," Leo murmured. "He looks completely harmless."

"It's just a pose," Mimi whispered back, eyeing Bun suspiciously. "Someone that cheerful must have something to hide."

"I'm with you," Freda agreed.

"And what do you fancy today, ladies and gents?" asked Bun, his face positively shining with good humor. "A nice sultana cake? A bramble pie, still warm from the oven? Or could I tempt you with some Princess Pretty Tarts, as served at the recent Crystal Palace ball?"

He gestured with modest pride at a rack of small, heart-shaped tarts glistening with pink fruit and topped with a fluff of meringue. "My own invention," he continued happily. "They melt in your mouth, if I do say so myself."

"Er, yes, we'll have a few of those," Conker said, feeling for his money bag.

"Five dibs apiece," Bun said cheerfully. "Or a dozen for a dab and six bread rolls thrown in — that's our holiday special."

"Excellent value," said Freda, eyeing the Princess Pretty Tarts with interest.

Conker nodded. "A dozen, then," he said grandly. "Why not?" He put a gold coin on the counter.

Bun picked up the coin and inspected it closely on both sides before putting it into the cash register.

"I've grown cautious," he said apologetically, catching sight of Conker's insulted expression. "I had a bad experience not long ago. The shop was full of customers — locals, mostly, when a fine-looking chap came in. He waited in line, nice as you please, listening to the local chat, and when it was his turn to be served he asked for three curry pies, a box of Princess Pretties, and a bag of cheese straws."

"So?" Conker said belligerently. "What's that got to do with —"

"I'm telling you!" Bun exclaimed. "Well, this fellow took the things from me, slapped some money down on the counter, all grand and careless-like, and told me to keep the change. Well, I thanked him very much and busied myself with the next customer. It was only afterward, when I went to put those coins in the till, that I realized I'd been taken in. They were nothing but gold-painted buttons!"

Leo jumped. He looked quickly at Mimi and could see by her startled expression that she was thinking the same thing he was.

"What did this man look like?" he asked, trying to sound quite casual.

"Oh, I don't know," Bun said vaguely. "Tallish. A mustache curled up at the ends and one of those little pointed beards. Gold eyeglasses with blue lenses — weak eyes, I suppose. Fancy clothes — hat and traveling cloak and all. He claimed to be a count or a duke or something. Said he was on his way to the Crystal Palace ball. All a pack of lies, I daresay."

"There are a lot of dishonest folk about," Conker said blandly. "Speaking of which, I hear you've had some even worse trouble here in Hobnob."

Bun's face relaxed into the smile that seemed to be his normal expression. "The Terlamaine in the Snug, you mean? Oh, you don't want to worry about that! There's a lot of bosh talked about Terlamaines if you ask me. They're no more dangerous than you or me — just a wee bit stripier."

Chuckling over his small joke, he took a white cardboard box from beneath the counter and turned to fill it with Princess Pretty Tarts.

"He didn't mean the Terlamaine," said Freda.

"Oh!" said Bun, transferring tarts from their rack to the box with a pair of tongs. "Oh, well, you don't want to worry about the cloud palace, either. Least said, soonest mended, as far as *that's* concerned. It'll be gone by morning, you mark my words."

Leo felt desperate. "Conker was talking about the disappearance of Wizard Bing and the arrest of Simon Humble, Master Bun," he said.

Bun turned, the tongs held stiffly out in front of him. His face was no longer cheerful.

"I don't know what you folk have heard," he said. "But, believe me, whatever happened to Bing was entirely his own fault. The Humble boy was in here all the time — looking for a free feed, poor chap — and we know him well. He's harmless, and his arrest is a travesty of justice — at least, I think so, and Patty, my wife, agrees with me."

"So I do!" a voice exclaimed vehemently. And a pleasant-faced woman, as round as Bun and wearing a white cap and apron, toddled from the back of the shop carrying a tray of little iced cakes decorated with the letters of the alphabet.

"If you ask me," she announced, putting the tray on the counter, "Bats Bing transformed poor Simon by mistake with that new invention of his, then got in a temper and blew himself up. That would be just like him. He was the most conceited, most irrational, most irritable man that ever was born."

"Now, Patty," her husband demurred, with an anxious glance at the quest team.

"Well, he was," the woman declared, snatching up a second pair of tongs and waving them in the air. "And he might have been very clever and all that, but he didn't have a speck of common sense."

She shook her head in disgust and began putting her cakes onto one of the racks behind the counter. "He blamed Bun and me for the price of bread," she said, her voice rising. "The truth was, he was poor as a squirrel because he'd run through all his money with that idiotic messenger lizard affair."

"And he wanted us in the poorhouse with him!" said Bun, abandoning discretion. "Sandwich tree, indeed! Times are hard enough for bakers these days. Dot security costs are crippling, and Renée has to sleep sometime."

He looked despairingly at the glass door, through which the fox could be seen sitting as still as a statue while dots danced and jeered on the cobblestones of the square, keeping well out of reach.

"Bing tried to make us get rid of Renée, you know," Patty rattled on, tossing cakes onto the rack with reckless abandon. "He complained to the mayor that Renée was a danger to his chickens. Just because Renée's brother had that bit of trouble with Bodelia Parker's parrot."

"What sort of trouble?" Freda asked curiously.

"He ate it," said Bun.

Bertha squeaked in horror. Freda turned to glare at the fox on the doorstep.

"It's not Renée's fault that her brother is a bad lot," snapped Patty. "Renée's a sweetie — and a hard worker, too. But Sylvester is nothing but a smooth-talking confidence fox. He told Bodelia he'd work for his keep, keeping dots off her vegetable garden. He charmed her completely. She went around boasting that she had the best and cheapest dot-guard in Hobnob. Gave him the run of her shop, after a while. And the first chance he got after that, he ate Patricia and left town. Poor Renée was *mortified*!"

"I don't suppose Patricia was too happy with the situation, either," mumbled Conker, who had begun jiggling with impatience and glancing at the door. "Well, we'd better be —"

"Going. Of course, of course!" chuckled Bun, handing the box of tarts and a bag of bread rolls to Leo. "You need to make the most of your holiday. It's been a pleasure to serve you, ladies and gents. You have a nice day, now."

"Do *you* think Bing blew himself up?" Leo asked as he and the others reached the bakery corner and walked down to where the rug was waiting for them.

"Nah," said Freda. "There'd have been bits of him lying around all over the place, and even Begood would have noticed that."

"That's true," Mimi agreed as Conker nodded and Bertha shuddered delicately.

They climbed aboard the rug and it rose into the air, its fringe fluttering peacefully in the breeze. As it sailed across the back street, they saw that the cooking pot was still dangling from the knob of the bakery's back door. Gentle, tinny snores floated to their ears.

"You see? It's quite comfortable," Conker told Bertha. "And it'll have a good home in the bakery. Plenty of work to do, plenty of other pots to talk to, and so on."

"Who cares?" said Freda. "The main thing is, it's Bun's problem now, not ours."

Bertha shook her head and sighed, but didn't say anything. She'd been very quiet since seeing the fox at the bakery.

"Leo and I think the man who cheated Bun could have been Spoiler," Mimi said abruptly. "The beard and glasses are an obvious disguise. And passing fake money is just the sort of mean, small-time thing Spoiler would do."

"The man who passed the counterfeit coins said he was on his way to the Crystal Palace ball," Bertha objected halfheartedly. "And Spoiler wasn't *at* the ball."

"That doesn't mean anything!" Leo exclaimed. "He could have been just trying to impress Bun. Or he could have meant to go to the ball, then changed his mind."

Conker rubbed his beard and exchanged dubious glances with Freda. Clearly they were both unconvinced.

"Look, I know you two don't think Spoiler is in Hobnob, whatever you said in town," Leo said. "You wouldn't have brought us with you if you'd thought he was here. But what if you're wrong? I don't think we should take any chances. We should contact Hal straightaway."

Conker frowned. "You're probably right," he admitted reluctantly. "As you say — it's better to be safe than sorry. Tell you what, we'll find Tye as soon as we've finished at Bing's house, and tell her your theory. If she thinks the lead's worth pursuing she'll send a message to Hal herself."

"Right, so that's settled," said Freda, eyeing the bakery box on Conker's lap. "Let's eat."

Conker opened the box and passed it around. The Princess Pretty Tarts proved to be just as delicious as Bun had promised, and a contented silence fell as the rug flew sedately over the town, heading west. The giant Snug trees and the smaller, paler trees of the grove were straight ahead, and behind them hulked the Strix's cloud palace, looking even more solid and menacing than it had when the day was new. Leo tore his eyes away from it and nudged Mimi to make her do the same.

"Don't look!" he whispered to her as she turned to him with a frown.

She hunched her thin shoulders in irritation. "You've got meringue on your lip," she said coldly, but Leo was relieved to see that she didn't turn back to face the cloud castle all the same.

Hastily he wiped his mouth. "It's just — you've got to be careful," he muttered, refusing to be put off. "It'll be easier for the cloud castle to suck you in because of — of what you're wearing. You know. I'm really worried —"

She rolled her eyes and to his great surprise smiled at him almost affectionately. "It's all *right*, Leo," she whispered. "Really, honestly, you don't have to worry about me. I admit I was really curious about the castle at first. And I *can* feel its magic, quite strongly. But it doesn't attract me in the slightest. It's fascinating to look at, but that's all. After what Tye said, the idea of going anywhere near it scares me to —"

"We're nearly there!" Bertha squealed, leaning recklessly over the side of the rug. "Bing's Wood straight ahead!"

CHAPTER 23

THE HOUSE OF BING

"Excellent!" said Conker, demolishing his second tart in a single bite. "Now, let's get organized. The first thing we'll do when we get to Bing's place is examine the scene of the crime for clues."

"What sort of clues?" Bertha asked excitedly.

Conker stroked his beard with great satisfaction. "Oh, hairs and footprints and buttons and threatening letters and handkerchiefs with initials on them and so on," he said airily. "The idea is to find proof that one of the suspects was at Bing's house *before* the alarm was given."

"Easy-peasy," said Freda.

"I *see!*" breathed Bertha, her eyes very wide. "And I suppose we'll look for Wizard Bing's body as well, while we're there?"

"Of course!" said Conker. "Bing's body would be quite a big clue in itself."

"This is so *thrilling!*" cried Bertha, sitting very upright, her hat ribbons blowing back in the wind. "Investigating a murder is even more fun than fighting wolves!"

Leo was glad to see Bertha looking happy again. Conker and

Freda were also looking eager and pleased with themselves. He hated to spoil their mood, but there was something he really had to say.

"I think you're all forgetting something," he said cautiously. "We still don't know that there *has* been a murder."

There was a short, disappointed silence.

"Don't we?" asked Bertha, her forehead wrinkled in puzzlement.

"No," Leo said gently. "All we know for sure is that Wizard Bing has disappeared. We've decided that he didn't blow himself up, but he might just have run away, like Stitch the tailor said."

"If Bing had run away, someone would have seen him by now and reported it," Conker said, recovering a little. "Wizards are very noticeable characters, and Bing's too conceited to stay hidden for long. Anyway, the chicken who gave the alarm *said* Bing was dead."

"That chicken sounded like it was one egg short of an omelet," Freda sneered. "It also said the sky was falling, if you'll remember."

"We'll interview it," Conker said firmly. "As soon as we've inspected Bing's house."

Freda made a disgusted sound, but Bertha looked pleased. "I've always got on very well with chickens," she confided to Leo and Mimi in a low voice. "The hens at home —" She broke off and blushed. "I mean, the hens at Macdonald's farm — were very good friends of mine. I often think about them, wondering how they are, and . . . and so on." Her lips trembled a little, but she lifted her chin bravely, refusing to give way to her emotions.

"Have another tart," Conker said hastily, pushing the box under her nose.

The rug began to lose height, and everyone looked over the side. The Snug was to their right, and the little wood where they had left Tye was directly below them. In the center of the wood was a ramshackle house completely encircled by a broad band of shining water.

"Lawks-a-daisy!" Bertha gasped, surprise driving away her homesickness. "Wizard Bing's house is on an island!"

"I don't see any sign of a boat, either," said Conker. "That's strange. I wouldn't fancy swimming across that lake. Bing obviously used it for defense purposes. There could be man-eating eels in it — or snapping turtles! Right, Freda?"

"Wrong," said the duck. "That water's so shallow it wouldn't cover your boots. It's just a dot barrier if you ask me."

Conker nodded grudgingly.

The rug drifted down, down past the crooked chimney of the ramshackle house, past the gray shingled roof dotted with birds' nests, the rusty, lopsided gutters filled with moss, and the creaking purple walls that all seemed to tilt in different directions. The wire mesh of a chicken pen glinted through the trees on one side of the house, and Bertha looked longingly at the path that led to it.

"Scene of the crime first, witnesses second," Conker said firmly, and Bertha sighed.

The rug landed in the littered front yard of the house, right beside a sandwich tree that was taller but even weedier and more depressed-looking than the one in the town square. The tree's sparse leaves were spotty and limp. Two gray sandwiches hung from the lowest branches, exuding a strong smell of very old fish paste.

"Someone should put that thing out of its misery," said Freda, looking at the tree with distaste.

"It must have been Wizard Bing's first try," Bertha said. "What a shame! As Master Sadd in the square said, a sandwich tree *sounds* like a very good idea."

"All Bing's inventions *sounded* good," growled Conker. "The trouble was, none of them worked — or if they did they went wrong or had horrible side effects. Look at this place! It's a disaster area!"

"There are blue butterflies here," Leo said in a low voice, pointing at some spots of blue dancing in a nearby puddle of sunlight. "I think they followed us from the square."

"Probably," said Freda. "It's their job, isn't it?"

They clambered off the rug and began picking their way through the weird assortment of objects that lay abandoned on the ground in front of the house.

The first recognizable one they passed was a rusting machine that looked a bit like a bicycle except that it had huge springs instead of wheels.

"Bing's Kanga Komet," Conker said, his lip curling. "He claimed it was the ideal form of transport because it could jump up and down stairs and cross chasms, and so on. Well, it could, if you had the muscles of a troll, the balance of a tightrope walker, nerves of steel, and a cast-iron behind."

They skirted a huge stack of tiny leather harnesses covered

with mold (probably left over from the ill-fated lizard experiment, Conker said), a vat of what looked like shiny brown concrete (which Leo thought was the remains of the superchewy toffee experiment), and a ghastly, quivering bright orange bucket that smelled strongly of oranges and waved stubby feelers at them as they passed (no one knew what that was, but they all kept well away from it).

"Wizard Bing certainly invented lots of things," said Bertha, with a touch of admiration. "He just kept trying, didn't he?"

"Unfortunately," said Freda, kicking aside a pair of frantically wriggling knitting needles that were trying to find something else to knit into the wobbly-edged scarf they were dragging behind them like a knobbly, bizarrely striped tail.

"I've just thought of something," Leo said. "What if Bing's new invention turned Simon into a mushroom, and made Bing himself *vanish*?"

"You mean — the invention was some sort of magic wand?" asked Mimi, suddenly alert.

Leo shrugged. "Maybe," he said. "I mean, Bing *was* a wizard. And he did do some amazing things — even if they usually didn't work out the way he meant them to."

"If he's invisible, he could be anywhere," Bertha whispered. "He could be here, watching us, right now!" She cleared her throat nervously. "Wizard Bing?" she called softly, peering around. "Hello? Wizard Bing? Are you anywhere about?"

Feeling rather foolish, Leo listened with everyone else, but there was no sound but the rustling of leaves in the trees, the clicking of the knitting needles, which had found a grubby piece of string to work on, and a soft clucking and crooning drifting from the direction of the chicken house.

"Well, if he's here he's not admitting it," said Freda at last.

"He's not here," Mimi said positively. "We'd feel it if he was, I'm sure we would, and I don't feel a thing."

"He might have gone into town," Bertha suggested. "He might have gone looking for Simon."

"More likely to sneak some chocolate bars from Candy Sweet," said Freda.

Conker shook his head. "I don't think we're on the right track with this invisibility business," he said. "It was a good thought, Leo — a very good thought, and well worth considering. But it would take a very special wand to make a fully grown man disappear for any length of time, and I can't see a second-rate wizard like Bing being up to it. The man-into-mushroom thing . . . well, that's powerful magic, too, but it's a bit easier to swallow."

"Is it?" Leo asked, rather put out to find his theory rejected so quickly.

"Oh, yes," Conker said confidently. "Person to plant transformations are more unusual than prince-into-toad, or hero-into-newt transformations, certainly, but there have been a few cases of maidens turning into trees over the years, and an old woman who'd hired Freda and me to exterminate her dots swore that this flower down by her duck pond was actually her son."

"She was just trying to make you sorry for her so you'd cut our rates," Freda muttered. "It worked, too."

"Oh!" Bertha squealed, making them all jump. "Oh, I've just thought! Powerful magic! Everyone says that powerful magic is one of the main things that attracts the — the S-thingy!" She jerked her head toward the looming cloud castle, being careful not to look at it. "If Wizard Bing's invention *was* a magic wand, and he used it to mushroomize Simon, on purpose or by mistake, that would explain why the cloud castle is here in Hobnob — and so close to this house."

"Yes!" Conker exclaimed, tugging frenziedly at his beard. "Oh, my guts and garters, we're getting close to the solution now — I can feel it in my liver!"

He shook off the knitting needles, which were attempting to knit his trouser hems into their scarf, and pushed open the door of the house.

A hideous howling filled the air. Yelling in fright, Bertha, Mimi, and Leo jumped back. Conker merely sighed and beckoned. "It's only a burglar alarm," he said, as the howling faded away. "Come on."

He and Freda vanished into the house. Bertha and Mimi went after them. Leo followed, still feeling rather shaky. Dimness closed in around him. He could see the shapes of Conker, Bertha, and Mimi moving ahead of him. He could smell herbs, ash, and dust mixed with faint traces of something sweet and vaguely nauseating that reminded him of cheap air freshener.

He paused, waiting for his eyes to adjust to the dim light. Thoughts of Spoiler crouching hidden in the shadows crawled through his mind. The door swung softly shut behind him, and he felt something touch the back of his neck. He yelled and spun around, his heart pounding.

"What is it?" shouted Mimi in panic. "Leo!"

"Ha!" Conker roared, turning on the spot, his dot-swatters already in his hands and Freda snapping her beak beside him.

"Leo, get back!" squealed Bertha, swinging around at the same time with her head lowered and her blunt teeth bared.

Leo gulped, blinked, and saw that what had touched him was the point of a crooked wizard's hat, which was hanging, together with a threadbare cloak, from a hook on the back of the door.

"Sorry," he said, trying to laugh. His heart was still thudding painfully.

"Lawks-a-daisy!" Bertha panted. "Oh, you nearly gave me a heart attack!"

"Pull yourself together, Leo," Conker said severely, shoving the swatters back into their holsters. "This is no time to give way to your nerves. We're supposed to be looking for clues."

"Well, Leo's just found one, hasn't he?" said Mimi. "In fact, he's found two."

"What do you mean?" Bertha asked in bewilderment. "What clues?"

"Bing's cloak," Mimi said, pointing at the limp shape hanging on the door. "And his hat. Didn't those people in town say he never went anywhere without them?"

"Yes," Bertha said, her eyes very wide. "But they're still here, and Wizard Bing's not. So that proves . . ."

"That wherever Bing went, he didn't go willingly," Conker finished grimly. "And he didn't vanish himself, either. If he had, he'd have put on his hat and cloak first. Wizards are very formal about things like that."

He clapped Leo on the shoulder. "Good work, Leo! Keep it up! Now, team, on with the search!"

Before Leo could deny that he deserved any praise at all for being scared by a hat, Conker turned and bustled away with Bertha and Freda hard on his heels. Leo looked at Mimi helplessly.

"You owe me one," said Mimi with a mocking grin, and turned to follow the others.

CHAPTER 24

BING'S LIST

The inside of Wizard Bing's house was just as messy and neglected-looking as the outside. Bunches of dusty herbs and two dark lanterns hung from the low beams, which were festooned with spiderwebs. The fireplace was heaped with ash. A greasy frying pan, a dented kettle, a basket half-filled with straw, and a large, lumpy turnip cluttered the threadbare hearth rug.

"Cozy," Freda commented, fastidiously shaking something sticky from her foot.

The wall beside the door was lined with shelves that sagged under the weight of a weird assortment of equipment, presumably used for spell making. Shelves on the opposite wall were crowded with brown jars and rusty tins, most without labels and some containing things that made sinister scrabbling, tapping, or oozing sounds. In one corner there was a narrow folding camp bed, where Leo thought Simon Humble had probably slept in his pre-mushroom days.

In the wall opposite the fireplace there were two doors, both sagging open. One door led to the wizard's bedroom, and the other to a poky little room that contained nothing but a huge, claw-footed bath filled with firewood.

A long table heaped with clutter took up most of the space in the center of the main room. On the side nearest the fireplace, a chair lay on the floor with its back broken and its legs sticking up in the air.

"Here's our third clue," said Conker, pacing around the chair and peering at it intently. "It looks as if Bing was sitting at the table and jumped up in a hurry."

"Jumped up or fell over backward," Mimi said darkly. "His enemy must have crept up behind him and taken him by surprise."

"I don't see how an intruder could have taken him by surprise," Bertha objected. "The burglar alarm would have gone off the moment the door was opened."

"So he was attacked by someone who was already inside the house," Leo said. "A person he trusted."

"An inside job," Freda agreed. "This is looking bad for Simon — and for our fee, I might add."

"Yes." Conker was looking gloomier by the moment. "I hate to admit it, but Begood might have had the right idea all along."

"We can't give up yet!" Mimi exclaimed. "For one thing, we haven't found Bing's new invention yet. Simon obviously hasn't got it — mushrooms don't have pockets. And if it isn't here, that's proof that someone else took it."

"You're right!" shouted Conker, suddenly invigorated. "Fan out, team! Leave no apple core unturned. Search every possible hiding place for anything that looks like it might be Bing's new invention. And while you're at it, keep an eye out for threatening letters, weapons, and dead bodies, and make a note of anything unusual."

Everything looked unusual to Leo, but as Bertha disappeared into Wizard Bing's bedroom, and Conker, Freda, and Mimi began searching the living room, he started to examine the jumble of articles on the table, starting at the end closest to the door.

He sorted through chocolate-smeared spell books, chewed pens, empty ink bottles, old chocolate wrappers, withered apple cores, odd socks with gaping holes in the heels, and countless burned-down candles. He examined notebooks filled with incomprehensible scrawls and scraps of paper on which Wizard Bing had scribbled reminder notes like "Self-chopping wood — good idea — work on this," "Glowworm feed expensive — invent cheaper substitute," and "Buy socks." He found numerous lumps of toffee, one of which had been used to plug a hole in a blackened saucepan. He found a thin leather purse that snapped at him when he touched it and that turned out to be empty.

After about twenty minutes he'd worked his way to the middle of the table, near the overturned chair. Behind him, Freda was poking around in the ashes of the fireplace.

Leo straightened up, feeling tired and frustrated. Something was niggling at the back of his mind. He kept thinking that something was missing from the room and he couldn't think what it could be.

He told himself that if he stopped worrying over the problem of the missing object, the answer would pop into his head of its own accord, and went back to work on the table. He found dirty plates, crusted knives, and an overturned goblet lying in a sticky puddle of evil-smelling wine. He found a moldy rind of cheese. He found three small, hard, misshapen bread rolls that made him wonder if Wizard Bing had resorted to making his own bread to beat Bun the baker's prices. He found a greasy white paper bag that by its smell had probably once contained the cheese.

He was just about to toss the bag aside when he noticed that there was something scribbled on the back. It didn't look like a threatening note or a plan for an invention, but just to be sure he turned the bag over and flattened it out.

Some letters had been scrawled on the white paper. They were in Bing's handwriting, which Leo knew very well after looking at so many reminder notes, and they straggled down the length of the bag in a single column, as if Bing had been making some sort of list.

More than half the entries had been crossed out, but Leo could still read them quite easily. They were S, FOD, M, T, and W. The letters that had not been crossed out were B, C, VOD, and G.

At the bottom of the list were two large, triumphant ticks, as if Wizard Bing was very satisfied with the results of his work.

Leo stared at the list, wondering why he was so certain that it was important. The bag looked like a piece of scrap paper. The writing seemed to have no meaning. And yet . . .

"I think I might have found something," he said.

Mimi turned from her inspection of the shelves of spell equipment. Bertha poked her head out of the wizard's bedroom. Freda jerked up from the fireplace in a cloud of ash, and sneezed. Conker looked around from the dark corner where he had been gingerly feeling under the mattress of the camp bed. Released from his weight, the camp bed instantly folded itself up, trapping him inside it like a chunky piece of meat in a spring sandwich.

Ignoring Freda's raucous laughter, Conker freed himself from the bed with as much dignity as he could manage. He saw the paper in Leo's hand, and his face lit up. "What is it, Leo?" he called. "A ransom note? A threatening letter?"

"No," Leo said slowly. "This is something else."

As they all hurried over to him he held out the paper bag, suddenly embarrassed to have made a fuss about something that was probably just a shopping list.

"Hmm," said Conker, peering at the list and thoughtfully stroking his beard. "In-ter-esting. Ve-ery in-ter-esting."

"Is it?" Bertha asked. "Why?"

"Well, that's obvious, isn't it?" Conker said in some confusion. "Tell her, Leo!"

"It's a list of initials," Mimi put in eagerly, before Leo could say anything. "It might be a list of people Wizard Bing owed money to, or people who had a grudge against him, or who he wanted to punish, or something like that. That B could stand for Bun the baker, or Bodelia. And the C could stand for Clogg, or for Candy — and VOD is for . . . um . . ."

"Violet Orpington-Dunk!" squealed Bertha.

There was a short silence.

"Who's Violet Orpington-Dunk?" Freda asked bluntly.

"Why, lawks-a-daisy, she's one of the leading hens at Macdonald's farm!" Bertha exclaimed, pink with excitement. "*Very* important socially, but not at all stuck-up and a dear, *dear* friend of mine."

Conker scratched his head in puzzlement. "How could Bing owe money to one of Jack Macdonald's hens?" he demanded. "Oh, my aching brain, this mystery gets stranger every minute!"

Leo cleared his throat. "It *is* possible that the letters VOD *don't* stand for Violet Orpington-Dunk, you know," he said as tactfully as he could.

"Just possible." Freda smirked.

Bertha gave a trill of laughter. "Don't be silly!" she giggled. "Of *course* they do! Look! Her sister's initials are on the list, too — FOD — Fiona Orpington-Dunk. They've been crossed out, but that's not very surprising. Strictly between us, Fiona isn't half the chicken that Violet is. And no one would ever be in debt to Fiona, because she hasn't got a dib to her name."

"S has been crossed out, too," Conker said thoughtfully. "So has M, W, T —"

"S for Stitch — and Sadd!" Mimi exclaimed. "M for Muffy! W for Woodley! T for . . ."

"*Tilly*," Bertha breathed. "Oh, how *shocking* of Wizard Bing to borrow money from a young maid like that. He must have had no conscience at all!"

"This paper mightn't actually *be* a list of debts," Mimi said soothingly. "That was just an idea, and I don't think it could be right. Stitch has been crossed out, and so has Woodley, and we know Bing owed money to them both."

"This isn't just a hate list, either, in my opinion," said Freda, tapping the paper bag with her beak and leaving a smear of soot on the edge. "It's too short for that. Bing seems to have been on bad terms with everyone he knew."

"He was certainly very unpopular," Bertha agreed. "No one ever writes to him. I found a few birthday cards in a drawer in his room, but they were very old and covered in dust."

"So," growled Conker, drumming his fingers on the tabletop. "The list isn't a hate list, and it isn't a list of folk Bing owed money to. So what is it? We have to find out. It's the key to the whole case, I feel it in my liver."

"What if it's a guest list?" Leo asked, suddenly inspired. "What if Bing wanted to sell his new invention, and he was working out who he'd invite here to see it?"

"Yes!" squealed Bertha as Conker punched the air and Mimi, strangely, grew very quiet. "Oh, why didn't I think of that? Wizard Bing was always trying to make money out of his ideas, wasn't he? And if this particular invention was very special, of *course* he'd think very carefully about who might buy it. He'd probably ask his prospects here one at a time, swearing them to secrecy . . ."

Leo nodded, excitedly thinking it through. "The initials that are crossed out must be people Bing decided not to invite, or people who refused to come," he said. "So we don't have to worry about them. We only have to look at the names still on the list.

"Brilliant, Leo!" said Conker, rubbing his hands enthusiastically. "We're getting on famously. What a team! So . . . our suspects are B, C, VOD, and G — that is, Bun or Bodelia, Candy or Clogg, Violet whatshername, maybe, and — and someone whose name starts with G."

"What about . . . George?" Mimi said, very quietly. "George *Langlander.*"

Leo's heart gave a great thud.

"Why in Rondo would Bing have *Spoiler* on his list?" Conker snapped.

"Why would he have a socialite hen on his list for that matter?" muttered Freda.

"Listen!" Mimi insisted tensely. "Say Bing did invent something really special — something really magic that worked, for a change. And say that the man with the fake coins in the bakery *was* Spoiler in disguise. Bun said the locals were chatting while they waited — and we know that Bing is one of the main subjects for gossip around here. Well —"

"You think people were talking about Wizard Bing's new invention!" Bertha exclaimed. "And Spoiler heard. So he changed his mind about going to the Crystal Palace to steal the wedding presents, and came here to steal the invention instead!"

Mimi nodded. "It would be just like him. He's used to magic because of the Blue Queen, and he'd do anything for an easy life."

Everyone murmured agreement and Leo felt his face beginning to burn. It still shamed him that one of his own family could be as weak and despicable as his Great-Great-Great-Uncle George.

"Oh, well, it's *possible*, I suppose," Conker said grudgingly. "It's true that so far we haven't found any sign of a new invention or wand or whatever it is. So either it's buried with Bing, which seems fairly unlikely, or it's . . ."

"It's been stolen," Mimi finished triumphantly. "Stolen by Spoiler. You see? It all fits."

"It doesn't 'all fit,' Mimi!" Leo said, very irritated by the way Mimi had taken over his discovery and twisted it into a theory that seemed to him completely illogical. "We can't assume the thief was Spoiler just because the letter G is on Bing's list! For a start, Spoiler wouldn't tell Wizard Bing his real name. He doesn't tell *anyone* his real name. When you and I first met him, he said his name was Tom."

Mimi pressed her lips into a straight, stubborn line.

"You don't have to sulk just because I don't agree with you!" Leo snapped. "So far we haven't got a single shred of proof that Spoiler has anything to do with this."

"Leo, you're so annoying!" Mimi snapped back. "You're the one who's kept insisting all along that Spoiler might have done something to Wizard Bing. And now that everyone's finally starting to agree with you, you've changed your mind!"

"I haven't changed my mind," Leo said hotly. "I just said that the list isn't proof that Spoiler's involved. That doesn't mean —"

"Leo! Mimi!" cried Bertha, looking in distress from one to the other. "There's no need to be so —"

"Let's *look* for proof, then!" Mimi broke in. "Let's see if we can find out for sure that Spoiler was here."

"I thought you didn't have any doubts about it," Leo muttered.

"I don't!" Mimi retorted. "I *know* he was in this house. I can *feel* it."

"You *feel* it!" Leo jeered. "Right. So how do you think you're going to prove it?"

Mimi looked at him, her face expressionless. "Well, perhaps you've forgotten, but we haven't questioned the witnesses yet."

"What witnesses?" Leo demanded. "The sandwich tree? Those crazy knitting needles?"

"No," Mimi said. "Wizard Bing's chickens."

CHAPTER 25

THE FLOCK OF BING

They left the house and moved around to the side, carefully avoiding the knitting needles, which were attempting to knit a spiderweb into their scarf while defending themselves from the web's huge, furious owner.

On Bertha's advice, Mimi was carrying the straw-lined basket from Wizard Bing's hearth rug.

"I'm sure Wizard Bing used it for collecting the eggs. It's just like the one they use at home — I mean, at Macdonald's farm," Bertha said, her voice wobbling only slightly. "It will reassure the chickens — help them to trust us."

"They'll trust us or I'll shake them till their feathers rattle!" Conker growled. He darted to the bare little path that led to the chicken house and began striding along it so energetically that the others had to run to keep up with him. Ahead there was a burst of anxious clucking.

"Slow down, Conker," Bertha called softly. "You'll upset them."

"I'm not going to mollycoddle a bunch of hens!" snorted Conker, without slowing his pace. "It's up to every citizen to assist an official quester in —"

His voice was drowned out by a shrill, hysterical cry. "Chicken thieves!" a voice screeched. "Run for your lives!"

There was a chorus of shrieks and a frantic flapping and scrabbling. The next moment a flock of hens came hurtling down the path, beaks wide open, beady eyes wild.

"Down!" squealed Bertha, throwing herself to the ground.

Mimi, Leo, Conker, and Freda obeyed her warning just in time. Leo had barely hit the earth when claws raked his back and his nose was filled with the smell of dust and feathers. His ears rang with frenzied cackles and the sound of desperately flapping wings.

In seconds the onslaught was over. The hens had run on toward the lake, their shrieks fading into the distance.

Shakily, the friends sat up and looked at one another.

"I did tell you we should approach more slowly, Conker," Bertha said resentfully, shaking a few stray feathers from her flattened hat.

"How was I to know the silly things would panic like that?" groaned Conker. "Whoever heard of a chicken stampede? Oh, my aching back!"

"Watch it!" Freda muttered. "We've got company."

A large red rooster was strutting down the path toward them, looking very far from pleased. Mimi, Leo, Conker, and Bertha scrambled hurriedly to their feet.

"What is the meaning of this?" the rooster demanded pompously. "How dare you disrupt my household in this disgraceful manner?"

"Who's asking?" drawled Freda, standing her ground.

The rooster drew himself up. His gleaming chest swelled. "I am Egbert, son of Egmont, Guardian of the Flock of Bing," he declared magnificently. "And who, might I ask, are you?"

"I am Bertha, wolf fighter, artist's model, and quest heroine of — formerly of — Macdonald's farm," Bertha said hurriedly, before Freda could say anything rude. "These are my companions Conker, Mimi, Leo, and Freda, who — whose achievements are renowned."

"Oh, really?" the rooster said, looking down his beak at her.

"Yes," said Bertha with dignity. "We are here to investigate the disappearance of Wizard Bing, and —"

"A large person has already been here to investigate the tragedy," the rooster interrupted. "His name, I believe, is Begood. I was not impressed with him."

"We are not associated with Officer Begood," Bertha said. "We have been employed by Simon Humble's aunt to prove Simon's innocence."

"Indeed!" Egbert's cold manner softened a little. "And am I to understand that you are seeking *our* assistance?"

"Oh, my liver and lungs, of course we are," exclaimed Conker, who had been growing increasingly restless during this polite exchange. "You're important witnesses — the *only* witnesses, as far as we can see."

Leo expected Egbert to swell with rage, but instead the rooster looked at Conker with supercilious approval.

"It is gratifying that someone has seen fit to consult us at last," he said haughtily. "The Begood person seemed to feel that our statements were of no interest." Without warning he threw back his head and gave an earsplitting crow. Everyone but Freda jumped backward.

Egbert lowered his head. "I have summoned the flock," he said unnecessarily. "Please proceed to our humble dwelling. We can speak in more comfort there."

He turned and stalked up the path without looking back. The quest team followed.

"I don't see why he thinks we'll be more comfortable squashed into a smelly henhouse," grumbled Freda. "Why can't we talk out here?"

"Shh!" hissed Bertha. "He's cooperating — that's the main thing. Roosters can be a bit annoying, I know, but they're easy to manage if you avoid ruffling their feathers."

"Yah," jeered Freda, but at a look from Conker she shrugged and walked on.

Soon they reached a large yard fenced with chicken wire. In the center of the yard was a neat wooden shed that seemed to be in far better condition than Wizard Bing's house. Through the open door of the shed Leo could see cozy-looking nesting boxes and perches fastened to the wall.

Egbert was waiting for them at the yard gate. As they approached, he pulled the gate open and inclined his head slightly, inviting them to enter. Bertha, Conker, Leo, and Mimi filed in obediently. Freda followed, muttering under her breath and dragging her feet.

"Please take a perch," Egbert said grandly, waving a wing toward a low wooden rail that stretched along one side of the yard.

"Outdoor seating!" Bertha exclaimed in admiration. "How *very* convenient!"

"Ah, yes," said Egbert, preening himself. "It was one of my better ideas, I think, to commission Simon to make us some garden furniture. Naturally we have indoor perches as well."

"Oh, *naturally*," Freda muttered.

Bertha leaned gracefully against the rail. Conker, Leo, and Mimi perched on it uncomfortably. As Freda joined them, looking disdainful, the yard gate swung open again and six hens wandered in.

"Ah, the ladies have joined us," Egbert said expansively. He raised his voice. "Hurry along, my dears! All is well. I have everything under control."

When the hens had gathered around him, he puffed up his chest and made a rather long-winded speech in which he explained the guests' quest, promised the full cooperation of the Flock of Bing, and tactfully made no mention of the unfortunate incident on the path. He then made formal introductions, consistently (and deliberately, Leo was sure) referring to Freda as "Ferdie."

The hens were all very different from one another. The first to be introduced was Cluck, a small, neat, and rather bossy-looking red hen. After her was Teeny, who was golden-brown, even smaller than Cluck, and so thin, talkative, and excitable-looking that Leo was sure she was the one who had given the alarm and caused the stampede. Next was the elegant, beautifully speckled Chickadee, who kept tossing her gleaming red comb out of her eyes in a rather affected manner. Then there was Scramble, a white hen who smiled vacantly and instantly forgot everyone's name, and Broody, a handsome, silent, intense-looking black hen who seemed rather depressed.

"And last, but by no means least," Egbert announced, with the air of having saved the best till the end, "may I present . . . Moult!"

The flock parted to reveal a worried-looking mouse-brown hen standing by herself at the back. The brown hen jumped nervously. "Very pleased to meet you," she mumbled, ducking her head.

The elegant Chickadee sneered and whispered something to Scramble behind her wing. Scramble giggled uncertainly. Moult looked hunted.

Cluck began bustling around the yard, kicking up a lot of dust and issuing orders to the others. Moult scuttled to help her, but no one else took any notice.

"Cluck!" called Egbert. "Don't exhaust yourself, my dear! Come sit down."

"How can I sit down, Egbert?" snapped Cluck. "We have guests, and *someone* has to make the refreshments! You would think that everyone would pull together on an occasion like this, but oh, no. As usual, everything is left to me." She shouted some more instructions to Moult, and in a few moments the two of them had dragged a large tin platter into the center of the group surrounding Egbert.

"There!" Cluck said, collapsing and fanning herself fretfully with her wing. "Please help yourselves."

As the refreshments on the platter were a bowl of water with a feather floating in it, a small heap of grain, some very brown apple cores, and a few dusty fish paste sandwiches, the friends politely said thank you but they weren't hungry. Cluck gave a martyred sigh and ate an apple core herself.

"In a day or two all the grain will be gone," Broody said in a low, throbbing voice. "The apples, too, I daresay. Then . . ." She sighed deeply.

"Oh, my beak!" quavered Teeny. "Do you mean . . . we're going to *starve?*" Her feathers began to fluff up ominously. Clearly she was preparing for another bout of hysterics.

"Beak up, Teeny," Egbert said bracingly, shooting a reproving glance at Broody. He leaned a little closer toward Bertha. "Teeny is a delightful hen, but a trifle . . . highly strung," he muttered out of the side of his beak.

"We noticed." Freda smirked.

Egbert gave her a cold look and turned back to Teeny. "Remember what I told you, my dear," he said soothingly. "Our guests are here to save Wizard Bing and bring Simon home. Soon all our problems will be over."

"Oh!" gulped Teeny, her feathers settling a little. "And so in the end we'll all live happily ever after?"

"As sure as eggs are eggs!" Egbert assured her.

"Absolutely!" Conker said heartily.

All the hens began chattering excitedly — all but Moult, who stood a little apart, looking troubled.

"Conker, we can't promise —" Mimi whispered indignantly, but broke off as Conker glared at her.

"Now," said Egbert, turning to Bertha. "It is my duty, since I clearly have the most highly developed brain in this gathering, to take the lead in our discussion. As I would prefer to speak to you and your party in private, I suggest we adjourn to the henhouse."

"I'm not going in there," Freda said flatly. "Nesting boxes give me the creeps."

"There's no need for any of us to move from this spot!" Conker barked. "*We're* the expert investigators here, so *we'll* decide what's going to be discussed and what's not."

"Conker —" Bertha murmured warningly, but Conker took no notice. "We need to interview *all* the witnesses," he said to Egbert. "Your theories can wait."

"Well, *really*!" Egbert snapped. He turned his back on Conker and stalked away to the other side of the yard, his tail feathers stiff with outrage.

The hens looked after him, murmuring uncertainly.

"There's no need for concern, ladies," Conker said, baring his teeth in a terrible smile. "All you have to do is answer some simple questions."

"Questions?" Scramble quavered. "Oh, I hope they won't be too difficult. I never *can* answer difficult questions. Or even easy ones, sometimes."

"When Simon didn't answer the policeman's questions, he got taken to jail!" cried Teeny, blinking rapidly and hopping from foot to foot. "Maybe *you'll* have to go to jail, too, Scramble! And if the questions are *really* difficult maybe *I* will, too. Maybe *all* of us will!"

"And then the Flock of Bing will be no more," said Broody with melancholy satisfaction.

"We're doomed!" wailed Teeny, fluffing up until she was twice her normal size.

"Lawks-a-daisy," Bertha muttered. "Here we go again!"

"Teeny!" Mimi snapped, putting her hands on her hips. "Do you want to help Simon or not?"

Teeny's beak fell open in shock. She swallowed. "Yes." She gulped.

"Well, pull yourself together and help, then," said Mimi crisply. "Stop working yourself up for nothing and wasting everyone's time."

Teeny blinked, shut her beak with a little click, and began to shrink like a slowly leaking balloon. In moments she had returned to her normal size.

"Oh, good work, Mimi!" Bertha murmured.

"She's very hard-boiled, isn't she?" Leo heard Chickadee whisper to Cluck, looking down her beak at Mimi. "It's not very feminine."

Cluck tossed her head. "It's a relief to hear someone talking sense, if you ask me," she whispered back. "All this coddling of Teeny is a mistake — I've said that since she first came here. She was spoiled as a chick, that's *her* trouble. All that addle-brained nonsense about hysterics running in her family . . ."

"But it does!" clucked Chickadee. "My dear, they say her grandfather caused a general riot in his youth. The family tried to hush it up, naturally, but these things always leak out."

"Have the questions started yet?" Scramble asked Broody. Broody shook her head somberly.

"Right!" said Conker, running his fingers through his hair. "Well, then. First question . . . ah . . ."

"We'd like you to tell us about any visitors Wizard Bing had just before he disappeared," Mimi said quickly. "Was there a stranger, fairly tall — with a little beard maybe, and blue-tinted glasses?"

The hens all shook their heads. "There have been no visitors," Cluck said. "Wizard Bing does not encourage them. He is a very busy man, and he values his privacy."

"There must have been one visitor at least," Mimi insisted. "We found a list —"

"They can't see the house from here," Freda muttered, as the hens shook their heads again. "Bing could have had a whole team of visitors without them knowing about it — especially at night. You can't hear much with your head under your wing."

"No," Cluck declared, overhearing. "If there had been visitors, Simon would have told us. He kept us *fully* informed of events in the House of Bing."

"Dear Simon," moaned Broody. "Gone but not forgotten."

Moult, standing alone at the edge of the crowd, gave a strangled sob, and a few of the others glanced at her again in what Leo thought was definitely an accusing way.

"It's as if they blame *Moult* for what happened," he whispered to Mimi, forgetting for the moment that he was angry with her. "But how could it be *her* fault?"

"They're probably used to blaming her for everything," Mimi muttered back, glaring at the other hens. "They pick on her, you can see that." Her hands were clenched into fists, and as she saw

Leo glancing at them curiously, she shoved them into her jacket pockets.

"Simon's not dead," Bertha was saying to the hens soothingly. "He's only a mushroom. And speaking of that, have you any idea how he became, um . . . mushroomized in the first place?"

"No," clucked Cluck, who seemed to have appointed herself spokeshen for the flock. "It is all *very* distressing. We didn't see him at all on the day of the tragedy. The last time we saw him — saw him looking like himself — was the day before. Thirstyday."

"Was it Thirstyday?" Scramble asked vaguely. "Or was it Flyday?" Her eyes crossed with the effort of trying to remember.

"Chickens in Rondo have their own names for the days of the week," Bertha murmured to Leo and Mimi, seeing them glancing at each other in confusion. "It's a very old tradition. Isn't it the same in Langland?"

"I don't know," Leo said.

"Probably," said Mimi at the same moment.

"Of course it wasn't Flyday, Scramble!" said Chickadee, tossing back her comb impatiently. "Flyday was a very *unusual* day, don't you remember? First, it was Teeny's hatching-day but Simon didn't come to the party. And then in the night the explosion happened. But Thirstyday was just an ordinary day."

"Just an ordinary day," Cluck agreed with a sharp little nod. "We were just thinking of going to the sleeping perches when Simon came to say good night. He was in fine spirits then."

"He brought us some bread rolls for supper," Teeny put in, "and we had a little singsong, as usual. Then Wizard Bing called him to make dinner and he had to go."

"Ah, little did we know we would never see his dear face again." Broody sighed.

"That's right!" exclaimed Scramble, thrilled to have remembered at last. "Thirstyday *was* the last time we saw Simon, and it was just an ordinary day, with an argument at the end of it."

"Argument?" snapped Conker. "What argument?"

"Just the usual thing," Cluck said dismissively. "Wizard Bing shouting at Simon, calling him a nincompoop, telling him he was sacked and so on."

"But *Flyday* wasn't an ordinary day at all," Scramble babbled on. "As well as everything else, *Flyday* was the day Moult laid the golden egg!"

CHAPTER 26

THE DEEP, DARK SECRET

There was a sudden, shocked silence in the chicken yard. Conker, Freda, Bertha, Leo, and Mimi turned to gaze in astonishment at the cringing Moult.

"Scramble, you *featherbrain*!" scolded Cluck.

"Scramble, you *addle-head*!" squawked Teeny.

Scramble's eyes widened. She clapped her wing over her beak. "Oh," she whispered. "Oh, I wasn't supposed to tell, was I? The golden egg is a deep, dark secret, isn't it? I forgot."

"*Forgot?*" Broody repeated in disgust. "You *forgot* the last words our beloved wizard ever spoke to us?"

"How *could* you, Scramble?" cried Chickadee.

"My heart, liver, and lungs, this is — incredible!" Conker gasped. "I've only ever heard of one other hen who could lay golden eggs, and that was before the Dark Time. Moult — are you related to Goldie Featherlocks? Was she your grandmother or something?"

"I don't know," Moult said in a small voice. "I'm an orphan. I never met my mother and father, and I don't know anything about the rest of my family."

"Moult doesn't even know her hatching-day," Teeny chipped in brightly. "We're fairly sure it must have been a Thirsty-day, because you couldn't get a hen thinner and sadder than Moult is, but it's not official so she never gets any hatching-day presents."

Moult shook her head sadly.

"Moult can't be Goldie Featherlocks's granddaughter," Freda said. "Goldie Featherlocks was stolen so often that she didn't have time to have chicks."

"She couldn't have had chicks anyway," Chickadee said, with a spiteful, sidelong glance at Moult. "There's no room for a chick in a fancy-ansy solid gold egg."

"Leave Moult alone!" Mimi snapped unexpectedly. "Can't you see she feels bad? Do you all have to be so mean?"

Chickadee tossed her head. Mimi, her face flushed, turned to Moult. "Did you really lay a golden egg?" she asked gently.

Moult shuffled her claws and nodded, looking more dejected than ever.

"Did it hurt?" Freda asked with interest.

Moult shook her head.

"Lawks-a-daisy," Bertha breathed in awe. "The new Goldie Featherlocks! Imagine what Scribble would say if he knew about this! Imagine what — oh!"

She drew a sharp breath and swung around to face the rest of the quest team. "Violet Orpington-Dunk!" she cried. "Now we know why she was on Wizard Bing's list! Farmer Macdonald must have been one of Wizard Bing's targets, and Violet was coming here as Macdonald's representative! Violet is Macdonald's

243

right-hand hen when it comes to matters of poultry. He'd know she'd recognize a fraud when she saw it."

"Fraud?" squawked Egbert, overhearing the last few words. "Do you dare accuse us of *fraud*? This is too much!" He bent rapidly to sharpen his beak on a stone and then began to stride across the yard, puffing himself up ominously.

"Oh, no! I didn't mean —" Bertha began hastily, as Moult gave a tremulous cry and all the other hens began clucking excitedly to one another.

"Swatters out," muttered Freda to Conker, trying to push her way in front of Leo and Bertha. "You go for his head. I'll take the underbelly."

"No, Freda!" Bertha whispered furiously, standing her ground. "Stay back! Leo and I will handle this."

"Leo, be careful," Mimi cried, as the hens scurried aside to let Egbert through.

"Don't worry," Leo said. "It'll be all right."

He certainly hoped it would. His voice sounded amazingly calm, considering that his knees had started to feel extremely weak and his hands were sweating. Egbert, swollen with fury and now far too close for comfort, was a truly terrifying sight.

"There was no *question* of fraud!" thundered Egbert, his eyes hard as small black pebbles.

"We know that, Egbert," Leo assured him, eyeing the sharpened beak nervously. "Bertha was talking about someone else who might have made that mistake."

"That very *foolish* mistake," Bertha added quickly. "One we would *never* make ourselves, of course."

"Oh," said Egbert, the feathers on the back of his neck flattening a little. "I see."

Leo breathed a silent sigh of relief and decided to press home his advantage. "Can you tell us what happened on, um, on Flyday morning, Egbert?" he asked. "We need to know."

"Of course you do," said Egbert huffily. "And you would have done so, long ago, if you had agreed to my proposal to —"

"That was a mistake," Leo said, glancing at Conker to warn him to keep quiet. "We should have listened to you, Egbert. We apologize. Most — most profoundly."

"We certainly do," Bertha agreed.

Conker made a strangled, choking sound, Mimi snorted, and Freda made a vomiting noise, but Egbert was fortunately too busy clearing his throat and settling his ruffled feathers to hear them.

"Very well," he said, with the air of one making a great concession. "On Flyday morning, Wizard Bing came to collect our eggs. Broody, Cluck, and Teeny were tidying the yard while I — ahem — supervised. Chickadee, Scramble, and Moult were still in their nesting boxes —"

"Taking their time, lolling around on the nice warm straw while the rest of us did all the work!" Cluck put in resentfully.

"It takes time to lay a high-quality egg." Chickadee sniffed. "I can't help it if I'm a perfectionist."

"I think I'd forgotten what I was supposed to be doing," Scramble murmured.

"I'd laid my egg, but I wasn't feeling very well," whispered Moult.

"I'm not surprised," Freda said.

"Wizard Bing went into the henhouse with the basket," Egbert went on, raising his voice determinedly. "He asked us to go with him —"

"He was in a very good mood," Teeny interrupted breathlessly. "He told Chickadee, Scramble, and Moult not to get up, and he wasn't even angry when he found that Chickadee and Scramble had empty nests. He just laughed and wagged his finger at them and said, 'I hope you'll do better tomorrow, my friends. Don't forget — an egg a day keeps the hatchet away.'"

"That was just his little joke," Cluck put in hastily as Bertha looked shocked. "Wizard Bing always joked when he was happy, and he was *very* happy that morning. He looked splendid, too! He was wearing his best robe and his tall hat, and he was carrying a fine new wand striped in *four* different colors."

"Ha!" Conker hissed, digging Leo sharply in the ribs.

"'Things are looking up!' he said." Broody sighed. "'What a lucky old wizard I am.' It's so *ironic*, when you think about it, given what happened that very night."

"Yes," Chickadee clucked tearfully. "'An excellent breakfast,' he said, 'a splendid flock of hens, a fine apprentice, the invention of a lifetime — who could ask for anything more?'"

"Then he felt in Moult's nest, under her feathers!" squawked Teeny, in a high state of excitement. "He said, 'Aha, what's this?' And he pulled out — a golden egg!"

"We all saw it," Egbert said, fixing Conker with a steely eye. "There was no trickery involved. The egg Moult was sitting on was pure gold."

Moult gave a strangled cry and tried to bury her face in the dust.

"It's so unfair," Chickadee whispered piercingly to Broody. "*Moult*, of all hens!"

"Personally, I'm grateful it wasn't me," Broody answered darkly. "I wouldn't like it on *my* conscience."

"I didn't mean to do it," Moult cried piteously. "It just — happened."

"You've made your nest and now you have to sit on it, Moult," snapped Cluck. "You were happy enough on Flyday morning."

"Gobbling up Wizard Bing's praise like hot mash," Chickadee sneered. "Fluffing yourself up at Egbert's compliments. Clucking and cackling away like a —"

"That's *enough*!" Egbert moved to stand protectively over the cowering Moult. He glared around till all the other hens fell silent, then turned to face the quest team.

"You now, perhaps, understand why I wished to speak to you in private," he said severely. "This is a delicate matter. It arouses high emotion in the flock."

"And for very good reason!" snapped Cluck. "That golden egg was the cause of all our trouble or I'll be fried!"

"It was a disaster," agreed Chickadee, with a malicious side-long glance at Moult. "How any hen could have been proud of laying it, I do not know."

"*I* wouldn't have been proud!" cried Teeny, hopping feverishly up and down on the spot. "Oh, my beak, I would have been so ashamed that I'd have — I'd have drowned myself in the pond. Or let myself be knitted up by the click-clacks."

"That cursed egg was the downfall of the House of Bing," droned Broody. "The day it was laid was a day of doom."

"That was Flyday, right?" Scramble asked anxiously.

"Don't take any notice of them," Mimi said to poor Moult, who was crouching in Egbert's shadow, the picture of misery. "They're just jealous."

"Jealous?" squawked Chickadee. "What an idea! As if any of *us* could be jealous of *Moult*!"

"I think *I* might be jealous," said Scramble doubtfully. "Just a bit," she added quickly as Cluck, Broody, and Teeny glared at her.

"Cut the cackle, will you?" snapped Conker. "We're wasting precious time here!"

"What did Wizard Bing do with the golden egg after that?" Leo asked hurriedly, before another argument could break out.

"He put it in the basket with the rest," said Egbert stiffly.

"He put it right on the top," Cluck added. "Which was not a very wise thing to do, I must say, because it looked very heavy and could have cracked the other eggs. I mentioned this to Wizard Bing, but he said it didn't matter if every other egg in the basket was smashed to smithereens as long as the golden egg was safe. I'm sure that was just his little joke, too."

"Oh, I'm sure," drawled Freda, rolling her eyes.

"Wizard Bing then swore us to secrecy and left us to take the basket back to the house," said Egbert, ignoring her. "We never saw him, or the golden egg, again."

"We didn't find a golden egg in the house," Bertha said, glancing at Mimi significantly.

Conker narrowed his eyes. "Who else knew about this golden

egg business?" he demanded. "Could anyone in town have found out about it?"

"Certainly not," Cluck said. "Wizard Bing told us it was to be kept absolutely secret." She frowned at Scramble.

"Well, obviously *someone* knew," Bertha exclaimed. "Obviously, the golden egg was the motive for the crime! It must have been! Golden eggs are quite valuable, I imagine."

"Not as valuable as a hen who can lay them," Leo said slowly.

Everyone looked at Moult again. She bowed her head.

"And that," Egbert announced heavily, "is the yolk of the matter, I fear. A hen who can lay golden eggs is not only supremely valuable, but a great oddity — a very great oddity indeed." He sighed deeply. Then he raised his eyes meaningfully to the sky.

His skin prickling, Leo turned to look with everyone else at the glimmering towers of the cloud palace.

"I knew it," muttered Freda. "I *knew* that thing was going to get back into the picture somehow."

And, weirdly, the sound of shrill voices chanting the Strix skipping rhyme floated to their ears on the breeze like a chilling refrain.

"Oh, they've started again!" Bertha gasped. "How *could* they?"

"Mush for brains," Freda said. She spoke with casual disdain, but the feathers on the back of her neck were standing up like spines.

"Egbert," Conker snapped, "are you saying that you think Wizard Bing has been — collected? That's your theory?"

249

"It is," Egbert said very gravely. "And not only mine. We all believe it."

"The Ancient One answered the call of the golden egg," droned Broody, her eyes rolling alarmingly. "The Ancient One took Wizard Bing for its Collection. Brave Simon tried to prevent it, and was . . . changed."

Teeny nodded tensely. "The Ancient One can transform people — and chickens — into anything it wants, just by pointing its bony old finger," she said. "My grandmother told me."

"Indeed," said Egbert, as everyone shivered. "And that is the only logical explanation for recent events."

"No, it's not," said Leo, fighting down a sick feeling in his stomach and trying to close his ears to the continued chanting from the Snug. "It doesn't make any sense at all. The cloud palace didn't arrive in Hobnob till the day *after* Wizard Bing disappeared."

"That was Saladday," said Scramble, nodding vehemently. "The day after Flyday, which is Teeny's hatching-day, was Saladday, which is *Broody's* hatching-day. And today . . . is Sunday, and we don't have any hatching-day parties on Sunday. I remember that *perfectly*!" She looked around as if expecting congratulation, but only Egbert paid any attention to her, and he just said "Very good, my dear" in an absentminded way.

"It doesn't matter what day it was," Bertha interrupted in a high voice. "The Str — the Ancient One — couldn't be responsible for Wizard Bing's disappearance anyway. The cloud palace isn't here on the island. It's over by the Snug. And the Ancient One can't snatch victims from a distance — everyone knows that. If it doesn't land on them directly it has to lure them into its palace, just like the Blue Queen does."

"That's right," Conker said bracingly, as the hens gasped and shuddered at the mention of the queen, who seemed to frighten them even more than the Strix. "There are rules for baddies as well as for us, you know."

"Very handy, that," Freda commented.

"What you have not considered," Egbert said gravely, "is that unlike Her Extreme Wickedness, the Ancient One can come and go at will. Its palace can appear in an instant and disappear just as quickly. Or so it is said."

"Indeed," Broody crooned. "Who can say what occurred in the depths of that Flyday night, when the Flock of Bing was sleeping and the lights of the town were dim? Who was there to see a cloud come down over the island, shrouding it in mystery?"

"Oh, my beak!" wheezed Teeny. She started to pant, and had just begun to fluff out her feathers when she caught Mimi's eye, gulped, and fell silent.

"You think the cloud castle settled over the island on Friday — Flyday — night, Egbert?" Leo asked uneasily.

Egbert bowed his head. "We do," he said.

"Then why didn't it just go back up into the sky where it came from?" demanded Bertha a little hysterically. "Why did it come back on Saladday and settle in Tiger's Glen?"

"Because," Egbert said heavily, "as every chicken knows, the cloud castle cannot land in the same place twice. And when it had regained the sky once more after taking Wizard Bing, the Ancient One discovered it had made an error. Wizard Bing was not the item it wanted for its Collection. The item it wanted was — Moult."

CHAPTER 27

CRASH LANDING

Moult trembled, opening and closing her beak as if she wanted to speak but couldn't find the words.

Chickadee tossed back her comb. "So it's all Moult's fault," she said, with a resentful, sidelong look at Mimi. "If she hadn't laid that golden egg —"

"It wasn't Moult's fault!" Mimi retorted hotly. "She didn't mean —"

"Oh, don't defend me!" Moult cried, breaking her silence at last. "I know I'm to blame! The Ancient One came for me. Wizard Bing nobly sacrificed himself in my place. And Simon — dear Simon who was always so good to me — tried to defend us both and . . . oh!" She burst into a storm of heartbroken tears.

Egbert cleared his throat loudly. "So now you have all the facts," he said to Conker. "How long do you think it will be before you bring Wizard Bing and Simon home?"

"Oh," Conker said. "Well . . ." He tugged his beard.

"Perhaps you cannot give an estimate," Egbert said. "I know little of the hero business. Let me just say that the sooner we are back to normal here, the better. As you can see." His razor-sharp beak gleaming unpleasantly, he nodded meaningfully at the weeping Moult.

"We'll bear that in mind," Freda said briskly. "Cheerio, then." She turned and made for the yard gate.

"Right," said Conker. "Ah . . . right!" He hurried after Freda, urgently beckoning to the rest of the team.

Murmuring awkward good-byes, Leo, Mimi, and Bertha began to follow. They had almost reached the gate when Moult shot from Egbert's side and ran awkwardly after them, her shabby feathers awry, her tattered comb flopping. "Take me with you!" she cried, collapsing at Mimi's feet. "I want to help. I *have* to help!"

Mimi hesitated.

"No, Mimi," Leo muttered. "You know we're not really going to —"

"Now, now, Moult," Egbert called benignly. "Enough of this foolishness! You're embarrassing yourself, my dear."

"Please!" Moult wailed, looking up at Mimi, her reddened eyes beseeching. "I would have gone by myself long ago if I'd been able to, but I couldn't get off the island. I can't fly over the pond — I'm not a Flyday's chick like Teeny. And I'm too short to walk across like Wizard Bing and Simon do. Oh, give me a chance to redeem myself, I beg you!"

"Moult, don't be absurd!" squawked Cluck.

"Just ignore her," Broody muttered. "She's only trying to draw attention to herself."

"Imagine *Moult* going on a quest!" giggled Teeny.

"As if she could do anything except get in the way!" Chickadee sneered.

Mimi pressed her lips together. She gave the flock a single scathing look. Then she bent, picked up Moult, put her in the egg basket, and stalked out of the yard without looking back.

"Oh, lawks-a-daisy!" Bertha nodded in a sketchy way to Egbert, who was staring after Mimi with his beak open, and hurried out of the gate.

"Sorry," Leo said, backing out of the gate himself. "Sorry. We'll — um — see you later." He turned and bolted after Bertha.

Conker was far from pleased when he saw the new member of the quest team. Freda was, if possible, even more unwelcoming.

Leo understood how they felt. Hunched in the egg basket, clearly exhausted by the emotional stress of her outburst in the yard, Moult was not an impressive sight. He was sorry for her, and furious with Mimi. When Moult found out that the quest team had no intention of trying to save Wizard Bing from the cloud castle, whatever they'd let Egbert believe, she'd be devastated. Leo felt hot at the thought of it.

Away from the shelter of the chicken yard, the skipping girls' chanting seemed louder. Leo could almost hear the thudding of the rope. He imagined the twins and the small girl called Skip running in to jump, one by one, egging one another on, daring Woodley to stop them.

Carrying the basket, Mimi picked her way toward the flying rug. It was still floating by the sandwich tree, its fringe curled up to avoid the knitting needles, which were clicking around it avidly.

"There's no room for extra passengers," Freda snapped, standing in front of the rug with her wings outspread in an attempt to bar Mimi's way.

"Of course there is," Mimi retorted, dodging her, crawling onto the rug and putting the basket down in its center. "There are still only six of us. There's plenty of room for Moult now that we don't have the cooking pot anymore."

"I never thought I'd see the day when I'd be sorry you ditched that thing," Freda said to Conker.

Mimi murmured something soothing to Moult and crawled off the rug again. She faced Conker, Freda, Bertha, and Leo with her hands on her hips.

"I had to bring her!" she whispered furiously. "The other hens would have made her life a misery if I hadn't. I'll look after her. You won't have to do a thing. You don't even have to talk to her!"

"I'll thank you not to take that tone with me, Mimi Langlander!" Bertha exclaimed. "If Moult comes with us, *naturally* I'll talk to her. I am *exceptionally* kindhearted, as anyone will tell you, and I have *perfect* manners."

She tossed a drooping poppy out of her eye. "Which is more than I can say for *some* people," she added, "who put their hands on their hips and hiss at *good* friends who have feelings just like they do, and are *only* saying what they think!"

"Hear, hear!" growled Conker.

Mimi's eyes flickered. Her mouth drooped a little at the corners.

"We're *all* sorry for Moult, Mimi," Bertha went on, shooting a warning glance at Freda. "But —"

"It's not just that I feel sorry for her," Mimi burst out. "It's just . . . I couldn't stand the way the others were treating her. It made me so angry I felt . . . sick. I had to help her — I *had* to! Oh, I don't know!" She pressed her hands together in frustration. "I can't explain it."

But Leo thought he could. As Mimi stood there alone, her thin shoulders hunched defensively in the old way he remembered from so many Langlander family gatherings, he suddenly understood what was happening. Mimi mightn't realize it, but Moult reminded her of herself.

Spending time with Mimi Langlander is like doing a degree in psychology, he thought ruefully, trying vainly to hold on to his anger. Then, remembering what Mimi had said in the past about his need for approval and his dislike of rule breaking, he wondered uneasily if she felt the same about him.

Agitated clucking was coming from the chicken yard.

"They'll be storming down here any minute," Freda warned.

"Quite apart from everything else," Conker said to Mimi seriously, "you do realize, I suppose, that you're planning to steal a hen that lays golden eggs? We'll have Begood after us next."

"It's not stealing," Mimi protested. "Moult *wants* to come with us. She wants to help save Wizard Bing."

"But we're *not* going to save him, are we?" Leo argued, lowering his voice to be sure that Moult wouldn't hear. "If he's been collected —"

"Then he can stay collected, as far as I'm concerned," said Freda.

"We *were* going to invade the cloud palace at one stage," Bertha said doubtfully.

"That was before," said Freda. "Tye's put me right off the idea."

"Me, too," Conker said gloomily. "Dying a hero is one thing. Floating around in a cloud forever with only a monster and a bunch of dreams for company is something else again."

"I don't think Wizard Bing has been collected at all," Mimi said. "There's no proof that the cloud palace ever landed on this island. That was just an idea of Egbert's."

With a small jolt, Leo realized that she was right. He felt very irritated — with himself and, perversely, with Mimi. *He* was supposed to be the logical one — the one who weighed up the evidence and stopped Mimi from getting carried away by crazy theories. How had their roles become reversed?

"That's right," he said, digging in his pocket for the list he'd found in the house. "It's just as likely — in fact, it's even *more* likely — that one of the people on this list is responsible for everything that's happened."

"Well, it wasn't Violet Orpington-Dunk," Bertha said at once. "Violet would *never* do anything dishonest."

"It was Spoiler," said Mimi. "I'm certain of it."

"You *can't* be certain of it, Mimi!" snapped Leo. "You —" He broke off as the squawks from the chicken yard suddenly doubled in volume and the gate squeaked ominously.

"Here's trouble," muttered Freda.

"Oh, quickly, quickly!" cried Moult from her basket.

"Moult!" screeched Egbert from the top of the path. "Return to the yard at once! Quest team, stay where you are! I order you, as Guardian of the Flock of Bing!"

"Oh, my guts and garters!" Conker growled furiously. "Mimi —"

He jumped, his eyes bulging. The skipping rhyme had suddenly broken off and shrill screams, like the wild calls of birds, had taken its place.

"That goose Woodley wouldn't make those girls scream like that," Freda shouted over the sounds of flapping and scrabbling from the chicken yard path. "Dabs to dibs it's Tye. She's heard them, and gone to —"

"Tye!" Conker groaned. "Oh, my heart, lungs, and *gizzards*!"

Everyone leaped for the rug, Mimi hurrying to the center to wrap her arms protectively around Moult's basket.

"The Snug!" Conker bellowed. "Fast as you like!"

Its fringe quivering in excitement, the rug shot into the air. Looking back, Leo saw Egbert and the rest of the Flock of Bing arrive at the edge of the lake and stand staring after them in astonishment.

"I'm flying!" Moult squawked. "I'm *flying*!" She stretched her scrawny neck to peer over the basket handle, her eyes wild with exhilaration, her ragged comb pressed flat by the wind.

259

"Moult, stay down!" shouted Mimi, gripping the basket tightly to stop it from being blown away. "Leo, what's happening? I can't see!"

Leo barely heard her. He was gripping the fringe of the rug, staring fearfully down at the scene below.

The Snug was seething with activity. Everywhere people were running — running toward some girls who were racing into the center, pointing behind them and screaming in panic.

And beyond the ring of giant trees, in the middle of the little picnic ground that lay between the Snug and the mists of Tiger's Glen, was Tye. The flower-spangled grass at her feet was littered with abandoned jackets and caps. She was coiling up the long skipping rope. As Leo watched, she slung the coil over her shoulder, ignoring Skip, who was raging at her and trying to snatch the rope back.

"They moved the game outside the Snug, so Woodley couldn't stop them!" Leo shouted.

"Young fools!" roared Conker. "Don't they understand — ?"

"Tye's in trouble," Freda said suddenly. "Those oafs from the Snug — they're lighting torches — they're going to hunt her down. Rug! To Tye!"

The rug cleared the Snug treetops and dived sharply. Tye looked up, her face expressionless. At the same instant, a small figure in a purple shirt burst out of the Snug trees and ran heedlessly toward her, shouting questions and waving a notebook.

It was Scribble. The rug was hurtling straight for him.

"Scribble, watch out!" Leo yelled.

As if in slow motion, he saw the gnome turn and realize his danger. Scribble froze, his eyes bulging in shock, his mouth opening in a silent yell of fear.

Skip screamed piercingly. Tye sprang forward, seized Scribble, and threw him to one side, rolling over with him on the grass. The rug swerved violently. It missed Tye and Scribble by a hair, bumped the ground with a sickening thud, and flapped sideways, out of control, tipping its passengers off and ending its disastrous landing by wrapping itself around the trunk of a tree.

Leo hit the ground with a thud and lay stunned for a moment, flat on his back. Spots of light were dancing in front of his eyes. Cautiously he moved his arms and legs. He felt bruised all over, but nothing seemed to be broken.

He rolled awkwardly onto his side and hazily saw Bertha sitting nearby, shaking her head as if trying to clear it. A little farther away, Skip was staring, tongue-tied, as Tye hauled Conker to his feet and Mimi limped over to rescue Moult, who was fluttering helplessly beneath the upturned egg basket.

Scribble, the cause of the accident, was lying facedown on the ground. Everyone could see that he was breathing, but he didn't stir. He was unconscious, or pretending to be.

"You triple-dyed galoot!" Conker bellowed at him. "Why don't you look where you're going? You could have got us all killed! Wake up and fight like a man! Freda, give him a nip!"

"Forget him," Freda snapped. "We've got to get Tye out of here."

"It might be wise," Tye agreed calmly, staring over Conker's shoulder.

Conker looked quickly behind him. The sounds of shouts and pounding feet were growing louder in the Snug, and bobbing torch flames were already visible through the gloom.

The rug had slid down to the base of the tree and was half-hidden in long grass. One of its corners was bent at an awkward angle and not a thread of its fringe was moving.

"Out cold," Freda said. "We'll have to run for it."

"You three go," Bertha panted, scrambling painfully to her feet with her hat hanging down her back. "Leo, Mimi, and I will stay here. You'll move much faster without us and be less notice-able as well."

Conker nodded. "We'll make for Bing's Wood," he muttered. "We'll wait there till the hue and cry dies down, then get Tye out of town."

Tye hesitated, frowning.

"Don't think about arguing, Tye!" Bertha snapped. "It would be madness for you to try to go through Hobnob alone, the way things are. Conker and Freda can come back here when they've seen you safely away. Don't worry about Leo and Mimi — I'll look after them."

"Go, Tye!" Leo and Mimi begged, as the angry shouts from the Snug grew louder.

"She has to give my rope back first!" shrilled Skip, finally find-ing her voice.

Tye glanced at her and hitched the coil of rope more firmly around her shoulder. Then she nodded to Freda and Conker, and the three of them ran swiftly into the trees, and vanished.

CHAPTER 28

A NARROW ESCAPE

"And then there were four," Moult said dolefully, blinking around at her companions.

"Conker and Freda will be back soon," Leo said, wishing he felt as certain as he sounded.

The shouting of the people crashing through the Snug was very loud now. Bertha hurried to the tree where the flying rug lay and turned to face the sound, lowering her head belligerently.

"It's too late to hide," she called to Leo and Mimi. "We'll just have to try to bluff our way out of trouble. Get behind me. I'll do the talking."

Leo wasn't confident that anything Bertha might say would pacify an angry mob, but he couldn't think of a better idea. Still feeling rather wobbly, he shrugged on one of the packs, picked up the other, and joined Bertha by the tree. Mimi, holding Moult's basket close to her chest, moved to stand beside him.

"That Terlamaine stole my rope!" Skip shouted at them in fury. "She stopped our game, and I was up to eight, *and she took my rope!*"

Leo glanced at her with dislike, but didn't trust himself to say anything.

"Tye was trying to stop something worse from happening to you," Mimi snapped. "That game's dangerous."

"The Strix isn't *real*," Skip said scornfully. "It's just a Langlander tale your parents tell you to make you be good."

"That is not true, young human!" Moult squawked earnestly, sticking her head out of the basket and twisting her scrawny neck to look at Skip. "I am a witness! The Ancient One swooped down upon my home. It took a great and powerful wizard for its own, and changed my dearest friend into a mushroom."

Skip stared, her eyebrows climbing high on her forehead, her lips silently shaping the word "mushroom." Then she turned and blinked at the cloud that had taken possession of Tiger's Glen as if seeing it with new eyes. Almost against his will, Leo looked at it, too.

White mist crawled between the dark trunks of the trees at the edge of the little wood. Farther in, the cloud massed thickly and smoky gray towers climbed into the sky.

"The palace is in the center," Mimi murmured. "That's where the magic is strongest."

Leo glanced at her uneasily, but she refused to look at him and at last he turned to stare at the cloud again. Now that he was so close to it, he found it more frightening than ever.

If I saw something like this at home, he thought, *maybe on a trip to the mountains or something, I'd think it looked really interesting but that it was just low clouds. And Dad would explain what sort of cloud it was, and why it was so near to the ground, and why it shone in some places, because of the angle of the light. And Mom would say, "It looks like a castle, doesn't it?" And Dad would laugh.*

Suddenly he found himself longing for the certainties of home. It was like an ache deep in his chest, and to his horror he felt tears burning behind his eyes.

"*Pssht!*" whispered a voice beside him. He jumped violently and looked around.

A small black circle, rather wobbly at the edges, had appeared on the trunk of the tree. "Might you want a hidey-hole, by any chance?" the black patch asked diffidently.

"Mimi!" Leo croaked. "Bertha!"

Bertha and Mimi spun around. They stared at the hidey-hole in joyful astonishment.

"Just say if you'd rather not," the hole said, pinching its edges as if bracing itself for a rebuff. "I'll *quite* understand, honestly." Its voice was rather weak and snuffly, as if it had a cold.

"No! We want you!" gasped Mimi with a quick glance at Skip, who hadn't taken her eyes off the cloud palace, and at Scribble, who was still lying where he had fallen.

"Indeed we do!" cried Bertha. "You're a lifesaver!"

"Oh, it's nothing," the hole mumbled, and abruptly widened like a yawning mouth.

Bertha stepped inside it and vanished into inky blackness. Mimi followed quickly with Moult. Leo went last, dragging the second pack behind him and only remembering as the familiar warm, thick darkness closed in around him how much he hated being inside hidey-holes.

This hidey-hole, moreover, was not only far less confident than the holes he had met on his first visit to Rondo but much smaller, too. As it shrank beneath the bark of the tree, he, Bertha, and Mimi were so tightly pressed together that they could hardly breathe.

"What a *marvelous* piece of luck!" Bertha said. "I never *dreamed* we'd find a hidey-hole way out here."

"This must be what it's like to be still in the egg," said Moult in wonder.

"It might be better if you didn't speak," the hidey-hole suggested, its snuffling voice coming from all around them. "Just a suggestion. I mean, speak if you like, it's up to you of course, but —"

"Sshh!" Bertha warned. "They're coming!"

In acute discomfort, with Moult's basket jammed against his chest and his nose filled with the smell of straw and feathers, Leo held his breath as the sound of running feet pounded past the tree. Then there was a yell of joy.

"Skip!" a man called. "My dear child! Are you all right?"

"Yes, Father," squeaked Skip, her voice muffled as if she had been enveloped in a joyful hug.

"There's a dead gnome here," another man said grimly.

"It's that reporter fellow from *The Rondo Rambler*," cried a woman. "Killed trying to save the little girl, I suppose. What a terrible tragedy!"

"He's not dead, Candy," someone else called. "He's just been knocked out. I'll see to him. Here, Stitch, give me a hand."

"That's Clogg's voice!" Mimi breathed in Leo's ear. "And

Candy Sweet and Stitch are here, too! Oh, I wish we could see what's happening!"

Leo would have liked to see, too, but more than anything he wanted to move. He was finding the cramped conditions in the hidey-hole almost unbearable. He felt himself starting to sweat.

"Well, there's no sign of that wretched Terlamaine," said a bossy female voice Leo recognized as Bodelia Parker's. "It ran off when it heard us coming, I suppose. We should have crept up on it — I said that from the first."

"We'll get it this time for sure," an unfamilar man's voice replied. "It can't have gone far. Which way did it run, girlie?"

There was a moment's silence.

"Skip?" prompted Skip's father. "Tell the kind gentleman. Where did the Terlamaine go?"

"There," said Skip, and Leo groaned to himself as he imagined her pointing to where she'd last seen Tye. *We shouldn't have hidden*, he fretted. *We should have stayed out there and tried to delay them . . .*

"The creature went into *Tiger's Glen*?" Bodelia exclaimed. "Into that — that cloud monstrosity?"

Leo felt a wave of astonished relief. Bertha breathed out gustily.

"Well, I'm not going in there after it, I can tell you that," the man said, and there was a general murmur of agreement.

"But why in Rondo would the Terlamaine have run into the cloud palace?" Stitch asked in his squeaky voice.

"If you ask me, that's where it came from," Bodelia said darkly.
"If you ask *me*, it's the cloud monster's servant."

There were exclamations from the crowd.

"Sent out to carry off children and other strange creatures for its master, I've no doubt," Bodelia went on, raising her voice. "*And to steal anything it can lay its hands on!*"

Oh, no, Leo groaned to himself.

"But most of the thefts happened before the cloud palace arrived, Bodelia," called Stitch. "All except Woodley's sausages."

"Don't split hairs, Stitch," snapped Bodelia. "Mayor Clogg, you'll have to declare this picnic area out of bounds. As you should have done long before this, I might add."

"Yes, yes, Bodelia," Clogg said fretfully. "As soon as I've had a chance to explain things to Woodley."

"I doubt Woodley can stand any more bad news," said a hollow voice Leo recognized as Master Sadd's. "That pig calling for his dismissal from the Snug has just about finished him off as it is."

Bertha gave a muffled squeak.

"It's a scandal that the newspapers would *print* such rubbish," Bodelia declared. "On the front page, too! I knew Woodley would be devastated."

"I suppose that's why you didn't waste any time rushing out here to show it to him, Bodelia," Stitch said mildly.

Bodelia sniffed. "I know my duty, I hope," she said. "And speaking of duty, you'd better get that gnome back to the Snug."

"Is the poor, brave fellow very bad?" Sadd asked mournfully.

"He won't need your services yet, if that's what you mean, Master Sadd," said Clogg. "He groaned a minute ago. A bucket of water should bring him around all right."

People began to tramp back the way they had come. Every muscle in his body twitching with the urge to move, Leo waited in a fever of impatience as the last stragglers drew level with the hidey-hole's tree.

"Ooh!" Candy Sweet's voice cried suddenly. "Look!"

She sounded dangerously close. It was as if she were leaning toward the tree, peering directly at it. Leo gnawed nervously at his lip. Was this hidey-hole inefficient as well as cramped? Was part of it still visible?

"It's the flying rug those ruffians were tearing about on in the square," exclaimed Master Sadd. "And it's damaged, by the look of it."

"There!" Bodelia cried triumphantly. "They crashed it and abandoned it. That *proves* they stole it! Well, we can't leave it here. Pick it up, Master Sadd. Candy, take the other end."

There was a series of grunts and sighs, and the sound of the rug rasping against the tree's bark.

"We'll really *have* to call Officer Begood now." Candy gasped.

"Yes, we will," said Bodelia. "Hobnob is in the grip of a crime wave! A Terlamaine carrying off children for a cloud monster is bad enough — but the theft and damage of valuable property is a *very* serious matter. Come along, then!"

They moved on. Gradually their voices faded away.

"They're gone," Bertha whispered.

"I think so," snuffled the hidey-hole. "You could get out now, if that's what you'd like to do. Or you could stay. It's up to you, of course."

"Aren't you going to check that there's no one left out there?" Mimi asked. "Just in case?"

"Oh, yes, of course!" fluttered the hidey-hole. "I forgot. Silly me!"

A pinpoint of light appeared in the blackness. There was a very long silence.

"Well?" Leo burst out, by now almost frantic to escape into the open air.

"Oh, sorry, sorry, I was waiting for you to say one way or the other," said the hidey-hole. "*I* can't see anyone, but I didn't like to take the responsibility —"

"Let us out!" Leo roared, unable to wait a moment longer.

The hidey-hole gave a trembling little gasp. The next moment Leo was sliding onto the grass beneath the tree, blinking in the light. Mimi tumbled on top of him, with Moult's basket still clutched in her arms. They scrambled to safety just before Bertha came crashing to the ground, closely followed by the second pack.

"Oof!" squealed Bertha as the pack bounced off her stomach.

"Oh, sorry, sorry," mumbled the hidey-hole, drawing its flabby edges together in a flustered sort of way. "I'm *hopeless* at the expelling side of things. I've just never really got the hang of it. My last client broke his glasses when he fell out."

"*Glasses?*" Mimi and Leo gasped.

"Lawks-a-daisy, I think I've sprained a trotter," Bertha groaned.

"Oh, I feel dreadful now," mumbled the hidey-hole. "I'll just go, shall I? Yes. That would be best. Sorry again."

"Wait!" Leo panted, crawling to his knees.

But already the hidey-hole had shrunk to inkblot size and disappeared beneath a loose piece of bark. Leo tried desperately to call it back, but it was clearly too downhearted to return. Mimi moaned in frustration.

"It probably wasn't Spoiler anyway," Leo said. "Lots of people wear glasses."

Still, the coincidence had made him jittery. He looked quickly around but could see nothing suspicious. At first he couldn't even see any blue butterflies. Then, with a little shock, he saw that there were, in fact, dozens of them, perched motionless on the small blue flowers that spangled the grass. His skin crawled.

"Bertha's with us," Mimi said in a small voice. "She's a match for Spoiler any day. And you've fought him before, Leo."

Leo nodded, strangely touched.

Moult stuck her head out of the basket, her small eyes bright. "What now?" she asked.

"In my opinion," Bertha said, getting up painfully, "we should sit down at one of these picnic tables and have a bite to eat. Food settles the nerves, I always find. Leo, could I trouble you to adjust my hat?"

"This isn't the safest place for a picnic," Leo said, fumbling with the hat ribbons and glancing at the mist swirling in Tiger's Glen.

"It's the safest place there is for us at the moment," said Bertha. "We'll be alone here if Clogg's going to declare it out of bounds."

Leo managed to secure Bertha's hat more or less straight on her head and followed her to the nearest picnic table, dragging the packs. He sat down on one of the benches with his back to the cloud palace. He could still feel the palace's presence like a cold, malicious beam trained on the nape of his neck, but at least he didn't have to look at it.

Mimi put Moult's basket down on the opposite bench and began pulling out packets of food from the pack at random and plopping them down on the table. Moult hopped awkwardly out of the basket and fluttered up to perch on its handle. "Those people took the rug that flies," she clucked regretfully.

"Nothing matters as long as Tye gets away all right," Mimi said, sliding onto the bench next to her.

"Yes." Bertha sighed as she sorted rapidly through the packets of food and helped herself to a bread roll and a large pickled cucumber. "Especially now the silly things have decided she's a servant of the Ancient One!"

Leo saw Mimi tremble like a leaf in the wind and opened his mouth to tell her not to worry, he was sure Tye would get out of Hobnob safely. Then he realized that Mimi hadn't heard a word of what Bertha had said. Her elbows on the table, her chin propped on her hands, Mimi was looking straight past him, gazing with total absorption at the palace of the Strix.

CHAPTER 29

PICNIC

Leo reached across the table and gripped Mimi's wrist. She gave a little jump, blinked twice, and looked at him. "What?" she said thickly, as if she had just woken from a deep sleep.

"I don't think you're as used to the cloud castle as you think," Leo murmured, being very careful not to sound as if he was accusing her of anything. "You were staring at it again."

She shivered. "It's the magic," she said in a low voice. "It's really strong."

"I know," Leo said, letting his hand fall from her wrist. "It must be strong, if even I can feel it." He saw her look of quick surprise and wondered if she'd heard the trace of bitterness in his voice. Hastily he grabbed a bread roll and looked around for something to go inside it. He could only see dried meat, onions, and more pickled cucumbers.

Moult and Bertha were still talking about Tye. "The young human will tell the adults that the tiger woman wasn't trying to hurt her," Moult clucked. "She'll tell them that the tiger woman was only trying to stop the game."

"They won't listen to her, Moult," Mimi said. "They'll say she's too young to know what was really going on."

"I can't *believe* how intolerant people are in this village!" Bertha frowned, biting into her cucumber as viciously as if it were Bodelia Parker herself.

"Yes," Leo said thoughtfully. "But they don't seem to have a problem with anyone else. Only Terlamaines."

"That's because —" Moult began, and stopped as everyone looked at her.

"What, Moult?" Mimi asked encouragingly.

"Simon says that once upon a time, before I was hatched, a flock of tiger folk lived near Hobnob," Moult quavered. "That's what Simon calls them — tiger folk — but I think he must mean Ter — Ter —"

"Terlamaines," said Leo.

Moult nodded. "That's why those woods over there are called Tiger's Glen," she said. "Terma — Terla — tiger folk lived there, when it was part of a much, much bigger wood called Old Forest that stretched all the way to the land of the Blue Queen."

Leo, Mimi, and Bertha looked at one another in astonishment.

"I had no idea Old Forest came down this far south!" exclaimed Bertha. "Of course, I've always been *hopeless* at geography."

"Tye must know," Leo murmured. "But she didn't say a word."

"She wouldn't," Mimi said somberly. "Go on, Moult."

"Well," Moult said, her eyes very wide. "Simon says that one morning, just before the Dark Time began, everyone in Hobnob woke up to find that the forest had vanished in the night. Just one little patch of trees was left." She bobbed her head toward Tiger's Glen. "And all the tiger folk had gone. No one could think how it had happened, but everyone was very happy, and there was a big celebration with fireworks, Simon says, and everything!"

"Why?" snapped Leo, more harshly than he'd meant.

Moult shrank back, fluffing her dusty feathers. "Well, because they were safe at last," she whispered. "Because before the tiger folk left, people were scared to leave their houses at night, or to go too near the forest, even in the daytime, in case they got eaten."

"Terlamaines don't eat people!" Bertha cried indignantly.

Moult set her beak and looked mildly stubborn. "They ate Broody's grandmother," she said.

"That doesn't prove anything," argued Leo. "Broody's grandmother was only a —" Mimi kicked him under the table and he stopped himself just in time.

"Only a what?" Bertha and Moult asked together.

"A — a long time ago," Leo finished lamely.

They stared at him curiously. Feeling his face growing hot, he cast desperately around for a way of rescuing the situation. "I mean . . . maybe Broody's grandmother's flock —"

"The Flock of Bing," Moult put in, with a touch of pride. "Broody can trace her ancestry right back to the island's founding fowls."

"Right, right," Leo gabbled. "Well, maybe the Flock of Bing just *suspected* it was Terlamaines who ate Broody's grandmother, and the story grew from there. These things do happen . . . over time."

Moult put her head to one side, considering. "You might be right," she said slowly. "I always wondered how it was that the tiger folk were able to cross the lake. Wizard Bing set it around his island especially, you know, because tiger folk hated to get their feet wet."

"We thought the lake was to keep dots out," said Mimi.

Moult nodded. "Dots dislike water also," she said. "Simon says it makes them fall apart. That's why Wizard Bing's idea was so very clever. The lake defended the Isle of Bing from two enemies at once."

She thought for a moment. "It doesn't defend it from foxes, though," she added. "Foxes don't mind water a bit. This fox called Sylvester waded over to our island twice before he went to work for Bodelia Parker. He was very nice the first time — asked all our names, and told us to call him Sly for short and everything — but then he came back one day while Egbert was busy having his dust bath, and tried to eat Scramble."

Bertha gave a little start and knocked her last bread roll from the table. She mumbled incoherently and bent to pick it up.

"If it hadn't been for Simon chasing him off, Sly would have got Scramble for sure," said Moult, clicking her beak thoughtfully. "Instead of running away, Scramble started running in circles. She does that sometimes, when she forgets where she's going. So Sylvester nearly caught her."

"That must have been terrible," Leo murmured.

"Oh, yes!" Moult exclaimed. Her eyes were very bright. She was obviously enjoying herself, and it occurred to Leo that she probably didn't get many opportunities to talk at home.

Except to Simon, he reminded himself, and felt a pang as he thought of the mushroom jumping up and down in Officer Begood's jail.

"Of course," Moult continued vivaciously, "Scramble's a Chewsday's chick, like Egbert, and she could have fought Sylvester off if she tried, but she never remembers her hatching-day. Even though she has one every week, Scramble's hatching-day party is always a surprise party — that's what Simon says."

She paused, and the light died from her eyes. "What Simon always used to say, I mean," she added in a small voice. Her drooping comb drooped even farther.

Bertha emerged from beneath the table munching her retrieved bread roll distractedly. She looked upset. The tips of her ears were very pink.

She's sorry for Moult, Leo thought. But Bertha didn't say anything. She just chewed, staring into space and taking no notice of the poppy dangling over her right eye.

Mimi, on the other hand, was looking interested rather than distressed. "Are hens hatched on, um, on a Chewsday always good fighters, or something?" she asked Moult curiously.

"Of course!" answered Moult, surprise at Mimi's ignorance jolting her out of her sad mood. "Don't you know the hatching-day rhyme?"

"No," Mimi and Leo chorused. They both glanced at Bertha, thinking that she probably did, but Bertha seemed not to be paying any attention at all to what was going on around her.

Moult shook her head in amazement. She cleared her throat,

settled her feathers, shut her eyes, and began to recite in a high, crooning voice:

> *Moonday's chick is fair and sleek,*
> *Chewsday's chick is strong of beak,*
> *Wormsday's chick is rich and glad,*
> *Thirstyday's chick is poor and sad,*
> *Flyday's chick has wings of steel,*
> *Saladday's chick lays eggs with zeal,*
> *But the chick that is on Sunday new*
> *Is brave and noble, good and true.*

She opened her eyes, caught sight of Mimi and Leo grinning at each other, and cringed. "Oh," she said in a small voice. "You *do* know the rhyme. You were just teasing me."

"No, Moult!" Mimi said hastily. "No, really! I promise you we've never heard those words before."

"Do you really believe that the day you were born — I mean, hatched — makes a difference?" Leo asked.

"Well, of course it does!" Moult exclaimed. "It makes *all* the difference! It's *everything*! Teeny can fly so well because she was hatched on a Flyday. Chickadee is so glamorous and confident because she was hatched on Moonday. Broody is so good at laying eggs because *she* was hatched on a Saladday . . ."

"Couldn't it be just that they, sort of, made themselves like that because they thought they had to follow the rhyme?" Leo suggested gently.

"Oh, no!" Moult insisted. "It's *definitely* the day that's important. I don't know my hatching-day, but anyone could guess it was Thirstyday just because — well, because of the way I am. And I'm sure that Simon is a Sunday's chick, though he doesn't know his hatching-day any more than I know mine, because he's an orphan, too."

She sighed, her head wobbling uncertainly on her scrawny neck. "When are we going to begin the quest to the cloud palace to save Wizard Bing?" she asked. "Will it be straight after our snack? Or will you want to have your dust bath first?"

There was an embarrassed silence. Moult looked from Mimi to Leo to Bertha and back again, blinking uncertainly.

Leo determinedly bent his head and bit into his bread roll. *This isn't my problem*, he told himself. *This is Mimi's problem and she can handle it.*

"Moult, we've been thinking," Mimi began awkwardly. "We — we've decided not to go to the cloud palace after all. We're not sure that Wizard Bing is there."

"But — but of *course* he's there!" cried Moult, her voice cracking with distress. "He's been collected in my place! You heard what Egbert said! It's the only explanation!" She fluffed up in agitation so that for a moment she looked as wild as Teeny in hysterics. Then she lost her footing, toppled off the basket handle, and fell under the table in a spray of shabby feathers.

Attracted by the commotion, Bertha turned her head stiffly. "What is it?" she inquired in a tense voice.

"They say you're not going to attack the cloud palace!" Moult wailed from under the table. "But Wizard Bing —"

"Dots to Wizard Bing!" Bertha shouted astonishingly, going very red in the face. "I've got more important things to think about than —" She shrieked and jumped backward as a little brown mouse popped its head through a knothole in the table-top, right in front of her.

The mouse emerged timidly from the knothole. It was so extremely small that its tail looked very long and its ears very large, as if it hadn't grown into them yet. Below the very battered-looking message clipped to the chain around its neck dangled a small badge reading TRAINEE.

"Oh!" gasped Bertha, the blood draining suddenly from her face so that she looked quite gray. "Is that message for me?"

"Are you Conker the dot-catcher?" squeaked the mouse.

"No," Leo said, as Bertha sat down heavily on the ground and closed her eyes. "Conker isn't here."

"Conker the dot-catcher is *supposed* to be here," the mouse said, stamping one of its tiny paws. "I have it on very good author-ity that —"

"Conker *was* here," Mimi broke in, "but then he went to Bing's Wood. If you hurry, you'll find him there."

"Bing's Wood?" The mouse's face crinkled up as though it were about to burst into tears. "Oh, not again! I'm so tired and hungry, and I want to go home! My shift should have been over ages ago."

It slumped onto the tabletop. "Well, I'm not standing for it," it said. "I'm taking this message back to headquarters for delivery at

a later time. At training school they said we were perfectly enti-
tled to do that if after a reasonable time the official addressee was
still unavailable, unconscious, drunk, fighting, enchanted, or
dead. I can't remember which bylaw number that is, but I remember what it said."

"Bing's Wood isn't very far from here," Leo said, his eyes fixed
on the message and longing to snatch it from the mouse's chain.

The mouse shook its head. "Deliveries to Bing's Wood are
banned," it said dismally. "The wizard who lives there once tried
to break the messenger service union by training unskilled lizards to do our job. I can't go there now any more than I could go
there this morning when I first arrived in this place. The union
won't stand for it."

"Then give the message to me," Leo said eagerly. "I'll pass it on
to Conker as soon as he gets back."

"Cheese Louise, I can't do that!" squeaked the mouse, looking
horrified. "'No message may be given to any person, being, creature, or other user of the messenger service who is not the official
addressee under any circumstances whatsoever.' That's Bylaw
Number One."

"We won't tell anyone," Mimi said coaxingly. "Here, have a
piece of bread."

"Bribery!" shrieked the mouse, drawing back and clasping its
paws protectively over the message. "Bribery and corruption
aimed at diverting the Rondo mail from its official addressee!
They told me about this in training school, but I never thought
I'd meet with it on my very first run! Wait till I tell them
at headquarters!"

With that, it dived headfirst back into the knothole and disappeared.

Mimi threw up her hands in comical dismay. "I tried," she said.

Leo tried to smile, but he couldn't. He was wondering what was in the message — the message that the mouse had been carrying around since the morning. He was realizing that he'd totally forgotten to tell Tye about the suspicious man in the bakery. He was also wondering what was wrong with Bertha, who was still sitting motionless at the head of the table.

"Where's Moult?" Mimi asked suddenly.

Leo tore his eyes away from Bertha. "Still under the table, isn't she?" he asked, and ducked his head to look.

But Moult wasn't under the table. She wasn't in the egg basket, either. Leo and Mimi got up and searched carefully around, but she was nowhere to be seen.

"Oh, she's gone off somewhere!" Mimi said wretchedly. "I should have kept my eye on her. I *knew* she was upset because"— she darted a reproachful look at Bertha —"because she thought we were trying to wriggle out of saving Wizard Bing. But that mouse distracted me and . . . oh, *no!*"

She was staring at the other side of the picnic ground. With the sinking feeling that he knew exactly what he was going to see, Leo turned and looked, too.

Just in time to see the scrawny little figure of Moult plunge into the crawling mists of Tiger's Glen and disappear from sight.

CHAPTER 30

EAVESDROPPING

Mimi began to run toward the mist, frantically calling Moult's name. Leo sprinted after her and caught her easily, seizing her around the waist and swinging her off the ground.

"Let me go!" Mimi raged, twisting and kicking. "Oh, poor, silly Moult! We have to go after her! We have to stop her! Moult! Moult, come back!" She burst into a storm of tears and redoubled her efforts to free herself.

"It's too late, Mimi!" Leo shouted, holding on grimly and hoping she wouldn't bite. "Moult's gone."

"Only into the mist!" Mimi sobbed, tearing at his fingers, trying to pry them loose. "She can't have reached the palace yet. Look, you can see the mouth of a little track there — that's where she went. There's still time! Leo! Let — me — *go!*"

Leo looked quickly over his shoulder. Bertha was limping toward them, looking angry and despairing.

"Mimi," he muttered urgently. "Forgetting about everything else, you can't go into that mist while you're wearing the Key. You can't risk the Strix getting hold of the Key. Do you understand?"

Mimi gave a gasping sigh, and went limp.

"Do you understand?" Leo repeated fiercely.

"Yes," she whispered.

He set her on her feet and released her, watching her narrowly just in case she tried to run. He didn't think she would, now that he'd reminded her about the Key, but he'd learned through bitter experience that it wasn't a good idea to trust Mimi Langlander too far when it came to matters like this.

"Mimi!" Bertha exploded as she reached them. "Just what did you think you were *doing*? Thank goodness Leo got to you in time! How *dare* you frighten me like that? Lawks-a-daisy, haven't I got enough to worry about?"

"It's my fault Moult's gone in there, Bertha — *my fault*!" Mimi cried, still hiccuping with sobs. "If it wasn't for me, she wouldn't even *be* here! You all told me not to bring her, and I didn't listen."

"Well, listen this time, then," Bertha snapped. "There is nothing you can do for Moult now. Once the milk's in the swill, there's no taking it out again, as my mother used to say. If Moult was mad enough to go charging off to her doom, that's her business. You should have had more sense than to try to go after her."

Mimi wiped her tear-wet face with the backs of her hands. "I wouldn't have gone too far in," she said. "Just far enough to get Moult back. The magic isn't so strong at the edge of the Glen."

"You can't possibly know that for sure!" Bertha exclaimed. "And even if the magic *is* weaker at the edge of the Glen, it's still magic, isn't it? It's still dangerous."

Leo felt cold prickling on the back of his neck. He hunched his shoulders and then, unable to resist the temptation, turned and raised his eyes to the cloud palace.

Strangely enough, it looked less solid, more cloudlike, than it had seemed from a distance. Its towers were straggly, and the shapes of its windows were blurred. But still there was no mistaking what it was. And there was no mistaking the sense of menace that beamed from it like icy breath.

Whatever I feel, Leo thought numbly, *Mimi must feel ten times more strongly. Not just because of who she is, but because of the Key. Yet she wanted to go into that evil mist after Moult, and if it hadn't been for the Key to Rondo she'd still be fighting me to let her do it.*

He wrenched his gaze away from the cloud palace, and looked down to the edge of the Glen, where the mouth of a narrow track lay wreathed in drifting whiteness and dark tree trunks stood like ghostly sentinels. He willed Moult to come into view, willed Moult to come to her senses and return to safety before it was too late. But of course there was no sign of her. No sign . . .

He froze. One of the tree trunks had moved — he was sure it had moved! He stared, saw another flicker of movement, and realized that it wasn't a tree trunk at all. It was a shadow — a tall, thin, wavering shadow, gliding through the mist. He drew a sharp breath.

"What is it?" exclaimed Mimi, whirling around and trying to see what he was looking at. "Is it Moult?"

"No," Leo managed to say. "There's something else there . . . moving in the trees. I don't know what it —" He broke off with a gasp. The shadow had passed into a drift of finer mist, and at last he saw it clearly. It was the dark shape of a man — an old man wearing a flowing cloak and a tall, pointed hat.

Mimi made a smothered sound, and as if he had heard her, the man turned to face the picnic area. For an instant Leo saw the gleam of white beard and hair and the flash of agonized eyes that seemed to be looking straight into his. Then the mist closed over the figure again, and it was gone.

"Wizard Bing!" Mimi whispered. "Oh, Leo, he *is* there. Moult was right all along!"

Leo swallowed. He felt sick. He wanted to say that the figure in the mist might not be Bing, that it might be some other wizard taken by the Strix in the past. But he didn't have the heart for it. And he didn't believe it.

"Come away," Bertha said behind them, and her voice sounded so odd that they both turned to look at her.

Leo was confused by what he saw. Bertha's eyes were full of pain and her brow was wrinkled. She looked years older. But at the same time there was a strange sort of energy radiating from her. Leo didn't know what to make of it.

"Come away," Bertha said again, her voice shaking slightly. "Wizard Bing has been collected. Moult has gone on to the cloud palace to offer herself in his place, I daresay, but all that will happen is that she'll be collected, too. There's nothing more we can do here. No more reason to stay. And there's something I have to do."

She turned to face the Snug. "Come with me," she said over her shoulder. "We're going to get the flying rug back — it must have regained consciousness by now — and we're going to leave this horrible town."

"We can't go yet, Bertha," Leo said in bewilderment. "Conker and Freda —"

"I'll send them a note," Bertha cut in. "They can explain things to Muffy Clogg if they like. I have to go and I can't leave you here alone, so you'll have to come with me."

"Come where?" asked Leo in bewilderment. But Bertha just pressed her lips together and began limping across the grass.

Seeing that Mimi didn't move, Leo took her hand and tugged till she stirred and began to walk, following him mechanically, her eyes on the ground. Clearly she was still terribly shocked by the sight of Wizard Bing trapped in the mists of Tiger's Glen, and by the loss of Moult.

And then there were three, Leo thought, remembering what Moult had said after Freda and Conker left them.

He saw that Bertha was ignoring the clutter on the picnic table, and making straight for the path that led into the Snug.

"What's the matter with her?" he murmured.

Mimi didn't answer. He doubted she'd even heard him.

Bertha was waiting impatiently at the mouth of the path. "Come on," she said, the moment they reached her. "Be very quiet. We don't want them to hear us."

"Bertha, what's going on?" Leo whispered. But Bertha was already moving and didn't answer. Sighing with frustration, Leo followed, pulling Mimi along behind him.

The moment they began to hear voices floating from

somewhere ahead, Bertha turned off the path and started to creep through the giant trees on the tips of her trotters. Once a twig snapped under Leo's foot and she looked back warningly. Otherwise, she didn't hesitate. Head down, she stole forward, bearing toward the right, moving closer to the voices.

"I do not think you can be quite correct, Mistress Parker." Woodley's precise little voice suddenly sounded very near. "The Ancient One collects oddities — oddities, you know."

Leo saw movement between the tree trunks ahead, and with his next step the edge of a green-and-white spotted tablecloth came into view. He realized that they had almost reached Woodley's fireplace.

"And there is nothing unusual about the child Skip," Woodley continued. "Except perhaps her name, which is most peculiar for a human girl-child. In every other respect she is *extremely* ordinary."

"Then the Terlamaine intended to eat her!" retorted Bodelia, her dominating tones unmistakable. Bertha, Leo, and Mimi pressed silently forward, and at last the woman herself became visible. A large black handbag over her arm, she was standing glaring down at Woodley, who was sitting in a chair with a knitted blanket draped over his knees and the flying rug, neatly rolled, under his feet.

"May I quote you on that, Mistress Parker?" asked another voice.

"Scribble!" Bertha breathed. "He's woken up." She tiptoed forward till she reached the next giant tree and peered cautiously around its trunk. Leo and Mimi joined her.

Scribble was sitting in a chair next to Woodley, wrapped in a second knitted blanket and with his feet propped up on the other end of the rolled-up rug. He had a bandage around his head and his notebook was in his hand. Standing beside him, drinking tea and eating Princess Pretty Tarts, were Bun the baker, Stitch the tailor, Master Sadd, and Clogg.

"We'll have to wait till some of them leave," Bertha whispered. "We can't fight them all. Oh, lawks-a-daisy!"

"Certainly you may quote me, Master Scribble!" Bodelia said patronizingly. "And please write down also how grateful we are for your heroic rescue of the girl. *She* may not have understood her danger, but we in Hobnob know only too well what Terlamaines are, and deaths, especially deaths caused by savage beasts, are very bad for the tourist trade."

"I only did my duty, Mistress Parker," said Scribble virtuously, coming to the end of one page of his notebook and flipping over to the next. "Now . . . Mayor Clogg, you'll naturally want to comment on the fact that when, after attacking a child and rendering me unconscious, this lone Terlamaine took refuge in the mist surrounding the cloud castle, not one of the villagers present was willing to give chase."

His pencil poised, he waited expectantly. The people gathered around his chair glanced at one another, and everyone but Stitch shuffled and looked awkward.

"It wasn't a matter of not being *willing*," said Clogg defensively. "We thought it was too dangerous."

"Ah," said Scribble, his eyes very bright, "but now you know, thanks to Master Woodley here, that the mist surrounding the cloud castle isn't dangerous at all, don't you? How does that make you feel, Mayor Clogg? Quite embarrassed, no doubt?"

"Well, really — I —" Clogg blustered, sweat breaking out on his broad forehead.

"It is quite common — quite common, you know — for folk to fear the fine mist that always surrounds the Ancient One's palace," Woodley said placidly. "But as I said before, the trees have assured me that the mist is just a natural phenomenon, caused by the chill of the cloud meeting the warmth of the land. The earth welcoming the sky, as Bliss puts it — the earth welcoming the sky, you know."

"Yes, yes," drawled Scribble, looking down his nose. "Very poetic, I'm sure. So, Master Clogg . . ."

Leo stopped listening. His mind was filled with one single terrible thought.

The mist wasn't dangerous. If they'd acted quickly enough, they might have been able to save Moult after all. They might have been able to find her before she reached the palace. Then they could have grabbed her and forced her to return to safety. Even Wizard Bing might have been saved and brought home. Now it was too late.

Leo clung to the bark of the tree, staring sightlessly at the people gathered around Woodley's fireplace. He didn't dare turn to look at Mimi. He couldn't bear to meet her eyes, burning with grief and anger.

I'll apologize when we're out of here, he thought. *I'll tell her, "Mimi, I thought I was saving you from doing something stupid. I* was even angry about always having to bail you out. And all the time you were right. I'm so sorry . . ."

Yet even as the words formed in Leo's mind, he knew he could never say them. Because in his heart he was glad, very glad, that he'd stopped Mimi from going into Tiger's Glen. In the center of the mist was the palace of the Strix, and Mimi, especially, had to be kept as far from that dread place as possible.

Tye had known that. Tye had warned her.

. . . you would be wise not to deny its fascination, Mimi Langlander . . . If I am in danger from the Ancient One, then so are you . . .

CHAPTER 31

BERTHA'S CHOICE

"For all we know, those rascally rug thieves are hiding in the mist as well!" Bodelia snapped, her loud voice breaking into Leo's thoughts. "If you ask me, Clogg, you should raise a search party and flush them all out!"

"Clogg *didn't* ask you, Bodelia, and he has too much sense to do any such thing," Stitch said, as Clogg mopped his brow with what appeared to be a knitted handkerchief.

"Even if there is no danger, Mayor Clogg?" Scribble asked nastily. "May I quote you on that?"

"But I did not say there was no danger!" Woodley cried, very ruffled. "The mist may not be dangerous in itself, but it would be most unwise to enter it all the same — most unwise, you know. In the past, the phantoms of the Collection have often been seen wandering in its shelter. No doubt they like to feel the earth beneath their feet again, but most folk would not care to meet them."

Leo's throat closed as his mind was suddenly filled with a picture of the wizard with agonized eyes staring out at the world beyond the mist — a world forever lost to him. At the same time, he was comforted to think that he had — he really had — done the right thing in stopping Mimi from doing what she wanted to do. Woodley's next words made him even more certain.

"And of course there is always the danger of straying too close to the center — too close, you know, and being drawn into the palace," Woodley continued fussily. "The lure of the Ancient One is very strong, for some folk in particular."

"Well, that settles it," Clogg declared. "We're not going anywhere. We're going to wait right here on this spot till Begood arrives."

"Hear, hear!" said Stitch. He turned to Scribble, his mouth turning down at the corners. "I'd also like to say that if the Terlamaine laid a finger on that child, I'm a jam jar! And you can quote me on that!"

Bertha pressed her cheek despairingly against the tree. "It's no good," Leo heard her mutter to herself. "They're not going to leave. I can't get to the rug. And the cloud castle's over the Gap. All right. All right. I'll have to go the long way — I'll walk all night. If I hurry I might still be in time. But first I'll send him a message. He might not believe it, he might ignore it, but I have to try —"

She broke off as someone hurried directly past the tree, heading for the group surrounding Woodley and Scribble.

"So there you are, Candy!" Leo heard Bodelia say loudly. "I've been quite worried about you. Why, you've been home and changed your dress! Isn't that your best floral? What have you done that for?"

"Begood's coming to town," Stitch said slyly, and Clogg guffawed.

"I was hot," Candy panted defiantly, coming into view wearing an elaborately frilled gown patterned with purple and yellow pansies. "But I'm worse now, because I've run all the way here. Mayor Clogg, Mistress Clogg called out the window to ask me to tell you to come home at once. She's in a shocking state because Tilly went out without saying a word, and hasn't come back."

"I always said that girl was a flibbertigibbet," said Bodelia, looking down her nose. "Her skirts are far too short and she has a *very* saucy manner. Muffy should never have hired her."

"Yes, Bodelia," gasped Candy. "And Master Bun, Patty caught me as I went by. She says can you please go back to the bakery right now. She's been having terrible trouble with that cooking pot you found on your doorstep. The moment it woke up it started screaming and crying. Even that fox of yours — Renée — can't make it stop. It just keeps howling that it's lost its conkie, whatever that means, and it's upsetting all the other pans in the kitchen. The last two batches of fairy cakes came out of the oven flat as the sole of your shoe, Patty said. She's at her wits' end."

"Why didn't she send me a mouse?" Bun asked, bewildered.

"Haven't you heard?" said Candy, fanning herself. "It's so lucky we got our message to Officer Begood away when we did. The whole messenger service has gone on strike. It seems that someone tried to bribe a trainee. Someone in *Hobnob!*"

"Oh, no!" Bertha breathed, and went so pale that Leo was afraid she was about to collapse.

"Bertha!" he whispered urgently, putting his arm around her. "What's wrong?"

Bertha took a deep, shuddering breath. "My friends at the farm," she mumbled. "The chickens — Violet, Fiona, Eglantine . . . all the others! They're in terrible danger. And now I can't even write to Macdonald to warn him. Oh!"

She closed her eyes. "He used the same trick. The same trick exactly. So friendly. So polite. So efficient. And all the time waiting his chance . . ."

"Who are you talking about?" Leo asked, completely mystified.

"Sly!" moaned Bertha. "Sylvester — the killer fox who tried to eat Broody. Who ate Bodelia Parker's parrot. He's called Sly for short — Moult told us. Don't you see, Leo? It's the same fox! It's Sly — the fox who took my job at Macdonald's farm!" She sagged heavily against Leo's arm.

"I should have known," she wailed softly, as Leo struggled desperately to hold her up. "I should have seen it! The fox at the bakery looked so like him . . . it upset me . . . I thought I was imagining things. But of course she looks like him. She's his sister!"

The people at Woodley's fireplace were talking about the messenger strike. They weren't paying attention to anything outside their small, noisy circle, but Leo knew that if Bertha fell they'd hear the crash for sure.

"Today is Sunday," Bertha said faintly. "Mary and Macdonald always go out on Sunday nights. Tonight Sly will make his move. And there's nothing I can do. Nothing!" Her knees began to buckle.

"Mimi!" Leo whispered. "Help me!"

Mimi didn't answer. Staggering under Bertha's weight, Leo twisted his neck to look behind him.

There was no one there.

Leo blinked stupidly at the place where Mimi had been. All that remained were the small indentations her feet had made in the soft ground.

He went cold, then blazing hot. He knew what had happened — knew exactly — but he couldn't believe it. How *could* she . . . ?

"Bertha," he croaked, digging his fingers into Bertha's back and shaking her roughly. "Bertha, stand up! I've got to move! Mimi's gone. Bertha, *please!*"

"Mimi?" Bertha mumbled. "Gone? Not . . . Spoiler . . . ?"

"No," Leo said grimly. "She left alone. I think she's gone after Moult."

Bertha shook her head violently. Leo felt her weight shift as she straightened herself and stood upright. He pushed himself away from her, spun around, and started running for the path, not caring how much noise he made.

He could hear Bertha limping after him as he reached the path and pounded along it, but he didn't slow down until he reached the picnic area.

The grassy field was deserted. Blue butterflies rested motionless on the flowers that matched their wings. Nothing was moving except the mist crawling in Tiger's Glen.

Panting, Leo went to the table still cluttered with the food from the picnic. He could hear Bertha stumbling from the Snug, but he didn't look around. Any false hopes he might have had were gone. Now he was certain that Mimi Langlander had crept out of the Snug the moment she'd heard what Woodley had said about the mist surrounding the cloud palace.

. . . just a natural phenomenon . . . the earth welcoming the sky, you know.

Mimi hadn't made a sound. She hadn't sighed, or gasped, or breathed a word that might have alerted Bertha and Leo to what she was planning, or given them a chance of trying to stop her. She hadn't waited to hear what else Woodley might say. She'd acted at once. She'd crept away as silently as a messenger mouse. She'd reached the path, and probably she'd run all the rest of the way to the picnic area.

Then she'd come to the table. Leo knew she had, because something was missing. Moult's basket. In its place was a note, hastily scrawled in Mimi's handwriting.

Leo — Have to try. Might still catch her. Don't worry. Will use basket to carry safely. Back soon.

"She's gone into Tiger's Glen," he said aloud, as Bertha came up behind him. His voice sounded strange. He was almost choking with anger. He was cursing the day he'd ever met Mimi Langlander.

Sneaky. Stubborn. Conceited. Stupid. Reckless . . .

Bertha nodded. Her small blue eyes were inexpressibly sad. Without a word she turned from the table and began limping rapidly toward Tiger's Glen.

"No, Bertha!" Leo shouted, pelting after her, his head roaring with fury and fear. "Bertha, don't go in there! You heard what Woodley said!"

"I'll be careful," Bertha called over her shoulder without slowing her pace at all.

"No!" Leo panted, catching up with her and darting ahead to make her stop. "I'll go. I'll find Mimi and bring her back."

He didn't want to do it. He didn't want to try to rescue Mimi Langlander from the results of her idiotic, self-willed, pointless attempt to save a scrawny little hen she'd only just met. But he couldn't let Bertha risk her life and forget everything that really mattered to her while he just stood by.

Mimi was *his* responsibility. Mimi was a burden *he* had to bear. No one else should be made to suffer for anything she did.

Langlanders stick together . . . The words chattered in his mind like an irritating advertising jingle.

"You will *not* go in there, Leo!" Bertha exclaimed in a high voice. "That's my job. Your job is to stay here and wait for Conker and Freda. You have to tell them where Mimi and I have gone. Tell them that if we don't come back, they're not to follow us. And tell them about Sly, and ask them to do what they can to prevent the slaughter of the Flock of Macdonald — to do what I would have done, if I could."

"Bertha, it's not too late," Leo said, seizing on the only weapon he could think of to make her change her mind. "You can still get to the farm in time if you leave now — I'm sure of it. You can still save your friends!"

Bertha faced him, her chest heaving, her eyes bright with unshed tears. "Mimi is my friend, too," she said. "I had a choice to make, and I've made it. Move aside, Leo! We're wasting time."

She was determined. Leo could see it. He wasn't going to be able to stop her. His mind switched automatically to thinking of ways to help keep her safe, and something occurred to him almost at once.

"Wait!" he begged. "Just wait — one minute!"

He turned and sprinted back to the picnic table. Frantically he delved into Conker's pack, throwing the contents out haphazardly till he came to what he was looking for, right at the bottom. The coil of yellow cord.

Seizing it, he raced back to Bertha. She had moved forward. She was standing right beside the mouth of the little track that wound into the Glen. But she had waited for him.

Before she could say anything, he had looped one end of the cord around her chest and tied it tightly, using a double reef knot — a knot he'd learned long ago from one of his Langlander aunts who was the leader of a Girl Guide troop. "There," he panted. "Now you can't get lost or go too far by mistake. I'll hold the other end . . ."

Bertha's hard eyes softened a little. She nodded. Then, without another word, she stepped into the mist.

Leo wrapped his end of the line twice around his wrist and let the cord play out as Bertha moved farther into the trees, her shape quickly fading to a ghostly shadow. "Mimi!" he heard her calling, her voice muffled by the mist. "Mimi! Answer me!"

And then, suddenly, he couldn't see her anymore. Suddenly all he could see were dark tree trunks and the cord feeding steadily into the mist.

He could still hear her, though. Bertha was still calling Mimi's name, her voice even more muffled than before, and Leo could still hear the sounds of her movement — the soft rustling of dead leaves, the tiny snapping of sticks.

Or . . . were those moving sounds really being made by Bertha? Didn't they seem — more to the left of the faint sound of her voice?

Phantoms . . .

Leo stood rigid, straining to listen, as the minutes crawled by. The cord continued to slide smoothly through his fingers. When he looked down he saw that the coil was three-quarters gone.

I didn't tell Bertha about the Key, he thought, astounded that he had forgotten. *I didn't tell her that Mimi has the —*

The sliding of the cord stopped. At the same moment he realized that the calls had stopped, too. He jerked his head up, staring blindly into the crawling mist — at the yellow cord stretching into impenetrable whiteness. His stomach knotted. "Bertha!" he shouted. "What's happening? Have you found her?"

There was utter silence. Not a leaf rustled. Not a twig cracked.

"Bertha!" he bellowed. "Answer me! Answer, or I'll pull you in!"

No sound.

Gritting his teeth, he tugged experimentally at the cord.

And it moved easily — far too easily. Sweating, panting, Leo dragged it in, hand over hand, till at last a large loop came sliding out of the mist to lie empty and tangled at his feet.

CHAPTER 32

AND THEN THERE WAS ONE

Leo gaped at the twisted circle at the end of the cord. He couldn't take it in. Only a few minutes ago that loop had fitted snugly around Bertha's chest. It couldn't have slipped off — it just couldn't! He crouched and examined the knot. It was as secure as it had been when he first tied it. Yet . . .

Slowly he stood up again. Slowly he freed the cord — the useless cord — from his wrist. The chill breath of the mist played on his sweating skin. He noticed absentmindedly that the afternoon was fading. Soon it would be dusk.

And then there was one.

"Bertha!" he yelled at the top of his voice. "Mimi!"

There was no answer. He hadn't really expected there would be. But faintly, faintly, he heard the furtive rustle of leaves as if someone — something — concealed by the mist had heard him and was moving stealthily away.

"Bing!" he bellowed. "Wizard Bing!"

A tall, thin shadow stirred deep in the mist. Then it was gone. Blood pounded in Leo's head. He clenched his fists. "Give them back, Strix!" he bellowed. "Keep the others if you want to, but give Mimi and Bertha back! You don't need them! They're not for you!"

But they are, part of his mind registered coldly. *They're oddities, both of them. Worthy of Collection. A Langlander and a wolf-fighting, questing pig.*

You are a most unusual pig, Bertha . . .

Hal had said that once. The Strix agreed with him, no doubt. And Langlanders might be very common where Leo and Mimi came from, but here they were curiosities indeed — mythical beings, magical creatures from another world, the stuff of fairy tales . . .

And Mimi Langlander carried the Key to Rondo. The key to entering and leaving this world at will. The key to being and unbeing. The key to life and death.

The greatest prize of all.

The Ancient One was covered and hidden as our world grew beneath the Artist's brush, but still it had life — of a kind.

Life — of a kind . . . Leo shuddered as Tye's words whispered in his mind. Could it be that after all these ages, the Ancient One had at last found the way to release itself from half-life?

There's nothing the Key can't do . . .

Leo stood rigid, the cord clutched in his hands.

Your job is to stay here and wait for Conker and Freda. Tell them . . .

Leo dropped the cord and turned his back on Tiger's Glen. Blue butterflies scattered as he walked stiffly across the flower-speckled grass, but he paid them no attention at all. Let them tell the Blue Queen everything. What did it matter now?

He reached the picnic table and methodically put everything back into the two packs. Then he sat down, took out his pen, and tore a page from the notebook he had tucked so blithely into his pocket in what seemed another life.

Dear Conker and Freda,

We saw Wizard Bing in Tiger's Glen. Moult, Mimi, and Bertha have gone in, too, and haven't come back. I'm going in after them. Don't follow us. Warn Farmer Macdonald that his fox, Sly, is a killer, and will attack the Macdonald flock as soon as he gets the chance. Macdonald should contact Bodelia Parker if he doesn't believe you. This is urgent.

Cheers, Leo

"Cheers" didn't seem the right way to end the note, but Leo couldn't think of anything better, so he left it as it was. He'd decided not to mention the Key. If the Strix recognized it, and decided to use it, Conker and Freda would find out soon enough. The whole of Rondo would find out . . . soon enough.

Leo put the note in the middle of the table, weighed it down with a stone, then trudged back to Tiger's Glen.

The cord was lying where he'd left it. His mind was quite blank as he picked up the loop, undid the knot that fastened it, and tied the cord afresh around his own waist. The cord hadn't kept Bertha safe, but any experiment worth trying was worth trying twice, just to be sure, and besides there was nothing else he could think to do.

He tied the free end of the cord to the nearest tree. He had to enter the mist to do it. The mist swept around him, clung to him, closed in behind him as he moved onto the leaf-strewn track and began to follow it.

It crossed his numbed mind that he was doing exactly what he'd always jeered at characters in horror movies for doing — blindly following one another into clear and obvious danger. Then he put the thought away. He was doing what he had to do.

On he walked, and on, the cord snaking behind him, rustling through the leaves. He didn't call out. He didn't even look from side to side, in case he saw something that he didn't want to see. The mist was so cold that it made his skin tingle.

Just the earth welcoming the sky . . .

Leo didn't think so. No mist he'd ever known had felt like this. With every step, he became more and more convinced that it was no natural, harmless thing. It curled and twisted sulkily, like something alive. It was cold but strangely dry. And it had an odor — a faint, metallic smell that mingled with the earthy scent of the wood.

A rough line showed where Bertha's trotters had disturbed the fallen leaves and pressed into the soft earth of the track. Bertha had definitely passed this way. But Leo judged that he had almost reached the point where she had stopped shouting to Mimi. He had to stay alert. Not far ahead, Bertha had fallen into a trap of some kind. He had to avoid doing the same. He had to watch every step he took.

He stopped. He checked that the yellow cord was still knotted tightly. He wet his lips. "Mimi!" he called softly. "Bertha!" He waited a moment, then called again, a little more loudly. His cry sounded thin and feeble. The words seemed to leave his mouth only to hang in the heavy white air.

"They cannot answer."

Leo went rigid. His heart gave a great, painful thud, then started beating very fast. The low, rasping voice had come from somewhere very near him — somewhere to his left. He made himself turn.

He saw dark tree trunks and drifting mist. Nothing else. "Where are you?" he croaked.

There was a sigh. Then the mist swirled as a shadow moved near the base of one of the trees not far from the track. Carefully, ready to jump back instantly at the first sign of danger, Leo took a step closer.

An old man was sitting with his back to the tree trunk. He wore a tall pointed hat and an old velvet cloak. His shoulders were slumped and his head was bowed so that his thin white beard hung almost to the ground.

"Wizard Bing," Leo heard himself say.

The man raised his head. His forehead was seamed with lines. He had a long bony nose and a wide, thin mouth. His eyes were almost black, and so heavily shadowed that they seemed to have sunk deep into their sockets.

"Go back, boy," he said in a toneless voice.

"Have you seen — ?" Leo began.

The wizard sighed again. "I have seen them all," he said, as if every word was an effort. "The pig . . . the girl . . . and my gallant little Moult. One by one they came, and one by one they were

taken. I could not help them any more than I can help myself —
or you, for that matter."

A shudder ran through the old man's body. His hands twitched.
"I cannot act against the Ancient One," he murmured. "I have
been in the center. I have been collected."

"But I haven't," said Leo. Now that his shock had subsided he
felt strangely calm. It was as if now that the worst had happened,
much of his fear had drained away. *It didn't make sense*, he thought
dimly, but it was so.

"*I* haven't been collected," he said in a stronger voice. "I can
still do whatever I want — whatever I need to do to make the
Str — the Ancient One — give Mimi and Bertha up. There must
be a way. There's always a way."

There are rules for baddies as well as for us . . .

The wizard's thin lips curved into a sadly mocking
smile. "Perhaps a way does exist," he said. "But I cannot tell you
what it is."

"Yes you can!" Leo gasped, hope flaring. "Talking isn't acting.
Just tell me what I have to do!"

Bing shook his head. "Impossible," he almost whispered.

"Please!" Leo insisted, hurrying forward and crouching beside
him. "Tell me! If I know, I might be able to help you, too — you,
and Moult as well."

Bing's eyes were suddenly lit by a fierce glow, and for a glorious
moment Leo thought he was going to give in. Then the glow
faded, and the eyes were dull once more.

"Go away, boy," Bing said hoarsely. "You speak of things you
do not understand. This night the cloud palace will leave. The

Ancient One has claimed the prizes it sought. Leave me in peace to bear my misery as best I can. My tongue is tied. I can tell you nothing."

Leo stared at him, fighting down the savage urge to shout at him, to grab him by the shoulders and shake him. The wizard bowed his head again. He clasped his hands in an attempt to stop their trembling. And suddenly Leo's feelings underwent a complete reversal, and he was overwhelmed with pity.

"I'm sorry," he said awkwardly. "But I'm not going to give up. I can't."

"Do what you will," the old man mumbled. "Just get out of my sight."

Leo stood up reluctantly. He took a step backward and almost tripped over the cord still trailing behind him. Quickly he checked the knot at his waist. It was still firm. A few steps on, he found the track. Only then did he look back.

He could no longer see the figure at the base of the tree. The mist had closed over it again and hidden it from view.

What will I do? he thought miserably. For despite what he'd said to Wizard Bing, he knew that to follow the track deeper into the Glen would be reckless and even pointless. He knew now, for sure, that Mimi and Bertha were in the cloud palace. He knew he couldn't save them. Meeting the wretched Bing had taught him that. Yet . . . how could he turn and leave them?

And the Key . . . the Key to Rondo . . . his only way home — and in this world the key to life and death.

Leo wrapped his arms around himself, rocking in despair.

"Good," he heard Bing say. "He has gone. Now he can no

longer torment me with his foolish promises. Poor lad, he does not understand."

It was eerie and terribly sad to hear the old man talking to himself, alone in the mist. Leo felt a lump rise in his throat.

"Ah," the rasping voice went on, a little more loudly, "but how I longed for my tongue to loosen. How I longed to tell him of the night-lights."

Leo froze. He listened intently, hardly daring to breathe.

"How could I tell him, when his presence locked the secret within me?" said the voice floating through the mist. "But if I had been free to speak I would have told him. I would have told him of the small white flowers called night-lights, each a single, perfect cup with a fragrant golden center, borne on a stem of palest green no taller than a blade of grass."

He knows I'm listening, Leo thought, his skin prickling. *He's telling me what I need to know. The enchantment stops him from saying this to me face-to-face, but if he talks to himself, and I happen to overhear . . .*

"The Ancient One is great, but it thirsts for these tiny blooms," Bing's voice continued, dry and rough as sandpaper. "Their magic comforts its bitter loneliness as nothing else can. The Ancient One is drawn to places where they grow, but it cannot pluck them. If plucked by those of evil will, the night-light withers and dies. If plucked by those of good heart, it is everlasting."

Breathless, Leo waited. He pressed his hands to his chest, trying to still his heart. It was beating so loudly that it seemed to be thudding in his ears. He was terrified that he wouldn't be able to hear the rest of what the old wizard had to say.

"If only I could have spoken to that boy," the voice went on, slowly and distinctly, penetrating the mist with ease, "I would have told him that night-lights grow beneath the trees of Tiger's Glen. I would have told him to pluck one bloom for each of his lost companions. I would have told him to go fearlessly to the cloud palace, knock three times on any door, and ask for entry. And I would have told him to offer the flowers in exchange for his friends. The Ancient One would not have been able to refuse him."

Tingling all over, Leo turned to face the center again.

"And before he left me," said the voice from the mist, rising even louder, "I would have asked that boy to remember who told him the secret. And I would have asked him to pluck two extra night-lights . . . to ransom little Moult and . . . me."

"I will, Wizard Bing," Leo whispered. "I promise, I will."

CHAPTER 33

NIGHT-LIGHTS

Leo walked on slowly, scanning the ground on both sides of the track, looking for night-lights. The strange, dry mist was becoming thicker and its metallic smell was growing stronger. He was getting close to the center. He knew it was vital to stay alert — not to become so obsessed with his search that he failed to see danger ahead — but it was amazing how much better he felt now that he had something practical to do.

Then, suddenly, Bertha's tracks ended. Leo stood still, his scalp prickling. The leaves around the last of the trotter marks lay undisturbed. There was no sign of a struggle. It was as if Bertha had disappeared into thin air.

One by one they came, and one by one they were taken . . .

Leo bit his lip, trying to quell the sick feeling in his stomach. He glanced over his shoulder, wondering if he should retrace his steps and continue the search closer to the edge of the Glen where it would be safer.

As he hesitated, he heard a twig snap somewhere to his right. He turned quickly, just in time to catch a glimpse of a vast, shadowy form slithering past a tree and then disappearing behind a curtain of white.

Leo caught his breath and instinctively gripped the cord around his waist, checking yet again that the knot was still firm. The shadow had been indistinct and wavering, but he had seen enough — more than enough — of that sinuous body, that lashing tail, and those three flat heads, jaws gaping wide to reveal fangs whiter than the mist.

The Ancient One collects oddities — oddities, you know . . .

Leo forced himself to breathe out and wiped his sweating hands on his trousers. *So three-headed dragons are oddities even in Rondo*, he thought numbly.

His skin crawling, he glanced over his shoulder. There was nothing to see but billowing whiteness. The mist had closed in behind him, swallowing the path and all but a small section of yellow cord no longer than his arm.

Slowly, fighting down fear and panic, he faced front again, automatically scanning the ground as he did so. And there, at the base of a tree only a step away, was a small white flower.

Now that he had seen it, he couldn't understand how he could have missed it. Standing upright on its pale, leafless stem, it seemed to glow against the dark tree roots.

. . . a single, perfect cup with a fragrant golden center, borne on a stem of palest green no taller than a blade of grass . . .

Leo stepped off the track, moved cautiously to the tree, and crouched beside the tiny bloom. It looked like a miniature tulip, except that it had no long stamens. Deep inside the snowy cup formed by its curving petals was a golden center shaped like a candle flame. He couldn't smell any perfume, but that wasn't surprising. His nose was so filled with the odor of the mist that he couldn't even smell the rotting leaves under his feet.

He reached down and hesitated. The flower was so exquisite that in other circumstances he would have thought it a great shame to pick it. Now his only fear was that it would wither and die, dashing all his hopes. Wizard Bing had said that night-lights only faded when picked by people of evil will, but what if Langlander hands had the same effect?

Stop wasting time, Leo told himself. He touched the knot at his waist like a talisman and picked the flower.

He stood up, holding the night-light gently by the base of its stem. The fragile white cup remained upright, and the golden flame in its center seemed, if anything, even brighter than before.

Sighing with relief, Leo moved a little past the tree and turned slowly in a circle, inspecting the ground. If one night-light grew in this spot, it was quite likely that others did, too. And sure enough he saw one immediately, this time growing in open space, its slender stalk almost invisible against the leaf mold so that the pure white flower seemed to be floating just above the ground.

He looked around again before he approached it, the memory of the three-headed shadow he had seen from the path still very fresh in his mind. He crouched and picked the flower, taking care to break the stem as far down as he could. *One for Mimi, one for*

Bertha, he thought as he stood up again with his prize in his hand. *I only need two more, and then . . .*

His mind sheered away from what he had to do then. *Two more*, he told himself. *You don't have to think about anything else yet.*

He forced his eyes down and scanned the ground one more time, sweeping his arms in front of him to disturb the white fog that hemmed him in. The mist swirled, clearing in patches, and his heart leaped as he saw, not far away, a familiar shape.

He stumbled forward and fell to his knees beside a small basket half-filled with straw. It lay abandoned at the base of a huge tree, in a mossy hollow between two of the tree's vast roots.

Don't worry. Will use basket to carry safely. Back soon.

"Oh, Mimi!" Leo groaned aloud. He picked up the basket and laid the two precious night-light flowers on the straw. He was just turning away when out of the corner of his eye he glimpsed a gleam of white.

A third night-light was nestled on the far side of one of the roots. Wincing at the thought of how nearly he had missed seeing it, Leo picked it and put it beside the others.

Doggedly he moved on, his feet sinking deep into the dead leaves. The light was fading. If he didn't find the fourth night-light soon, it would be too dark for him to see.

This night the cloud palace will leave . . .

His stomach knotting, Leo gripped the handle of the basket. *I could just take three flowers to the Strix*, he thought. *One for Mimi,* one for Bertha, one for Wizard Bing. That would mean leaving Moult behind, but . . .

. . . *my gallant little Moult.*

A picture of Moult seriously reciting the hatching-day rhyme flashed into Leo's mind. He screwed his eyes shut and shook his head, as if that would make the picture disappear, but it didn't.

This was getting him nowhere. He opened his eyes and took a deep breath. *Get back to the track*, he told himself. *Move on toward the center. If you find a fourth night-light, you can ransom Moult as well as the others. If you don't* . . .

Grimly he stepped forward, waving his free arm in front of him to try to clear the mist. One step . . . two . . . three . . .

A bulky shadow loomed up in front of him. His heart leaped into his throat. His ears rang with his own strangled shout of fright.

But the shadow didn't move, and almost at once he saw that it was just a tree branch bowed low by the weight of a thick, tangling vine that covered it like a lumpy curtain and trailed all the way to the ground.

His heart still thudding, Leo began to skirt the leafy mound. The basket snagged on one of the vine strands as he passed. Stopping to free it, he discovered that the mound was hollow inside. The vine that had sprawled over the tree branch had formed a sort of tent. On impulse, Leo bent, parted the vine a little more, and glanced in.

The hollow was almost dark, but he could see enough to realize that it was a perfect hiding place — exactly the sort of secret place he would have loved when he was younger. Then he blinked. There was a white spot on the ground at the back of the hollow.

Leo fell to his knees. Pushing the basket in front of him, he crawled through the vine curtain and into the hidden space.

The night-light was growing beside the trunk of the tree that formed the back wall of the little enclosure. Leo picked it carefully. He could barely see the basket as he put the flower inside it with the others. He could barely see his own hand. But the four night-lights glowed in the darkness, gleaming, perfect . . . everlasting.

Clutching the basket, Leo began to turn around. It was hard to do in the cramped space, but there was no way he was going to crawl backward through the vine curtain, unable to see what might be waiting for him beyond it.

He had almost managed the turn when his elbow struck something hard. At first he thought it was a tree root, but as his hand brushed it in the darkness he realized that it was too smooth for that.

Gingerly he felt the object with his fingers. It was long and thin. Its sides were rounded and it felt cool, as if it were made of metal or glass. A shallow groove not much wider than his thumb ran down its whole length, and at one end of the groove there was something that felt like a small lever. *Well, it's not just a piece of pipe*, Leo thought. *Someone's made this. But what's it doing just lying here? Maybe it's some sort of weapon or . . .*

The thought struck him like a thunderbolt. Heat rushed into his face. He took the rod in his free hand and wriggled rapidly out of the darkness of the vine cave.

He scrambled to his feet, panting, and looked at the thing in his hand. It was a long metal tube. Its top quarter was painted white. Below that was a band of brown, then a band of green. The bottom quarter was yellow.

He was in a very good mood . . . he was wearing his best robe and his tall hat, and he was carrying a fine new wand, striped in four different colors . . .

"Wizard Bing's wand," Leo murmured. The tube didn't look anything like he'd imagined, but he knew he was right.

The groove that ran down the tube's length was black. Four white marks were dotted evenly from top to bottom, each mark in line with one of the colored bands. Leo squinted at the marks. He thought they might be letters or numbers. If only he could see them more clearly. If only it weren't so very dim . . .

So very dim . . .

His chest tightened. He'd only been inside the vine cave for a couple of minutes, but now he saw that it was much darker than it had been when he went in, and the swirling mist was faintly tinged with pink. Above the mist, in the world outside the shrouded Glen, the sun was setting.

And when night came, the Strix's palace would disappear, taking Mimi and Bertha with it. There was no time to waste. He had to find the track. It was to his left, he was sure. To his left . . .

Leo began to walk quickly through the darkening mist, bearing to the left, the basket in one hand and the wand in the other. He doubted he could use the wand to make magic, but at least he could use it as a club if necessary. It was quite heavy enough to stun an attacker.

He stumbled with a gasp as something jerked him backward. It took him several seconds to realize that it was the cord — the lifeline linking him to the edge of the Glen. It had stretched as far as it would go.

He put down the basket and the wand and tore at the knot that fastened the cord around his waist. His hands were shaking, his fingers clumsy, but at last the loop was undone and the cord fell to the ground. Only then did Leo look up and see that the mist around him was moving — not languidly as it had drifted before, but purposefully, and fast. It was tumbling silently past him, toward the center of the Glen. It looked like cloud blown before the wind, but there was no wind. The Glen was utterly still.

Leo snatched up the wand and the basket. He knew without doubt that he didn't need the track anymore. All he had to do was follow the mist. The four night-lights glowed in the dimness as he plunged on blindly, swept along by rolling waves of fog. Once he looked over his shoulder, and what he saw chilled him to the bone.

The mist behind him was thinning. Already he could see more tree trunks, bushes, even spreading branches in the distance. The mist was withdrawing from the edges of the Glen, streaming back toward the center. And that could mean only one thing. The Strix was reclaiming it. The Strix was preparing to depart.

Thrilling with panic, his breath coming in painful, choking gasps, Leo blundered on. Surely he must be nearly at the palace now. Surely . . .

He stumbled into what seemed to be a clearing — at least there were no trees he could see or feel — and suddenly the palace was looming in front of him like a great, billowing wall.

He stopped, and stared. Clouds of mist from the Glen were flowing toward the palace, lapping against it, sinking into its fluffy surface like water soaking into a sponge. Oddly, however, the palace looked smaller and more shapeless — even more cloudlike — than it had before. Leo could still see ragged towers rising into the red-stained sky. But they looked fainter, and the outline of the whole palace was wavering, as if the magic that had created it were gradually being withdrawn.

Vague outlines of windows and balconies still floated in the cloud wall, however. And straight ahead, there was a huge white door.

Leo ran forward. There was no time to be afraid. No time to think of anything except finding the Strix and making the bargain that would save Mimi, Bertha, and the Key before it was too late. He stuck the wand into his belt, raised his hand, and knocked on the door.

CHAPTER 34

CLOUDS

Leo's knuckles went straight through the cloud. They shouldn't have made a sound, and yet they did. A hollow knock echoed eerily in the silence.

Beyond shock, beyond fear, Leo knocked a second time, and a third. And as the echo of the last knock faded away, the door shimmered and thinned till all that remained was a fine, translucent veil of mist. Behind the veil, gray cloud swirled, and in the depths of the cloud, something moved.

"Do you wish to enter?" a voice whispered.

"Yes," Leo said, and watched as the veil of mist melted away. Gripping the basket tightly, he stepped in.

The room — for he didn't know what else to call the formless space he'd entered — was very cold, cold as a cavern of ice. He had been prepared for horrors, but saw only rolling waves of mist, dry, metallic-smelling, and faintly luminous.

The trapped curiosities of the Collection were kept somewhere else in the palace, then. The three-headed dragon, the ancient Terlamaines, Mimi and Bertha, Moult and Wizard Bing . . . drifting in misty gloom while the Ancient One gloated and dreamed.

Leo felt rather than saw the cloud door form again behind him. It was like the brushing of icy wings on his back. In front of him, mist writhed. The thing in the cloud was silent, waiting.

But it was eager. Leo could feel it. His skin crawling, he held out the basket.

"I have brought these night-lights to you," he said, his voice a husky croak. "I offer them in exchange for my friends — for Mimi, Bertha, Moult, and Wizard Bing."

"Come closer," the voice hissed avidly. "Let me see."

Leo took a step forward. The cloud rushed into his nose and mouth, dry and sour, making him cough. *It isn't cloud at all*, he thought suddenly. *It isn't mist. It's smoke. Cold smoke.*

There was a long sigh of pleasure. A wrinkled, mottled hand stretched out of the smoke and took the basket.

"You have done well," the voice said softly. "Now it is time for us to meet face-to-face."

A tall, thin figure moved out of the smoke.

It was Wizard Bing.

Leo gaped, unbelieving. "Where is the Strix?" he asked wildly.

The wizard smiled. Negligently he swung the basket in his hand.

A wave of smoke rolled over Leo, blinding him. When it cleared, golden bars surrounded him. He was in a cage.

"What — what are you doing?" Leo stammered, pressing against the bars, tugging at them helplessly. "Wizard Bing, don't do this! Let me out! I've brought enough night-lights to save you as well as the others. You can be free."

"Oh, I am free already," said the wizard, his smile broadening to a ghastly grin. "I am freer than I have been for a long, long time."

"No!" Leo shouted. "Wizard Bing, please! You have to let me out. I have to find Mimi and Bertha. I have to —"

The wizard began to laugh. And as he laughed his face began to melt. The white beard vanished. The pointed hat bent and collapsed. The mottled hands shrank and paled. The tall, thin body rippled like water, changing and reforming. The laughter rose, became shrill. There was the rustle of silken skirts. And there, before Leo's horrified eyes, stood the Blue Queen, her face flushed with triumph.

The queen looked older than Leo remembered. There were shadows under her eyes, and her skin looked as if it were stretched too tightly over her bones. But she was still as beautiful as ever, and to Leo she seemed even more terrifying. Gems glittered at her throat, on her ears, arms, and fingers, and on her magnificent gown of midnight blue. Her braids of white-gold hair coiled around her jeweled crown like snakes. Her eyes sparkled with malice.

Leo's first thought was that he was dreaming. This wasn't possible. This must be a nightmare — the sort of nightmare in which the very thing you have been dreading comes to pass no matter what you do to prevent it.

The queen is only powerful inside her castle . . .

"This isn't true," Leo whispered aloud. "You can't be here."

"Ah, but I am," purred the Blue Queen. "And so is my castle — or the essence of it, the center that is the source of my power. It has traveled here as smoke, innocent as a cloud, and I have traveled with it. Rumors of the Ancient One made it easy . . . all so

321

easy! And when you disappear this night, no one will seek you. You will be considered lost for good, in the palace of the Strix."

She smiled at the expression on Leo's face. "Surely you did not think that I would be content forever to stay silent and powerless on my hill when once I controlled the whole of Rondo?" she jeered. "Long before you and Mimi Langlander blundered into this world, I had been experimenting with a spell that would release me from my bondage. Your treachery in destroying the Key made me all the more determined to succeed, and in succeeding to make you pay for defying me."

"It — it was you in the Glen," Leo stammered, fumbling for understanding. "Not Wizard Bing . . . *you*! And . . . and you created that three-headed dragon, to convince me that the cloud castle belonged to the Strix."

"You already believed that, fool," sneered the queen. "The dragon phantom was simply to draw your attention to the first of the night-lights I wished you to find. I saw you hesitating on the path and could not risk your turning back. Ah . . . extending my power to the limits of this vile little wood was tiring, but it was worth it. Here in the center I am supreme, but even there, thin as the magic had been stretched, it was strong enough for me to do . . . what had to be done."

A tiny crease had appeared between her perfect eyebrows. She put her hand to her forehead and closed her eyes. For a second her beautiful image seemed to waver. The smoke behind her began drifting upward.

She's exhausted, Leo thought slowly. *Creating the palace, holding it together for such a long time, pushing the magic to the edges of the Glen . . . it's all weakened her. She's spread herself too thin. That's why she let the smoke rush back to the cloud palace the moment I'd found the night-lights. It's why the palace is losing shape and getting smaller. The magic is breaking down.*

The queen still had her eyes closed. A muscle at the corner of her mouth twitched. The furrow on her brow deepened. Leo looked around rapidly. The walls of the palace were growing more insubstantial by the moment. Already he could see through them to the little clearing and the dark shapes of the trees beyond. The walls were paling, thinning, becoming translucent exactly as the door had done on his third knock, but he was certain that this time the thinning wasn't intentional. And . . .

His heart leaped. Was it his imagination, or were the bars that surrounded him becoming less distinct as well?

He slid silently to the back of the cage. The bars seemed to ripple beneath his fingers as he took hold of them. With all his strength he strained to pull them apart. They bent very slightly, but not nearly enough to make a gap big enough for him to climb through. He took a breath and tried again, willing strength into his arms, willing the bars to weaken.

"You cannot escape!" The queen's voice cut through his concentration like an icy blade, making him jump. Stiffly he turned, striving to keep his face expressionless, to mask his bitter disappointment.

"You cannot escape," the queen repeated. "You are mine now."

Leo swallowed, fighting despair, clinging to hope. The queen was tiring. If her withdrawal to her castle in the north could be delayed, there was still a chance. He made himself walk to the front of the cage again. He grasped the bars and looked out at the queen. She smiled cruelly.

"You came to Hobnob because you found out we were on our way here," he said, as if trying to take it in. "The blue butterflies at the camping shop . . ."

"Quite so," the queen said languidly, stroking her pale gold hair as if it were a treasured pet. "You have tried to hide from me, but I knew that at last you would have to show yourselves. The moment you did, my spies alerted me. They told me that the dingy town of Hobnob was your destination — some ridiculous quest to find that pathetic dabbler Bing, who calls himself a wizard. So to Hobnob I came. I formed the castle over the Gap from Flitter Wood. It should have been a simple capture. You should have slipped straight out of the Gap into my hands, but you chose to travel by another, far longer way. Why, I cannot imagine."

To spare Bertha's feelings, Leo thought. *Something you would never understand, Blue Queen.*

"So then it was a matter of luring you into my power," the queen continued. "That task presented some difficulties, I must admit. I have been forced to remain here far longer than I intended. But with the help of my spies, some strokes of good fortune, and your gullibility, success is mine at last. I have you all."

I have you all.

Leo's stomach turned over. For some reason he had taken it for granted that Mimi and Bertha were not in the castle but were wandering lost in the mist — led astray, perhaps, by the queen's phantoms. He had assumed he was the queen's only prisoner.

Why did I assume that? he thought in confusion. His head felt

324

as if it were full of cotton wool. Fear and shock seemed to have dulled his senses. Even now, he realized, he couldn't quite come to grips with what the queen had said. Some part of his mind was sure she was lying. He stared helplessly at the woman's gloating face. She didn't look like someone who was lying. She was shimmering with triumph.

"When that foolish hen braved the mists of Tiger's Glen I knew that Mimi Langlander would follow," the queen said, clearly relishing her story. "I heard that she had formed a bond with the scrawny little creature. She has a weakness for eccentric outsiders, being one herself. The pig who boasts she defeated me, and thinks herself so brave, would come next. And you . . . well . . ." Her lip curled. "You are the image of your old uncle Hal, are you not? You have inherited Hal's tedious sense of duty, and his childish taste for heroics. I knew you would not leave your friends to be carried away in the cloud palace of the Ancient One."

She smiled mockingly. "The cloud palace of the Ancient One," she repeated. "The perfect camouflage. I will be able to use it again and again before the fools realize that oddities are not the only ones disappearing. I have many other scores to settle."

The cold gleam in her pale eyes turned Leo's bones to ice. His numbed mind drifted to Conker and Freda, to Hal and Tye, to Jim, Polly, and Suki, the Blue Queen's hated stepdaughter. He even thought of Spoiler, though this time with little sympathy.

"But you impertinent Langlanders had to come first," said the queen, gazing at the rings on her smooth fingers with satisfaction. "And if I have caught the boasting pig in my trap as well, so much the better. She can take the place of Mimi Langlander's loathsome little dog. I had hoped the dog would be with you, but it is still in hiding, no doubt. Well, I will seek it out later. In the meantime, we will see how long the pig's pride lasts when she is starving in my dungeons. How I will enjoy watching her beg for crumbs and husks! How I will delight in refusing her!"

Anger rose in Leo like a flame. The paralyzing numbness that had gripped his mind melted away, and he could think again. In a flash he remembered everything he'd ever heard about the Blue Queen's power. He knew why he was certain she lied. Desperate — hopeless — as his own situation was, relief flooded through him.

He stared defiantly at the woman preening in front of him.

"You're lying, Blue Queen," he said. "You're trying to trick me. But I won't be tricked. I know too much about you. You *can't* have Bertha in your power — and I doubt you've got Mimi, either. Moult might have come in here willingly, like I did. But I don't think Mimi would have knocked at the castle door, however much she might have wanted Moult back. And I'm *certain* Bertha wouldn't."

"Perhaps not," the queen purred. "But there is another way for a great sorceress to claim slaves, my dear Leo. They can be brought to her by another."

Blood surged in Leo's veins like liquid fire. Energy thrilled through him, driving out despair, dissolving fear and doubt, and leaving something pure, hard, and bright in their place. He gripped the golden bars and laughed in the woman's face.

"Is *that* the plan?" he jeered. "That *I'll* bring Mimi and Bertha to you? You're a fool! You don't understand anything! I'll *never* bring them to you — I don't care what you do to me. I'll never —"

He broke off. The queen had begun to smile again, and this time her smile was so full of gleeful spite that his throat had closed.

"You do not understand, Leo," she said softly. "Your companions are here with us now. You delivered them right into my hands, just as I planned. Now they are mine, and you are, too. Is it not amusing?"

And she looked down at the basket — at the four night-lights gleaming on the dusty straw.

CHAPTER 35

IN PERIL

"Ah, yes," said the queen, watching Leo's appalled face, greedily drinking in his horror. "The magic in the outer Glen was thin — strained to its limit. But it was enough to enable me to transform intruders into any form I wished. Something small, I thought. Something easily carried to me by the dupe I had chosen for the task. Night-lights were perfect. They are flowers I have always disliked."

"Did you change Simon into a mushroom, too?" Leo asked dully.

She laughed. "The wizard's apprentice? What do I care for him or his bumbling master? Whatever happened to them is nothing to do with me. Now — we have talked long enough. You have amused me with your feeble attempts to delay our departure, but there will be plenty of time for further amusement when we are safely behind stone walls."

She was gazing over Leo's shoulder. He glanced behind him and saw that while they had been talking, while he had been concentrating on her alone, the whole front wall of the palace had melted away. A full moon had risen above the trees, and the small clearing was flooded with light. Slowly, as he turned back to face his enemy, he realized that the light was shining in from all sides and from above. The smoke had thinned and contracted till all that remained was a misty column stretching up into the sky with the queen and the golden cage at its base.

"It is enough," the queen drawled, smiling cruelly at the renewed hope that Leo could not help showing in his face. "It is what I came with to this place, and it is all I need to leave it. But just to be sure, I will rid myself of one burden at least . . ."

She plucked the four night-lights from the basket and threw them negligently into the cage, muttering a few words under her breath.

The tiny flowers twisted in the air, transforming as they fell. In seconds they had disappeared and four figures were rolling, dazed, on the ground — Moult, Mimi, Bertha, and . . . a cloaked man with a broad-brimmed hat, long black hair, a pointed black beard, and gold-rimmed, blue-tinted glasses.

Hopelessly tangled in his cloak, the man thrashed from one side to the other, struggling to get up. His hat fell off — and his long, glossy hair fell off with it.

Leo stared. "Spoiler!" he gasped.

And George Langlander it was. Without the wig there was no mistaking the man who now staggered to his feet with a smear of dirt on one cheek, torn frills on his fancy shirt, and a web of cracks disfiguring one lens of his glasses. There was no mistaking, either, the look of cringing terror that he shot at the Blue

Queen before backing as far away from her as he could. He ran his fingers through his greasy hair, and a stale, flowery scent drifted to Leo's nose.

That was the smell in Wizard Bing's house, Leo thought. *Spoiler's hair oil. That smell was what made Mimi sure that Spoiler had been there, though she didn't know why. I wouldn't listen to her. I thought she was being illogical and crazy. But she was right all along.*

And before that, I was right, his thoughts ran on. *Spoiler was here, in Hobnob. He came here from Innes-Trule, and for sure he stole those clothes and things from Winkle's cart. He was the so-called count who cheated Bun the baker. He was probably the one responsible for the rash of thefts in the town as well. And he was the one who stole Wizard Bing's wand.*

Leo remembered the night-light he had found in the tent of vines. The wand had been there, too. In a flash he saw what must have happened. After stealing the wand, Spoiler had stayed in Bing's Wood — unable to slip away easily because of all the villagers coming to investigate the explosion. In the morning he had crept to Tiger's Glen, planning to escape through the Gap, but he'd found the Glen crawling with children on a nature tour, so he'd hidden in the vine cave. Then, having been up all night, he'd probably fallen asleep. So he'd still been in the cave when the castle landed in Tiger's Glen at sunset. How delighted the queen must have been to discover him and make him her first victim.

"What happened?" mumbled Bertha, sitting up and shaking her head till her ears flapped. "I feel very strange. One minute I was walking through the wood following Mimi's tracks and the next minute . . . oh!"

She had seen Spoiler glowering down at her. She had seen Leo, Mimi, and Moult. She had seen the golden bars of the cage.

She blinked, turned her head, and saw the Blue Queen. "Eek!" she squealed.

The Blue Queen's lips curved in a very nasty smile. "Is that a pleasant way to greet your new mistress, pig?" she purred. "Your manners must be improved. And they will be, I assure you."

Bertha's eyes narrowed.

"Where are we?" Moult quavered, her head nodding on her scrawny neck as she peered from side to side. "I'll be fried if *this* is the palace of the Ancient One! Where is Wizard Bing?"

"We've been tricked," Leo said loudly, his eyes on Mimi as she stood up unsteadily. "Wizard Bing isn't here. The Strix's palace isn't here, either. It's all been a hoax. It was a trap set by the Blue Queen to capture Mimi and me. And there's nothing we can do to help ourselves. We have no magic to fight her."

Mimi turned and looked at him. He held her gaze and casually touched his hand to the base of his neck, as if he were simply scratching an itchy spot. Her eyes darkened, and slowly she shook her head.

Leo felt his face grow hot. Was Mimi telling him she wouldn't use the Key even now? Even when it was certain that eventually the queen would discover the Key hidden under Mimi's clothes and take it for herself? What sort of time was this for Mimi suddenly to decide to obey Hal's orders? Was she crazy?

No, a small calm voice whispered in his mind. *You know she's not. You're making the same mistake again. Trust her, for once.*

Leo's anger died as quickly as it had flared. He pushed past Spoiler to get to Mimi's side. As he passed, Spoiler saw the wand in his belt, gave a yell, and grabbed it.

"Hey!" Leo shouted instinctively. But Spoiler was already rushing to the front of the cage, waving the wand at the Blue Queen.

"See here, Your Glorious Highness!" he cried. "This is a miracle! It can make us rich! Look at this!" He fumbled in his bulging pocket with his free hand and pulled out a gleaming golden egg.

"My egg!" squawked Moult.

"This wand will make anyone who owns it all-powerful, My Most Exquisite Majesty!" gabbled Spoiler, shaking the wand at the Blue Queen. "I took it from the wizard who made it. And I have brought the wand to you, Your Extreme Wonderfulness! I stole it for *you*!"

"Oh, yes?" said the queen, raising her eyebrows. "Then you had better give it to me, hadn't you?"

Timorously Spoiler poked the wand through the bars of the cage. The queen took it without comment and turned away.

Spoiler wiped his mouth with the back of a trembling hand. "W-well?" he stammered, with false jauntiness, pushing the golden egg back into his pocket. "Aren't you going to let me out? I mean, we're partners again now, aren't we?"

"Oh, I don't think so," said the queen, turning back to him and smiling slightly. "In fact, the more I see you behind bars, George, the better I like it."

"But the wand —" Spoiler whined.

"As we both know, you stole the wand for yourself, George," the Blue Queen cut in coldly. "Whatever you say now, you stole it to enrich yourself, to help you live in comfort while you hid from me. Well, that is no longer necessary, is it? Because the hiding is over. I have found you. And what I will do with you . . . or *to* you . . . in the future, is my concern alone."

She smiled. Spoiler cringed and shuddered. Clutching the golden bars, he sank to his knees. The queen raised her arms, closed her eyes, and began a low, muttering chant. Slowly the column of smoke began to swirl as if stirred with a spoon.

"Mimi," Leo whispered, "what's wrong? Why don't you want to use —"

"I don't have it, Leo," Mimi said.

He gaped at her, thunderstruck.

"I took it off when I went after Moult," Mimi said, her lips barely moving. "Just in case anything . . . happened to me. I *told* you! Didn't you read my note?"

For a wild moment Leo thought she really had gone mad. Her note? There was nothing about the Key in . . .

Don't worry. Will use basket to carry safely . . .

He wet his dry lips. "You put it in the basket," he said huskily. "Under the straw."

"Of course," Mimi muttered. "I had no choice. I couldn't wear it, in case I was captured. There aren't any Safe Places in the Snug, and I couldn't find any in the picnic area, either. And I couldn't just leave it in the open where someone might steal it. So I carried it in the basket. I *told* you. Well, I couldn't write 'Key' because of Bertha, but I put 'Don't worry' as a clue. Didn't you get it?"

Leo shook his head. It crossed his mind that only Mimi Langlander could think that any normal person would understand something so vague. Then he thought again, and a wave of sadness rolled over him as he saw the truth. Mimi had assumed that "Don't worry" would make him think instantly of the Key to Rondo because she had felt sure that his first concern would be for the Key's safety, not hers.

"I must have dropped the basket when the queen got me," Mimi murmured, rubbing her forehead. "*That* plan worked, anyway. But how *did* she get me? How did she get any of us? How could she be here? She's not supposed to be able to —"

"The new spell," Leo managed to say. "It frees her power from the castle center — lets her move with it, in smoke . . ."

Mimi nodded. Her eyes looked enormous in her pale face. "It's my fault you're here, Leo," she said in a low voice. "I didn't think you'd come after me, after all you said, but I should have known you would. You and Bertha are heroes — everything heroes should be. There's no point in saying I'm sorry. This is too bad for 'sorry.'"

Leo's face was burning. He felt as if something were twisting inside his chest. "It wasn't just your fault," he said. "It was mine as well. I —" The thought of telling her what he'd done, how he'd been tricked into delivering them all into the queen's hands, made his throat tighten. He swallowed. "At least —" he began, and stopped.

He'd been going to say "at least we're together," but had decided at the last moment that it was a stupid thing to say.

"Yes," Mimi agreed soberly, misunderstanding him completely.

"At least she hasn't got the Key. That's something I did right, anyway."

And as she spoke, she looked down and saw the basket on the ground at the Blue Queen's feet. Her lips parted, but she uttered no sound. She pressed her back against the bars of the cage, shaking her head, her eyes appalled and disbelieving.

"Leo! Mimi!" Bertha hissed. "Look!"

She and Moult were at the back of the cage, staring out at the moonlit clearing.

The clearing was bright as day. Some children were standing there, staring in awe at the column of smoke. Leo could see Skip among them. She was wearing a red dressing gown over black-and-white spotted pajamas, and she had slippers shaped like white rabbits on her feet. The twins were standing on either side of her, whispering excitedly. Behind them stood the girl with the long braid, looking rather frightened, and some boys Leo had never seen before. The boys had their hands in their pockets and were trying to look casual and unconcerned, as if they investigated strange phenomena every night of the week.

"Why have they come?" Moult cried. "It's so *dangerous*!"

"It's all that Skip child's doing or I'm a mushroom," Bertha said grimly. "She probably noticed the castle shape changing and persuaded the others to sneak out of the Snug to have a closer look. Their parents must be busy cooking dinner or something."

"It might be a good thing," Leo muttered. "They've seen us. They'll be able to tell people what really happened — tell everyone that it wasn't the Strix who took us at all."

"They won't tell anybody anything," said Mimi flatly. "They're not supposed to *be* here, are they? I bet when we're gone they'll creep back to the Snug thinking they've seen something really cool and swearing to each other not to tell a soul."

"I'm afraid you're right," said Bertha. "Oh, if only —"

"Something's happening," quavered Moult.

And something was. The queen's chanting had grown louder, drowning out Spoiler's moans. The smoke was swirling upward as if it were rising from an underground chimney.

The cage began rocking slightly. Leo's throat closed as he realized what this meant. The queen's magic was coiling beneath it, preparing to lift it from the ground.

He staggered away from the bars with some idea of trying to distract the queen from her chanting. As he did so, he heard screams from the clearing.

"Oh, my beak!" Moult screeched. "Oh, I must . . ."

There was the sound of clumsily fluttering wings. Dusty feathers drifted past Leo's nose and he sneezed.

"Moult got out, Leo!" he heard Mimi shout. "She flew up and squeezed through a little gap in the bars! She hurt her wing but she's . . . she's out of the smoke! She's safe! But what is she — ? Oh! Oh!"

Leo kept his eyes fixed on the queen. He told himself he was glad that Moult at least had benefited from his struggle with the bars. He hadn't been able to push them very far apart. Even for a skinny little hen it must have been a tight squeeze. He only wished . . .

"Lawks-a-daisy!" Bertha shrieked. "Conker! Freda! Tye! . . . *Hal*!"

CHAPTER 36

CHILD'S PLAY

The Blue Queen's eyes snapped open. She glared into the clearing and made a rapid circling gesture. The column of smoke was suddenly enclosed in a shimmering transparent shield.

Leo spun around. The children had scattered. Only Skip had stood her ground. She was glaring at Tye, who was running into the center of the clearing with Conker, Freda, and Hal while Moult fluttered lopsidedly to meet them.

Hal's here, Leo thought dazedly. *He must have worked out what the queen was doing and rushed to Hobnob. And Tye's here. She, Conker, and Freda must have seen the cloud palace change shape and come back . . . Moult saw them arrive. That's what made her fly for the first time in her life, and force her way out of the cage.*

Skip called out something. She was pointing at the coil of skipping rope looped over Tye's shoulder.

"She's asking for her rope back!" Bertha hissed. "Lawks-a-daisy, how can she be so *callous*? Doesn't she realize what's happening here?"

"She doesn't understand it," said Mimi slowly. "To her, it's just weird and exciting — like a movie she's watching."

Tye, Freda, Conker, and Hal took no notice of Moult or Skip. They ran straight at the column of smoke, and the Blue Queen laughed mirthlessly as they dashed themselves against the shield she had raised around herself and her prisoners. She lifted her arms and resumed her droning chant. The smoke began to whirl faster than ever, compressed by the shutting spell spiraling upward like steam in a giant test tube.

Leo watched helplessly as Hal, Tye, and Conker staggered to their feet, looking devastated. He saw Moult squawking at them urgently. He couldn't hear what she was saying, but what did it matter? The cage was beginning to rock again. Soon it would be lost in the spiral of smoke, swept up into the sky. Soon it would be locked in a smoke cloud floating toward the Blue Queen's castle.

And that would be the end. Conker, Freda, Tye, and Hal had followed Leo, Mimi, and Bertha into the castle once, but they wouldn't be able to do it again. This time the queen would be prepared for attack. Her sorcery would shield the castle just as it was shielding the column of smoke.

Tye and Conker seemed to be arguing about something — what to try next, perhaps. Hal was taking no part in the conversation. He was staring into the smoke, his lean face bleak. *Hal knows*, Leo thought. *He knows that this time we're lost.*

He pressed his forehead against the cold bars of the cage and shut his eyes. What would Hal think if he knew that the Key to Rondo was lost as well?

Hal saved Rondo and I'm about to destroy it, Leo thought. *Hal took the Key from the Blue Queen, and I carried it back to her.*

"Skip!" Tye's voice was loud and commanding enough to penetrate both the shutting spell and Leo's despair. Leo opened his eyes and blinked out at the clearing. In slow surprise, he saw that Tye was holding out the coil of rope and beckoning to Skip. The girl hesitated, then approached Tye cautiously, her eyes fixed on the rope, while the other children peeped fearfully from behind the trees that edged the clearing.

"Yes!" Mimi whispered, clasping her hands as Tye spoke urgently to Skip and Moult nodded frantically beside them. "It's worth a try! Fight fire with fire!"

Leo met Bertha's eyes and raised his eyebrows. Bertha shook her head. She had no idea what Mimi meant, either.

"Mimi," Leo muttered. "What — ?"

"Wait!" Mimi whispered, her face pressed to the bars. "Watch!"

Skip took the rope, looking very surprised and excited. She turned and beckoned imperiously to her friends. The twins edged out of hiding and walked uneasily toward her, glancing under their eyelashes at Tye, Hal, Conker, and Freda. The two boys quickly followed. The girl with the braid hung back.

Astonished, Leo saw Skip uncoil the rope, give one end to the taller of the twins, and take the other end herself. The two girls stretched the rope between them and began to turn it.

The rope hit the ground once, twice. And as it rose for the third time, Tye, dark and slender, her tiger-striped face set, ran into the center and began to jump.

The children were chanting. Leo's stomach turned over as he heard the familiar words.

Dare to call the Strix!
Show the Strix your tricks!
One, two, buckle your shoe,
Who will meet the Strix?

At the third line, Tye bent and touched the toe of her boot, straightening again in time for the next turn of the rope.

The cage rocked. Leo glanced over his shoulder. The Blue Queen's eyes were open. She was staring venomously out into the clearing. But her arms were still raised, her lips were still moving, and the smoke was whirling around her, faster and faster. If Tye's plan had been to distract her, it wasn't working. Leo looked back at the clearing. The children were still chanting.

Dare to call the Strix!
Show the Strix your tricks!
Three, four, knock on the floor,
Who will meet the Strix?

At the third line, Tye crouched and knocked on the ground so fast that she was upright again before Leo could blink.

The cage rocked. The chanting went on. It was loud now — very loud. Dazed, Leo saw that Conker, Hal, Freda, and Moult were chanting, too. The girl with the braid had crept out of hiding and joined her friends. And behind them, deep in Tiger's Glen, lights bobbed and swayed. People in the Snug had heard the noise, had discovered the children missing. They were hurrying, following the sound of the voices.

Dare to call the Strix!
Show the Strix your tricks,
Five, six, pick up sticks . . .

Tye touched the ground on either side of her feet and effortlessly rose again in time for the next fall of the rope. The chant rose to a shout.

Who will meet the Strix?

Leo stood frozen, staring through the bars and the smoke. The sight was dreamlike. Lights bobbing in the darkness of the Glen. The rope turning in the moonlit clearing. Children chanting and clapping, wild with excitement. Hal, Conker, Freda, and a scrawny little hen chanting, their faces very grim. And, strangest of all, the slender, alien figure of Tye the Terlamaine jumping the rope, her tiger-striped face intent, playing a children's game as if it were the most important thing in the world.

Leo's whole body tingled as at last he understood what was happening. He understood what Moult's idea had been, what Tye was trying to do, what Mimi had meant by "fight fire with fire," what a terrible risk was being taken . . .

Dare to call the Strix!
Show the Strix your tricks!
Seven, eight, lock the gate,
Who will meet the Strix?

When Tye spun lithely around on the third line, landing as gracefully as a ballet dancer, all the children cheered. The girl with the braid was squealing with excitement. Hal looked very tense. Conker was scowling ferociously. Freda was watching the sky.

His heart in his mouth, Leo heard the last verse of the rhyme begin.

> *Dare to call the Strix!*
> *Show the Strix your tricks!*
> *Nine, ten, tumble and then . . .*

Tye turned a perfect somersault, so fast that her body was a blur. She regained her feet just as the rope thudded down again, and cleared it effortlessly.

YOU WILL MEET THE STRIX! the children screamed, and suddenly the rope was turning at twice its previous speed, whipping the ground relentlessly, and Tye was jumping very fast, and the crowd was bellowing and clapping in time.

STRIX . . . STRIX . . . STRIX . . . STRIX . . .

Leo found himself shouting the word with everyone else. Mimi and Bertha were shouting, too. Behind them, Spoiler groaned in terror. The queen's voice rose to a shriek, but she couldn't drown out the chanting.

. . . STRIX . . . STRIX . . . STRIX . . . STRIX . . . STRIX . . . STRIX!

And as the last shout died away, the stars went out. A thick, swirling, glittering mist had tumbled from the sky, had fallen to earth, overwhelming the smoke, overwhelming the cage, the shutting spell, the queen. The mist was damp, bountiful, whirling with color, and in its center something was alive.

Life of a kind . . .

What have we done? Leo thought numbly. He felt his teeth beginning to chatter. He heard Bertha moan.

The children were shrieking piercingly. Spoiler was rattling the cage bars, howling to be let out. The queen was silent.

Leo, Mimi, and Bertha huddled together, lost in a sparkling haze. Before their eyes, glittering particles in every color of the rainbow, borne in a soft white mist, formed and reformed into the dreamlike shapes of living things — huge, exotic flowers, mermaids with sea-green hair, dancing zebras, twisting sea serpents, unicorns, giants, dragons . . .

Then they heard a voice slowly rumbling above their heads like distant thunder, infinitely peaceful and as old as time.

"Who called my name?" the voice said. "Who disturbed my dreams?"

Leo heard Mimi catch her breath. He looked up, straight up, but could see only a faint smudge in the heart of the glittering cloud. *The Ancient One.* He felt an ache of longing in his chest and quickly looked down again, his eyes dazzled and his heart thudding with fear. Through the mist, through the endlessly changing dream shapes, past Spoiler clinging to the cage bars, he saw the Blue Queen staggering back, one arm pressed over her eyes.

"Ahh," sighed the old, old voice. "Here is powerful magic. Ah, it warms me. It reminds me of the olden times, when the Artist strolled with the Terlamaines in the glades of Old Forest. And of later ages, too, when Langlanders trod the world, and played their tricks, and made their magic. And of . . . a darker, more recent time that . . . I would prefer to forget."

It feels the Key, Leo thought in terror, glancing at Mimi. But Mimi seemed unaware of him. She was gazing, awestruck, at the visions drifting around her. Her eyes were filled with tears. He looked quickly back at the queen.

The queen had uncovered her face. She was looking at the wand still clutched in her shaking hand.

She doesn't know about the Key, Leo reminded himself. *She thinks the Strix is sensing the magic in Wizard Bing's wand.*

"The wand is mine, Ancient One," said the Blue Queen in a low voice that trembled only slightly. "It is but a trivial, commonplace thing, made by a trivial, commonplace man. It would not interest you for long, and nor would I. But see what I have here! Something far better!"

She pointed into the cage.

Shrinking back, Leo felt a strange, cool sensation sweep over him like a soft, steady breeze. He knew without a doubt that he was being examined curiously from somewhere high above him, somewhere in the center of the dancing visions, the dazzling mist. He began to shake. He wanted to hide himself, but he couldn't move.

"Langlanders," said the rumbling voice softly, almost dotingly. "Young ones . . . the youngest I have seen . . . and an old one with them — a bad apple, rotten almost to the core . . . and a pig with fine intelligence and a great heart. How interesting! How very curious and interesting!"

Leo felt the coolness intensify. He gripped Mimi's hand.

"Then take them, Ancient One," the Blue Queen gabbled, her lips stretching into a ghastly smile. "Take them all! I give them to you!"

"Give?" said the Strix, sounding puzzled. "How can you give? What I want, I take."

Leo shivered, shivered all over. He heard Bertha take a sobbing breath.

Her mouth twitching uncontrollably, the queen edged aside. She trod on the basket, stumbled awkwardly, and staggered a little, reaching for the cage to stop herself from falling.

In a split second Spoiler's arm had shot between the bars and his meaty hand had fastened on her arm. She screamed with rage and fought to tear her arm away.

"Sell me, would you?" Spoiler shouted hysterically, tightening his grip. "Trade me for your own miserable life and steal my wand as well, would you? Think again, witch! Wherever I go, you go!"

Wild with fury, the queen swung around and smashed the wand down on his hand.

Spoiler gave a strangled squeak, dropped her arm, and froze. Then, bizarrely, he began to swell. His head ballooned. His eyes vanished from view as his cheeks and forehead rose in doughy mounds. His arms and legs puffed out. His skin browned, thickened, and crusted. And suddenly the cage was filled with the strong, unmistakable scent of newly baked bread.

Mimi and Bertha screamed. Leo yelled in horror. They shrank back as Spoiler, hideously changed, blundered blindly around the cage, his swollen arms and legs stiff as jointed breadsticks, his bulging, crusty head crashing against the bars, spraying the floor with crumbs.

The queen shrieked with surprised laughter — a shrill cackle of pure, wicked delight. There was a low, ominous rumble from above, and abruptly she stopped laughing. Her mouth was still half open, the laughter lines still creased her face, but her eyes were suddenly wide with terror. She began to tremble. The wand dropped from her hand.

Leo, Mimi, and Bertha fell to the cage floor, paralyzed by the icy breath of the terrible anger gathering above. But the anger was not for them. It was for the woman cowering on the other side of the golden bars — the queen who to them was a towering monster of evil, but who was a child compared to the ancient being in the mist.

"You have learned nothing since first the Artist painted you in your pride, Blue Queen," growled the Strix. "You have not grown. You have merely grown old. You are not interesting. Leave us, and return to your own place."

The queen threw up her arms. Smoke swirled about her, cocooning her, lifting her off her feet. As she struggled, howling with baffled rage, her eyes fell on Leo, lying in the cage, gaping at her. She bared her teeth and hissed at him like a snake.

"Be gone!" thundered the Strix.

The queen shrieked. The whirling cocoon spiraled upward into the night, carrying her with it. And in an instant she had vanished, leaving behind only the echo of her screams.

CHAPTER 37

AMAZING SCENES

The cage bars had vanished with the queen. Spoiler had blundered away. But Leo, Mimi, and Bertha didn't move. They were lost in the dreams of the Strix.

Phantoms formed and reformed around them. Laughing dwarves and scowling goblins. Treasure chests and trees with faces. Bears and witches, growling griffins, sweet-faced girls with golden hair. Cats and rats and spotted dogs. Children playing, knights on horses, farmers, dragons, fisher-kings . . .

A scraggy brown hen, her feathers fluffed up in fright, her eyes filled with terrified determination.

Leo blinked. The hen was real. It was Moult. He stirred from his waking dream. Suddenly, as if plugs had been taken from his ears, he heard the sound of many murmuring voices. Suddenly his dazzled eyes were able to see beyond the visions.

Moult was standing in the moonlit clearing, peering into the glittering haze. Behind her were Conker, Freda, Hal, and Tye. Behind them, keeping well back, was a goggling, muttering crowd of people. Leo could see Bodelia, Master Sadd, the tailor

Stitch, and Scribble, gaping, his notebook hanging limply in his hand . . .

"Please let my friends go free, Ancient One," croaked Moult, her head bobbing, her ragged comb flopping. "Take me, instead. I am the one who laid the golden egg. And — and my flock can well do without me."

"Oh, Moult!" Mimi whispered.

The Strix was silent.

"Or take me." Tye moved forward, very upright, pulling away from Hal's restraining hand. "All my kin were killed in the Dark Time. I am the last of the Terlamaines. That, surely, makes me oddity enough."

"No, Tye!" Leo murmured, his heart wrenched by Tye's proud stance, by Conker's despair, and Hal's stiff, expressionless face.

"No, Terlamaine!" shrilled Skip. "Don't go! If you're the only one, you should stay!"

The crowd moved restlessly.

Tye took another step forward. She stared into the haze. The glittering dream particles moved and separated, circled and drifted. And suddenly the mist was filled with visions of ancient trees, lush vines, huts of bark and woven grass, cool, dappled light, and Terlamaines, Terlamaines by the hundred, climbing, laughing, swinging, sleeping, embracing, playing with their children.

The visions danced like shadows on the surface of Tye's hard golden eyes. The eyes softened and filled with tears.

"Take me, Ancient One," she repeated softly. "This world no

longer has a place for me. It is time for me to leave it, and dream with my kin."

There was a long moment's silence. Tye waited. Moult bowed her head. The crowd leaned forward breathlessly. A redheaded man who was surely Skip's father was clutching his daughter's arm, preventing her from running to Tye's side.

"Ahh," the Strix rumbled at last. "How full of passion you young beings are! I had forgotten. It is good to remember."

It paused. In the hush, the visions whirled. The Terlamaine phantoms shifted and blended with the images of owls, donkeys, goose girls, old women making porridge, children lost in a wood, and wolves disguised in sheepskins. They dissolved and reformed as pictures of a blundering bread man, a striped wand, a short-haired girl in a green and gold tunic, a boy in a brown leather jacket, a pig in a flower-laden hat, a rugged man with steady eyes holding the hand of a tall, proud Terlamaine, an awestruck crowd, a basket half-filled with straw, and a small, scruffy hen with a dragging wing.

"You see?" the rumbling voice said gently. "I do not need to take you, gallant Sunday's chick, or you, brave Terlamaine. Nor do I need the young Langlanders or the most unusual pig. It has been long, very long, since living creatures have been necessary to my comfort. My memories are my dreams, and this night has given me fresh dreams enough to last many of your lifetimes. May your own dreams be interesting ones."

And without a sound, the Ancient One and its memories melted away into the moonlight.

Mimi and Leo took a long time to wake fully from their dream-like state, and afterward there were gaps in what they recalled of the time following the Strix's farewell.

Leo remembered Hal and Conker alternately shouting at him and joyfully banging him on the back as they hauled him to his feet. Mimi remembered crawling to the basket, and furtively reclaiming the Key to Rondo before setting the exhausted Moult on the straw and slipping the handle of the basket over her arm. They both remembered what happened when Bertha got up, shaking her ears dazedly and mumbling about Sly the fox.

"Bertha, we found Leo's note, and I did try to send a warning to Jack Macdonald before we came in here," Hal said gently. "But the mice are on strike."

Instantly Bertha set off in a lurching gallop with Freda flying grimly after her and Leo, Mimi, Hal, Tye, and Conker close behind.

They must have chased Bertha through the Glen, and the picnic area, but neither Leo nor Mimi had any memory of it. By the time they came to themselves they were running through the Snug trees, gradually becoming aware of shouts and wails drifting from the field in the center.

"Catch it, Officer Begood!" screamed someone who sounded like Candy Sweet. "Save us! Oh! Oh! Oh!"

"Silence in the Snug, if you *please*!" Woodley's squeaky voice pleaded.

Bertha put on a fresh burst of speed. She thundered out of the trees and skidded to a halt, her trotters digging deep trenches in the grass. Freda fluttered to the ground behind her. Panting after them, Leo, Mimi, Hal, Tye, and Conker also stopped short.

The Snug glowworms, it seemed, had recovered from their illness, for lanterns blazed in the trees around the central field, illuminating a scene of chaos. The field was ringed with people. In the middle of the ring the bread-man floundered, flailing his crusty arms. Whichever way he lunged, people scattered, screaming, as if they were playing a bizarre game of blindman's buff. Dots swarmed over the grass, gobbling up crumbs.

Officer Begood was inside the ring, too, struggling to keep hold of a chain attached to a plunging giant mushroom in a red-and-white striped beanie.

"Police brutality!" screamed Muffy Clogg from the edge of the crowd. "How *could* you bring poor Simon into danger like this?"

"I had to bring him!" Officer Begood bawled, crimson with frustration. "There's no one to look after him except me. What if he'd suffocated in his pillow or fallen over and broken his stem while I was away? Who'd have been blamed for that, may I ask? Me, that's who!"

Everyone was far too interested in Officer Begood, the mushroom, and the bread-man to notice the newcomers.

"This is our chance!" hissed Bertha. "Quick! To the rug!"

The flying rug was still lying by Woodley's fireplace, but it was awake and unrolled itself eagerly as the quest team appeared. It didn't flinch when Bertha clambered on, despite the painful-looking crease in one of its corners.

"Take care of yourselves," Bertha said. "I don't know when I'll be back. It — it depends on what I find when I get to the farm." She bit her lip.

"Tye and I will go with you, Bertha," Hal said quickly. He stepped onto the rug and thrust the striped wand at Leo. "Be careful with this," he said, entirely unnecessarily as far as Leo was concerned.

Tye joined Hal silently. Her face was expressionless — almost vacant. *She's still thinking about the Strix*, Leo thought suddenly. *She's still thinking about what she saw in the mist — the dreams of Terlamaines.*

"To Jack Macdonald's farm!" cried Bertha, and the flying rug shot upward, quickly vanishing over the treetops.

"Oh, I hope they get there in time," squawked Moult, poking her head out of the basket.

"Never mind about that," Freda said sourly. "That's their business. *Our* business is to find Bing, and as far as I can see, we're back where we started."

"Not quite," Mimi said, staring hard at Leo. "Now we know for sure that it was Spoiler who stole Wizard Bing's wand. If we can change Spoiler back into himself we can make him tell us what happened."

Leo knew what she meant. She was going to use the Key to Rondo. But everyone would see . . . *Trust her*, a voice whispered in his mind. He swallowed and nodded.

"It's too risky to use that wand," Freda objected. "We don't know how it works."

"I wasn't thinking of using the wand," Mimi said. "I'm going to use the wishing well. All we have to do is get Spoiler close to it . . ."

Leo shook his head in rueful admiration. Mimi Langlander, he thought, was the most devious person he'd ever met.

No one took any notice of them as they pushed their way back into the center of the field. As they ran toward the wishing well, however, the people who had been in Tiger's Glen burst out of the crowd right in front of them.

"There they are!" squealed Skip. "But where's the Terlamaine?"

"Rug thieves!" screeched Bodelia. "Allies of Terlamaines! Summoners of cloud monsters! Blue Queen attracters! Encouragers of disobedient children!"

"Put a sock in it, Bodelia," said Stitch, and dodged as she swung her handbag at him.

"Keep back!" Conker bellowed. "This is vital quest business!"

"Conkie!" howled an all-too-familiar voice from the back of the crowd.

The bread-man turned. He saw Conker, Freda, Leo, and Mimi standing by the wishing well. He began lumbering toward them, his crispy jaws snapping with fury. Dots swarmed around his bulbous feet, carrying away large flakes of crust. The crowd gasped in horror.

"We've got to stand our ground," Mimi said tensely. "He has to be right beside the wishing well before — before I try to wish him back to normal."

His sunken eyes fixed on the wand in Leo's hand, Spoiler lumbered on, making small, horrible crunching sounds with every step. He stretched out his arms, and his fingers, smooth and glossy as dinner rolls, began opening and closing in a threatening way.

353

Leo backed against the well, wondering how it would feel when those plumped-up, crusty fingers closed on his throat.

"It's going to throttle them!" shouted Stitch, pushing past Bodelia. "Why are they just standing there?"

"Tragic events at the notorious Hobnob Snug . . ." muttered Scribble, writing madly.

Spoiler lunged at Leo, reaching for him over Conker's head. Conker swatted ferociously at the crusty body. Freda attacked the feet and legs. Nothing they did made the smallest difference except to provide more crumbs for the dots, which swarmed around the well squealing in a feeding frenzy.

"Conkie!" Out of the crowd hurtled the cooking pot, trailing a piece of frayed rope. Screaming Conker's name, it shot between the bulging legs of the bread-man and threw itself at Conker, knocking him sideways. The bread-man rocked on his swollen feet, flailing his arms like windmills, then toppled forward, rigid as a falling tree.

Leo leaped away and fell sprawling onto the grass just in time to avoid being crushed as the bread-man's chest thudded against the well.

"Perfect!" Mimi breathed. And suddenly the bread-man was no more, and it was Spoiler who was draped over the well's rim. Finding himself suddenly able to move freely again, he stood up and looked around blearily.

"Why, it's Count Éclair!" shouted Bodelia in astonishment.

"*Count?*" roared Bun the baker. "If he's a count, I'm a Princess Pretty Tart! He's that scoundrel who passed counterfeit coins in the bakery!"

Spoiler's bloodshot eyes bulged. Pushing Mimi roughly out of his way, he ran.

"Stop that man!" screamed Bodelia. "He owes me for a very valuable antique trinket box!"

But so desperate and ferocious did Spoiler look that the people in his path jumped aside. He shot into the Snug trees and vanished from sight. Conker, Freda, Stitch, and a few other brave souls went after him, but Leo doubted they had any chance of catching him in the dark.

Leo and Mimi crawled painfully to their feet, dazed by the utter failure of their plan. The Snug was now noisier than ever, and the departure of the bread-man hadn't calmed the giant mushroom in the least. In fact, the mushroom seemed to have become more enraged than ever.

"Simon is usually such a sweet-natured boy," wept Muffy Clogg, clutching her husband's arm for support. "I can't understand what's got into him!"

"I think he's trying to get to the wishing well," said Clogg. "Take him over there, Begood. He saw what it did for the bread-man, and he wants to try it, too."

"Well, he should have thought of that before he misbehaved," Officer Begood said huffily. "He has to learn that tantrums won't get him what he wants."

At that point the mushroom seemed to snap. It reared back, then sprang straight at Officer Begood, butting him so hard that its beanie fell off. Officer Begood yelled, flew backward, and sat down with a thump. The chain slipped from his hand.

With a mighty bound, the mushroom was free. The crowd cheered it on as it bounced desperately toward the wishing well, its chain jingling behind it. Leo and Mimi jumped out of its way as it reached them. It crashed against the side of the well. There was a puff of smoke . . .

And when the smoke cleared, there beside the well stood a tall, thin man with a long, hooked nose and a trailing white beard, wearing a shabby purple robe and an expression of absolute fury.

"Wizard Bing!" shrieked Muffy Clogg, and collapsed in her husband's arms.

CHAPTER
38

REVELATIONS

"What's all this?" said Officer Begood, striding up to Wizard Bing with Scribble at his heels and the entire crowd following, giggling at the red-and-white striped beanie stuck to the seat of the policeman's trousers. "Impersonation of another person is a very serious offense, you know, and you are clearly *not* Simon Humble!"

"I never said I was!" snapped Wizard Bing.

"Nevertheless," said Begood, taking out his notebook and licking his pencil in an official sort of way.

"It was just a case of mistaken identity, Officer Begood," called Stitch, clearly trying hard not to laugh. "The beanie gave everyone the wrong idea."

"Muffy made that beanie for Simon with her own hands!" said Clogg, fanning his unconscious wife. "This is an outrage!"

Wizard Bing scowled as Conker, Freda, and the rest of the search party trailed empty-handed back to the well, staring at him in astonishment. "That thieving scoundrel who just made his escape under all your noses stuck Simon's beanie on me with a piece of toffee after he'd turned me into a mushroom," he said angrily. "Thought it was funny, I suppose! Then he shut me in the house and ran off with my wand. By the way, I'll have it back, if you don't mind." Imperiously he held out his hand for the wand and Leo gave it to him, with some misgivings.

Bing's temper improved visibly once the wand was safely in his possession. He brandished it enthusiastically, and everyone took a hasty step backward. "The secret's out now, so I might as well announce that this wand is my greatest invention yet," he said. "It changes useless things into other, more useful, things, depending on where you move the lever. It's clearly marked, you see?"

Leo peered at the slot on the front of the wand. Now that he looked at it closely he could read the letters written in white inside the slot. "B," he read. "C, VOD, G." He glanced ruefully at Mimi, Conker, and Freda.

"The list!" Mimi exclaimed.

"Violet Orpington-Dunk indeed!" growled Conker.

"Bread, Chocolate, Vegetable of the Day, and Gold," said Wizard Bing, tapping the letters proudly. "I considered other things — marmalade, sausages, tea, wine, fruit of the day, and so on, but I found I could only fit four items on, so I chose the most important."

He sighed. "Mind you, the wand's still not perfect by any means. The main snag is that it's not everlasting. The gold section, for example, is more or less exhausted. The golden egg took most of it."

Moult, sitting wide-eyed in her basket, gave a little jump. He nodded at her absentmindedly. "I couldn't resist playing a little trick on the flock," he said. "I was in such a good mood that morning."

"You caused Moult a lot of trouble," Mimi burst out angrily.

But Wizard Bing had already turned his attention back to the wand. He weighed it in his hand, then waved it about experimentally, missing Conker's nose by a whisker.

"Oh, my heart and liver, you be careful with that!" Conker exploded.

"It's quite safe," said Wizard Bing regretfully. "It's tuned to bread at present — that villain must have changed the setting after he stole it, wanting something to eat — and the bread section's completely drained."

"I suppose it would be," said Freda, "given what happened to him."

Everyone shuddered at the thought of the bread-man.

"I never intended the wand to be used on living creatures," Wizard Bing said crossly. "It was only supposed to be used on *things* — sticks and stones and rusty horseshoes and so on. Perhaps it would be a good idea to put some sort of safety switch into it."

"A *very* good idea," Leo agreed. "I suppose the Vegetable of the Day was mushroom, the day you were — um — changed?"

"Of course," Bing said. "I do like mushrooms for breakfast. And we had mushroom omelets for dinner — Tom cooked them very nicely, I must say."

"*Tom?*" squawked Moult. "Who's Tom?"

"That rascal who just ran away from here," said Bing. "At least, he *said* his name was Tom."

"His real name is Count Éclair!" snapped Bodelia, pushing forward. "He's a disgrace to his noble title. It is an outrage that he was allowed to escape. I wish to protest in the strongest possible terms!"

"Your complaint is noted, madam," said Officer Begood sadly.

"His name *isn't* Count Éclair!" Conker roared. "Oh, my lungs and liver, Begood, didn't you recognize him? The bread-man was Spoiler! Spoiler!"

Horrified exclamations rose from the crowd. Bodelia snorted in disbelief.

"Do you want to hear my story or not?" Wizard Bing snapped. "I'm the one who's been a mushroom for days."

"Everything in good time," said Officer Begood sternly, but he flipped over to a fresh page in his notebook and raised his pencil expectantly.

"Well, I'd hired Tom, or whatever his name is, to be my new apprentice, you see," said Wizard Bing. "It seemed a good idea at the time. And it seemed a great stroke of luck that he turned up the very night Simon left for good."

At the mention of Simon's name, Muffy Clogg stirred and her eyelashes began to flutter.

"Left for *good*?" clucked Moult. "You mean, Simon went away after that argument you had on Thirstyday night and didn't come back? But Simon *always* comes back!"

"He didn't this time," said Bing, shrugging. "I can't understand it. I've sacked him dozens of times and it's never worried him before. Anyway, later that night this fellow calling himself Tom arrived. He said he'd seen Simon leaving town, so he'd come straightaway to offer himself as Simon's replacement."

"That sounds bad," croaked Master Sadd.

"Tragedy in Hobnob," Scribble muttered, writing frantically in his notebook. "A vicious bread-man, believed to be the confidence trickster Count Éclair, is suspected of foully murdering brilliant young wizard's apprentice Simon Humble in order to take his place and steal —"

"He wasn't a bread-man then, you fool!" Bing said irritably. "Mind you, even if he had been I'd probably still have hired him. I couldn't do without an apprentice, could I? *Someone* has to wash the test tubes and cook my meals and feed the chickens and chop the wood and so on."

He stared around resentfully, but finding that no one looked at all sympathetic, he went back to his story.

"Everything was all right that night, and all the next day," he said. "I didn't mention Simon's treachery to the chickens. He's a bit of a favorite with them for some reason, and I was too busy to cope with a scene."

Moult made a strangled sound and all her feathers fluffed up so that she almost filled the basket. The wizard either didn't care or didn't notice.

"I showed Tom my invention, and he was most impressed," he went on. "I was very pleased with him. But after our omelets, when I had dozed off at my table for a moment, he tried to sneak away with my wand and my golden egg. And when I woke up and tried to stop him, he hit me with the wand and there I was — a mushroom myself! The wand was still tuned to Vegetable of the Day, you see."

"A mushroom isn't actually a vegetable, you know," Conker said knowledgeably. "It's *actually* a fungus."

"Is that so?" Officer Begood asked with interest, and wrote it down in his notebook.

"It just goes to show you can't be too careful with apprentices," Bing said. "I was better off with Simon — even if he did change my good cauldron into a turnip."

The cooking pot in Conker's arms wriggled with interest but didn't say anything. It seemed rather overawed by Wizard Bing.

I knew something was missing from Bing's house! Leo thought. *That's what it was — a cauldron! How could a wizard brew potions without a cauldron? And I actually saw that huge turnip on the hearth rug.*

"So that's what happened on Thirstyday night, is it, Wizard Bing?" Moult asked, in the frostiest voice Leo had ever heard her use. "That's why you called Simon a clumsy nincompoop and told him to get out and never come back?"

"Oh, yes," Bing said carelessly. "Another little snag I've struck with this invention is that it hasn't got a reverse gear. It can't undo its transformations, so it's very aggravating if you touch something by mistake. Naturally I was a little annoyed with Simon. I was already feeling rather low because the Vegetable of the Day was turnip. I'm not fond of turnips."

"Me neither," Conker agreed, wrinkling his nose. "Turnip and chili mash, for example, must be the worst pie filling ever invented."

Leo grinned, remembering Conker's feud with Crumble the pie seller. It seemed so long ago that he had stood by Crumble's stall with Conker and Freda, while Crumble complained about people asking for free samples. But it wasn't long ago at all, he reminded himself. It was only yesterday.

And suddenly an idea came to him — an extraordinary idea. *It couldn't be*, he told himself. But the more he thought about it, the more he remembered little things that, added together, seemed to make a very complete, very convincing picture.

Feeling slightly dazed, he turned his attention back to the conversation going on around him.

"Simon was a terrible apprentice," Wizard Bing was telling Conker in injured tones. "Stupid and clumsy and always wanting me to pay him — as if he was worth paying! He got his meals free, didn't he? I even let him build a new chicken house in his spare time. And how did he reward me? He left me in the lurch so I got changed into a mushroom!"

Moult drew herself up. "Wizard Bing," she said, in a trembling voice. "I have always been loyal to you, but no hen of honor can put up with being lied to and tricked and hearing her friends insulted. I hereby resign as a member of your flock."

"Don't be silly, Moult," said Bing. "You've got nowhere else to go."

"I will be homeless, certainly," said Moult with dignity. "But better a nest on the side of the road than a snug coop with a bad master."

"As you like." Bing shrugged.

"Oh, poor Simon!" Muffy Clogg moaned. "Whatever can have become of him?"

Officer Begood cleared his throat with the air of one determined to take control of a difficult situation. "Brace yourself, madam," he said to Muffy. "I fear you must expect the worst concerning your unfortunate nephew. As to the whereabouts of your maid, I can make no comment at this time."

"Dabs to dibs that villain Count Éclair disposed of them both," Master Sadd said with gloomy relish.

Muffy Clogg began to wail. Candy sniffled. Bun, Patty, and Woodley looked sorrowful. Even Clogg rumbled in distress.

Leo knew he had to speak up. He couldn't let everyone grieve when he was sure there was no need for it.

"Don't give up hope, Mistress Clogg," he said. "I think Tilly and Simon are fine."

"And what would you know about it?" sneered Bodelia. "You're nothing but a rascally rug thief. Master Sadd is no doubt perfectly right. We'll never see that flibbertigibbet Tilly or that poor fool Simon Humble again!"

"Well, it seems you're wrong for once, Mistress Parker," called a laughing voice. And to the astonishment of everyone except Leo, Tilly the maid came tripping through the crowd, smiling prettily and holding the hand of a skinny, bashful-looking young man with popping pale green eyes.

"Simon!" shrieked Muffy Clogg.

"Simon!" squawked Moult, hurtling out of the basket and into the young man's arms.

364

"I went away secretly to seek my fortune, Aunt Muffy," said the young man. "I met a kind man called Count Éclair in the woods, and he told me it was the only way I'd ever be able to marry Tilly. But today I read in the paper that I'd killed Wizard Bing, so I wrote to Tilly to tell her I hadn't."

"And I wrote back at once," said Tilly, "telling him to come home as soon as the cloud castle had stopped covering the Gap, because I didn't want a fortune, I just wanted him."

The young man grinned and blushed.

"Oh, my lungs and liver!" Conker roared. "I don't believe it! It's — it's that straw-haired chap who's just started work at The Black Sheep!"

CHAPTER 39

CELEBRATIONS

"I knew it!" crowed Leo, as Simon and Tilly were swamped in a sea of rejoicing people. "Someone had started asking Crumble for free pies — just like Simon used to do with Bun here. Wizard Bing had been working on a new sort of glowworm food — and the glowworm plague had only struck in Hobnob and at The Black Sheep. And everything we'd ever heard about Simon reminded me of Jolly's new assistant."

"Do you know what this means?" Freda muttered in disgust. "It means we could have solved the whole mystery without ever leaving home!"

"Oh, sure," Conker said. "But that wouldn't have been any fun."

"*Fun!*" Freda quacked. "Tye nearly got lynched by an angry mob, Leo, Mimi, and Bertha nearly got snaffled by the Blue Queen —"

"Oh, I hope Bertha's all right!" Mimi exclaimed. "I hope they got to the farm in time."

"We'll go and find out," said Conker, rubbing his hands. "Our work here is done."

"We're not going anywhere till we've been paid," Freda said, setting off into the crowd.

Music had begun playing, and many people were dancing. Woodley was whirring overhead, beaming and waving. The trees were swaying and whispering with pleasure.

"You two might like to tidy yourselves up a bit before we see Mistress Clogg," Conker said as he, Mimi, and Leo hurried after Freda. "You've still got Strix sparkle stuff all over you."

Leo looked down and saw that Conker was right. His clothes were thickly spangled with tiny glittering flecks that sparkled in the moonlight.

My memories are my dreams . . .

"It doesn't matter, Conker," Mimi said quickly.

"It does," Conker insisted. "We don't want to give Mistress Clogg the wrong impression, do we?"

Since the cooking pot was still clinging to Conker like a large black limpet, sneezing repeatedly because of the bread crumbs thickly encrusting Conker's hair and beard, Leo thought he and Mimi weren't the only ones who might look strange to Muffy Clogg. Nevertheless, to be obliging, he brushed at the flecks of color on the front of his jacket.

Some sparkles flew upward, and the next moment a white unicorn with a golden horn was plunging in the air before him.

Leo gasped. The people around him yelled, scrambling to avoid the rearing animal's golden hooves, but Leo didn't move. Transfixed, he stared at the unicorn. He'd seen it before, in the palace of the Strix. But now it was so close, floating in the air right in front of him, and it was the most magnificent thing he had ever seen. His chest ached, and tears burned behind his eyes. He knew it was a vision, but it seemed so real.

And that's because it is *real,* he thought. *It's a memory, one of the Ancient One's millions of memories, from the time since Rondo began.* He sighed as the unicorn memory softly dissolved into pinpoints of light and vanished.

"Oh, my guts and garters!" Conker exclaimed.

"Don't touch that stuff again, Leo!" Mimi snapped.

Leo put his head down and hurried after his companions, trying to close his ears to the excited whispers of the crowd and feeling annoyed with himself because Mimi had obviously known what would happen when the colored flecks were disturbed, and he hadn't had the slightest idea.

But I saw the unicorn, he thought suddenly. *I saw it, right up close!* And as the wonderful memory filled his mind again, he felt a delicious warmth spread through him, and smiled.

They found Muffy sitting by Woodley's fireplace, fanning herself and looking confused but very happy. Simon, grinning broadly and still clasping the elated Moult, was with her, and so were Clogg, Tilly, and Wizard Bing, who, naturally, had claimed the only other chair. Scribble was hovering at the edge of the group, busily taking notes.

"Simon and I kept our engagement a secret, because we knew you wouldn't approve, Mistress Clogg," Tilly was telling Muffy. "Oh, I've been so unhappy, thinking that Simon was a jailed mushroom! That's why I suggested you write to Bertha's quest team. I knew Bertha could help. My sisters have always said that she's a true heroine."

"Mercy!" cried Muffy, with a flustered glance at Clogg.

"Well!" said Wizard Bing. "I don't usually allow my apprentices to have wives, but I'll make an exception in your case, Tilly. You seem a sensible, hardworking girl. You'll clean up my house in no time."

"Thank you, sir," said Tilly composedly, "but you dismissed Simon from your service, so he is no longer your apprentice. After we're married, he and I are going to live on a farm."

"Ridiculous!" snapped Wizard Bing. "How can Simon have a farm? He hasn't got a dib to his name!"

"No he hasn't, thanks to you, sir," Tilly said pertly. "But I have. I've been saving a little from my wages every week since I met him, and this afternoon I bought a nice piece of land on the edge of town. Simon will build our house and the farm buildings. He's very good at building, aren't you, Simon?"

Simon nodded and grinned at her adoringly. "We're going to keep chickens and sell the eggs, Moult," he said to the shabby little hen nestled in his arms. "Will you come be the founder of our flock?"

"*Me?*" Moult gasped.

"Why not, Moult?" said Mimi, smiling at her. "You're a Sunday's chick — the Ancient One said so. And I think it's only right that Simon and Tilly's flock should have a founder who's brave and noble, good and true."

"A Sunday's chick!" exclaimed Tilly, clasping her hands. And everyone, even Wizard Bing, regarded Moult with great respect.

"Well, I'm not so sure about all this," Muffy said in a high voice. "After all, Simon is *my* nephew. And Tilly is only a *maid*!"

"You were only a maid when I met you, my love," Clogg said gently. "Such a pretty one, too."

Muffy blushed, dimpled, and pressed her handkerchief to her eyes.

"Right, so everyone lives happily ever after," Freda said briskly. "Now, Mistress Clogg, to business! We've come about our fee."

Muffy Clogg glanced nervously at her husband again.

"Don't worry, my love," said Clogg. "I don't blame you for not telling me you'd hired the quest team. I've been very bad-tempered lately, I know. It's just . . . my little problems have been getting me down." He shot a resentful glance at Wizard Bing.

The cooking pot sneezed and struggled in Conker's arms. He put it down and at once it ran to Wizard Bing. "You've got a pretty dress, Bingle," it said admiringly.

"Hmmph!" said Bing. As Muffy began rummaging in a frilly handbag, he stood up and stomped crossly away from her. "I don't know what you've got to complain about, Clogg!" he snapped over his shoulder. "You're rolling in money and you've got assistants coming out your ears. All thanks to me, I might add. My word, that was a clever spell! I wish I could remember how I did it."

"So it *was* you who magicked those elves on me!" hissed Clogg. "Well, I'll thank you to just magic them away again!"

"I can't do that, my dear man," Bing said patronizingly, turning to face him. "They're not warts, you know. They've got a will of their own. They'll leave when they want to and not before."

Clogg clenched his fists and took a menacing step forward. Bing brandished his wand in alarm.

370

"Wizard Bing," Leo said hurriedly. "I was thinking . . ."

Bing swung around, his eyebrows bristling, the wand held high. Leo resisted taking a step back. "Master Clogg has elves doing all his work, and he doesn't want them anymore," he said carefully. "And you have lots of work to do, and no one to help you do it. So maybe if you were to explain this to the elves they might . . ."

Wizard Bing lowered the wand. "You know, Clogg, the boy might have something there," he said thoughtfully. "If there's one thing elves love, it's work. And my house might interest them — it's a mess."

"Wonderful!" cried Clogg. "Let's go ask them now."

They shook hands, beaming as if they were the very best of friends.

"Now!" said Wizard Bing. "All I need is a new cooking pot."

The cooking pot sprang into his arms. "Bingle," it crooned. "Clever, famous Bingle! *You* have a magic wand. *You* don't have sneezy crumbs in your beard! And *you* have a very nice dress. Take me to live with you, pleeease!"

"It's a robe, not a dress," Bing said with dignity. "Still . . ." Glancing furtively at Conker, who was cunningly pretending to look the other way, he hurried off with the cooking pot in his arms and Clogg at his heels.

"What next?" Leo gasped, as soon as he and Mimi had stopped laughing.

"Next we visit the bathhouse," Mimi said. "As soon as we've stolen Woodley's tablecloth."

———

When Leo and Mimi returned to Woodley's fireplace, they found it deserted except for Conker and Freda, who were sitting in Woodley's chairs happily dividing a large heap of coins into five equal piles. They looked up as Leo and Mimi joined them.

"You look a lot less sparkly than you did," Freda remarked.

"We had a bath," said Mimi. "Conker, give Leo my share to keep for me. We've —"

Two identical mice emerged from beneath a clump of grass by Conker's foot. "Message for Conker the dot-catcher," they said in unison.

"So the strike's over, is it?" snapped Conker, scowling at them as he took the two messages, one very frayed around the edges, the other crisp and new.

"Talks are continuing, but we have returned to work for the moment as a gesture of goodwill," droned the right-hand mouse.

"Oh, really," Conker snarled. Freda snapped her beak. The mice squeaked and dived back under the clump of grass.

Conker scanned the old message rapidly. "This is the one Hal sent me this morning, saying he'd just discovered that the queen had left her castle and he thought she must have gone up in smoke." He sighed. "Oh, my heart, lungs, and liver, we would have saved ourselves a lot of trouble if we'd had this before. The messenger service is really getting beyond —"

"Conker, read the other one!" Mimi begged.

Conker unfolded the second note. Everyone waited anxiously

as he looked at it. His face broke into a broad grin and he held the note out so everyone could see it.

Arrived just in time. Massacre foiled. Bertha magnificent. Sending rug back to you at Snug. See you at The Black Sheep.
Hal

Leo and Mimi cheered. Freda shrugged as if she'd known all along that everything would be fine, but Leo thought she looked mightily relieved all the same. "Let's go get the packs," she said, turning away. "We'd better be ready for a quick getaway in case Begood gets funny about who the rug belongs to."

When the rug landed at their feet not long afterward, however, even Bodelia could see that it regarded them as its rightful owners.

Good-byes took quite a long time. Word of the quest team's exploits had spread, and everyone, it seemed, wanted to shake hands with the heroes. Woodley made a little speech saying that, despite some inaccurate and sensational press coverage, it had been an honor to have them in the Hobnob Snug. Simon banged them on the back, too moved to speak. Moult, utterly content and already looking glossier, blinked away tears and said she would never forget them. Tilly kissed them all on both cheeks and said she wished they'd change their minds about leaving and stay for the wedding.

"We'd like to," said Leo. "But we'll be . . . somewhere else tomorrow."

Home. It was hard to imagine.

"Somewhere else?" asked Scribble, his long nose twitching. "Where would that be?"

"None of your business," growled Conker. "And don't ask for a lift back to town, either, gnome."

"I don't want a lift," Scribble said scornfully. "I am going by Woffles Way to test my new purchase — a unique pair of seven-league boots from Clogg's Shoe Emporium. It's quite amazing, the distance they cover with every stride."

He grinned at the envious look on Conker's face. "Ah, yes," he said carelessly. "They cost a fortune — almost every dib I had left on me, as a matter of fact — but you have to pay for quality. Something *you* wouldn't know much about, dot-catcher."

He left hurriedly as Conker clenched his fists. To everyone's surprise, Mimi darted after him. She said a few smiling words to him, then came running back to take her place on the rug. Conker glowered at her.

"To The Black Sheep," Freda said, and the crowd cheered as the rug rose rapidly into the air. For a brief moment the lights of the Snug were twinkling below, and Leo was looking down at a sea of upturned faces and waving hands. Then the rug swooped over the treetops and on into the night.

Conker touched his cheek rather wistfully. "I don't know what a clever girl like Tilly sees in Simon Humble," he complained. "He might have a good heart, but he's got no brains at all."

"She's got enough brains for both of them," said Freda. "A bit like us, really."

Conker lunged at her fruitlessly, then turned his back on her. "What do you mean by giving an interview to that villain Scribble, Mimi?" he growled.

"Oh, it wasn't an interview," Mimi said, looking down at her hands. "I was just recommending a place where he could get some breakfast on his journey home. He was very grateful. He'd never heard of The Tavern of No Return."

CHAPTER 40

FAREWELLS

A long, breezy ride later the rug settled to the ground in the lane behind The Black Sheep. Not long afterward Conker, Freda, Leo, and Mimi were reunited with Bertha, Tye, and Hal, who were waiting up for them in front of the fire in Merry and Jolly's private sitting room.

For a while everyone talked at once. Bertha, Tye, and Hal had to hear about the amazing events at the Snug. The newcomers had to hear about how Bertha had leaped upon Sly from the flying rug, saving Violet Orpington-Dunk, whose head was actually in Sly's mouth at the time, from a horrible death.

"Bertha was the hero of the hour," said Hal. "As soon as the mice went back to work I sent word to Jack Macdonald, and he and Mary came rushing home. They were so grateful to Bertha. Jack's begging her to come back and work for him again."

"He didn't have much choice," said Bertha, tossing her head. "The flock made it *very* clear that they would no longer stay on a farm that offers substandard security."

"It's not just that, Bertha," Hal said. "Jack's really missed you. Mary told me the farm wasn't the same without you. The dots had gone, but all the fun had gone out of life, too, she said, and Jack's been moping ever since you left."

"Oh," said Bertha in a small voice. "Well, that's . . . very nice." She blinked away a few happy tears.

Jolly came in with a huge tray of sandwiches, a whole apple pie, a big brown pot of tea, and a foaming jug of cider, and all talk ceased while everyone ate and drank. The newcomers were ravenous and so was Bertha, though she'd eaten earlier. She said that saving hens from vicious foxes always made her hungry.

"I'm only sorry that I didn't hit Sly harder," she said regretfully, swallowing the last of the sandwiches. "Somehow he managed to get up and sneak away while we were giving Violet first aid. He could be anywhere by now."

"Like Spoiler," grumbled Conker. "He's on the loose as well. I wish we'd let him stay a bread-man. At least then he'd have had trouble creeping around without being recognized."

"I'm surprised he was able to use the wishing well to change himself," Bertha commented. "He hadn't been in Hobnob very long. It's a wonder he knew that the well worked backward."

"Indeed," murmured Hal, and glanced at Mimi. She returned his gaze unblinkingly, but two red patches appeared on her cheekbones.

He knows, Leo thought, feeling his own face grow hot. *He knows Mimi didn't leave the Key in the Safe Place — that she used it on Spoiler.*

Hal leaned forward, his steady gray gaze fixed on them, and Leo held his breath. But Hal said nothing about the Key. Instead, he started talking about their escape from the Blue Queen.

"I thought we'd lost you," he said gravely. "I cursed myself for not realizing till too late that the queen had left the castle without my knowledge, in a way I'd never imagined."

"I kept telling them the Blue Queen was no problem," Conker said, tugging dismally at his beard. "'She's got no power outside her castle,' I kept saying. Well, all that's changed now."

"Yes," said Bertha. "Now she can go anywhere she likes! And we can't depend on the S — the S-thingy — to save us next time."

"The Ancient One will not return," Tye said somberly. "Not in our lifetimes." Firelight flickered in her golden eyes like the living memories she had seen in the mist.

"The Blue Queen won't try to impersonate the Strix a second time, either," said Hal. "She knows that the story of this night will soon be all over Rondo. She'll use her new power in a different way."

Leo wet his lips. "You don't think she's been hurt at all by — by what happened?"

Hal shook his head. "The Strix dismissed her from its presence — sent her back to her castle, that was all. When her shock and rage have died down she'll realize that the first important toot of her new spell was successful in every way but one. Certainly she failed to capture you, Mimi, and Bertha, but she succeeded in moving herself and her power to another place. It won't be long before she starts planning her next move."

"What do you think that will be, Hal?" asked Bertha.

"If I knew that I would be a happier man," Hal said with a wry smile. "What I do know is that the queen is now free to wander

Rondo at will, and there is nothing we can do to stop her. From this night on, life here will be far more dangerous — especially for us."

"Folk will have to be warned," growled Conker.

"Yes," Hal said. "Bertha, I fear you'll have to hold one more press conference before you return to the farm."

"Oh," cried Bertha. "But why me? Why not you, Hal?"

"Folk are far more likely to listen to Bertha the quest heroine than Hal the burned-out wizard," Hal said with a tired grin. "I think I'll be more useful working in the background with Conker, Freda, and Tye — and with Mimi and Leo, if they still want to be involved."

"Of course we do," Leo said instantly. "We're not going to leave you to fight the queen alone."

Mimi hesitated. The red patches on her cheeks had faded, leaving her very pale. "I can see why you'd want Leo, Hal," she said abruptly. "Leo's smart, and he's . . . reliable. He notices things, and he can work things out. And he's brave as well. He's . . . a hero, like you, Hal — like all of you. I'm different. All I do is cause trouble."

"Mimi, that's not true!" Bertha cried.

"It is, Bertha," said Mimi. "I did it again this afternoon. You and Leo nearly died because you came after me."

"*That's* true," said Freda, and squawked as Conker trod on her foot.

"The trouble is, I can't promise it won't happen again," said Mimi, staring straight ahead, looking at no one. "I'm — not good at being on a team or listening to other people. At home I've got used to just — listening to myself because . . . because a long time ago I realized that people don't see things the way I do, and they think I'm . . . you know . . . a bit weird." Her lips twisted into a mirthless little smile that made Leo's heart ache.

"Mimi —" he began, but she shook her head.

"I'm not making excuses, Leo," she said, avoiding his eyes. "I'm just saying how it is. And things have got really serious here now. Hal and the others can't afford to have someone with them who's going to be trouble."

She took a quick breath. "So I've decided not to come back," she said in an offhand voice. "I'll give you the Key, and you can come alone, next time. The queen won't suspect anything as long as her spies see you. She'll just think I'm hiding somewhere with Mutt."

Her face was quite expressionless. Only the stiffness of her body and her tightly clasped hands showed what her decision was costing her.

This is what I wanted, Leo thought. But he found that now he didn't want it at all. He remembered Mimi coping efficiently with Bertha's trouble at the well, murmuring reassurances to Bliss, wading, laughing and fully clothed, into the Snug bath. He remembered Mimi seeing that Bing's cloak and hat were clues, insisting Spoiler had been in Bing's house, defending Moult, saying that Leo was a hero, telling him not to brush away the sparkling memories of the Strix . . .

It's up to me to make her change her mind, he thought. *I'm the one who's been fighting with her from the very start of all this.*

He struggled to think of something to say — something that didn't sound feeble, sentimental, and unconvincing. But to his surprise it was Tye who broke the heavy silence.

"You may feel a stranger in Langland, Mimi, but you are not a stranger here," Tye said slowly. "You may find you will be less inclined to take matters into your own hands if you understand how much we value you. In the time to come we will need Leo's courage and practical intelligence, certainly, but your instincts and imagination will be just as important."

"I agree!" Bertha exclaimed.

"And I," said Hal.

"We *all* agree," said Conker. "Right, Freda?"

"Absolutely!" said the duck.

"I think so, too, Mimi," Leo said awkwardly, finding his voice at last. "They need us both. You can see things I can't. We think — differently. And you're more at home in Rondo than I'll ever be." He paused. It had been so hard to admit that, but suddenly he wondered why. Suddenly he wondered how he could have begrudged Mimi's feeling at home in Rondo, when in her own world she felt like such an outsider.

Mimi's eyes widened. She went crimson, and a delighted smile began tugging at the corners of her mouth.

"Excellent!" said Conker, rubbing his hands. "So it's decided. The team's still intact."

"There's just one thing, Mimi," Hal said. "While you're here, especially now that the queen is free, the Key to Rondo must always be kept in a Safe Place. No arguments, no deceptions."

"Absolutely," Conker agreed. "Why, my heart and lungs, just think what might have happened if you'd had the Key on you when the queen trapped you this time!"

Mimi looked hunted. "I understand," she mumbled. "I really do."

Bertha suddenly yawned hugely. "Oh, pardon," she said. "It's just that it's been a long night, what with all the fighting and the emotional strain . . ."

Hal grinned and stood up. "We all need rest," he said. "And it's time for Mimi and Leo to leave us."

They all went up to Bertha's room, climbing the stairs quietly so as not to wake the sleeping tavern. Everyone waited outside while Mimi went through the charade of recovering the Key from the empty Safe Place. Then Bertha opened the doors to her balcony and they all went out into the cool night air.

"I *will* miss this balcony when I go home to the farm." Bertha sighed. "Balconies are *so* romantic."

"You won't have any trouble persuading Macdonald to build you one for your sty now," Hal said. "I think he'd give you the moon and the stars if he could."

"Oh!" said Mimi. "That reminds me." She dug in her pocket and brought out the little drawstring money bag Conker had given her. It was round and plump. She pushed it into Tye's hands.

"What is this?" Tye asked, frowning.

"Strix dreams," Mimi said. "The sparkles fell out of our clothes and hair after we had a bath in the Snug. But they didn't sink into the moss because we stood on a tablecloth while we were drying off. We gathered them up — as many as we could — for you."

"For me," Tye repeated. Her lips hardly moved. Her voice was expressionless. It was impossible to tell what she was feeling.

"Yes," said Mimi, rather breathlessly. "I — *we're* sure that some of the dreams of Terlamaines will be among the rest. They were very thick around us when the Ancient One first looked at you. And we thought . . . you should have them."

Tye was silent for a moment, gazing down at the little bag in her black-gloved hands. When she looked up, her eyes were like liquid gold. "Thank you," she said softly.

Bertha sniffled. Conker wiped his eyes roughly with the back of his hand. But Hal's face broke into a grin that made him look ten years younger. "Good-bye, you two," he said. "Till we meet again."

Leo took Mimi's hand. She put her free hand to the pendant at her throat. "Home," she said softly.

Chiming rainbows closed around Leo, whirled around him, bright as the dreams of the Strix. He felt himself falling, drifting weightless, his head filled with music . . . Then his feet hit solid ground and the rainbows cleared from his eyes. He was back in his room. He saw his bed, his desk, the black-and-white rug on the floor. Dust motes swirled in the air, shining like tiny specks of glitter in the mellow afternoon light. The sound of laughter drifted up from the garden.

"Open the box, Leo."

He looked around. Mimi was beside him, blinking owlishly. "Open the box," she repeated. "So the music will run down."

Leo moved unsteadily to his desk and opened the lid of the music box, releasing the sweet, chiming music, the music of the rainbows. He stared at the front of the box and suddenly his knees felt weak. He slumped down in his chair. *What did I expect?* he thought. But it was so strange. He felt Mimi move up behind him and knew that she was staring at the box, too.

The bright, painted colors had dimmed. The sky was gray-blue, paled by the light of an enormous moon, spangled by the gleaming pinpoints of a thousand stars. Near the top, a tiny village was ablaze with light.

"They're still dancing in Hobnob," Mimi murmured.

With one movement, she and Leo both leaned over to look at the back of the box. Moonlight flooded the rolling grass, turning it to silver. The willow trees clustered by the river were dark. The castle on the hill shone with sulky blue light.

Leo sank back into his chair. He stared at the front of the box, and with a trembling finger traced the line of the road that led down from the bright village to the square bulk of the camping shop. Somewhere along that road, skulking in the shadows, was Spoiler, the golden egg safe in his pocket. Somewhere Peg prowled, huge, shaggy paws padding, white teeth gleaming.

The street at the bottom of the box was deserted. Streetlamps shone on the dark police station, the shuttered shops, and the red-and-white striped awning drawn down over Posy's flower stall. But soft light glowed in an upstairs room of The Black Sheep. And on the balcony outside that room stood five familiar figures — a tall, lean man with graying hair tied back in a warrior's tail; a slender woman in black, her arm raised in a wave of farewell; a short, chunky man with a wild beard; a masked duck; and a pig wearing a flower-laden hat.

High above them, the pale sky gleamed. A few tiny shreds of cloud drifted across the brilliant moon. But of the Ancient One's cloud palace there was no sign. No sign at all.

This book was designed by Tim Hall. The text was set in 11 point Minion. The book production was supervised by Joy Simpkins. The book was printed and bound at R. R. Donnelley in Crawfordsville, Indiana, in the United States of America. Manufacturing was supervised by Jess White.